Liberation Square

Liberation Square

GARETH RUBIN

MICHAEL JOSEPH
an imprint of
PENGUIN BOOKS

MICHAEL JOSEPH

UK | USA | Canada | Ireland | Australia
India | New Zealand | South Africa

Michael Joseph is part of the Penguin Random House group of companies
whose addresses can be found at global.penguinrandomhouse.com

First published 2018
001

Copyright © Gareth Rubin, 2018

The moral right of the author has been asserted

Set in 13.5/16 pt Garamond MT Std
Typeset by Jouve (UK), Milton Keynes
Printed and bound in Great Britain by Clays Ltd, Elcograf S.p.A.

A CIP catalogue record for this book is available from the British Library

HARDBACK ISBN: 978–0–718–18709–5
OM PAPERBACK ISBN: 978–0–718–18710–1

www.greenpenguin.co.uk

Penguin Random House is committed to a
sustainable future for our business, our readers
and our planet. This book is made from Forest
Stewardship Council® certified paper.

For my parents, a psychologist and a historian

N

DEMOCRATIC
UNITED
KINGDOM

Aberdeen

Glasgow   Edinburgh

Newcastle

Belfast

Leeds   York

Dublin

Liverpool   Manchester

Sheffield

Birmingham

Oxford

Cardiff

REPUBLIC OF
GREAT BRITAIN

Bristol   London

Gravesend

Plymouth

London

DEMOCRATIC
UNITED
KINGDOM

REPUBLIC
OF

GREAT
BRITAIN

0   100 km

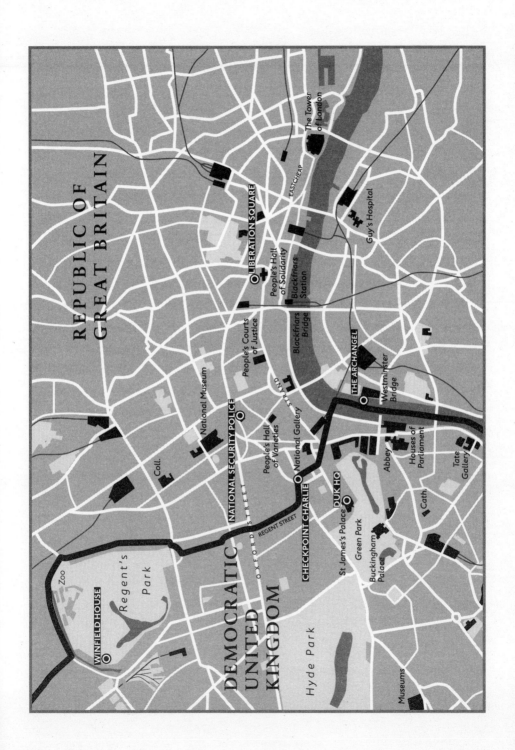

I

We walked all the way to Checkpoint Charlie that day. At the end of the road, the grey autumn light made the barbed wire and the concrete guard towers disappear into the sky, so that you could believe they kept on rising forever. I stood watching crowds of people stare at the only opening in the Wall for twenty kilometres, and tried to pick out those who had come for a day trip just to gaze at it from the locals who could remember it being built and still felt the loss. But the faces all showed the same mix of anger and quiet sorrow.

The soldiers in their muddy-brown uniforms looked bored as they paced back and forth between the metal barriers. They always look bored. I once saw one grinning and winking at the girls in the crowd, but he was the exception – they stand there for six hours straight, rain or shine, and you wonder if they hope for the occasional attempt to jump the Wall, or an attack by the Western Fascists, just so they can put their training into practice. Even I, when I had a gun placed in my hands for my Compulsory Basic, felt a bit of a thrill as I pulled the trigger. The kick from the Kalashnikov nearly knocked me over, though, and my instructor laughed before taking it from me and replacing it with a single-shot rifle.

So the boys in the watch towers were looking for a spark of excitement while the people below were looking for some sort of understanding. They wouldn't find any there, I knew.

Nick appeared through the crowd then, carrying the drinks that he had bought from a man with a cart. He handed one to me, and we both turned to silently gaze at the barrier.

'What do you think, when you look at it?' he said after a while.

My eyes ranged over the barbed wire and thick camouflage netting that prevented you from seeing through the ten-metre opening in the concrete. 'I suppose it's hard to put into words,' I replied. 'It feels like we've lost something, something we won't get back. But, well, maybe it's necessary, just for now.'

He peered up at the guard tower. 'So they say.'

A group of schoolboys shuffled past, clutching the red paperbacks that were to be the map to our future. One broke off and wandered right up to the soldiers, but his teacher caught him and dragged him away, to the laughter of the others. They were just like the ones that I used to teach. I suppose children are the same everywhere.

'Do you remember it going up?' I asked.

'Vividly,' Nick said. 'Yes, vividly.'

I understood and twisted his warm fingers into mine. After five months of marriage I could recognize the ridges and wrinkles in his skin. 'At least we're on the same side of it.'

'Yes. That's something.' He sighed. 'I do have friends over there, though.'

I looked over at the guards, wondering what they were thinking as they stared back at us. It must all have seemed very different to them. Perspective changes things. 'I expect you'll see them again. They might be on the other side right now, looking this way.'

'Perhaps.'

A man approached the schoolboys, offering photographs of the Wall to be used as postcards. 'Strange things to send,' I said.

'Presumably you give them to people you don't like.' I smiled.

The school party stopped in front of a hoarding showing the country split in half, with ten occupied babies' cots on the other side, and nine on ours alongside an empty one bearing the slogan YOUR CHILD. STRENGTH IN NUMBERS! The boys' teacher reached into his briefcase, took out another copy of the red book, in which the First Secretary had set out our nation's course, and began to read out a passage.

Nick nodded in his direction with a sceptical smirk. 'Does he think it's all going to work so beautifully?' he said.

I glanced around to make sure we couldn't be overheard. 'Well it's worth trying, isn't it? Surely if the state makes certain everyone is fed and has a job, nine tenths of all the fights and arguments we have with each other will be gone.' And really it did make sense – God knows there were difficult aspects to our new life, but the argument seemed entirely logical, and rehearsing it in my mind made me hopeful for the future.

'Overnight. In a puff of smoke.' He tried to suppress a smile.

'Oh, you're a horrid man.' I poked him in the ribs. 'So what's *your* big idea, then?'

'I'm glad you asked,' he said. 'A gliding wing.'

'A gliding wing?'

'That's it. We build it on the roof in the dead of night,

wait until the wind picks up, then soar over the Wall like a couple of birds. Down a pink gin and slip into the best hotel we can find for an hour.' He did some calculations in his head. 'Make it ninety minutes.'

'You need a cold shower.' But my hand slipped around his waist.

'Maybe I do.' A soldier crossed from one side of the watch tower to the other, scanning the crowd with his binoculars. 'Awful job,' Nick said.

'People surprise you. What they can do.'

'That's true. That's always true.' Above us a flock of black birds drifted so high that they became specks of dust. 'Shall we go?'

I nodded. 'Yes, let's.'

As we left, north towards Oxford Street, I gazed back at the statue of Eros, his attempt to leap over the Wall permanently frozen, caught by the concrete and the wire.

In my very soul I believe that there is nothing on this earth as wonderful as the land we have inherited from our forefathers. Tomorrow we will mark seven years since the shining *Archangel* sailed up the Thames to liberate us from Fascism. In those seven short years we have sown the seeds of peace to realize the promise of our ancestors. Capitalism, you see, sees greed and mutual mistrust as the most desirable of human attributes. Communism answers that claim with a belief in the fundamental goodness of humanity. And we have believed it for a very long time – for what was the cry of the French Revolutionaries? *Liberté. Egalité. Fraternité.* Now I won't paint a rosy picture of the future. At times it will be difficult. But some day we will be truly free, and that means living in equality and brotherhood.

Anthony Blunt, interviewed on RGB
Station 1, Monday, 17 November 1952

A few weeks later, I walked the same route north to Oxford Street, part of a mass of people trudging slowly with scarves or cotton masks tied over their mouths to keep out the heavy November smog. The few cars on the road sprayed one by one through the gutter, so that regular waves of oily water swept on to the pavement, leaving pools clouded with dirt. It had been less than a month since that day, but so much had changed.

I stopped to look down Regent Street. With their faces covered, the swaddled bodies seemed like a strange crowd of moving shop mannequins, reeling about on the pavement in patterns only they understood. Someone's shoulder knocked into mine and a man in a raincoat seemed to mumble an apology through his scarf, but before I could say anything he had melted into the throng, disappearing among countless others shambling in every direction. I took a moment to wipe the grime from my face before I set off again.

Along the way, I peered into the shop windows. Some were well stocked with winter clothes that could keep the cold out and the warm in. My shoes would do for another year, but I needed a new pair of leather boots and I hoped Nick could find me some. One of his patients could get hold of good clothes – the yellow woollen overcoat he had somehow come up with was the best I had ever had. Even before the War, I could barely have afforded it and there was certainly nothing in the shops now that came close. I thought about asking if he could buy another one and keeping it in a box until needed – you never knew when you would see anything like that. Nick said the man had connections with the factory, that's how he had first go at what they turned out.

Looking in one misted window, I found myself staring into a baby-goods store. Its sole display was a wooden cot, painted bright pink for a girl and my eyes traced the delicate flowers etched up its sides. But then the migraine that

I had felt brewing all morning seemed to worsen and I knew that I needed to sit down and let it pass. I thought of the little café around the corner where the coffee was ersatz but the staff were friendly and didn't bother you if you ordered something small from time to time. The owner was a plump and matronly woman who seemed to treat customers like members of her family who had dropped by for a chat, and she served little scones for five new pence, which was good value. 'All I can charge, love,' she had told me, although I didn't think that was true. They were edible too, unlike what was offered by some of the places around there. Or Nick's surgery wasn't far – I could go there instead and sit in one of the soft armchairs and he would tell me a silly joke he had heard that day, busying himself while I let the pain subside.

'Are you just going to stand there?'

I looked around to see a cheaply dressed woman my own age staring at me. 'Sorry,' I said, my cheeks flushing red as I stepped aside to let her enter the shop. 'Miles away.'

'Hard enough as it is,' she muttered. 'Probably nothing in there anyhow.'

'Oh, I'm sure there will be.'

She looked at me as if I were an idiot. 'And you would know all about it, would you?'

'I mean –'

'Don't matter what you mean, do it?'

She pushed past me into the store and I blushed again, embarrassed, before hurriedly edging into the flow of muffled people descending the steps into Oxford Circus Tube Station.

The concourse wasn't too bad, but when I got to the

Oxaloo Line platform I found it so packed that I thought I would never get on the train, and the closeness of the coughing bodies and lack of air made my head worse. As the carriages came to a halt, we all shoved in, staring straight ahead, not speaking to each other, and I only just managed to get on. While we shuffled around, my eyes fell on a poster above the seats, warning of the threat of infiltration, showing tunnels burrowing from the DUK land – everything north of a line stretching from Bristol to Norfolk, plus the north-western quarter of London – into our Republic of Great Britain, covering southern England and the rest of the capital. Constant vigilance was needed, it said. Then a man pushed in front of me, blocking my view of the poster.

The train started up and rattled away from the now-deserted platform. They say that during the Blitz, the men and women who used the Underground as a shelter at night would just take themselves off to quiet corners without even knowing each other's names. No doubt, thinking you might get blown apart as soon as you set foot above ground makes you realize that there are some things you don't want to go to your grave never having tried. And I think it was seen as patriotic too if it were some young man being sent to the front who might never come back – to give him something to smile about when he was on the ship going over.

Not many did come back, of course, and I knew some of those who didn't: boys I had grown up with and would never see again except in my mind's eye. I had held those sickness-inducing photographs of the D-Day beaches, though – countless bodies with their heads or limbs missing. Tens of thousands of corpses floating in the water. The Germans had taken a lot of images to celebrate how victorious they had been over us. Then, after the Red Army had, in their turn, defeated the Germans, we had been shown those images to learn how lucky we had been that the Soviets had come to our aid. Either way, the photographs had left me feeling ill for a very long time.

After forcing my way out at Waterloo, I passed the broken remains of Westminster Bridge that invited you to step off the bricks and into the river. That's if you could somehow scale the electrified wire and stay hidden from the guard towers and their searchlights, of course. Everyone had heard of someone who had managed it, but the stories were always second-hand, and there was a line of simple white crosses on the other side for those who had slipped silently into the black water at night and tried without success.

As I walked, the paving stones echoed to the sound of Comrade Blunt's daily radio address leaking from a government building. He was speaking of the new day ahead of us: a day of peace and plenty. My footsteps rang in unison with his words as I passed the gloomy block, followed by sparsely stocked grocery shops, a pub or two, and little tobacconists.

And then, finally, Nick's surgery shifted into view, at the top of one of the old Georgian blocks on the south side of the Thames, opposite the Houses of Parliament.

From his consulting room, you could see Big Ben – or what was left of it. The glass had been smashed out of the four clock faces, leaving ugly dark holes like blinded eyes. Apparently the Luftwaffe had shot them to pieces as they scented victory over us and there was no more RAF to stop them – it must have been nothing but sport to them then. Below the tower, most of the Palace of Westminster still stood, but the far end had been turned to rubble in the final battle and no one had rebuilt it. And, in front of it all, the American 'protection troops' stood along the river with their rifles pointing at us. It was that sight, more than any other, I think, that seemed to sum up for me what extremities our nation had been forced into.

'Good afternoon, Mrs Cawson,' Mr Paine, the ageing porter, greeted me from his chair just inside the building entrance.

'Good afternoon.'

'Smog's heavy today.'

'Yes, it is,' I said, doing my best to be friendly despite the thudding pain in my head. He touched his cap in salute and I smiled at his lovely old-fashioned manners. I hoped some things from the past would stay with us.

'Would you like a cup of tea to warm the bones?' He reached into a leather bag and took out a flask. 'My sister sends me honey from her own bees. It's nicer than the daily teaspoon of sugar. Better for you too.'

'Yes it is,' I said happily. 'That would be very nice.' I loved the taste of honey and you didn't see it all that often.

'Good.' He pulled another chair over and poured warm nut-brown tea into a cup. The tip of his tongue pushed between his lips as he concentrated, spooning bright yellow mounds from a jar to the cup and stirring five times in each direction. He took such pains with it.

'Thank you. And you must call me Jane.' I tasted the brew. He was right, the rich honey made it taste far better than the few grains of sugar we were allotted each day.

'And I'm Albert.' He blew on his own cup. 'My granddaughter's called Jane as it happens.' He put his hand inside his jacket and drew out a wallet of photographs. There was one of a little girl playing the violin. She had the same tongue-between-the-lips expression of concentration.

'She looks very good at that.'

'She is. She's going to one of the special music schools soon.'

'Oh, I'm sure she'll love it there. I'm a teacher and someone I used to work with is at one of those schools now. She says they're wonderful – the children really flourish. I rather wish I were that age again so I could keep up my clarinet practice; I was never conscientious enough.'

He chuckled. 'Children. They never change.'

'No they don't. No. But music is such a gift. Maybe one day I'll be able to hear your granddaughter perform.'

'I hope so. You and your husband can be her first audience.'

'Yes we could.'

'Then one day when you have a child I can come to his recital.'

I drank a little more as we looked through a few more photographs and talked about his four grandchildren. He was so proud of them all. 'Now, thank you so much for the tea,' I said after a while. 'I have to go up to the surgery.'

'It was nice speaking to you. Mind how you go.'

'You too.' I waved as I began to climb the stairs.

A welcome surge of warmth drifted over me as I reached the top of the stairs and entered the surgery. Charles, Nick's secretary, was staring out the window.

'Mrs Cawson. I'm sorry, but Dr Cawson isn't here,' he

said, moving to his well-ordered reception desk. It had a little wooden block with his name, CHARLES O'SHEA, on it, that he had pestered Nick for. Charles was always neatly turned out, his fine hair flipped artfully over on the left side, but his figure was squat and somehow shapeless.

'Oh.' It hadn't crossed my mind that Nick wouldn't be there to sit me down and help me stave off the pain.

'You should probably call first next time.'

'Yes, you're right.' I looked at him keenly. I always felt self-conscious in front of Charles. 'Where has he gone?'

'He went out for a walk,' he said, comparing two sheets of paper on his desk. He appeared to have some sort of unpleasant rash on his left hand and when he caught me looking at it he put it in his pocket.

'But the smog has come down.' He shrugged, a very slight movement. 'Well, it's not too bad today,' I said, trying to fill the silence.

'I can give Dr Cawson a message.'

'It's nothing.'

'Nothing?'

I felt more stupid now. 'I have a migraine.'

'I see.' I wondered if he knew what had happened, how things had changed between Nick and me.

'When did he leave?' I asked.

'About an hour ago.'

'An hour ago?'

'As I said.' He sounded as irritable as ever.

'Yes, of course. Sorry.' It just seemed a bit odd. Nick's Mondays were usually his busiest time – people would store up their problems all weekend and demand to see their GP first thing. Nick's patients – many of them Party officials – brooked no refusal and he would normally just snatch a sandwich at his desk for lunch in order to meet all their expectations. And yet he had gone out for a walk at noon. 'The schedule is usually packed, isn't it?' I asked.

'Sometimes.'

'Do you know when he'll be back?'

'No, I don't.'

'Well, I'll wait for him.'

'As you wish.'

I sat in one of the plush seats that Nick had rescued from the lines of bombed-out houses – there was something luxurious about sinking into an armchair that had come from a townhouse once lived in by Lord Such-and-Such – and watched Charles glancing at me out of the corner of his eye as he returned to his work, obviously annoyed by my presence. Lorries shuddered noisily along the road as I waited, and somewhere below us two people seemed to be having a blazing row about the cost of office stationery.

After a while the second post arrived, fluttering through the letterbox, but that was all the excitement to be had and I wished Nick would come back. The time ticked slowly and interminably by, marked by a carriage clock in the corner of the room.

Eventually, I grew tired of watching Charles use two fingers to laboriously type up letters, and I could see that the door to Nick's office was unlocked and ajar. So, ignoring Charles's protestations, I wandered in. The desk was chaotically strewn with the usual mess of pens, a stethoscope, wooden tongue-depressors in a short vase, drug phials spilling out of cartons, a pharmacology textbook and buff folders of medical notes. And there was something else: torn yellow paper in which a small package had been wrapped. Curious, I took it in my hand.

The paper was embossed with the name of a Bristol shop that had once sold perfume to society ladies and now sold it to the wives of Party men. As I lifted it and held it in the air, a scent drifted up, the remnant of what had been bound in the paper. Its sweet, sultry notes were familiar, but I couldn't place it. It was a strange thing to find. 'Charles?' I called out.

'Yes, Mrs Cawson,' he replied, in the same tone as before.

'Why has . . .' But then I stopped. I remembered where I had smelled it before. And my eyes gently closed in utter pain.

I had breathed it twice, that perfume. Once at a party and once, terribly, in my own home. I slowly placed the paper back on the desk and began looking among the items on the desktop, searching through the jumble of instruments and papers for something that would speak of her. The scent was based on rich Virginia tobacco, she had said.

I shoved the instruments and pens aside and rifled through the letters and papers, checking for anything with her name. The package could only have contained a gift for her, I was certain. I searched through it all, turning it all over.

But no, there was nothing else. No note, no letter. And I took a step back, smoothing my palms down my skirt, berating myself. Such a fool I had been, and so wrong. I had been jumping to conclusions, nothing more. I stared out the window and the broken Houses of Parliament filled my view. Would I have acted like this a month ago? Before that party when she had shone like the sun? The party that surely led to a death that still has me twisted in a pain that won't let go? No, no, I was sure that I wouldn't have. A gunboat on patrol passed slowly along the Thames, its searchlight eerie in the smog, and I watched it disappear from sight.

So I pulled myself together, took another deep breath and turned to leave. I would wait calmly for Nick to return and never breathe a word of this to him. That would be for the best.

But then, just as my fingers touched the brass handle, I caught sight of a side table by the door. It had a short pile of brown folders stacked haphazardly on its polished surface; and there was something strange slipped into the middle of the pile. It looked like the edge of a large photograph, seemingly out of place among the medical notes, as if it had been deliberately hidden. I went over and lifted the upper folders and, as I did so, I found that it wasn't a photograph I was holding, it was the cover of a magazine – an old society glossy full of pictures of actors and young debutantes in furs outside nightclubs – the type of frivolous publication that had entirely disappeared under the new, classless regime. Its title, *On the Town*, was blazed across the top in red lettering.

Tensely, I opened it, feeling the smooth paper on my palms, and flicked through a few pages of scattered black-and-white images and unattributed gossip before I noticed that the corner of one page towards the centre of the publication was dog-eared – as if Nick had opened it time after time. My fingers turned quickly to that spread of paper. The pages fell away. And there she was.

In a flashlit scene before one of her film premieres, the faces and smiles around her seemed to drift into the background, their owners blurred and lifeless. It was as if they had stepped back into a whirlwind. And, in the centre of it all, she stood gazing into the camera. Yes, you could see in her eyes that the whole world could go to hell and she would still be there in that light. That blaze of light. I understood why Nick had been unable to leave her in his past.

My hands trembling, I put the magazine back as I had found it and fought to control myself before casually returning to the outer room, where Charles was writing something.

'When is Nick's next appointment?' I asked.

'I'm afraid I can't discuss patients' details,' Charles replied, without looking up.

I paused. 'I just want to know when he'll be back.' He put his pen down but eyed me coolly and didn't reply. I spoke as calmly as I could. 'Is he with someone?'

He took one of those foul Soviet cigarettes from a packet and put a match to it, sending a stream of smoke to the ceiling. 'Dr Cawson has gone for a walk.'

It felt as if the smog were seeping into the room. I went to the window and looked out. With my back to Charles, I gripped the sill and closed my eyes. The words left my mouth but felt distant even as I spoke them. They could have been someone else's. 'Is he with Lorelei?'

In the corner of the room, the clock ticked and the sound of rumbling traffic came and went again. There was a long silence before Charles spoke. 'He has gone for a walk.'

I felt myself collapse inwardly. 'Would you tell me if he were with her? No, don't answer that,' I laughed bitterly. 'I already know.'

'Will there be anything else, Mrs Cawson?' he said, with an unmistakable undertone of anger.

'I . . . Just . . .' I couldn't stay there another second with the seed of humiliation growing in me.

Standing on the kerb, I knew that what I was doing was a mistake, that nothing good would come of it, but I couldn't help myself. I put out my hand and a car stopped. It looked like one of the black vehicles that Party officials used and I wondered if the driver were really a Party chauffeur making a little cash on the side. I gave him the address in our sector on the north-eastern side of the river, close to the Tower of London – an address that had been Nick's too until their divorce. He still received mail there occasionally. The driver mumbled a price, let out the grinding clutch and we moved into dirty traffic ringing with the sound of tram bells and car horns.

We rattled along the road before turning at speed into a one-way street populated with new blocks of flats, and I fell forward as the driver stamped sharply on the brake pedal. A line of vehicles was crawling one by one through a police stop point. My driver swore and turned tightly, accelerating away to take another route through narrow backstreets. The police watched but didn't stop us, probably because we were in a Party car. A stroke of luck. Well, perhaps.

We drove through ruts and past the many trenches where the road was being dug up because the Soviet system of communalized heating was being installed: it would pump hot water from a central station to all the homes in the new tower blocks. It was happening alongside a big overhaul of the telephone network too. First, our lovely old exchange names had been replaced with drab numeric codes: no longer could we ask the operator to connect us with 'Whitehall 5532'; we had to ask for 'Exchange 944, Number 5532'. And then residential numbers had changed in readiness for a mass expansion that would see us all connected with one another for the common good.

As we charged past wrecked houses, my mind tumbled with thoughts. One moment I was sure Nick was with her; the next I told myself that Charles was right: he had simply gone for a walk and nothing more.

Still, my fingers were white with tension when we eventually pulled up outside a row of Edwardian townhouses, and I handed the driver a pound note emblazoned with Marx's grey image. Out in the smog again, I hesitated before pushing the porcelain doorbell button on a house with its plaster cracking away like an old mausoleum. If I pressed it, would she open the door and confusedly ask me why I was on her doorstep? Would she know full well and laugh at me? There was no way of telling. I had to push it home.

A dull ring sounded somewhere inside. I waited.

Nothing. Behind me, a platoon of Young Pioneers marched past. 'When you salute Comrade First Secretary Blunt, just remember what you all owe him,' their CO called out. 'The peace that you live in.'

I tried the bell again. Still nothing.

But then, if Nick were there, they wouldn't answer, of course. They would be in her room. He would be slipping off her dress.

I looked up and down the street, past the marching

Pioneers. And I thought: most of these high houses had rear entrances through which they had once admitted tradesmen: butchers with boxes of fresh meat and soot-crusted chimney sweeps. There would be one for her house.

At the end of the road I discovered an alleyway giving access to the back gardens and counted along until I located the right gate. The wood had long since rotted – little need for the rear entrance now that we were all entitled to use the front – so it was easy to force it open. It led into a wildly overgrown garden, full of weeds and creeping creatures hiding among the stalks. It probably hadn't been touched since Nick had lived here too.

Quelling my fears, I waded in, kicking through wide leaves and pulling myself free from thorny bushes. The back door was unlocked, I found, and I opened it on stiff hinges to reveal an old-fashioned kitchen with a dusty floor. I wondered if she ever ate here or if it was always at restaurants and public events, surrounded by fat Party apparatchiks having their photographs taken with the celebrated actress: Lorelei, the beautiful face that our young Socialist state had once presented to the world.

It would have been a cosy, welcoming room with a family cooking in it, I thought, yet it was quite wasted and barren like this. I passed through and into the hallway, but stopped with a jolt. There was life somewhere. From upstairs, light dance music was echoing in the chill air.

And then she laughed. It was an unbridled, whooping laugh that flew through the house, wrapping itself around me. Just as quickly, it died away to leave only those playful notes from unseen instruments.

I hesitated, afraid now of what I was doing and what I might learn. I stared back towards the kitchen and the door that would take me away from there; but I couldn't leave – really, I had to know. And so, in the cold air, I forced myself to put my foot on the bottom stair.

As I began to climb the steps, a new sound came: some-one else speaking. A man.

I stopped, my hand gripping the bannister so tightly it hurt, straining to hear, to make out his voice. But it was muffled by the music, and I couldn't hear properly, no matter how hard I tried. I told myself that it might not be him; I could be mistaken. The voice might belong to a total stranger. I began to climb again.

My feet took me upwards step by step. And, without really knowing it, sensing rather than hearing it, I became aware of another sound, a thudding like wood hitting wood every five seconds. I couldn't understand what it could be.

'Champagne!' Her voice burst from the music. 'Oh, yes, let's drink up, because what else is there to do?' I pictured her filling their glasses to the brim and a little more hope seeped away.

Now as I rose, the boards creaking under my weight, I saw a strange spread of water on the carpet slipping down like fingers, touching a new stair and another, and another. They were talking more quietly, their voices masked by the music, but I caught the occasional word or phrase from Lorelei. 'Rome'. 'Absolute madness'. 'It was so very dull, but the . . .'

The carpet was soaking now; each footstep into it sent a little flurry of dampness down to the next stair. And finally

I reached the top of the staircase, where a cold draught seemed to swirl around. In front of me was a bedroom door, open just enough to let a blade of light escape; as I watched, it began to move back slowly, pulled by an unseen hand. Wind rushed through. Without warning, it flew away from me, crashing against the wall. The air caught in my chest as I waited for an accusation against me and my unwanted presence. A humiliating dismissal. A sneer.

But all I saw was an empty room. No one stood in the doorway to push me out or to smirk at Nick's betrayal. The room held only furniture covered in dust sheets – a box room of abandoned things; and it was the wind through an open window that was sucking the door open and closed in that five-second rhythm. Through the gaping window I could see one of the new tower blocks topped by the hammer and compass, ready to house families harried out of their tumbledown slum homes. The door slammed shut again, leaving me staring at the blank wood.

Behind me, I heard Lorelei's laughter once more. Gentler than before, but with an undertone that suggested something more . . . more what? Selfish? Lascivious? It was coming from the door opposite and water was spilling out under the door – it must have been the bathroom – to form a stream right down the stairs. 'More Champagne,' she cried. 'Come on, see it off!'

The man laughed and I groped again for the thought that it might not be Nick. The flood ran around my feet, and it seemed that if I stood there long enough I would be worn down by it, like a statue in a river. But I took a deep breath, and decided: to hell with them both.

I grabbed the handle, wrenched it down and threw open

the door. For a moment I was blinded by a lamp shining straight into my eyes.

And in my mind, I have only flickers of what comes next: her face in the light; my feet moving swiftly across glittering, shifting water on black-and-white floor tiles; a figure in a mirror.

Then a mist falls. A darkness, like the smog outside. It sweeps in from the edge of my vision, taking over, fading the lines between everything that I can remember, turning it all black, so that around me there is nothing.

I don't know how long I was there before there was a pain that pulsed on the side of my head – a pain that told me I was waking up. Before I had memories again.

I let that pain pull me out of the darkness, and gradually my eyes opened. Little by little my vision focused to show me the smooth squares of the black-and-white floor. For a second, I had no idea where I was. I only felt my cheek against a floor that was awash with freezing water, and when I raised my head it throbbed. Then I glimpsed the door on the other side of the room and I knew where I was. As my mind cleared, I could just about remember coming in, something happening, and then hitting the floor, with my head feeling like it had split in two.

Now I ached all over, wincing as I prised my shoulders from the floor. A gilt full-length mirror on the wall filled my vision, reflecting nothing but the flowing water. And I heard Lorelei's voice again.

'Just for tonight, sweetheart,' it whispered to me, soft and close. 'That's all.'

For a moment, all I could see were the mirror and the

tide through the room, spilling from the edge of the copper bath, until I twisted to take in an empty bottle of Russian Champagne lying on the tiles. And high above it, unmoving, like an alabaster statue, Lorelei's delicately manicured hand hung, with beads of moisture running slowly along her slim pale wrist. The droplets glistened as I dragged myself upright. I watched them slip down towards her curving shoulder, gathering others, down and down, until finally they melted into the surface of the water, where a dapple of sunlight through a window hit her skin, shining it bright silver. Under the rippling surface, the light fell on little white teeth, a narrow waist and long, pale, graceful limbs made for dancing, or to be seen draped over grass in the heat of summer. And then it touched green eyes open wide, ruby hair swimming like threads in the sea and a mouth frozen open as if it were silently crying out.

Under water, the dead look like the living. They have smiles on their lips, soft skin, hands that seem to reach out for you with feeling. And yet you know that you are looking at a hollow shell.

From the corner of the room her laughter shrieked out again, drawing my gaze to the radio set, its dial glowing orange. Then there was her voice. 'I'll dream of you tonight, darling, if you'll dream of me. If you'll only dream of me.'

I didn't know which of her plays it was. One from before the War, probably.

3

'Oops-a-daisy!'

No, Nick's first words to me weren't what most people would think of as romantic. But then he had caught me falling out of a train carriage on platform four at Waterloo when I was up for the day from Herne Bay with my best friend, Sally. And, anyway, I think it *is* quite romantic that we met entirely by chance.

Sally and I were like two peas in a pod: one hundred and sixty centimetres (my mum would have said five foot three, but you get in trouble these days for imperialist measurements), fresh-faced blondes soon to turn thirty. We had bought matching jackets for the January chill and done our curly hair in the same Greta Garbo style, giggling for a week that we were coming up to find ourselves chaps. The War had robbed us of men in our early twenties, so seven years after it ended we were still trying to make up for lost time. Sally had insisted on Victory Red lipstick and I had gone along with what she wanted, even though I thought it was a bit much.

When the train came to a halt, I opened the door and she saw Nick on the platform, waiting to climb in after our departure. So Sally – never one to hold back – shoved me right on to him, and 'Oops-a-daisy!' was what I heard as I fell straight into his chest. I think it was about two seconds before my cheeks turned the same colour as my lipstick.

'Oh, I'm so sorry,' I said, feeling the flush spreading to my neck as I pushed myself off him.

'No, she's not,' Sally called from behind me.

'I am.'

'She isn't.'

I wasn't completely, if I'm being honest. He just laughed. Nick always had a nice laugh – free and easy; and a handsome, puckish face that could have been eighteen years old or forty. There were a few silver strands in his brown hair, though, giving the game away. He insisted he dyed them that way just to look distinguished.

'Well, if you're not sorry, then you should be,' he said. 'You've got lipstick all over my shirt.'

'Oh, now I'm sorry again.' I blinked down at the cream cotton and saw that it really was stained bright red. 'I could . . .' I ran short of anything I could do. 'Buy you a new one?'

'This one was two pounds.'

'I can't buy you a new one.'

'She can do other things,' shouted Sally, who remained in the doorway, leaning against the frame with her arms folded, enjoying every second.

'Will you shut your trap?' I demanded over my shoulder.

'Only trying to help.' She jumped down. 'All right, let's have a look at you,' she said, examining him. I always marvelled at how forward she was – it must be nice to be like that. She should have been in an infantry regiment or something. 'Nice and tall. Ooh, all your own teeth, I see.'

'I'm a doctor. I don't want to see a dentist if I can help it. Matter of professional pride.'

'Doctor. Right, that's it: looks like I'm up on my own

for the day. I'll see you on the six thirty train,' she told me, striding away past the propaganda posters. 'But if I'm not here, don't wait for me. Oh, and her name's Jane, doctor. She needs some medical attention. You should probably take a look at her.'

'I've seen worse,' he said. I slapped his shoulder and he laughed. There was a moment's hesitation when neither of us knew what we were meant to do next. 'Well, I don't usually perform consultations on the platform at Waterloo Station, so I suppose we had better go somewhere else,' he said.

'Weren't you on your way somewhere?'

'It can wait,' he said with a smile.

Oh, that charm of his. You really could lose yourself in it.

4

As I sit in my study in Winfield House, an old house in Regent's Park, I am but a few hundred yards from the iron curtain that fell across our land some six years ago. It is a wretched and ugly line. Indeed, I am but a few hundred yards from the raised guard posts where young Britons have their rifle sights fixed on their fellow citizens – men and women forced by the Marxist authorities to doubt their friends and family and to fear those whom they should most trust. Tomorrow is their national celebration. A day their self-deluding masters call Liberation Day. And yet I believe that one day the true liberation will be when they break their rusted bonds of servitude.

Winston Churchill, Radio Free Europe address,
Monday, 17 November 1952

'Lorelei!'

Her name echoed all around and rang off the walls. I stared at her, her mouth pulled into that silent scream, her hair wafting under the surface and her eyes as bright as coral. The flood at my feet made it seem like the floor itself was shifting. The black-and-white squares were losing their familiar shape, twisting into one another.

And then a thought pushed into my mind. An urgent

and desperate hope that forced away all the others: perhaps she was still alive.

Perhaps I had mistaken what had happened. There might still be a pulse beating in her wrists. I thrust my hands into the water and tried desperately to lift her, but her head arched back and the sides of the copper bath were too high. As the taps continued to pour down a torrent, I pushed my arms deeper until I was half submerged. 'Lorelei!' I shouted again, fighting against the radio in the corner as it blared her voice, the lines from a play recorded long ago.

Her body against mine as I wrenched her up with all my strength, I cried out her name for the last time. Then her face burst through the surface, her mouth open, as if she were gasping for air, and I stared into her eyes, waiting for them to turn to me. I stared from one to the other.

But there was no breath, no flush of colour on her cheek. And, as I felt it against me, I knew her body was as cold as stone. In that moment, with her in my arms, I collapsed downwards, my hair trailing in the water like hers, some of the strands intertwining and drifting in the tide. At the last I held her against me, feeling my arms shake, feeling numb, before I let her slip back under. Nothing but the icy water now.

The radio crackled as I stumbled out of the room, down the stairs and out the front door. 'And what have you been to me, my love? What have you been to me?'

It was, I suppose, an hour later that I stood again on that landing. The floor was still awash but the radio was broadcasting a man's voice. 'In readiness for tomorrow's magnificent celebrations for Liberation Day . . .' I didn't know when the programme had changed.

The house seemed full of men now. One asked me a question and I think I told him the answer. And Nick was there too – someone must have called him, though it hadn't been me. I was thankful that they had: just having his familiar presence there made it feel like I was still in this world.

'Did you touch her?' It was an older man with square glasses and white hair, thin as a rake, who was speaking to me. He gently guided me away from the doorway so that I couldn't see into the bathroom. 'Did you touch her?'

I turned my bewildered eyes to Nick, wishing that he – or anyone, really – could answer the questions for me. I struggled to form any words: it was as if they had been locked away from me. 'I . . . I tried to pull her out,' I mumbled.

'You tried to lift her out?'

'Yes,' I said. My mind was focusing, fighting through the shock of the body. 'How did she . . . Did someone do that?'

He didn't answer me. 'Go back to the beginning. You entered the room – what then?'

I put my hand to my forehead. As I touched it, I felt a stab of pain. 'I . . . fell. I think I hit my head. On the bath. Then I woke up on the floor.'

He wrote it down in a notepad. 'That's when you saw her, tried to pull her out, couldn't, and ran for help. Is that right?'

My head was throbbing. I saw her image under the water. Shimmering and perfect. White all over. As I tried to remember, it hurt more. 'Yes, that's right,' I said.

'She was definitely dead at the time?' I looked at him now. He had an air about him like one of the houses that had been bombed in the night Blitz, leaving a sad shell that, when the morning came, threatened to collapse in on itself.

'Sergeant, as my wife told you –' Nick interjected.

'Please stay out of this, sir.'

'She was dead. I know she was,' I pleaded. I saw her again.

'Mrs Cawson?'

I realized the policeman had asked me another question but I hadn't heard it. Nick put his arm around my shoulders. 'Sergeant, I'm taking my wife home,' he said. 'She can't remember because she has concussion. It's very common after an accident. You can speak to her later.' He turned to me. 'Just rest. You'll be fine in a couple of days.'

'I'm afraid you can't take her, sir.' I stared at the hammer-and-compass insignia on his cap. Even after years of seeing it, the sight still jarred.

'I can and I will,' Nick insisted, taking me by the arm.

We started to leave and I felt an overwhelming rush of gratitude to him. It wasn't just gratitude, though – mixed in was a sense of guilt that was spreading as I recalled more. I had gone to the house in the mad, unjust belief that Nick was there, making love to her. I looked at him, trying to tell from his face if he knew what I had done, hoping that he didn't, but I saw only concern for me. My eyes blurred with tears and I realized that, until then, I had been too shocked to cry.

But the policeman put an open hand in Nick's path. He wasn't young. He looked as if he had been in a few hard situations in his time and was prepared for another one if politeness wasn't enough. 'Dr Cawson, I can't let your wife leave here until I've spoken to her. It's the scene of a death. We have to know what we're dealing with. You understand, don't you, sir?'

Nick looked as if he were considering knocking the officer's hand aside and taking me home regardless. 'Good God, she's concussed!' he said. 'If you just leave her be, she'll get better, she'll remember more. Talk to her tomorrow.' He rubbed his hand over his eyes. 'And I have to leave. I have to tell my daughter.' My God, I hadn't even thought of Hazel, his daughter with Lorelei. Telling her would be a burden far greater than looking after me.

'I understand, sir, but we'll see what she remembers now. We won't keep her too long.' His manner was kind. I looked up at Nick and nodded. 'I'll make sure she's all right, sir.'

Nick seemed to relent. But there was something else in his manner, and he hesitated. 'Officer,' he said. He took the policeman to one side and said something very quietly.

'I'm sorry to hear that,' muttered the other man. 'When was it?'

'A few weeks ago.'

I knew what Nick had told him. It was something that should have been just for us. The pain of that night, of what had happened at the party where Lorelei had shone so, had not gone away – would never go away – and now he was telling this policeman. It's agonizing to have a stranger know your grief. They looked at me for what seemed a long time. 'Come this way, please,' the officer said to me gently.

'All right,' I said.

He led us into the master bedroom. The walls were covered with theatre playbills and film posters but it didn't register that they were Lorelei's productions until I saw her name in big letters at the bottom of one of them. 'And just what were you doing here, Mrs Cawson?' he asked. I didn't know what to say. The shame I felt, the stupidity – they held the words in my throat. 'Mrs Cawson. What were you doing in Miss Addington's house?'

'Tell him,' said Nick. 'Whatever it is, you have done nothing wrong.'

I gulped down air. 'I thought . . .' The humiliation set fire to my cheeks and held my tongue so that no matter how I tried I couldn't make another sound.

'Sergeant –' began Nick.

'I thought Nick was here,' I blurted out. 'I thought he was here. With her. With Lorelei.'

The policeman looked at Nick with his eyebrows raised. I could see his mind working. Mapping out a chain of events. Nick's mouth fell open a little and he clamped it shut again. I could see his forehead furrow in anger.

'And why did you think that?'

'I don't know!' I cried out. 'I don't know,' I repeated to Nick. 'I'm sorry.'

How I wished I could somehow take back what I had done. If only we could do that in life, as children do when they play games, to save themselves.

'I think you do know,' the officer said.

Nick looked as if he wanted to shout at me but was forcing it down. 'It was nothing,' I insisted.

'Tell me.' The policeman moved between me and Nick,

blocking him. I lifted my hand to Nick, but he made no motion to take it.

I turned over in my mind those little signs that had made me think Nick would be there: the perfume in his office and how it had once been in my home; Nick's absence from the surgery that Charles wouldn't explain. The magazine.

But now I knew my suspicions had been wrong they seemed so transparent and weightless that a breeze would blow them away.

'It was . . . nothing.'

'Nothing?'

'There was a package at his office. Perfume. The one she wears.' For a second, I actually looked to the officer for confirmation that that did, truly, look suspicious, just so I wouldn't feel so idiotic and disloyal.

'What?' Nick burst out, amazement in his voice. 'The . . . I bought a bottle for you. Not her brand, a different one. I thought you would like it.'

It was awful. I was a patient in a madhouse being watched by the sane.

The policeman tapped his pencil on his notepad. 'Where were you today, Dr Cawson?' he asked.

Nick looked like he was about to explode at the implication. 'I went to my surgery and saw my patients. At lunchtime I went for a walk and then to a house call. Comrade Taggan, Deputy Secretary at the Department of Labour. I was there for an hour and a half. After that I returned to my surgery and your station called to say what had happened. I came straight here. Feel free to check.'

The policeman nodded. 'Long house call. It was at his home?'

'Yes.'

'Was anyone else there?'

'Of course not. It was a medical consultation.' Nick became exasperated. 'For God's sake, this was just an accident. They happen all the time.'

'He's not married? Housekeeper? No one else?'

Nick's face darkened. 'He is married. His wife was not there. He has no housekeeper as far as I'm aware. He is a senior government official and also Secretary of his Party branch. I should think his word would be sufficient.'

'Thank you.' The officer nodded. 'Would you please wait downstairs?' Nick glanced at me as he passed. I saw anger in his eyes. I couldn't tell who had inspired it but some of it was probably directed at me. I think I would have felt better if he had torn into me. 'Do you work, Mrs Cawson?'

'I'm a teacher. English.'

'Which school?'

I fluttered my hands. 'I don't have a job right now.' I didn't want to explain that for the half-year since I had married Nick I had been writing to education boards hoping for a position in one of the new schools opened by the Republic and hadn't been offered one. But I realized that it wasn't just my hands that were fluttering – my whole body was shaking. I stared at my limbs.

'It's the shock,' he said. 'It's normal. You'll be all right.'

The bedroom door opened and a well-built man in his thirties with an aquiline nose and a bald head entered, looking around the room in a methodical way. He didn't wear a uniform and the old policeman seemed annoyed at the man's presence, smacking his notepad against his hip in irritation. The newcomer leaned against the wall and waved his hand in a manner that said we should continue. 'When did you get married?' the white-haired policeman asked.

'May the twelfth.'

'This year?'

'Yes.'

'Where?'

'Lambeth Records Office.'

He wrote it down. For another ten minutes we went through what I had seen and not seen, heard and not heard. There wasn't much. I kept looking at the other man, bemused by whom he could be. He said nothing and yet somehow had an air of authority. I can't properly explain it – it was just something about the way he held himself. 'Was there anyone else here?' the policeman asked. I was about to say no, but hesitated. He noticed. 'Think very carefully.'

I put my hands to my temples. And, as I concentrated, I saw those flickers of memory from just before I fell. I closed my eyes.

I had climbed the stairs; thrown open the bathroom door. And then, in the light, there was Lorelei. I saw her again now, red hair, pale skin. Her beauty unmistakable. But was she alive or dead? Ready to cry out or past caring about this world? I couldn't be certain. After seeing her, my feet had moved over the wet tiles; and as I looked up, there had been something reflected in the gilt mirror above the bath. Something dark – a figure. I tried to make it out now but it was too obscure, too shifting.

After that, I had fallen, cascading on to the solid metal

of the bath, down into the black. And I had woken to find her drifting under the water. I ran then for the police.

I dropped my hands and looked at the officer. 'What is it?' he said.

'There might have been someone behind me.'

'Who?' He spoke urgently.

'I don't know. There's a mirror there. I think I saw someone in it.'

'Man or woman?'

Desperately I tried to picture the rough form. I wanted to turn the fading edges into clean lines and the greys into colours, but I couldn't. It remained a ragged silhouette. I shook my head. 'I'm sorry, it's too blurred.'

'You have to try.'

And so I tried again, seeing the shifting water reflected in the glass. Waves of light ran across its surface and I tried to focus on them, telling myself that if I remembered, it would mean an end to this terrible day and Nick and I could go home. He would loathe me for my unfounded suspicions about him, but we could get through it and pick up the pieces. Yet, no matter how hard I reached for the memory, feeling my head pulse with the effort, it stayed locked away from me as surely as if it had never formed. 'I can't,' I whispered.

'*Try.*'

'I can't, I just can't!' There was silence. I looked at the other man in the room. He said nothing.

The policeman rolled his pen in his fingers thought-fully. Then he went back to asking me more questions and I answered them. Questions about my family and how long I had been in London, that sort of thing. From time to time he would softly return to the image in the mirror but what remained of the memory seemed to crumble and become less real every time.

He wrote everything down in his notebook and I had to sign each page to say it was a true statement of the facts. My fingers could barely hold the pen as I did so – the shock still, I supposed. I might be required to attend the station to make another statement soon, he told me. 'What happened to her?' I asked, with my eyes cast down. 'To Lorelei.'

He cleared his throat. 'That's what we're going to find out.'

And then, finally, the other man spoke. 'I think that will be all,' he said. His voice was calm and controlled.

At first I presumed he was speaking to me. But the policeman replied, 'Is that so?' I could tell by his face that he was beaten, though, and I got the sense that there was something going on that I couldn't see.

'Thank you, Detective Sergeant. May I have your notes, please? They will go in our files.' And that's when I realized who he was. I had thought he must be a senior plain-clothes policeman, but I was wrong, of course.

The old police officer paused briefly to critically appraise him, but he didn't challenge him before ripping the pages out of his notebook, handing them over and walking out.

The bald man spoke. 'My name is Grest. I'm an officer of the National Security Police. Mrs Cawson, you'll be free to go soon.' I had never come face to face with a NatSec officer before. If I had started feeling less tense, less taut about where I was and what had happened, his presence reversed that.

'I'll go now,' I said, feeling a seed of fear in my stomach.

'No. Not yet, I'm afraid.' His tone was smoother than the other officer's, yet the message underneath it was far harsher and he made me nervous. I went for the door but he moved more quickly than I could and jammed his arm against it, stopping me in my tracks. There was something frighteningly mechanical and practised about the way he plucked me away and pushed me back into the centre of the room to sit on the bed. It made no sense because I had explained all I knew and I just wanted to leave with Nick.

'Please let me go,' I said.

'Soon.'

I sank a little into the bed and stared around. Lorelei's face gazed out from posters on every wall. The theatre bills were the more sedate, with just the name of the show, an inked image or two and the performance dates, but the garish film posters seemed crass, her presence in those films a mockery of a life that was now consigned to the past. *The Whole Deal*; *A Month in the Country*; *Daisy Daisy*; *Victory 1945*. Her image would still laugh and move and dance in them, but the human being was gone.

I stared blankly at *Victory 1945*. Lorelei's finest hour. It was a film we had all seen many times, its poster dominated by the image of her character's boyfriend wrestling a Gestapo officer to the ground. At the side she stood on a plinth, rousing the crowd to rise up against the Nazis and welcome our Red Army liberators arriving on the *Archangel*.

Below it, her cosmetics and hairbrush lay on the dresser still, objects as strangely lifeless now as her images on the posters. I touched the brush; it was made of fine bristles, with an ebony handle and silver detailing. A few of her hairs were entwined on it, long and shining. I put it to my own hair. Then in a moment I caught myself and dropped it, remembering where she was now.

After a few minutes, Grest checked what was happening outside. He seemed satisfied by what he saw and opened the door wide, indicating that I could leave. At that sign I felt an inexpressible surge of relief and hurried out to the top of the stairs, but, as my feet touched the top step, something pulled me up. The terrifying sight below was of Nick being pushed out the house by a heavyset man, his wrists in handcuffs. I couldn't understand. He looked up at me. 'It will be fine. I haven't done anything,' he called up. But his face betrayed the worry he clearly felt and I could only stare open-mouthed. 'I'm all right. I'm all right.' He was shoved out the door.

A second later my mind began to work again and I started to rush down, but the thin, white-haired police-man was at the bottom and he caught me before I could run outside. 'Don't,' he said. 'Best not.'

'Is he under arrest?' I asked, frantic for someone to tell me what was going on.

It was Grest who spoke again. 'It would be best if you go home, Mrs Cawson,' he said from above us.

The suggestion seemed to me nothing but a joke at my expense. Amid all the madness and confusion, I had been clinging to Nick, and now all that was left was the chaos.

'Is he under arrest?' I pleaded.

'Yes,' replied the old policeman.

'Why?' I couldn't think why they wanted him. It made no sense. He couldn't have been involved in Lorelei's death. He hadn't been there. I wanted to shout it to them to make them understand. What were they not telling me?

The policeman just looked up at Grest. 'Ask him.'

The Sec spoke: 'We will speak to you again later, Mrs Cawson. But for now I can have a car take you home.'

I looked to the white-haired officer. He seemed to shake his head very subtly. With an effort, I quelled my nerves. Nick hadn't done anything, I told myself, so he would be safe. 'No, I can find my own way,' I said, forcing the words out as if things were normal. 'Thank you.'

'Your choice,' Grest replied.

'When will my husband be back?' I asked.

'That depends on him.'

I wanted to scream out that we weren't criminals. 'Where are you taking him?'

I looked again to the policeman, and his uncomfortable silence gave me my only answer.

5

Our house was in a street of semi-detached properties built for the Edwardian middle classes, close to the southern end of Blackfriars Bridge. When I first saw it, I was taken by its simple, solid lines. It wasn't grand but it had four bedrooms – twice as many as the little house where I had grown up – so it seemed huge to me. I wondered how Nick could afford such a place on a GP's salary but his dark eyes had twinkled when I asked and he led me around the back to show why it was so cheap: the rear wall had been shorn away by a doodlebug in '44, leaving a pile of rubble and a scar in the ground. A hastily erected wall in the middle of what had once been a rear parlour was the new back to the house, and a split in the bricks halfway up gave a pair of jackdaws access to the wall cavity, wherein they had built a nest.

If there hadn't been a shortage of labour due to all the new flats being put up, Nick said, he could possibly have had the back of the house repaired properly, but as things stood we would just have to lump it. It didn't seem such a hardship, in fact, I was excited about changes like the government's push for housebuilding.

There were people who grumbled about the new way of things, but I couldn't understand them, really – it would be wonderful, as far as I was concerned, to see an end to people living in slums and tenements. That would be the first great achievement of our new system and it did seem that the future could only be brighter. I had even been allowed to attend a couple of Party meetings in Herne Bay – although I had been quietly shown the door when I unwittingly broke the rules by mentioning the wrong thing.

Before the outbreak of the War, the Soviet Union had signed a peace agreement with Germany and had stuck to it, watching while the Nazi soldiers marched into Warsaw, Brussels, Paris and, finally, in 1944, London. That was when the Royal Family had fled to safety in Northern Ireland, then exile in Canada a month later, for it seemed all was lost. Six months after that the Red Army's twelve million fresh troops had overrun the over-stretched German lines to claim all that territory for themselves; and the Soviets' ensuing advance up through Britain had been halted only when the Americans had arrived in the North. The Royal Family had followed and taken up residence in Holyrood, their Edinburgh home. But, in the drizzle outside the Herne Bay Party meeting, it was explained to me that, while the glorious arrival of the Red Army was to be frequently celebrated, no reference was ever to be made to the Soviet Union's prior agreement with the Nazis. It was no longer history. Well, I had my misgivings, but I tacitly agreed. After all, the past was less important than the future.

As I drew close to our house now, I saw someone on our doorstep: Charles. I felt such a rush of relief. We were hardly friends but here was someone who knew Nick, who would sympathize and help. Maybe he even knew something about why they had taken Nick, or what could have happened to Lorelei, and could lead me through the confusion.

42

'Mrs Cawson. I have been calling for an hour. Is Dr Cawson here?' he asked as soon as I was within earshot.

'Oh, God, he's been arrested,' I said.

He stopped, confused. 'The police?'

'NatSec.'

Confusion turned to amazement. 'They took him to Great Queen Street?'

'Yes. They —'

'No.' He looked around to see if anyone had overheard. 'Tell me inside.'

I was gabbling, I knew, as we hurried to the parlour. Charles had a limping gait, the result, Nick had once told me, of taking a round to his hip on D-Day, and I was rushing ahead of him. 'Lorelei. She's . . .' The shock came back to me as we reached the room. 'I found her dead.' His mouth fell open. 'In her home.'

'Her home?' He could only repeat what I had said, as if it couldn't be true.

'The bathroom. She drowned.'

'Why?' he asked after swallowing hard. 'What —'

'I don't know. I don't know. They've taken Nick. Why do you think they did that?'

He stared at me. 'I have no idea. Was he there?'

'No,' I said, fighting back tears.

'What happened to her?'

'They're trying to find out. Can you think of anything about her, why it could have happened?'

He shook his head, scratching that rash on his hand until it became an angry crimson. 'What did they tell you?'

'Nothing!' I related what had happened. When I had finished, he went to the window and stood there for a

43

while, before pulling the curtain fully across and sitting in the wing-backed chair. 'What shall we do?' I begged him. Now that the shock was wearing off, my stomach was twisting at the thought that it was my baseless suspicions that had resulted in Nick being taken in. If I hadn't gone there, he would never have been sent for and would probably have come home from the surgery like any other day.

Charles rubbed his forehead. Mine still ached from where I had hit it on the bath, although the pain was lessening. 'It's hard to say. I have some friends in the Party. I'll contact them and ask them to find out the situation.'

'Can they get him out?' It was a glimmer of hope.

'I believe they can try.'

'Well, please call them. Please. Do anything you can think of. Anything.' That guilt, I knew, would tear me to pieces if things turned worse.

'Yes, yes, I will. Straight away. Can you think of any friends of your husband's who might be able to exert some influence?'

I sat mentally running through all of Nick's friends and colleagues who might be of use. But my mind just wasn't working properly. And, besides that, I didn't really know many or what they could achieve. Charles put forward a few names but I was only vaguely aware of them. He knew them and their potential far better than I did, so I just agreed to whatever he suggested. I ran out of words. I had never known anyone taken away by NatSec.

We were interrupted by a knock on the front door and my heart leaped at the thought that it might be news of Nick's release. When I dashed to answer it, I found a woman in police uniform on the doorstep and I felt sure this must be it, she had come to tell me Nick was coming home – but then I saw, behind her, a tall, thin fourteen-year-old girl, her orange hair falling across her face from under a school cap, and I realized that the officer's visit was for a different reason. 'Oh, Hazel,' I said, going to the girl with my arms outstretched.

'Are you her stepmother?' asked the policewoman.

'Yes.'

Nick's daughter had been at one of the state's dreary boarding schools until the beginning of the new academic year, when she had come back to live with her mother and go to a normal school. I had only met her a handful of times and now she was here. Nick's parents were dead and Lorelei's mother was old and frail, I knew, so there was no immediate place of safety and familiarity to take her in. I tried to put my arms around her shoulders in the hope that I could bring her some comfort, but she pulled back and hugged her bag to her torso. My arms hung in mid-air before I let them drop.

'She was at a friend's. Got home and found us there, packing up,' the officer explained quietly, as if the girl wouldn't hear her. Why do people think children can't see what's right in front of them?

'Come in,' I said. The girl shuffled into the hall. She looked like all the blood had been drained from her.

'Will she be staying with you?'

'Oh, yes. Of course.' Hazel looked at her feet and seemed to shrink further into herself. 'She'll be all right here.' The officer nodded, glanced at the girl and left, joining a male colleague stamping his feet to keep warm in the five o'clock twilight.

45

Charles had appeared behind me. 'Are you really going to look after . . .' he began, with a sceptical look on his face.

'Yes.'

'As you wish.' He returned to the parlour.

'Hazel.' I lifted her satchel from her hands, placed it on the floor and wrapped my arms around her. She was shaking. 'You'll be staying with us now. You'll be all right.'

She tried to speak but could hardly form the words. She was in shock too, I could see; the grief hadn't yet hit her. 'Where's Dad?' she managed to stutter.

I didn't know what to say. I had presumed the policewoman had informed her about Nick, but the girl had been told only that her mother had died.

'He's not here right now,' I said.

'Where is he?' There was need in her voice, but in her eyes there was something else. A flash of what? Resentment? She wanted her father and instead here I was swanning around in his home.

It was best she knew, I thought, or she would become more frantic the longer it was delayed. 'The National Security people are talking to him.'

'He's in Great Queen Street?' she gasped. I had hoped she wouldn't know much about 60 Great Queen Street. A forlorn hope.

'Yes, but he'll be fine,' I said quickly. 'He's done nothing wrong; they just think he can help them work out what happened.' She dropped on to the stairs and buried her face in her arms. I could do nothing but stroke her back. She flinched from my touch. 'He'll be with us soon.' Her mouth opened as if she were trying to form words, but closed again as tears began to course down her cheeks. 'I have to . . .' she

46

sobbed, trying to speak. 'My mum. I . . .' But she couldn't go on and I gave her a few minutes just to cry.

'You'll be all right,' I said again, at a loss for anything else to say, anything with depth to it. I wanted to talk more to Charles, to see if there were anything we could do for Nick, but right now this girl needed me.

'No,' she whispered.

'You will.'

She gazed up at me and her expression changed, as if she were making her mind up about something. 'I have to go back to my house,' she said, her mouth still twisted by sadness.

'What?' I couldn't understand. Did she want to say goodbye to her mother? 'Why?'

'I just have to go there. I need to get something.'

'What is it?'

She froze. I turned to see Charles with his arms folded. Hazel looked at her feet. 'What are you talking about?' he said. 'Perhaps I can help.'

'Thank you, but no,' I said forcefully.

'As you wish.' He walked back to his chair and I closed the door behind him – this looked to be something that Hazel wanted to keep private.

'Hazel, you can't,' I whispered. 'It's . . . you just can't. The police won't let you.'

'I'm going!' she said defiantly.

What could I say? 'Oh, Hazel, I can't think what you're going through, but I have to make sure you're all right. Do you want your clothes? I'll lend you some.' She looked at me, then suddenly broke away and ran out the door. She was in such a state of distress that I was worried what she would

47

do. 'Hazel!' I shouted, as I grabbed my purse and keys from the table and chased after her along the smog-filled road. I caught up with her after twenty paces and pulled her, struggling, to the side of the pavement. 'You can't go there. It's not safe!' I insisted. I was becoming almost as wild as her. I held her tightly and she tried to fight me off. 'Hazel, that's enough. It's not safe for you or for your dad.' She kept tugging away from me, but with less fervour.

'I need to get something,' she said to the ground.

'What? Tell me.'

She wiped her face. She was trying to remain defiant but it wasn't really in her. 'Something of Mum's.'

She stopped again. Charles was walking towards us. 'I'm going to see what I can find out,' he said.

'All right,' I said, exasperated by his interruption.

'You should go inside. Both of you. Wait until I come back. Don't do anything else.'

'Charles, he's my husband.'

'I'm as concerned as you are. But we have to understand that the state takes precautions when it feels a citizen may be endangering society.' He had changed his tune.

A fury hit me. 'Is that what you think he's done?' I demanded. 'Put the state in danger?' It seemed so absurd. He seemed absurd. I saw the curtains of the house beside ours twitch.

'It doesn't matter what I think. It is what the state thinks that matters. And that is precisely what I'm going to find out.' He stalked away without another word. I had no time to argue with him too.

Hazel had composed herself. 'Please, can I go?' she said.

'No.' But there was clearly something she was keeping to herself, and I softened. 'Hazel, whatever it is, you can tell me. I only want what's best for you and your dad.' She hesitated, unable to decide whether to tell me. But the girl was fourteen and her need to trust someone was winning. 'Hazel?'

'I think . . .' she stammered. She lowered her voice and I had to lean in to hear her properly. 'I think Mum was hiding something. In my room.'

I glanced around. 'What do you mean?' But already my mind was racing on. It made some sense out of a situation that seemed inexplicable: the Secs wouldn't normally attend a domestic death; their work was political – subversives, plots against the state. So what had Lorelei got herself into? 'Is that why NatSec was at your house?' I asked, with some trepidation. She nodded, and I began to understand why the girl was so desperate. I gripped her hand in mine and stared straight ahead as my mind worked double speed. 'Hazel, what was she hiding?'

She was about to answer but halted at the sight of a young couple walking past, wearing worker's caps with Spartacist badges on them. They were probably off to a meeting in advance of Liberation Day. Hazel waited until they had gone before she spoke. 'I'm not sure.' She put her hands to her cheeks. 'She did it even before Mum and Dad split up. They didn't know I knew about it.'

'Where is it?'

She hesitated. 'In the ceiling. You can take the light fitting out and there's a sort of hole you can put things in. Mum put them there when she thought I was asleep.'

It wasn't unusual for people to have hiding places – for fake food coupons, foreign currency or pro-American

49

samizdat leaflets surreptitiously circulated among the most trusted friends. But somehow this sounded different.

'What was she hiding?' I made her look at me. 'It's important.'

She glanced nervously at the backs of the Spartacist couple as they disappeared into the smog. 'I'm not sure. It was boxes, white boxes made out of card. This big.' She held her palms about thirty centimetres apart.

Card boxes that size, well, that could be anything. 'Do you know what was in them?'

'I never looked. I thought Mum might catch me.'

'I'll get them,' I said.

I had no idea if Lorelei's house had been searched. If it had been, the police or the Secs might have found whatever it was she had been storing. They might have thought Nick was involved and that was why they had taken him. On the other hand, if the house hadn't yet been searched, I felt that I had to get there before it was, or that evidence could be held against Nick and he might never be released. Perhaps if I hadn't felt so guilty for suspecting him earlier, and desperately needed to make penance for it, I wouldn't have had the courage. It just wasn't the sort of reckless thing I would do.

'Will you?'

I pulled together as much resolve as I could find in myself. 'Yes.'

We talk of love as such a powerful driver of what we say and do, but sometimes guilt is just as strong.

It took me half an hour to walk back to Lorelei's house over Blackfriars Bridge, past the bombed-out shops and even an old Victorian doss house where the destitute once slept in coffin-like boxes for a few pence per night.

I had lived through the hunger of the Depression and the sheer brutality of the War, and I would never shake those memories; yet from that massed rubble we would create something to be proud of. I was certain of that. Ending the slum poverty was the first step, and all those new tower blocks were proof of our intention. No, our new nation wasn't spotless – people talked quietly of NatSec's visits during the night; and it felt low after five hundred years of parliaments to have a government choose itself – but the free hospitals and schools we were promised had to count for something. Soon there would be no more private healthcare; it would all be provided by the state, with the same for everyone; and education for the sons of bricklayers would be as good as for the sons of dukes. Sometimes to get out of the wood you have to pass through the brambles. That's what I told myself any time I began to doubt.

There was a police notice on the front of Lorelei's house, warning people not to enter, but no one was around to enforce it. Once again, I stole in through the back gate. In the dusk the garden seemed different – thicker and danker as I trod through finger-like tugging weeds and over mounds of earth to the kitchen door.

I didn't dare turn on the lights when I got in, so the house stayed hidden from me, until, slowly, my eyes adjusted to the weak glow from the streetlights outside. I slipped silently through the hall and up the damp stairs, and I couldn't help but open the door to the bathroom, to see stagnant pools of water on the floor. Even though I knew

Lorelei's body was long gone, my stomach twisted when I gazed at the copper bath, before my eyes rose to the gilt mirror on the opposite wall. And then, as my heart began to beat faster, I tried to picture someone in the dark glass, to bring the memories back. Something began to form.

A sound made me stop: creaking from somewhere in the house. I froze, nervously trying to hear; all I could make out, though, was the wind outside and a draught through the cracks. After a while, not moving a muscle, I decided that it had only been the house settling, but I knew I shouldn't spend any longer here than was necessary, so I hurried out to find Hazel's bedroom in order to collect what I had come for.

One of three on the upper floor, Hazel's bedroom was pleasant and airy despite the gloom. She liked books, I could see from her shelves. They were filled with a mixture of classics – Dickens, the Brontës, Louisa May Alcott – and the sort of girlish romances that I used to read at her age. If I had been there any other time, seeing this would have made me smile – to know that, when it came down to it, each generation was just like the last. But the circumstances hardly allowed for sentimentality.

There was a desk and a chair that she had covered in a velvet throw. I pulled the chair underneath the wide brass light fitting and stood on it to reach. Just as Hazel had told me, the fitting unscrewed. It came away quite easily, hanging from the cable, to leave a roughly cut hole in the ceiling. I stretched up so that I could see into the cavity above it and gingerly, worried about what I might find, slipped my hand inside. I felt about until I touched something smooth, something that moved as I probed it. Reaching further, I managed to twist it out.

A white box made of card lay in my hands, looking quite plain, quite unremarkable, yet I couldn't help but hope that this was the key to how and why Lorelei had died. The key to getting Nick released.

It was about the size of a dinner plate, ten centimetres tall, without a single mark on it to denote its contents. I lifted the lid. It tipped up to reveal that the box was divided into a dozen identical little segments – but, crushingly, whatever had once been in those compartments was now gone. The thing was empty and meaningless.

I was about to cast it aside in anger when something struck me, though: a sense that there was something familiar about the box, something that I recognized. I was sure that I had seen one like it before. And yet I couldn't think where.

It had been years ago, I was sure of that – when I was younger, although not a child – but when? Where? I racked my brains trying to remember more.

It was the clamour of a police-car bell outside that made me stop. Nervous, I eased back the curtain and looked out the window. The car came close to the house, charging through the ruts and black water, but continued straight past without slowing. It wasn't coming here – but, my God, what they could do to us just with the sound of a bell.

I returned to the box, weighing it in my hand and trying to picture another like it. I paced thoughtfully around Hazel's room, surrounded by her books; the pictures on her wall; the soft pink ballet shoes tied to the back of her door; her navy school skirt and blouse slung over the back of a chair. I could have kicked myself for not being able to remember. The dank house, it was as if it were taunting me. Then I halted and looked back at the chair.

That uniform. I stared at it. And suddenly I was back in another time, a time when I had worn a muddy-brown uniform, my feet damp even through thick leather boots as thin rain drizzled down. Yet a thrill of excitement was running through me as I looked along the barrel of a bolt-action rifle. I and twenty other girls were all lined up for our Compulsory Basic at a run-down former naval base in Kent and I reached into a carton just like this one to lift out a round, before slotting it into the breach and squeezing the trigger. Then came the explosion and a kick into the muscle of my shoulder. Followed by the dark, distant hole appearing in the target.

I held up the box, my mind churning, the speckled light making the white box a dull grey. Is that what it had held? Those little metal spears? And, if so, what the hell was Lorelei hiding them for? I couldn't for a single second picture the beautiful actress who wore furs firing a weapon. The idea seemed wholly impossible.

Of course, they could have been for someone else – but then, in a sense, it didn't matter: whatever her purpose in storing them, it was placing us all in danger. Another creak from the house startled me and made me catch my breath.

I put the box on the bed and stepped back on to the chair. Once more I reached into the void and patted my hand around to see if there was anything else up there. I felt nothing and was about to jump down when my fingers touched the corner of something hard. Stretching up, with my feet unsteady on the chair, I just managed to pull it out.

It was a thin hardback book with plain leather covering, like a ledger I thought, and about the dimensions of a school exercise book. Curious, I opened it to find blocks of writing, but before I could examine them, I heard a violent metallic ringing from outside that told me the police car was coming back. I crept to the window with my heart in my mouth. The car was drawing closer, from the end of the street, then to within fifty metres, finally stopping abruptly on the other side of the road, a few houses up. I waited to see, trying to think if I could run – but where to? For a few moments nothing happened, then three plain-clothes officers jumped out and charged up to the nearest house, where they began hammering on a red door until it opened and they all rushed in. I felt relief. They hadn't come for me, but I knew that I should leave.

After replacing the light fitting, with my hands trembling a little, I went into Lorelei's bedroom in search of a bag to hide what I had found. At the back of a wardrobe I found one with a stiff flat base inside. I tore away some of the thread and managed to slip the book between the base and the outer fabric. The box that I had taken was designed to fold flat, so that went in too. I dropped in my purse, handkerchief, and a silk scarf I found on the floor of the wardrobe to cover it all, put the bag over my shoulder and went out the back of the house, checking around carefully before hurrying away in the dark.

As soon as it felt safe, I stopped walking. On the other side of the road a little corner café was still open and advertising fresh mutton in the stew, rather than the spam and corned beef that still made up the meat staple of our diet. It seemed a good place to sit for a while to examine what I had taken.

I sat at a cracked table to order a tea, carefully lifted out the book and opened it to discover the pages were fine old paper, thick and creamy, thinly lined. I didn't recognize the handwriting that appeared – it could have been Lorelei's and I knew it wasn't Nick's, unless he had gone to some pains to disguise it. It was compact yet spiderishly untidy, and it made me wonder about the person who had made those little marks and dashes on the page – can you really tell someone's personality from their handwriting? It seems a silly idea, and yet, as I traced the careless lines and reckless curls, they seemed to conjure the woman I presumed was their author. I pictured her rapidly scratching a pen across the surface of each page, with the doors locked and bolted to prevent anyone catching her. The writing filled page after page, but it was all in a strange form, nothing like what I had expected.

6

'Lucky old Democratic United Kingdom. All the best parts of London are over there,' Nick said, peering through the wire fence, across the Thames to the fenced-in north-western sector and the American troops guarding its borders. 'I always fancied myself as a bit of a boulevardier, you see. No chance of that now. Goodbye, Westminster, farewell, Buckingham Palace. Hello, Croydon.' He rubbed his chin. 'And hello, American soldiers too.'

We were beside the wreck of Westminster Bridge – the first stop on a sightseeing tour upon which he was taking me that first day that we met.

I looked through the fence too. The other side seemed very far away. 'Were you in the army?'

'Yes.'

'D-Day?'

'Yes,' he said.

'POW?'

He dropped his cigarette and ground it underfoot. 'In Belgium.' I never knew what to say to men who had been through what he had been through. There were so many of them, and yet I was always lost for words. He didn't want to talk about it either, it seemed, and instead gazed up at the huge grey battleship towering above us. 'Do you know about the *Archangel*?' he asked.

Of course I did. Everyone knew about the iron angel

that watched over London, with her searchlights sweeping the water of the Thames at night to prevent American spies coming over to our side. It was aboard her that the first Soviet troops had arrived in 1945. 'Yes.' I paused. Before we started chatting about the *Archangel* and all the other strange things that had fallen on London, there was something I needed to ask. Sally was always getting in trouble with married men, and it had made me cautious. 'You're not married, are you?' I said.

He hesitated before bursting out laughing. 'Well, you're direct. All right, the truth is I'm getting divorced, but it's not yet final. And I have a daughter. She's a lovely girl. Very sensitive. Not like her mother.'

I wasn't sure how I felt about all that. 'You sound like you can't wait for the divorce.'

'I can't.'

'Is she that bad? What's she like?' I tried not to sound jealous.

'An actress. She was a bit of a star for a couple of years.'

'Fancy.' I hated her.

'Sometimes. But not me, I'm just your average family doctor.'

'You're not, though, are you?' I said, meaning it. 'Average, I mean.'

'Well, who wants to be average?' He thrust his hands in his pockets and suddenly he seemed like one of the boys I had had to tell off for making the others giggle in class. 'Right, well, let's head for Covent Garden. Scene of drunks and reprobates for four hundred years.'

'All right.'

We spent the day wandering around Covent Garden,

watching the musicians and Punch and Judy shows. The big theatre there was once Britain's finest opera house, Nick told me. Now it sported mass entertainment for the workers' tastes – vaudeville acts, gay singers and slapstick comedy. We arrived back at Waterloo Station as the sun was setting but didn't say much – we were a bit too thought-ful, I think. I climbed up to the carriage and leaned out the window.

'I would like to see you again,' he said.

'Why?' I asked. I genuinely couldn't understand why someone like him would be interested in someone like me.

'Kindred spirit,' he said.

7

Checking to make sure that the waitress was in the café kitchen, I flicked quickly through Lorelei's book. It was written in watery ink, spread through twenty-odd sections. Each section was separated from the next by a blank page. Each had two columns. The first was a column of strings of two letters followed by thirteen digits. The second was a column of three-letter strings.

The first section in the book had four lines. They remained throughout the book, but more lines were added from time to time, growing to seven lines in the final section:

DD2261033445298	wfn
VN1081209994632	str cor
TW3284408109028	pro wfn
AM7126026369346	cor
VN4653310089328	cor str
DO5574301038201	wfn pro
TL2159414038033	nor

Throughout the book, the first column of letters and numbers would always be complete, but sometimes the second column would be blank.

I spent a long time trying to guess what it could all mean, but in the end I could make nothing of it other than that Lorelei had had something to hide and had gone to some effort to do so.

I suppose I have never had the sort of mind suited to deciphering codes: I was the very last person you would describe as devious, I just tended to take things at face value. It made me a pushover for my pupils, of course: if they had failed to complete their homework or turned up late, I would believe any excuse if it were told with an honest-looking face.

It would take some puzzling over – and Hazel was waiting at home for me, I reminded myself. So I placed the book back into Lorelei's bag and set off for home. I would try to decipher it there.

Outside, I kept up a good pace despite the smog and it wasn't long before I caught sight of our house. It seemed like a sanctuary now, and it was a relief just to come within a hundred paces of it. With Lorelei's secrets in my possession, Nick might soon be back with us, I told myself.

As I drew close, a beam of light from the front window pierced the mist and I saw my two-year-old ginger cat, Julius, sitting neatly on the step, watching my approach. His amber eyes blinked at me but he jumped up and bounded away when a noise spooked him. I glanced around to see a vehicle coming to a stop behind me: a delivery van with its passenger door open. A man got out, silhouetted by the van's headlights. 'Jane Cawson?' he demanded.

'Yes,' I replied, taken aback and worried by the thought of who he might be.

He took me forcefully by the arm and pulled me around to the back of the vehicle. 'Come on, be a good girl.'

'Have I done something wrong?' I asked fearfully. I was just metres from my house but couldn't reach it.

'You'll find out.' Someone opened the van's rear door and I was pushed inside to find two narrow little cages made of fine steel mesh. I tried to protest but the sound wouldn't come and a slender young man who had been waiting inside grabbed my leather bag, before shoving me hard into the far cage. The van door slammed closed and for a moment we were in perfect darkness. Then a very dim blue light came on above his head. Under its pale glow, he flicked open the bag's tarnished brass clasp and turned it all upside down. My purse and the handkerchief dropped out. I prayed that neither the book nor the card box that I had taken from Hazel's room would fall out from under the stiff base where I had slipped them.

The guard opened the purse and turned his nose up, as if its contents weren't even worth pocketing. 'Load of shit,' he muttered, tossing it aside.

'Please,' I said. He just snorted. 'Why are –' He smacked a baton across the steel and the vibrations went through me, making my teeth grind. He took hold of a hand grip set in the roof, flicked a switch and the light was off again. 'Please, are you NatSec?' I said, just wanting to know what was happening. The only answer I got was the sound of the engine gunning, and the wheels turning on the tarmac.

We bounced along through potholes for a while before turning this way and that. I tried to keep my mind focused, but the panic was rising and I had to fight a surge of sickness as I braced myself against the two sides of the mesh cage. The floor of the van shook hard under me and I gave in, slumping down. It was all a whirlpool.

We stopped from time to time, once coming to what seemed to be an emergency halt that slammed me against the side of the cage. The guard must have been thrown too, because he mumbled something angry under his breath. And then, finally, after what must have been half an hour, we slowed and made a series of small manoeuvres.

I stood up, trying to find some sort of purchase on the wire mesh, but didn't dare say anything. The back door was opened and I had wild thoughts of somehow breaking free and running out into the darkness, although I knew it was impossible. Instead, I watched the young man squeeze out, his feet clunking on the floor as he went, and wondered if I would be dragged from the vehicle, to some unknown building like so many others were said to have been. But the guard's place was instead taken by another, bigger man who clambered inside before closing the door behind him, making everything black again.

The faceless man trod gently from the back to the front of the van, shifted his weight and leaned on the side, saying nothing. In the silence I had no choice but to listen to every breath he sucked in, heavy and long like an athlete's, until, finally, the dim bulb clicked on and I saw a face I recognized: Grest, the NatSec officer from Lorelei's house. His eyes were no more than a hand's breadth from mine but in the blue light everything was indistinct. He stayed silent, tilting his head to the side to examine me. His heavy muscles made him look like an animal through the mesh of the cage.

Slowly, he pulled back the bolt and opened the cage door. I began, hesitantly, to step forward, fixing on the thought that he might have come to release me; but he thrust me hard backwards so that I fell against the rear panel, before following me in and coming so close that when his chest rose, it pressed against mine. The metal tang of his sweat mixed with the smog seeping into the van, and he waited for a long time, staring straight through me.

'Now,' he said. 'We're going to talk about you and your husband.'

The faint blue glow that wept from the bulb above us threw long spindly shadows of my limbs on to the floor, making me inhuman in my own sight.

'Please let me go.'

'I can't do that, Mrs Cawson.' Despite the closeness of the cage, I tried to twist my body past his, but it was so tight he barely fitted into it. 'What were you doing at Lorelei Addington's house?' At those words, my legs became weak and I nearly fell. They must have seen me there searching for the box and the book hidden in Hazel's bedroom. I wanted to lie, to make something up, but my mind was empty.

'I –'

'Why did you think your husband was there?'

I stopped short, failing to understand. Why did I think Nick was there? I hadn't thought that. I was just going to collect what Hazel had said was hidden in her room. Then it dawned on me: Grest was asking about the first time I had gone to the house, the time when I had found Lorelei. He didn't know that I had returned and found the ledger-like book. I forced myself not to look at the bag on the floor that held it, and stammered an answer to what he had asked. 'I thought . . . I thought he was having an affair with her.' The shame I felt at those words was nothing compared to my need to hide where I had just been.

'Did you?' He slid his hand across the wire mesh side of the cage. I looked at my feet, feeling guilty once more of my unfounded suspicions. 'How long have you been married to Nicholas Cawson?'

'Six months.'

'Not very long.' A pause. 'Do you know where your husband really was this afternoon?'

'With a patient.'

'Who?'

He knew who. He had been there at the house when Nick told the policeman. He was testing me. 'I can't remember.'

'Think.'

It came to me. 'Taggan! Comrade Taggan.'

'And do you know who this man, Taggan, is?'

'No.'

'So how do you know your husband was there?'

'Nick said so.' But, as I said it, I realized how weak that sounded.

Grest nodded. He stepped half a pace away and picked up the scarf I had taken from Lorelei's house. He played with it in his fingers. I was terrified about what he might do with it. 'But you don't know, do you?'

'No.'

'So he could be lying.'

Was that right? I supposed it had to be. 'I don't know,' I said quietly.

The reasons I had had for doubting Nick had been absurd when I came to examine them in the clear light of day. But this man's questions were confusing me, making me uncertain. Had Nick really been at Taggan's? If he hadn't, why would he say he had, when it could be checked quite easily? 'What other secrets does your husband keep from you?'

'He doesn't . . . nothing.'

'There must be something that he keeps from you, Mrs Cawson,' he said. 'Everyone keeps something back. What would it be?'

I heard the sounds of life outside: people nearby, traffic moving. I tried to think of something to tell him – to please him, somehow, so that he would leave me alone. 'The . . . maybe something about being a doctor. He can't tell me about his patients.'

'He could if he wanted to.'

'It wouldn't be allowed.'

'He could if he wanted to.' He repeated it in the same precise tone.

'Yes,' I relented.

'Yes.' He looked me up and down and his voice changed: curious now, instead of accusatory. He let the scarf fall from his fingers. 'Are you a Socialist, Mrs Cawson?'

'Yes.'

'Not a Party member, though.'

'No. I'll join if –'

'Do you support the state?'

'Yes. Yes, I do!' That was still true, although right then I would have believed in or supported anything.

'Some people don't.' He watched for a reaction.

'I do.'

'I believe you.' He seemed satisfied and retreated just enough so that I could breathe freely and let my mind and body relax a little.

He glanced at his wristwatch. 'Where were you this

evening?' He said it plainly, as if any response held no real interest for him, and yet I realized straight away this was the question he had really wanted answered from the beginning. Somehow, though, because the other questions had been so invasive and this one was put so simply, without threat, I felt a strange urge to tell him the truth.

I forced myself to take a moment, however. 'I'm sorry?'

He wound the watch. 'You were away from your house. Where were you?'

'I went out to think.'

'Where?' He looked up with an expression of mild surprise on his face.

'I . . . just walked.'

'With your husband in custody?'

'I do it when I'm upset.'

And then he dropped the pretence, his eyes boring into me once more. 'You returned to Lorelei Addington's house.'

'No,' I cried. 'I didn't.' If he found out, the consequences . . .

'Why did you go back there?'

'I didn't. I just walked.'

'Don't lie to me!'

'I'm not!' I shouted.

'You are!'

'No,' I sobbed, genuinely breaking down. 'No.'

He waited, considering me in the blue light. Deciding whether I was telling the truth. My nerves felt like they were on fire. 'Where were you walking? Which streets?'

My mind sped. I picked a route – the one I took to go to the bakery and greengrocery. 'Calward Road. Then into March Street.' His eyes moved to the side, as if he were picturing the path, mentally checking if it were possible. I prayed he wouldn't find some fault, such as a road closure that would have prevented me from taking that route, or a street that I had missed out along the way. Then his eyes returned to mine.

For what seemed an age he simply stared, unblinking, at me before thumping twice on the panel separating us from the driver. The engine started up again and we began to move.

He was silent while the van shuddered and the wheels turned through potholes. Eventually, with a whining of the brakes, the vehicle stopped. 'Do you know where we are?' he asked. His voice was calm again. I shook my head.

He stepped out of the cage and pointed to the rear door. Hoping that this really was the end, I frantically scrabbled on the floor for my purse and bag, before shuffling to the back of the vehicle, grabbing the handle and turning it.

'Have you got a stepdaughter?'

I froze, my back to him. His words echoed metallically off the sides of the van. It took me a while to answer. 'Yes.'

For a moment there was silence. 'How old?'

'Fourteen.'

Another pause. 'Nice age.'

The air was damp as I hauled myself out, clutching the leather bag.

8

I found we were in a little side street facing Liberation Square, site of the People's Hall of Solidarity – the great grey dome of which had dominated London's skyline for four hundred years. But the golden cross that had once adorned the former cathedral had been melted down and turned into the hammer and compass on the main door; and inside you could see the bullet holes that the trigger-happy Soviet troops had made when they tore into the city. There were no priests there now; those licensed by the state conducted their services in grey concrete basements, regularly harried and harassed by the authorities but clinging on to what they could of the old ways. For how much longer? It was anyone's guess.

With a hum, the NatSec van pulled away and I collapsed on a wooden bench to catch my breath. I had never been so close to one of these men before; I had never been able to smell their sweat. I wish I could say that it had demystified them, that up close they were just flesh and blood, no more terrifying than the local drunken bully in a pub. But he had been just as inhuman as the pamphlets or the broadcasts on Radio Free Europe portrayed them. I wondered what had made him like that. We had seen it with the staring-eyed Nazis who had marched through our streets in '44, but that had taken years of brutalizing propaganda. I couldn't understand how it had come down on us. The Marxism that I had read, and of which Blunt spoke, was about peace and cooperation. It said nothing of such savageness.

From where I sat, I could make out the northern side of the former cathedral, which now seeped stone blocks twenty metres into the square. The blocks formed a platform where the high and mighty would stand to give all the Liberation Day speeches tomorrow, marking the seventh anniversary of the day that the Soviets arrived to drive out the Nazis. If the Red Army had pressed on right up to the North and Scotland when they arrived, of course, the whole island would be celebrating their arrival. Instead, the Soviets had been as surprised as the rest of us when American paratroopers dropped into the Midlands a month later, closely followed by their ships docking in Liverpool. And a year later, as Churchill said, 'The iron curtain fell across our land.' So tomorrow we would all cheer the streams of tanks, troops, Pioneers, bands, boilermen and fishermen as they paraded past us after marching defiantly along that curtain.

It was a day when we all felt we could do anything as a nation, and when I had first moved to London, I had been excited that I would be able to watch the parade and go to all the celebrations afterwards. But the prospect had soured for me somewhat when I had passed by the square one afternoon in mid-July and stopped to watch a platoon of Pioneers drilling in preparation.

'Platoon will advance left turn,' their CO had barked, although their fifteen-year-old faces showed they weren't entirely concentrating on their task. 'Platoon right turn.'

Behind scaffolding, I had seen red marble panels with the unmistakable outlines of Marx, Engels and Blunt lining a platform that was still being constructed, while, tucked away in a corner of the square, a gang of cleaners was attempting to scrub away something that had been crudely painted on a plinth: a sort of vampire with blood-dripping fangs, wearing a military uniform and cap. STALIN, its artist had scrawled below. Nearby, soldiers manned little machine-gun turrets on strange beetle-like armoured cars. There were a few people milling about, but it was a dreary day so the square was largely empty.

I had watched, curious, when the armoured cars suddenly started up, pouring thick black exhaust fumes into the air, and the soldiers began shouting to each other. In a rush of sound, they sped off into the square and I followed their path, trying to work out what was happening. Then I saw: an aged-looking couple – in their sixties or thereabouts – were hurrying towards the platform. The man was carrying something in his arms.

The few sightseers stopped. Workmen who had been bolting together the scaffolding let their tools fall idle and watched as the couple scrambled to the front of the stage, jointly took a hold of whatever it was the man was carrying and stepped apart to unfurl a home-made banner: a sheet, with the words DEMOCRACY NOW in red letters roughly made from sticky tape or such like. I had only heard of this sort of thing – the weak political protests that happened occasionally. What did they really expect to come of it? A public uprising? After thirteen years of conflict and upheaval, all we wanted was peace. No one was going to join them to see their last remaining friends and family

71

destroyed by more war, whether it was against a foreign enemy or against our own countrymen. And out of the corner of my eye I noticed a young man discreetly taking photographs of them. His presence was no coincidence.

The old couple stood there for a second before two of the workmen gingerly took hold of them and tried to push them away – probably more for the pair's own protection than out of loyalty to the state – but they were too late: the soldiers were already jumping from the back of the screeching armoured cars. At that, the workers slunk into the background – they could predict what was coming next. Seeing the soldiers' arrival, the young man also realized it was time to leave, placing his camera in his coat pocket before quietly but rapidly walking away. He didn't see one of the soldiers smack the butt of his pistol across the old man's cheek and kick his legs away; or how, when the woman screamed, they hit her too. I, however, winced with each blow.

Between them, the two soldiers – boys no more than twenty – shoved the man from the platform down to the concourse of the square, and I felt another shiver of pain as his head connected with the ground. For a moment, no one moved: we all just watched him lie there, complicit in our inaction; and then, haltingly, he tried to push himself to his knees. But there was something impossible about his attempt – the lower half of his left leg had broken clean away and I realized that it wasn't made of flesh, but of wood and metal, articulated at the knee: a product of the Blitz or a battlefield mortar.

One of the soldiers made a beckoning gesture across the square, and I looked around to see a tarpaulin-covered army truck burst into view. Four more soldiers scrambled out – their insignia showed them to be a sappers' regiment – and surrounded the injured man as he tried to crawl off, with his broken false limb still dragging uselessly behind. He was thrown into their truck before the troops jumped in after him and I heard him cry out an indistinct word or two. I could do nothing except watch.

The woman was also pushed into the van, albeit less harshly, and, as soon as the vehicle's wheels could turn, they careered on to the main road, leaving only a strange silence. It had all taken barely more than a minute.

The air was broken then by a new sound: a mocking, whining human voice. It was jeering, coming from the ranks of the Pioneers – just one boy at first, and then a few more joining in, until they were all doing it. One pretended to break his leg and hop in mockery of the man until their grinning CO quietened them down with a 'That's enough, now' and had them return to their drilling. I walked away, my feelings about Liberation Day a little more subdued.

That had all happened in the summer, and now I sat on a bench in the November evening smog, recovering my breath and thoughts after my ordeal with Grest. It felt so raw. After a while, my hand fell on something poking up between the bench's wooden slats: a little piece of paper that had been folded up and stuffed there to be found. I would have ignored it but it had been placed so as to expose large bold type at the top, with words that couldn't be missed. POLITICAL PRISONERS HELD AGAINST INTERNATIONAL LAW IN MENTAL HOSPITALS. I pulled the page out, to find it was a small sheet of closely printed black type: the sort of cheap samizdat that one saw gummed to walls here and there before it was ripped down.

'They are prisoners for what they believe! We do not know where they are. Please do not forget them,' it added below the top line. There was a long list of names, most of them male.

I had heard – we had all heard – of the new usage that the mental hospitals were being put to. Those poor people. They didn't deserve what had happened to them, but there were so many names on the sheet that I would never recall them. I looked along the road. With the paper in my hand, the memory of the couple, and the NatSec van receding into the distance, I began to wonder where on earth the Republic was going.

Grest's words were still ringing in my ears and the sharp smell of his sweat was still on me when I arrived home. I needed to wash it off or I would be ill. As I entered the house, I found Hazel on the crushed silk sofa – one of Nick's rescues from bombed-out houses – and the room warm, with a fire going in the grate. I usually loved returning to the house when Nick had the fire going, so we could cuddle and warm up. Now there was heat, but no warmth.

'Did you find it?' she asked the second that I stepped in. 'You've been gone so long.' She was still keeping her distance from me, but most of the resentment and defiance seemed to be gone. I think she had probably cried it away – her cheeks were wet with more tears – and she was now feeling sad and alone, rather than angry at me and the world. I wished that I hadn't had to leave her when I went to search Lorelei's house.

'No, I'm sorry, there was nothing there,' I said. I didn't like lying to her, but I couldn't have her involved any more. She sat down heavily. 'But this will all be over soon. You don't need to worry.'

Her expression changed. She struggled to get the words out. 'Do they think Dad killed my mum?'

I looked into her eyes and saw such a rush of conflicting emotions that I didn't know where to begin: her fear for her father, her grief for her mother, even a suspicion that perhaps her father was guilty. And what then? I hadn't even come to terms with my own fears; I had no idea how to address hers too.

'I don't know,' I confessed. 'I don't know what they think. But I know he didn't do it. These people, they just . . .' I waved my hand, unable to finish the sentence because my eyes were also seeping tears. The adrenalin had got me through the time in Lorelei's house and the van with that foul man, but now I broke down next to her. I was glad she was there so I wasn't alone.

We spent the evening on the sofa telling each other that we would hear Nick's key in the lock any minute now, that he would saunter through the door, smile at seeing us together and make some joke about having escaped from NatSec's cells. My cat Julius came in and wound himself around our ankles. I made myself feed him, and he did his best to show his affection afterwards, rubbing himself on our legs, but it meant nothing as the time stretched on and Nick never returned home.

Twice I slipped away to my bedroom – first to stow in my wardrobe the book and white carton I had found in Lorelei's house; and then to open that book again, desperately

75

staring at its contents. I think I was hoping for inspiration, a lightning bolt that would turn those letters and numbers into meaningful words and messages, but they remained a mystery.

At eleven o'clock I told Hazel it was time she went to bed and we would see her father in the morning. When she had got herself ready, I went in to see her and I realized just how young and vulnerable she was. Only fourteen. I stroked her hair and told her everything would be all right and she seemed to believe me. Yet, in the space of a day, the girl had lost both her parents and I, a virtual stranger, was all that was left for her.

9

All of the Republic of Great Britain is looking forward to today's celebrations for Liberation Day. Dignitaries from the Soviet Union, France, Jugoslavia and our friends in Africa are among those attending to show their support and celebrate the day when the Red Army drove the Nazis from our shores. What a day it promises to be!

News broadcast, RGB Station 1,
Tuesday, 18 November 1952

I slept for two, perhaps three hours that night before I was woken, disoriented, by the *Archangel*'s bright searchlight beams sweeping the clouds and rooftops, shining in through people's windows to make the rooms brighter than day. I lay there thinking of those lost moments in Lorelei's house, of what I had seen but couldn't recall. And I tried to recover the memories but the effects of the concussion still kept them from me. I wondered if Hazel, in the next room, had had any more rest than I had had, or if she too had stayed awake hoping still to hear the sound of Nick's key in the lock.

It was about seven, I think, when I heard the newspaper rattle through the letterbox. I hurried down to intercept it because I wanted to see what they knew of Lorelei's death – maybe it would lend some hint as to who or what lay behind it – and I also didn't want Hazel presented with the lurid details. I flicked through the pages before going back to the beginning, confused. There was no word of her. Well, perhaps it had been too late for the edition.

I sat on the stairs, thinking. Nick's continued absence had me frightened, but, after what I had done the previous day – taking the book from Lorelei's house and surviving the encounter with Grest – I felt more able to cope. Was there something I could do to help Nick? One idea occurred, even though it was itself daunting.

I called Number Enquiries. I had to repeat my request because it was hard to hear down the crackling line, but they connected me and the call was answered immediately.

'National Security Police,' said a gruff voice when it connected. There was a pause while I told myself that I really was doing this. '*National Security Police*,' it repeated with annoyance.

I shook myself into action. I had to concentrate if I were going to find out anything about Nick. 'Hello. You have my husband in custody,' I said. Despite my resolve, it was painful for me even to pronounce the words, and, at the back of my mind, there was the worry that calling might somehow make matters worse. 'My . . . his name is Nicholas Cawson.'

'And?'

'Can you tell me if you will be releasing him soon? His daughter is here. Her mother died yesterday.'

'We can't discuss any case. But what did you say your name was?'

My heart skipped – it felt dangerous even to give these

people your name – but there was no point in withholding the information, because they would have it all on file anyway. 'Jane Cawson. Can you tell me anything at all?'

'No. But I'll make a note that you called.'

'Please, just something.'

'I will make a note that you called.'

I didn't doubt that. It was clear too that I was going to get nothing more from him. 'Thank you. Goodbye,' I said. The words seemed strange and self-mocking under the circumstances.

I thought it over. I had no influential friends in London – hardly any friends at all, in truth. But I remembered one man who had seemed kind, who might be able to help. Once again, I requested a line from Number Enquiries.

'Borough Police Station.' There was no love lost between the regular police and NatSec, and I was banking on that.

'Hello. I hope you can help. I wanted to speak to an officer I met yesterday.'

'His name?' The accent was Cornish, I wondered how he had ended up in South London.

'I don't know.'

'It'll be hard to find him, then, won't it?'

I remained as polite as I could. 'He's about sixty, thin, white hair. A sergeant, I think. Detective. And he attended a death yesterday in Eastcheap.'

'Eastcheap?'

'Yes, that's right.'

'Won't be us, then. You want Tower Hamlets Central.'

'Oh. Right. Thank you.'

I hung up and went through it all again. Repeating my

request to a man at Tower Hamlets Central Station. I heard him mumbling to someone else in the background. Then he came back to the telephone. 'Well, we don't know who it was. But most of CID's not in till eight. We can try them when they get here. What's your name?'

Half an hour later I made breakfast for Hazel. She looked even more wan than yesterday. 'You have to eat something. Your dad would want you to,' I said, persuading her to take some bread and butter and a glass of milk. 'It's going to be all right now. Today's the day he comes back.' I squeezed her hand in mine. She didn't squeeze back but neither did she immediately pull her hand away, which was something. Six years of war had taught us how resilient kids could be: they had seen their families buried in rubble or graves and still those children managed to survive. I just hoped she could find it within herself to keep going until her father was free.

When the telephone rang, I jumped and hurried to it. 'Hello?' I said, lifting the receiver.

'Mrs Cawson?'

'Yes, that's me.'

'This is Detective Sergeant Tibbot at Tower Hamlets Central. We met yesterday.'

The relief washed through me. It was a step towards getting Nick back. 'Oh, thank you so much for calling,' I said. 'Thank you.'

'I haven't done anything yet,' he replied. 'Why did you want to speak to me?'

'My husband. You know who took him.'

There was a pause. 'Yes, I know.'

I tried to weigh up his tone of voice. Given his age, Tib-bot had probably joined up forty years earlier. He had been there long before the Soviets arrived, long before they had helped Blunt's comrades set up NatSec. A lot of the older police felt the same way about them as the rest of us, and I had seen Tibbot's anger when Grest had pushed him aside at Lorelei's house. But I didn't want to tell him that Grest had come for me: it would put him on guard, wondering if anything he said would get back to them. 'Can you help me find out about him?'

He hesitated. 'That's not really for me to do.'

'Please, I just want to know if he's all right and if he's coming back or . . .' I left it hanging because my own words brought home to me the fact that he might not. I waited.

'I'm sorry, I can't help you,' said Tibbot.

'He has a daughter.' I was growing desperate.

There was another pause, and he answered in a voice harder than before. 'I can't help you.'

He hung up and the line hummed with a mechanical buzz. By now Nick had been in their custody for eighteen hours. At least they hadn't found what was in Lorelei's house, I told myself. But suddenly, thinking of that, a thought struck me.

According to Hazel, Lorelei had been storing those secret items in the house even when she and Nick were together – meaning there was a good chance he had been involved. In that case, if NatSec were to search our own house, there was no telling what they would find. If there were something incriminating, I had to get to it first.

The place to start looking would be Nick's study, where he did his paperwork. That door was always locked and he said that was because it contained confidential medical records, but now I wasn't so sure. And I knew the key was in his chest of drawers in our bedroom.

I looked through the doorway to where Hazel was waiting to see if the call had brought news about her father. 'I'm sorry, it was nothing. Do you have a friend you would like to go to today?' I asked, even though I presumed they would all be at the Liberation Day events. 'As soon as your dad is back, we'll come and collect you.'

She shook her head, dejected that it wasn't news that Nick was coming home. 'I want to stay here with you,' she said. I was surprised by the closeness of those words. Our shared fears for Nick seemed to have brought us together. 'Can I?'

'Yes, of course. I just have to do some things upstairs. You could listen to the radio or to some records. Take your mind off things.'

'OK.'

She went to her room and I looked up towards Nick's study. Perhaps it would provide the key to what I had found hidden in Lorelei's house.

10

In May, four months after he caught me falling out of a train at Waterloo, Nick met me outside Lambeth Records Office, where we signed the marriage register. He had bought a bunch of sunflowers and Sally threw a packet of confetti over us as we left the building.

I think Sally had a bit of a soft spot for Nick herself, and it was the morning of October the twenty-fifth, a few weeks before Liberation Day, when I received a letter from her that ended with: *So tell me about the dashing doctor. When will he do the decent thing and get you knocked up? After all, IT'S OUR DUTY TO THE STATE.* I wondered if any censor reading the last line would hear the irony in her words.

What she didn't know was that I already was pregnant. When, in August, I had missed my first period the thought had occurred but I didn't pay too much attention. Then I'd missed another and soon each morning had become a scramble to the bathroom to be sick. I would see women with children in pushchairs and I couldn't stop myself smiling. They always smiled back and I was sure they could tell. Nick had performed a test – he called it an hCG test – and told me I was definitely pregnant. While he had been closely monitoring my temperature and blood pressure, I had been thinking about names.

It was chilly that October evening as I walked up and

down the steps of the Brookfield Hotel until Nick arrived at last, wearing his evening suit. I was in the simple white dress I had worn at our wedding, and we were there for some dreary function with a bunch of Party dignitaries, welcoming Comintern delegations from Poland and Russia. Nick thought he might be able to make some connections that would be helpful for his career, but I had felt ill all day and didn't want to be there. 'Hello, darling,' he said as he started out of the cab. I was about to kiss him but as he fully emerged I saw that he wasn't alone. Charles was behind him. I took Nick by the arm and led him away as Charles paid the fare.

'Why is he here?' I asked.

'He was the one who got me invited. He heard there are going to be some very important people here tonight. You know Charles – always star-struck.' He looked at me, concerned. 'Are you all right?'

'No, not really.'

'Let's go inside.' We went to the corner of the lobby. Charles waited a little way off. 'What's wrong?' Nick asked.

'I'm feeling quite sick.'

'Oh.'

'This is bad timing, isn't it?' I said, forcing a smile.

He smoothed down my hair. 'All right. It's just morning sickness – they really should call it something else. But shall we go home anyway?'

I was grateful to him and was about to say yes, I did want to go home and curl up by the fire or listen to the evening concert on the radio, when Charles strode over. 'Dr Cawson, I really do think we should try now, before he sits down to dine,' he said, keeping his voice low. 'He won't be here very long. Just for Comrade Burgess's address, then he'll probably go.'

I must have looked confused. 'A patient of mine is at the Ministry of Food,' Nick explained. 'He's offered to introduce me to one of Burgess's people tonight.'

'Who?'

'Ian Fellowman. Assistant Secretary of State Information. In charge of broadcasting.'

'It would be excellent to meet Comrade Fellowman,' Charles added. 'Of course, there's no real chance that we can meet Comrade Burgess himself. He –'

'Charles, could you give us a minute?' Nick said, without looking at him.

'Yes. Of course, Dr Cawson.' He went through into the ballroom.

There was a silence between us. I really didn't want to be there. 'Would it be useful to you?' I asked.

He sighed. 'An Assistant Secretary is a useful contact, and perhaps things could develop from there. I've heard his usual GP is planning on retiring soon.'

'Will you get a chance to meet him again?'

'Who knows? To be honest, I don't know how well my patient really knows Fellowman. That's why this looked like the best chance – a social gathering.'

'Where you can charm him,' I said, mustering as much of a smile as I could. 'How long would you need?'

He paused. 'If I could have just five minutes ... God, it's awful, isn't it? The lengths we have to go to. But look –'

'No. Of course you must meet him.'

'Are you sure?'

'Yes, you might not get another chance.'

He took my hands in his. 'All right. If you're sure.' I wasn't. I felt dreadful, but I knew it was important to him and I didn't want him to go home and miss his opportunity, so I resolved just to keep a lid on the nausea. I did my best not to let on how I felt as we crossed the lobby to the ballroom, had our identity cards checked against an approved list, and stepped inside.

There were no shortages where Comrades Burgess and Fellowman ate, that was clear. There were waitresses in black skirts and perfect stockings handing around trays of genuine French Champagne; plates of canapés stacked on tables; food I had never seen even in the pages of an old *Vogue* I had found in a pile on the floor of our wardrobe. All around it was as if the previous decades had never taken place, and we were still in the roaring twenties. The era of *The Great Gatsby* and all that excess. I couldn't help but feel a shade of anger at the hypocrisy.

Burgess and Fellowman weren't in the room – they had probably been escorted through to a more private place – and Charles was nearby, talking to a tiny man who kept wiping sweat from his head with a handkerchief. Nick was known here too, I found. Within seconds he had been grabbed by a fat Party apparatchik, accompanied by an unhappy-looking young woman, who wanted to know if Nick was treating any of the Politburo and if he had heard anything about the health of Comrade First Secretary Blunt. The tiresome man allowed his jacket to fall open so that we could see a copy of Blunt's ruby-coloured treatise on our future, *The Compass*, tucked into an inside pocket. I sighed within myself. Men like this were the most irksome

86

manifestation of the new regime, trying to ingratiate themselves here and intimidate others there.

It was Charles who intervened. 'Dr Cawson,' he said, attempting to suppress his excitement as he came towards us. 'Comrade Honeysette is over there.'

'So he is. I really must speak to him. Excuse us.' Nick walked over to the small, sweating man, who was evidently his patient with the connection to Ian Fellowman, leaving me with Charles and the apparatchik.

'So you're just married, Comrade Cawson?' the paunchy man asked me.

'In May,' I replied.

'Church wedding?' He was trying to sound friendly, not sly.

'Lambeth Records Office.'

'Ah.' My distaste for this man made my stomach turn. But then I realized it was more than that. There was a sharp pain there too. I rubbed it involuntarily. He cocked an eyebrow. 'Are you hungry? There is so much food here, all proof of the bumper harvests we have had recently.'

Charles volubly agreed. 'Oh, yes,' he said. 'It is important to eat well. As Comrade Blunt said himself: we are the thriving muscles of the body politic. Just as the head relies on the limbs for movement, so those limbs rely on the head for . . .' His voice drifted away.

Despite my lack of interest in his second-hand thoughts, I waited for Charles to continue, but then I realized that his attention had moved elsewhere, and I followed the direction of his gaze to the doorway I had come through a minute before. There, under its lintel, stood a tall, slim woman with bright red hair twisted up in the French style.

She was in a scarlet dress that flared slightly at the bottom, exposing equally red high heels. Such heels were officially scorned nowadays as a bourgeois affectation, and yet she seemed to have gone for the reddest pair she could find. Although in her late thirties or early forties, she was still striking – by far the most striking woman in the room. A waiter offered her a gilded box of long, thin cigarettes, and she took one and held it to the flame on his lighter. For a moment it seemed like everything around her face had darkened. The flame flickered down as she let a stream of smoke drift from her mouth. When it had all gone, there was a smile left on her lips like an aftertaste.

'She's . . . very beautiful,' I said. It was all that I could say.

The apparatchik nodded vigorously. 'Oh, yes. Yes, sometimes I used to watch her films three times over.'

I realized then who she was.

'Is that Lorelei?' I said.

'You didn't recognize her?'

I looked at Charles. He appeared surprised. 'No,' I replied, self-consciously.

It was strange that I hadn't. *Victory 1945*. It was shown on a loop all day long on Liberation Day. Lorelei had stolen the film as the resistance fighter with a pistol and untold courage who, upon discovering her soldier boyfriend had been killed by the Germans, had roused her cell, and then the crowds in the streets, to throw off the Nazis and welcome our Soviet liberators. But it had been more than a film: it had been the declaration of our statehood, the way we told each other that we were a new country. Lorelei was the image of everything that we were going to be: beauty and courage personified. It had affected me just as much as the other young men and women of my generation, because after the disaster that had engulfed the entire world for a decade – the Nazis, the War – it was up to us to change it for the better.

'I suppose you have never been introduced – your husband is hardly likely to do that, is he?' said the apparatchik. He gave out a hearty little chuckle. 'I wish I could do the honours. She did so much for our nation.'

'She did,' said Charles wistfully.

Yes, it was strange that I hadn't recognized her. From the film's release in 1946 and throughout the following years, her face had rarely been absent from newspaper pages and posters, but where had she been for the past few years? I hadn't seen her in anything.

A man she seemed to know approached her, offering his arm, and she accepted, gliding through at a sedate pace. As she passed us, I could smell her perfume: sweet and playful, it seemed to be drifting through the whole room, and the man at my side looked from me to her, then took a sip of his Champagne.

She stopped walking to tap on Nick's shoulder, and he turned and broke into a smile. What was he thinking at that moment, with us both in the room? Her and me. I would have loved to have known that. So I hesitated, but, well, jealousy got the better of me and I walked over, with Charles following in my wake. 'Hello, darling,' Nick said, as I approached.

Lorelei turned her head ever so slightly to look at me. One of the curls from her hair swung to brush her cheek. 'You must be Jane,' she said. Her voice was airy but full of confidence. Now that I was beside her, I felt weak in her presence, like the new girl at school. Up close, I could see the cat-like curves of her green eyes, and I must admit I was pleased to see the traces of crow's feet there.

'Yes. Lorelei?' I tried to sound unconcerned by her presence.

'That's right. Hello, Charles.'

'Miss Addington. It's very nice to see you again.'

She smiled weakly at him, before examining me and the glass of white wine that I was clutching for security. 'Good God, if you're married to Nick, you'll need something stronger than that,' she burst out, taking it from my hand and grabbing a passing waiter. 'Brandy for the lady.' He scuttled away to find some.

It was not what I had been expecting, and I hoped it wasn't some trick that she was pulling on me.

'Will it be that bad?' I asked. I didn't know whether I needed to be guarded or to go with the joke.

'Marriage to Nick? Probably. It's hard for me to tell: I was squiffy for most of my sentence.'

I was taken aback. She really was being friendly. Yet, somehow, I found that harder to deal with than outright hostility. Charles looked, as Nick had said he might be, star-struck. And Nick was clearly amused by his former wife. 'I'll have to take that as a tip,' I said, still uncertain how I should respond.

'A tip from me? Golly, I'm the last person you should take one from.' She took the glass of brandy that had arrived with the waiter, put it in my hand and swapped her empty Champagne glass for a full one from his tray. 'Now, see that off and we can take it from there.' She knocked back her drink and indicated for me to do the same.

Nick intervened. 'Following Lorelei in anything tends to result in madness or severe injury,' he said.

'Preferably both,' she added.

'Well, let's see where this gets me.' I threw half of it down my throat.

'Mrs Cawson,' began Charles. 'If you would like –'

'Good girl,' Lorelei interrupted. I felt like my throat was on fire. 'We'll make a flapper of you yet.'

'What's that perfume?' I asked.

'This?' She held out her wrist. 'Tabac Blond. By Caron. Do you like it?'

'Yes.'

'Based on sweet Virginia tobacco, of all things. Hard to get now. Order Nick to get you a bottle. Place in Bristol does it – he knows which one. Now, Nicholas, I want to spend some time with you tonight, but I must go over there and sweet-talk the Ruskies, since they're our masters now. Cheerio, Jane. We'll compare notes later. I've got some tips for controlling Nick. I got them from a wild-animal keeper at the zoo.'

My throat was still raw from the brandy and I had to struggle to pronounce more than a crackle. 'I'll look forward to it.' That was true. I felt intimidated by this force of nature but also drawn to her. Some people are like that, aren't they? You just can't help yourself around them. 'Goodbye,' I said, waving my empty glass.

Nick focused his attention back on me. 'This is Comrade Honeysette. He's in the Ministry of Food.'

'I'm very pleased to meet you,' Honeysette said, shaking my hand. He had a quick, rattling manner of speech.

Charles looked across the room and spoke. 'Comrade Honeysette is a friend of Comrade Fellowman.'

'Known him since Oxford. Solid man. Very committed. Came over in '47.' So when scores of people were being thrown into Brixton Prison for attempting to escape from our side to theirs, Ian Fellowman was one of the handful who had made the journey in the other direction. I had seen and heard men like him interviewed on the radio and television, speaking about the corruption and hunger in the DUK that they were leaving behind, but I had never seen one in the flesh. I was quite intrigued. I felt another pain in my abdomen but managed not to let it show.

At that moment, a murmur went through the room and heads turned as, in the corner, a small train of guards and assistants strode forth. In the midst was someone familiar to me from the pages of the *Morning Star*: Guy Burgess. He was tall, medium build, with a rectangular face, and in his wake followed a clutch of eager apparatchiks, like seagulls chasing a trawler.

But it wasn't him that Charles and Honeysette were watching, it was someone else: a very big man with thin ginger hair who was following at a distance of only a couple of paces, and yet seemed somehow alone. He wore a drab grey suit, and there was something strangely transparent about him as he slipped between people, as if he could disappear right in front of you. They all entered a small area divided from the rest of the room by silk ropes.

'That's Fellowman, isn't it?' said Nick.

'Yes, that's right,' Honeysette replied, thoughtfully. 'Shall we go over and I'll see if I can catch his eye?'

'Yes, let's.'

We walked through the throng. Comrade Fellowman was whispering in Burgess's ear as we arrived, before stepping back to instruct a couple of junior assistants. 'Ian,' Honeysette called over. Fellowman glanced at him. 'May I introduce a few friends of mine. This is Comrade Nick Cawson and his wife, Jane.' He was about to speak again, but it was just then that a man appeared on the stage, tapped the microphone twice to make sure it was on and spoke, his voice distorted by the wires and speakers.

'Comrades. It is my great honour tonight to welcome some very special guests,' he said. 'First, our colleagues in the struggle for democratic Socialism from the Russian league of Communism International.' Clapping resounded around the room as we all turned to a group of ten men standing near the stage. I felt a hot flush and sweat forming on my brow, my stomach clenching. 'And also to the Secretary of State Information, Comrade Burgess.'

Burgess raised his hand to louder clapping, which died out as the speaker returned to the microphone. I saw Charles grin widely at me. But then something different passed over his face. Something like shock. It was reflected in the faces of all the men immediately around me. They were looking down to the floor at my feet. A few paces away, Lorelei seemed to have frozen in the act of clapping, her hands resting in mid-air as she too stared at the floor below me. Nick's eyes rose, wide, to mine. Then there was a bolt of searing pain through my whole body, and I felt the glass slip from my fingers. It shattered on wood stained with droplets of wet blood, the shards exploding across the polished surface.

'Christ,' someone said.

II

Nick's study was a small, necessarily tidy room at the back of the house – it would have been larger had it not been foreshortened by the doodlebug that had blown the back off the building. Although I was doing it for Nick, searching the room for anything that could incriminate him, I still had a sense that I was somehow invading his privacy. Before I began, though, I waited to make sure Hazel was in her room and listening to the radio. The sound of voices and a laughing audience through the wall told me that she was doing as I had asked – I didn't think for a second that she would take much of it in, but at least it would give her mind a rest from her fears and sadness.

Boxes of files were stacked untidily around the study walls. One wall also displayed a map showing how Britain had been divided. I traced the border along the complete southern shore of the Thames, and along the eastern part – our part – of the northern shore. Those stretches were all fence. The solid concrete wall, ranging from five to eight metres high and topped with barbed wire, ran up from the river near Trafalgar Square in the middle of the city, through Piccadilly Circus, where Checkpoint Charlie had been built, then north for fifteen kilometres to Barnet, at which point it curved west down to meet the Thames again at Twickenham.

For those in DUK London, the only way out of it was the heavily fenced-in road that the Westerns had named 'the Needle' because it pierced the cordon we had thrown around them. That ran from Checkpoint Bravo, on the western limit of DUK London, out through our land to Oxford, which was the beginning of the main part of the DUK. It was Nick who had explained to me that a convoy of supply lorries – and a few civilians with the right visas – passed along the Needle each day. The DUK's London citizens actually ate better than the rest of their country because the Americans sent so much food – mutton and pork and fish – along the road just to make sure they couldn't be starved into submission if we were to cut it off.

That border. Even if we did need it to reduce conflict with the DUK, it was awful how it also kept us divided from ourselves and from our vital, collective history. I couldn't help thinking that even my own mind was taking on its character by locking away the memories I needed the most: those lost moments in Lorelei's house. I suppose on some level our thoughts will change to reflect and resemble the world around us.

Under the map stood Nick's writing desk – one of the lovely old roll-top ones with leather and brass all over. It looked so intriguing that I started my search there, lifting the top to find a few letters ready to post, the normal assortment of pens and notepaper; some old correspondence in the drawers; and, in the very bottom one, a clutch of letters neatly gathered in ribbon. Although the ink on the envelopes was fading, I knew the hand: it was the same as in the book that I had stashed under my shoes in our bedroom. With some trepidation, I untied the ribbon. The notepaper was scented – it must have been old because you couldn't get that sort of paper any more.

It's one thing to know that your husband was once in

love with another woman. It's another to know that he kept her letters.

28th April 1942

Darling Boy,

I've just landed in New York. Eleanor and Harry met me off what they think is called an 'airplane' ('Well, it flies through the air, don't it?') and drove me straight to their little place on Long Island. I say 'little place' but they have clearly dug up Canada to build their garage and drained most of the North Atlantic to fill their swimming pool. I therefore made sure to chuckle loudly at all the inconsistencies in architectural style and smile in a condescending manner at their attempt to re-create Versailles in a town where they think Versailles is a type of fish. I think they got the message. Well, if you can't insult two of your closest friends, who can you insult? Although it's now after midnight and I'm almost as tired as their wallpaper, I'm lying on my four-poster bed and dreaming of the best ways to insult their children. Will write again when they have asked me to leave.

Kiss Hazel for me.
L

20th August 1942

Darling Boy,

Hollywood is a God-awful place. Yes, yes, all the sunshine is nice, and they seem to have pink gins coming out of their ears, but the town is full of the worst sort of harpies ready to fall backwards with their legs in the air if it means an audition. Half of them have a permanent

96

grin like a hyena. It's stuck on with lipstick and regular injections from a doctor, Max Jacobson, who everyone here calls Dr Feelgood. I have no idea what's in those shots, but I have to say that after I gave one a go I was dancing from Friday night until lunchtime on Tuesday. He was telling me how he could get hold of the latest medical drugs in big quantities when a Yank officer marched over, announced that his name was Colonel Hank Dee, that he was a huge admirer of mine and that he would be honoured to take me out for a drive. I politely told the good doctor I would talk to him later about his offer and allowed Col. Dee to escort me away. You would have been endearingly jealous, as you always are, but don't worry – the dear Colonel is sixty if he's a day (not that that stops them over here!).

He says he's in the Education Corps and he has all those lovely manners of the old-fashioned Southern gentleman – but behind Col. Dee's eyes there's a light that's burning just a little bit too bright for the classroom, if you know what I mean. So when we were in his car, taking a nice evening drive through the hills, we chatted about Britain right now and is it true that half the House of Commons and a smattering of the idiot sons of the Lords are red to the bone? They absolutely loathe Stalin over here. As well as being a commie, they think he's a coward for staying out of the War. Not surprising, really. And my new friend IS terribly sweet, with all that 'Why ma'am, ah'm jus' a simple country boy from South Carolina' flim-flam. Do you think I should see him again?

And don't worry, Darling Boy, I've only got eyes for you. Well, when I'm in London anyway. Right now there's a charming little cornball from somewhere called 'Iowa' with muscles like a Studebaker car who keeps following me around. Maybe tonight will be Chuck's lucky night!

Kiss Hazel for me.

L

I checked the date on Lorelei's letters. They had been written when Hazel was about four. The marriage had lasted another seven years, give or take.

'What are you doing?'

I spun around to see Hazel standing behind me. I stared at the page in my hand. 'It's nothing,' I said quickly. It was like being caught stealing – and I *was* stealing something: a part of Nick's past. My first instinct was to hide the letter, but it was too late for that. Hazel came closer and looked down at it.

'That's my mum,' she said.

'It's an old letter to your father.'

She took it out of my hand and read it. 'She was in Holly-wood for a bit,' she said.

'I'm sure she missed you.' I realized that I was speaking as if I knew her. Strange to be so famous, a household name to millions, and yet so unknown. I wondered if Nick had really known her, or if she had always played a part with him too.

'Did you meet her?' Hazel asked.

'Just once. At a party.' I couldn't help but think of that night as I put the letters back in the desk.

'She told me that I could do anything. That I would be more beautiful than her.' She tried to smile but it didn't work. 'She said people would write films just for me to star in them.'

'It's going to happen,' I said, stroking her cheek and hoping a real smile would come. But her expression changed to confusion.

'What are you doing in here?' A note of suspicion, of faint mistrust.

'It's nothing. I just need to find something.'

'Is it to help Dad?'

'Yes. I think it will help.'

98

'I'll do it with you.' She probably just wanted something to take her mind away from her mother for a short while.

'There's no need.' I was sorry to push her away, but I couldn't involve a child in this. I sat in Nick's chair; it shook slightly. 'And it's not always safe to go poking around in the past.'

'That's what you're doing,' she insisted.

'Yes. But I know what I'm getting into.'

'All right.' She looked down and her eyes teared up again before she left. Poor girl.

There was nothing else in the desk. I even searched it for secret compartments, which some of these old desks have. After that, I took a look inside the boxes lining the walls, which proved to be full of medical records. Perhaps the reason that the Secs had arrested Nick had nothing to do with Lorelei after all, and the reason really lay in these records – a powerful patient with a secret illness, or someone who had died when he shouldn't have done – but they may as well have been written in a foreign language for all that I understood of them.

I moved back to the desk and hesitated, far from sure that I was doing the right thing, but I gripped the tarnished brass handle on the bottom drawer and pulled it towards me, lifting the letters out again. As I did so, I noticed something new. The bottom of the drawer felt different to the others – papery where the others had been smooth wood. I pulled it out entirely and turned it upside down, to find that what I had thought was the bottom was, in fact, a sheet of white paper cut to perfectly fit the base. It fluttered out and fell to the floor; and with it fell a photograph.

I recognized the pair in that picture, their faces displaying happy and confident expressions that seemed to say the sun would never dim. But it would one day. And I saw too that Nick and Lorelei weren't alone. They stood beside a car, an expensive open-roofed one, and at the wheel sat a pale woman with her black hair tied back. All three had wine glasses in their hands, seemingly toasting something. Across the bottom, in Lorelei's handwriting, were the words, 'To a brighter future!' I pondered them. Such optimism and confidence, but it wasn't high hopes for the state – no, this was a private affair. There was something between them that they thought was going to work out well.

I knocked on Hazel's door. 'Come in,' she said.

'How's the radio show?' She shrugged. 'Well, I hope it's nice. I have to ask you something. Do you remember your parents ever having this car?' I said, showing the photograph. She had been crying and I wanted to comfort her, but I had to keep on with what I was doing. Time could be short.

'No. Why?'

'It's nothing. Do you recognize this woman, maybe?'

Hazel looked at me with curiosity and took the photograph. 'I don't know. I've seen her at our house, I think. But I don't know who she is.'

'Do you remember anything about her?'

'No, it was a few years ago.' She looked bemused that I would ask about such trivial matters at a time like this. 'Jane, what's going to happen about my mum? The funeral.' She stuttered over the final word. It was heart-breaking.

I sat on her bed. She had a scrapbook open, displaying articles cut from the *Morning Star*. Each was a story or photograph about Lorelei in the years after *Victory 1945*. There was even a grainy picture of her meeting the First Secretary outside the gala premiere for one of her films – the art historian Anthony Blunt loved the highest forms of art, but he also understood the reach of the lower ones. The power of giving people a narrative to live through.

'I don't know. I think we can arrange that in a few days' time. Your dad will do it later.' I tried to make it sound like I had no doubt he would be back soon.

'OK.'

I leafed through the scrapbook. 'These are about your mum, aren't they?' I noticed that the stories about Lorelei stopped abruptly in 1948, even though there was still space left in the book. That must have been when she disappeared from view.

'Yeah.'

I had to ask her again about the photograph from her father's desk, though. 'So this woman was at your house.'

'I think so.'

'Do you —'

The sound of knocking on the front door, rapid and demanding, made me stop. Cautiously, I went downstairs to answer it. I didn't know who it would be. I just hoped to God it wasn't the Secs.

The second I turned the latch, however, Detective Sergeant Tibbot entered without a word. He waited until the door had closed behind him and indicated I should lock it firmly. Then he spoke.

'There are some things you don't talk about on the phone.'

12

The look on Tibbot's face as he entered the house was serious. He came close. 'Do you know all your neighbours by sight?'

'All the immediate ones, yes.'

'Seen anyone new?'

'No.'

We went into the parlour. 'Your husband is still in Great Queen Street,' he said. 'They're accusing him of killing his ex-wife.' I felt the air rush out of me. I wanted to cry out that it wasn't possible, but he wasn't finished. 'I'm sorry to say that's worse than you think.'

My voice caught in my throat. 'How?' I stammered.

'Do you remember when I saw you at the location of the incident, your husband told me he had been on a call at a patient's house when the death occurred?'

'Yes.' I could tell what was coming. Nick had lied. He had been at Lorelei's after all. Somehow I hadn't seen him.

'Well, you see –'

I heard Hazel's door open. Tibbot halted abruptly.

'Hazel?' I called up the stairs.

'Yes?'

I went to the foot of the staircase. She was on the landing above. 'Someone has come to see me, to help make sure your dad is OK,' I told her. 'It's very important that I speak to him. Could you do something for me?'

'What?'

'Could you stay in your room while he's here? It won't be for too long.'

'All right,' she said, although she looked unhappy as she went back to her room.

'Is that his daughter?' Tibbot asked when I returned.

'Yes,' I said.

He paused in thought for a moment, then shook himself out of it. 'Well, as I was saying, I checked with the man concerned, Comrade Taggan, this morning just after I called you. NatSec hadn't spoken to him. He claimed that Dr Cawson came for over an hour, conducted his consultation and left. No one else was there.'

I couldn't understand what he was saying. Nick's story was true – he hadn't been with Lorelei and he had had nothing to do with her death. And yet Tibbot looked severe. 'But that's good,' I insisted. 'It proves it, doesn't it?'

He hesitated. 'No, I'm afraid that's the problem. Because your husband told NatSec exactly the same thing. And they haven't bothered to check.' It slowly dawned on me what he was saying. 'It means that they want him to be found guilty whether or not he actually did it.'

I gasped. Despite the fire, the room was freezing. 'But why?'

He cleared his throat, uncomfortable with having to bear such news. 'There could be ten different reasons: they think somehow he did it; or they're under pressure to find someone – anyone – to blame for it and he'll do; or just incompetence. But I don't think it's any of those. I think it's because they want him for something else they seem to think he has done. Mrs Cawson, NatSec investigates

103

crimes against the state.' His voice dropped and his eyes found mine. 'You know what that means.'

I did. It meant a military court and the rope. I groped for the chair and felt Tibbot's hand under my shoulder, holding me and leading me to it. I fell on to the seat and wiped the sweat from my brow. 'I'm sorry,' I mumbled.

'You'll be all right. Do you have anybody you want to contact?'

I thought of my parents, long gone. 'No.'

I couldn't understand what was happening. I had hoped, when I rang the station earlier, that he would tell me that Nick was coming home in an hour or that the Secs were dragging their heels and it might even be a day or two before he was back, but that he would come. The idea that Nick might actually be charged, and that NatSec were after him because they believed he and Lorelei were involved in crimes of subversion, was devastating. 'Maybe he's innocent,' I insisted. 'They must be wrong.' But there was what I had found at Lorelei's house.

He sat down and looked at me closely. 'Mrs Cawson, are you *political*?'

I knew what he meant. It was a very dangerous question to be asked by any official: did we harbour ideas that the state deemed troublesome? 'No. We're not.' There was a pause.

'All right.'

Without wanting to, I pictured life without Nick – sitting alone in the house, Hazel in one of the awful communal schools for the children of dissidents. And I thought of the family I would never have with him. Such a sterile and bleak existence, devoid of the brightness and excitement and the hard-to-explain sense of *things to come* that he had brought to my life just half a year ago.

'What can we do?' I asked. Maybe there was a way to show that Nick had had nothing to do with Lorelei's death; and that, even if she had been subversive, he hadn't. Tibbot looked uncomfortable. I realized I had said 'we' as if he were going to help me. There was no reason that he would. 'Thank you for coming. You're putting yourself at risk just being here,' I said. 'If they found out you had been talking to me like this, it wouldn't be good for you, would it?'

'No, not good.' He stood up and went to the drinks cabinet. There was a bottle of vodka and a small bottle of scotch. 'Whisky. Don't often see it. May I?'

'Please. I think it was a gift from a patient.' It was very early to be drinking.

He poured himself a small glass and drank it thoughtfully. There was something melancholy about the way he did it. 'His daughter,' he said into his glass.

'Hazel.'

He kept staring into the drink. 'How old is she?'

'Fourteen.' Forgive me for hoping that her vulnerability would help turn his mind.

He rubbed his brow and drank again, before staring back into the glass. I began to understand his air of sadness. 'Do you have –'

'She died.' There was a long silence before he went on. 'In '47. When things weren't like now. Less stable.'

'What happened?'

He shook his head and poured a little more into his glass. It looked like an action he had performed many times. 'If he's gone, what happens to her?' he asked.

'I have no idea,' I said, truthfully. 'Lorelei's mother is alive, but she's old. She can't look after a child.'

He drank for the last time and put down the glass. He remained quiet for a while. 'If we find that he is working against the state, will you drop it?' he asked.

There was a long pause while I thought of what it would be like if that turned out to be true. 'Yes. I suppose I would have to,' I said. There would be no point going on. He would be lost no matter what I did and it would only make things worse for Hazel and myself. I hoped to God it wouldn't come to that. 'They questioned me too, last night,' I said.

He stopped. 'The Secs?'

'Yes.'

I described how they had shoved me into a wire cage in the back of one of their foul vans.

'You got off lightly,' he said, after thinking it over. 'I've heard some of what goes on in their HQ. The cells below.' He shook his head. 'Though that officer, Grest, I've come across him before. From what I hear, if you'd given him a tenner he would've let you walk. I would try that next time.' He sat down. 'Does your husband often make house calls?'

'Sometimes. Why?'

'Oh, nothing. Just that this Comrade Taggan went into work that day, after your husband went to see him.'

'So?'

'Well, I thought doctors only make house calls for people who are too ill to get out.'

'I expect if they're very important, Nick will go to them.'

'Yes, you're probably right. Could anyone else verify your husband's whereabouts? His secretary?'

'I doubt it. Charles doesn't go on calls with him.' I gazed at him. 'Do you know yet how she died?'

'The force medical officer said at the scene that it looked to him like drowning – no injuries on her – but he couldn't be certain until he had the body back at the morgue.' I shivered at the harsh image.

'And what did he say then?'

'Nothing. By then NatSec had taken over. So I don't know any more than you on that score.'

'Wasn't it just an accident?' I appealed to him. 'There was that Champagne bottle next to her. So she was drinking and slipped in the bath.' If someone could prove that it had been just an accident, they would have to release Nick – unless, that is, they could find evidence that he had been involved in subversion. If he had been involved with a dissident group – maybe even one of those encouraged by the Americans – it would be a very serious situation.

Tibbot sounded sceptical. 'Well, it happens – someone falls and knocks their head. But there wasn't a mark on her. And her eyes open like that . . . Strange.'

'So what do you think?' I was just desperate for something to hold on to. It was like he was playing with me, holding out the prospect of an innocent explanation that would give Nick his freedom, then pulling it back.

'Well, I think we need to know two things: first, why NatSec want your husband, and, second, why his former wife died. You can put money on it that one will tell us the other. Was *she* political?'

'I don't think so, but I only met her once.'

'Did she make any political statements?'

'No, nothing like that. Not that I heard, anyway.' That

evening I had met her, and the letters of hers that I had read, had left me with the impression that she was, by nature, interested in little more than her own world, floating above the rest.

'Can you remember anything else about the scene of death that you didn't say before?' Tibbot asked.

'No.'

'There must be something. Think.'

'There isn't!' And in a moment it all hit home. I needed air.

I ran out of the room, out the back door, and stood sucking in the air, damp as it was, in an attempt to cool my brain. In a neighbouring garden a little boy was kicking a football around, shouting to an unseen friend about the tally of goals between them. The friend yelled back at the same childish volume.

I calmed myself down and looked towards the house. This man, Tibbot – I knew nothing about him. Should I be telling him so much? For all I knew, he would report it all straight back to NatSec. It was a risk. But I thought it over a hundred ways and each time I decided that, no matter how dangerous it was, I had little choice. I needed to help Nick and I couldn't do that alone, I needed someone who had been in such a maze before and could guide me through.

Still, I hadn't yet told him about the book and carton I had found at Lorelei's house, and I decided to hold off for now until I was a little bit more certain about him.

The boys nearby shouted again as one of them seemed to score a goal and, after another minute getting my breath back, I returned.

The second I stepped back inside, however, a sight

made me stop dead. Tibbot was standing with the hall telephone in his hand. I imagined the line running straight to NatSec. 'Who are you calling?' I demanded.

'No one,' he replied, taken aback by my tone. 'Someone's called you.'

I snatched the receiver out of his hand. 'Nick?' I said urgently.

I glanced up the stairs towards Hazel's room. The sound of the radio news was drifting down: '. . . since the Republic erected a barrier to prevent residents of north-west London from looting our stores for low-priced but excellent-quality food . . .'

'Mrs Cawson?' came the cautious reply. 'It's Charles O'Shea.'

It wasn't Nick. Shattered, I dropped the receiver and walked away. I didn't care how I must have appeared to Tibbot as he picked up the handset from the floor. 'Can I help you?' he muttered into it. I leaned against the wall as Charles's voice buzzed from the other end. Tibbot looked over at me and covered the mouthpiece. 'He wants to speak to you.'

I reached for it. 'It's all right,' I said, recovering a little. 'Hello, Charles.'

'Who was that?'

'A policeman.'

'You're with a policeman?'

I glanced at Tibbot. He went into the parlour. 'It's fine. You can speak.'

'Dr Cawson is still where he was?' he asked.

Tibbot had warned me that there were certain things you didn't talk about on the telephone and Charles too was being guarded. 'Yes. It doesn't seem to be changing.'

'Is there any more information? Regarding his former wife?'

'No.'

'I understand.' He paused. 'I tried my contacts in the Party; they are looking into it for me.'

'Of course.' I suspected now that if he really did have any friends in the Party, they were on the lowest rung of the ladder.

'I'll continue to keep the practice running as best I can. I would, of course, appreciate it if you could keep me informed about any developments.'

'I will.' I slipped the receiver back into its cradle. 'Why did you answer that?' I called out to Tibbot.

He came back into the hallway. 'You were outside; I thought it might be about your husband and you wouldn't want to miss the call. Mrs Cawson, you asked to speak to me. I can go if you don't want me here.'

I relented. 'No, I'm sorry. Please stay.' But I couldn't shake off the fact that I knew nothing about where his loyalties lay.

'Can I ask who that was?' Tibbot said as we went back into the parlour.

'Is it important?'

'It could be.'

'Charles O'Shea. Nick's secretary.'

'Right,' he said. He glanced at the clock on the mantelpiece. It was nearly half past nine. 'Well, there's something else we have to think about.'

'What's that?'

He brushed something unseen from his brow. 'It's that I'm not sure how much time we have. You see, I don't know how to put this, but NatSec . . . sometimes people hang themselves in those cells.' My heart thumped and he paused as I struggled with the idea. 'If that were to happen, the case would be closed with his name on it. It's a tick in their records.' I had been picturing Nick before a military tribunal. Now, in a moment of panic, I saw him buried.

I couldn't be sure that I could trust this man. I didn't know why he was helping me. But I had to know what Lorelei had been involved in.

'There's something I need to show you,' I said.

'Cryptography,' Tibbot muttered, flicking over the pages of the book I had retrieved from Lorelei's house. The white box I had found sat beside it on the table; it had meant nothing to him, and I hadn't let him into my suspicion that it had contained rifle rounds, for fear that he would immediately wash his hands of us. 'From the Greek *krypto*, meaning "hidden thing". It's NatSec's department, really, not the police's.'

I was surprised by his knowledge of Greek. He was a working-class Londoner and not many of them had been to the sort of school that taught Classics. Maybe I had been jumping to conclusions.

'So do you know anything about it?'

He scratched his white-bristled chin. 'We've had a few pointers in CID. There'll be a key – a set of numbers or letters. If you have it, it's easy to decode. If you don't, you have to look for patterns.'

'I don't think we've got it.'

'No.' We peered at the book again. The strings of letters

and numbers varied only occasionally between its twenty-odd sections. 'Might as well start here,' Tibbot said, tapping the final section. I slid my finger down the page through the first column of two letters followed by a series of numbers.

DD2261033445298	wfn
VN1081209994632	str cor
TW3284408109028	pro wfn
AM7126026369346	cor
VN4653310089328	cor str
DO5574301038201	wfn pro
TL2159414038033	nor

Two of the seven strings began with *VN*. 'That's a start,' I said hopefully. 'A way in.'

'Possibly,' he said. 'Our best shot, anyhow.' He didn't sound very positive.

We tried making phrases from the letters, turning them around and thinking of names for which they could be the initials. But half an hour later we were no further on. 'What if we're going at this the wrong way? What if it's not a code?' I said.

'I've been thinking about that. They could be identification numbers, say, but for what? Phone numbers are seven digits, including the exchange code. Identity cards have three letters at the beginning of the number.'

'Bank notes?' The new decimal currency still felt strange to many of us.

He pulled a pound note from his wallet and examined it. 'No. Nothing like it.'

'Map reference?'

'They're much shorter.'

We sat reading the numbers backwards and forwards. I saw them spinning in the air, but it did no good. It drove me mad to think that these marks on a page might tell us who was responsible for Lorelei's death and – more importantly – why it wasn't Nick. But no matter how much I stared at them, all they did was mock me with their impenetrability.

Then, as Tibbot went to the kitchen to draw a glass of water, I suddenly had a thought. 'I know where I've seen something like this,' I said, jumping up. 'At school.'

'What do you mean?' he said, coming back in.

I was overjoyed at the thought that we might now have it – we might be able to decode what she had been writing. 'Library codes. To identify books.'

He nodded thoughtfully. 'Library codes. Yes. Could be. Where's your nearest library?'

'Southwark.'

'Better get there soon. If it's open at all, it'll probably close early for Liberation Day,' he said.

We copied the codes on to a small slip of paper and put the book back in its hiding place. I had a hurried word with Hazel – with what was going on now, I thought it best if she went to a friend's house and she reluctantly agreed to go. She had a key and could let herself back in for supper that evening.

Leaving the house after seeing her off, I saw a figure at the window of the house next door. She was perhaps twenty-two and dressed in a plain blouse and trousers cut like those you had to wear in the army, and her appearance made me suddenly very nervous. It must have shown, because Tibbot discreetly asked who she was.

'Patricia. Our neighbour. She's in the Party.'

'Serious about it?'

'Very. Nick told me to watch what I said around her.' This slip of a girl could be as dangerous as the men who beat on your door in the night. So strange that raw muscle power – the power of men – was being quietly supplanted by the power of a whisper behind hands, a force that we women were better at employing.

Tibbot took my arm. 'Well, try to keep calm,' he said. 'Don't attract attention. Smile. Look around you. Stop to button up your coat. Just think of it as a normal day.'

He was right, of course: what we were undertaking was dangerous enough without doing anything to signal that we were engaged in something that made us nervous. After all, we were probably the only people in the city that day not happily getting ready to celebrate the arrival of the ship that had fired the first Soviet shot against the Germans.

'Right. Yes,' I said, and I did my best to smile.

13

I don't remember the journey home with Nick from the Comintern party at the hotel, the moment when he, Charles and Lorelei had stared as the world had seemed to fall to pieces around me.

He gave me a sedative when we got in and told me not to say anything, simply to sleep and we would talk about it in the morning. I couldn't have spoken if I had tried. He stroked my head and wiped my cheeks dry, and I felt warmth spread over me like a blanket as the memory of what had happened that evening melted away. It was something that had happened to someone else.

I have images of the days that came after; but nothing is clear now. Just Nick sitting patiently by my side. But there is a memory I do have, distinct in my mind, of a time when I woke up and he wasn't there. It was an afternoon and I heard a woman's voice downstairs, strong and clear. I lifted myself out of bed and rubbed my clammy skin. I wasn't sure how long I had been asleep. Opening the door just a crack, I heard the voice again.

'. . . anything I can do for her?'

'No, no. I don't think there's much anyone can do. Time. That's all.'

'Yes, that's right. You're still coming for Hazel on Sunday?'

'Yes.'

'Stay to dinner?'

'Thanks, but no, I should come straight back. I'm needed here.'

There was a pause. 'Nick, I wanted to say something.'

'About this?'

'About something else.'

'Oh, yes?' he said.

'It's your choice, of course, but – Ian Fellowman. I saw you were angling for an introduction. You have heard about him, haven't you?'

'Heard what?'

'He has a side to him.'

'Meaning?'

She hesitated. 'Well, I saw George Orwell – Eric – on the street just last month, walking past that restaurant that used to be Rules. I was meeting a chum there. I pointed him out and was about to call over because I hadn't seen him for ages, but then Sabrina grabbed me and warned me off. It seems he was put in one of those re-education camps for that silly story he wrote about the animals. And it was Ian Fellowman who put him there.' She paused again. 'Darling, I've met real fanatics, and they don't look like fanatics: their eyes don't swivel or stand out on stalks; they just look like middle managers in off-the-peg suits. Really, I'm serious, Fellowman's damn well toxic. You must watch yourself.'

'Thanks for the warning.'

'All right. Yes. Well, look, I really must make tracks.' There was silence. I wondered why they weren't speaking. 'Do you think she'll be all right? It's a terrible thing to happen.'

'She's in a pretty bad state. I'll go and check on her in a minute,' he replied.

'Yes. Do be kind. Cheerio.'

'Goodbye.'

I returned to the bed. I didn't want him to catch me listening. The creaks on the stairs told me he was coming up, and I pulled the bed sheets up to my chin as some sort of protection and waited. He gently pushed the door – I don't know if it registered with him that it was ajar – and slipped into the room.

'Oh, you're awake,' he said, sitting on the bed and taking my wrist. He laid his hand on my forehead. 'How are you feeling?' As he bent over me, I smelled that sweet perfume on him. The one she had held out to me on her wrist that night at the party. Tabac Blond.

'I don't know. Numb.'

'Do you remember what happened? Why you have been unwell?'

I blinked. The question was awful. 'Of course I remember.' And then I was furious. I don't know where it came from but I could have torn my hair out with the rage. 'Do you think I could forget that? What are you . . . Are you mad?' As I started to shout, he stood up and retreated to the wall, but remained facing me. I threw back the covers and looked down at my stomach. I had half expected to see some sort of evidence there. But there was nothing, no record. The child had been and gone without a mark on this world other than in my mind. Nick too just stared at the place where I would soon have been swelling.

'Do you want some time alone?' he asked.

'Yes.' I couldn't look at him. 'Was that Lorelei?'

He hesitated. 'Yes.'

'Why was she here?' I was so bitter.

'Just so –'

'I don't want her here again!' All the anger I had was swept up into him.

'She just came to collect something for Hazel.' I picked up a wooden-framed photograph from the table and threw it against the wall. The frame broke in two and dropped to the ground. I half recognized an image of the two of us on a day out. There was a long pause. 'Please don't do that, my darling,' he said. 'You nearly hit me. We'll get through this. I promise.'

I wanted desperately to believe him, but my mind was echoing with a thought that I knew was unfair but I couldn't put away from me: *If you had taken me home when I told you I was ill, I might not have lost the baby.*

14

Southwark Library was only a fifteen-minute walk away, so Tibbot and I reached it by ten thirty. It stood at the end of what had once been a small parade of greengrocers and tobacconists and was now a large Closed Shop for Party members. The little windows were hung with curtains to prevent your seeing inside, but everyone knew that its shelves were always stocked. You could get bacon and legs of lamb all year round, and, in summer, strawberries. French wines for the price of beer. The stories got bigger all the time, so if you asked some people you would hear of whole pigs roasted on spits in the centre of the shop or whisky sold by the gallon. Others would tell you that their sisters' friends worked there and they were allowed to take home a kilo of sausages each day. You never knew whom to believe.

A group of Teddy Boys were standing around outside, smoking. The Teddies had arrived about a year ago and seemed to be everywhere now, wearing their grandfathers' Edwardian clothes, dressing like dandies in velvet frock coats and narrow-legged trousers, but in their pockets they carried flick-out knives and brass knuckles. They were harassed by the police, told to move on from their pavements and milk bars, and sometimes there would be a scrap between them but rarely anything serious. Secretly, many people admired them and their refusal to conform.

When we got to the library door, we were met with a sign saying that it was already closed, but Tibbot spotted movement inside and banged on the door. It was opened by a fidgety young man who, I noticed, was holding a collection of T. S. Eliot's new work as National Poet – verses lauding our leaders that I couldn't help but think were pretty thin.

'Sorry, we're closed,' the young man said.

'I know, I'm terribly sorry,' I said, being as polite and friendly as I could. 'We need to find a book. A particular book. Please. It will only take a second.'

'I can't.'

'Please, it's for my daughter's homework. Just one second.'

'I –'

'She's going to get in trouble if I don't.'

He relented. 'Oh, all right, come this way.' He led us to his desk.

'All we have is the long code,' I said.

'The decimal?' he said, going to a thick hardback catalogue. 'Well, unless it's a common book, there's no reason why we would have it ourselves. And, in that case, I won't know which one it's for.' I felt deflated. 'Now, let's see.' I handed him the note with the code. He tapped his finger on the first string in the column, DD2261033445298, and counted them with his finger. 'Thirteen numbers. It can't be the Dewey at all, then,' he said. 'On the Dewey system, three digits will tell you the subject quite precisely. This one, two-two-six, would place a book in' – he checked down the list in his catalogue – 'religion; then the Bible; then the Gospels. The following three digits would narrow it down further on the shelf if need be – if you have a lot of books about the Gospels, say – but the rest of the digits in this number wouldn't mean anything. You can only have six in total. And these letters at the beginning, well . . . Sometimes you can put letters at the end of the sequence to denote the author's surname, but not at the beginning.'

I was crushed, I had been sure we had made progress. 'Are there other systems?' I asked.

'None that look like this, I think.'

'Let's put the code to one side for a minute,' Tibbot said, back in our parlour. 'Let's say it's nothing to do with her death. And let's say that her death wasn't an accident either. Who might have wanted to do her harm?'

'I hardly knew her,' I said. Did anyone really know her?

'Most killings are just domestic,' he mused. 'Someone gets angry, drunk. It's the boyfriend or husband.'

'Nick's not –'

'I know. Did she have a boyfriend?'

'I have no idea.' I wanted to get back to what I was sure was the way in. 'But this, this code. She was doing something secret, something NatSec wanted to know about. That has to be it, doesn't it?'

And yet, if she had been involved in subversion, as Nat-Sec's presence seemed to suggest, what could have brought her to it? Her friend George Orwell had been through one of the re-education camps at Ian Fellowman's behest. Had there been other friends who had suffered? Perhaps that had hardened her feelings and pushed her to make contact with people who thought as she did. After all, during the

War, we had seen acts of extraordinary courage from people one wouldn't have expected to act that way – housewives who had joined SOE and lived in occupied France with the prospect of Ravensbrück hanging over them; quiet family men who, when the time came, led battalions into the teeth of the German guns. I suppose we all have the capacity within us – it's only a question of circumstances.

'We're stuck there,' Tibbot sighed. 'Unless we can get into this book of hers, we're blind.'

I had a thought. 'There was something else I found,' I said.

'Go on.'

'Stay here.' I went to my room and fetched the photograph of Nick, Lorelei and the dark-haired woman. I had put it from my mind because the book had seemed far more important.

'The car isn't theirs, I think, so it's probably that woman's,' I said, handing the photograph to him.

'Probably,' Tibbot said. 'But I can't see that it means anything.'

'But it's how I found it – it was hidden at the bottom of a drawer, covered in a sheet of paper.' I was trying to convince myself as much as him.

'So? I've got photographs in my desk under paper. It protects them from dust.'

'Well, yes, but I thought,' I hesitated, not wanting to tell a police detective his job. 'It's Nick and Lorelei together. How many men keep photographs of them with their ex-wives? It's strange.' And at the back of my mind was the thought that it was also disturbing – was it something that I wouldn't want to know? 'And she's written on it, "To a brighter future!" That must mean something, mustn't it? It's something we can try.'

He looked unconvinced. 'Jane, it's something to look into, but please don't get your hopes up. Most of these kinds of . . . odd things, turn out to be nothing to do with what you're investigating; they're just a distraction. The truth is, nine times out of ten, it's just a nasty little domestic incident. No big crime.' He sat back in his chair and pointed to a badge on the car's front grille. 'Nice machine. Sunbeam. I remember them.' He closely examined the woman in the driver's seat holding a glass of wine. 'So who is she?'

At least he was taking an interest. 'I don't know. Hazel says she recognizes her a little but doesn't know who she is.'

'Is there anyone else who might know? Someone you can trust to keep all this to themselves – you understand?'

'Yes. I suppose I could try Charles. I'm not sure it will help, though.'

'Give it a go.'

I knew he was right. I went to the telephone. My call was answered as immediately and efficiently as I had come to expect.

'The consulting rooms of Nicholas Cawson, Charles O'Shea speaking.'

'Charles, it's Jane Cawson.'

'Oh, Mrs Cawson. Has Dr Cawson been released?'

'No. Not yet.'

'I'm sorry to hear that,' he said.

'Could you do something for me?'

'I will try.'

'Could you come here? There's something I want you to look at.'

123

'Mrs Cawson, I am at work, running the surgery.' He sounded irritated.

'I fully understand that, Charles. Please come here.' I was firmer with him than I had been before.

'Very well.'

'You put him in his place,' Tibbot said, as I returned to the parlour.

'Yes, I suppose so. He can be very difficult.'

'How do you mean?'

'Oh, nothing much. He's just very off-hand. Nick says it's because Charles went to Harrow and resents having to take orders from a grammar-school boy, let alone from me.'

'I'm sure that's quite the comedown in his world.'

After twenty minutes, Charles stood in the hallway, brushing down his jacket and muttering about the cost of having come by cab. Tibbot was waiting out of sight upstairs. On the way to the parlour, Charles tripped over the paraffin lamp that Nick used when the smog was heavy or when the electricity to the house cut out, refilling it from one of the nearby bottles of oil that also went into our heaters. He swore in annoyance.

'Do you remember this photograph being taken?' I asked when we had sat down.

He glanced at it. 'No.'

'You weren't the one holding the camera?'

'No, I don't believe so.'

'What about this woman?' I said, pointing to the driver of the car.

'No idea. A friend of your husband, I presume. And his wife.'

'You're positive you don't know?'

He took out one of those foul Soviet cigarettes, tapped it on the packet and lighted it. 'Yes.'

'Do you know when it was taken?'

Charles looked at it again briefly and shrugged. 'Pre-War?'

'Pre-War? Nick doesn't look that young. A few years younger, perhaps. And, look, there's bomb damage to the street.'

'If you know yourself, why are you asking me?'

'Charles,' I soothed my own voice. 'Nick is in trouble. I think we can help him. But I need to know who this woman is.'

'I haven't the faintest idea.' He shifted in his seat. 'But, Mrs Cawson, one thing I do know is that if you do anything that the Secs don't like, such as poking around or talking to people about his arrest, it won't go in Dr Cawson's favour. Or in anybody else's. If Dr Cawson has done nothing wrong, as I am sure is the case, he will soon be released and we can go back to how things were. It's not worth the risk.'

He was being cagey and I knew why. I had once asked Nick why Charles didn't get another job if he disliked being a secretary so much. 'Frankly, no one else would give him one,' Nick had replied. 'His parents ran off to Northern Ireland with the Royals, you see – I believe his father's from Dublin and was supposed to be some sort of envoy to the Irish government – and they're up in Edinburgh with the new Queen now. So no one wants to touch him for fear of being tainted by that. But he was in my regiment on D-Day and when you've gone through that together, well . . .' He drifted off and his face took on a

125

troubled, faraway expression that I saw from time to time when the War came up. All I could do was place my hand on his arm and hope he understood.

'Charles,' I said, 'I appreciate what you're saying.'

'I'm glad,' he replied coldly.

'I know your parents are in Edinburgh with the Queen –'

He jumped up. 'What does that have to do with it?'

'So you don't want NatSec knocking on your door, but –'

'I am not responsible for what my parents do.' He angrily stubbed out his fag on the grate. My eye was drawn to the livid clutch of little blisters on his hand.

'Of course not. I only meant –'

'Are you responsible for what *your* parents do?' he demanded.

Damn it. I had wanted to reassure him, but all I had done was to alienate him more. I was losing what little help he had been giving me. 'I was saying that –'

'Will there be anything else, Mrs Cawson?'

I gave up. I couldn't think of anything worth asking and he probably wouldn't have answered anyway. 'No.' He glared at me for a long time before he went to the front door. Just as he was about to open it, however, he whirled around and dashed up the stairs. 'Who are you?' he said angrily. He was staring at Tibbot. Tibbot didn't reply.

'A friend of mine,' I said.

'A friend? Just waiting up here?' His tone wasn't pleasant.

'It's none of your concern.'

'Isn't it?'

'No,' Tibbot replied.

'Well, I'm going to ask you again.' He stabbed his finger at Tibbot. 'What are you doing here?'

'Look, mate, do you really fancy your luck?' the old policeman replied. 'Only that pricey bit of schmutter you're wearing won't look very nice ripped apart.'

Charles twisted around to look down at me. 'I don't know what this is about, but you had better stop it.' Realizing that he would get nowhere, he looked icily at Tibbot once more and stomped out to the street.

'He's not very happy, but that doesn't matter,' Tibbot said as he descended the stairs. 'It's a bigger problem that either he doesn't know who this woman is or won't tell us.'

'So what do we do?' I replied, annoyed not by Charles's attitude – I couldn't have cared less about what he thought of me at that moment – but by the fact that it had been a waste of precious time.

He rubbed his jaw. 'I can try a friend in the Transport Division. It might be Liberation Day, but if I know Kenneth he'll be in the office enjoying the peace and quiet while everyone else is out jumping up and down for Comrade Blunt. He never really *goes in for* Liberation Day, if you know what I mean. Always prefers to be the one minding the shop.'

'Will he help us?'

'I think he'll try. That might not be enough, though. A lot of the records went up in smoke thanks to the Luftwaffe. Of course the Party has more than made up for it with those new files in Somerset House.' It was strange to hear a policeman talk that way. The scepticism was almost dissident. I knew what sort of files he was talking about. 'But we might have a record of the registration plate.'

'The telephone is in the hall,' I said.

'Better from somewhere else.'

*

127

A vagrant sat sleeping inside the call box across the road from our house, slumped against the glass walls. His legs, which were bare below the knee, were covered in a damp film of soot, and he had strange bumps under the skin on his nose and cheeks. 'Wake up, mate,' Tibbot said. The man stirred and, without a word, hauled himself up and staggered away.

'What was wrong with his skin?' I asked.

'See it quite a lot with the vagrants. Caused by a social disease they have. One of the ones that doesn't exist.'

He reached into his pocket and drew out a little leather-bound notebook. Inside, in tiny slanted handwriting, there were lists of telephone numbers and he ran a stubby finger down one page, then the next, until he found what he was looking for. He picked up the receiver and gave the operator the number.

'Hello, Kenneth?' he said, once connected. 'It's Frank Tibbot. Oh, not so bad. Not so bad. Getting old and doddery. Yeah. And tell me, what was your lot up to on Saturday? Two against Portsmouth? I could beat Portsmouth meself. Yeah, you can try. That's right. Anyway, work call. I've got an old reg for you. Can you check it? Well, just do your best. Ta. It's YXA 998. Old Sunbeam. Got that? Good. How long, do you think? And Ken, do you want to meet for a drink – you can give it to me then? You got it in one. All right. No, you're right. Yes. Cheerio.' He hung up. 'He has to get the files from storage – if they still exist.'

'You're meeting for a drink?' I said, amazed. 'It's urgent.'

'You never know who's listening, even to police lines,' he explained calmly. 'Especially to police lines. You don't want to raise any suspicion, so you keep things social.' I regretted my naivety. 'He's in Somerset House. I'm meeting him at two, at a pub round the corner from there.'

'Are you sure it's safe to go anywhere near the Strand?' I asked. 'Today of all days.'

He shrugged. 'No worse than anywhere else today.'

15

The First Secretary is now making his way to Highgate Cemetery to visit the tomb of Karl Marx. It was Comrade Blunt's leadership of the Communist Party of the Republic of Great Britain that resulted in the fulfilment of the promise that Marx and Engels made: that Communism would flourish in the land of Britain.

News broadcast, RGB Station 1, Liberation Day,
Tuesday, 18 November 1952

The stream of tanks and armoured cars, ranks of men with Kalashnikovs, girls with shining pistols and fresh-faced Pioneers holding up photographs of Comrade Blunt stretched for three kilometres along the swept-and-washed Strand, up Fleet Street, where the crowds were held behind steel barriers, and around the People's Hall of Solidarity like a noose. Tibbot was meeting Kenneth alone in a pub around the corner, because it could have made Kenneth nervous if I had turned up too; and watching the parade was the best way for me to avoid attention while I waited nearby.

A squadron of Air Pioneers marched past with little wings stitched to the lapels of their uniform. They were the boys who had shown the most aptitude in their dexterity tests and now dreamed of piloting Soviet-made Yaks in dogfights with the Americans above London. They wore proud expressions as they passed their yelling parents and jealous schoolfriends. After the boys came the older girls in the boiler suits of engineers, followed by honoured assembly-line workers. And then a crowd-pleasing moment as a cavalry regiment trotted through, the kids behind the barriers scrambling forward to get a closer look at the stamping horses.

Liberation Square was unnaturally warm and humid due to the surrounding jets of paraffin flame that constituted the Smog Dispersal System: the intense heat from the circle of bright fires evaporated the suspended droplets of water in the smog, thinning it until there was just a light smoky mist. It had saved the lives of countless air crews during the War who would otherwise have been unable to find the landing strips, and now it enabled us to see our leaders in all their glory. Along with boiling the air, its light threw a strange dark glow on us, accentuating the lines and shadows in everyone's flesh.

And, finally, there he was: borne on a wave of cheers, Anthony Blunt, standing upright in a huge, open-topped car sweeping along the road. Officially, Blunt's role in the day's ceremonies was to pay respect to his forebears, not to receive it for himself. So he had first visited the desk in the National Museum Reading Room at which Marx had sat while he composed *Das Kapital*, and then the great man's grand mausoleum at Highgate Cemetery. Now Blunt was serenely climbing to the platform as the crowd shouted his name. At precisely one thirteen, the time that the *Archangel*'s guns had fired for the first time on a German cruiser, a squadron of Red Guards shot three times into the air, and Comrade Anthony Blunt stepped to the microphone.

He stood for a moment surveying the crowd as we waited upon his words. A breeze slipped among us. Then he leaned in and spoke, his aristocratic voice dripping with confidence. 'The destiny of man is a river. It has shallows and rapids. Eddies and calms. There are times when it is so dark that it cannot be made out, and others when it is so bright that a child knows where it is heading. We know where we are heading.' He waited as people whispered to their neighbours. His address was different from those he broadcast on the radio: there was less delicacy and nuance; these were words for a huge audience. 'We know because for the first time in the tide of human life, we, the people, can steer our course.' More whispering, excitement. The wind blew the heat from the paraffin jets over us.

He grew more forceful. 'For the first time in history, no one who falls sick will die from want of care; no one will sit idle for want of work; no one will lie hungry for want of bread. For the first time in history, all men and all women can choose their rulers; can walk where they want, can say what they believe.' I couldn't help but wish that were true, and somehow, as he said it with confidence and commitment, I almost believed that it were. Atmosphere can do so much to what you feel and think. 'We know what we believe.'

He pulled back from the microphone and, like a ballet, behind him the other Secretaries filed on from the sides. Kim Philby and Arthur Wynn took their seats at the side of the dais. They looked self-assured. Today was the day they jostled for public recognition, building popularity among the people, while their backroom deals for influence stayed hidden. Yet someone was missing: the Secretary for Information, Guy Burgess, never appeared. And he was said to be the most ambitious of all.

'Have they purged Burgess already?' I heard someone snigger. 'Gone like Cairncross?'

'Shut up,' a woman muttered angrily.

The man must have been drunk. Nobody dared mention John Cairncross in public these days. Not since he had been caught sabotaging our industrial effort in order to aid the Americans. His trial had been broadcast on the radio, and he had famously broken down in tears when the verdict was announced, mumbling an apology to the nation that he had betrayed for money. At the end, it was said that he had looked up towards the public gallery, as if hoping to spot someone there, but the only spectators were feverishly clapping the judgement.

Blunt's speech boomed for half an hour through the damp air. He spoke of our place in the world and our commitment to the peoples of other nations before returning, at the end, to ourselves. 'We are pioneers,' he said, his voice alive with self-belief. 'Ahead of us is a new land of equality and justice and plenty for all, where the people who create the wealth have equal shares in that wealth, instead of being forced to stand by and see it leached away by birth right and privilege.' The crowd bristled with energy at his words. 'Yes, we are pioneers of a new land, yes, we are pioneers of a new, better humanity!' And they burst out in cheers, men and women crying for their golden future. The Red Guards fired into the air. And again. And again.

And yet, when Blunt retired to a wall of applause led by Comrade Philby, who thanked the First Secretary for his inspirational words, he had been on his feet for far less time than in previous years. That sign, we all knew, would be pored over in the privacy of people's homes that evening – not to mention at the DUK's London head-quarters in St James's Palace.

Among all the joy I was itching to leave, and as soon as I felt I could do so without turning up too early and worrying Kenneth, I pushed my way through the crowd and down a street leading in the direction of the Thames. The road turned out to hold a picture house that, like all the cinemas that day, was showing Lorelei's crowning glory, *Victory 1945*. It was one of a triple bill with Charlie Chaplin's old anti-capitalist satire *Modern Times* and the new one he had produced since moving back to the Republic from Hollywood, *The Old Soldier*, in which a thinly dis-guised Churchill rants all day at his peaceful and bemused neighbours and ends up shovelling himself into a hole that he can't get out of.

There was something queer about the street, though. It was filled not with the normal mix of damp people and dirty vehicles, but with a hundred former army motor-bikes, all painted black. Their riders sported old-fashioned clothes and greased-up hair: Teddy Boys, many with girls perched behind them on the machines. They swarmed like bees around the entrance to the cinema and there was a constant buzz of engines as more arrived or departed.

I should have expected to see Lorelei's image that day, of course, but still it was a shock suddenly to come across it on the film's poster outside the cinema. I had seen it in her house after her death but out in public like this it seemed almost to bring her back to life.

I hadn't watched the film since meeting Nick, because seeing her light up the screen would only have made me more envious of all that she had, and left me wondering again what Nick could possibly see in me. But, as I stared at the poster, her character rousing her resistance cell to rise up against the Nazis, something fell into place like a tumbler in a lock. Tibbot had said there would be a key to decipher the book code. Well, there it was, I was sure, right in front of me. Lorelei's face was whispering it: whispering the name of the film. *Victory 1945. Victory Nineteen Forty-Five.*

'I think you're lost,' a voice close to me said. It was an oily-haired boy, little older than the ones I had tried, with mixed success, to interest in *Romeo and Juliet*. 'This is our street. Not yours.'

'Not now,' I said. I couldn't tear my eyes from Lorelei's.

He seemed taken aback. 'Yes, now.'

'Come on, Alfie,' called one of the girls. 'Just tell her to piss off.'

I looked at her. 'I used to teach little girls like you,' I said. 'I used to rap them across the knuckles with a ruler.'

Her friends hooted with laughter at my words and the boy broke into a grin. 'I like you,' he said, making a low, sweeping bow. 'Yeah, I think I like you. All right, where you going?' I pointed to the picture-house entrance. It was surrounded by the other Teddies like a guard. He started leading me towards it. 'Right, you sods, out the way. Lady coming through.' He pulled a few out of my path and I made it to the doorway to stare at the poster and Lorelei's image, working things out. From inside the cinema, there was a chaos of shouting – it looked like the management were trying, and failing, to maintain order while the

Teddies were milling around, throwing drinks and food from the kiosk, juggling with bottles of milk. A man in a suit kept shouting that he had called the police. I could hear the film playing; it must have been the scene in which the *Archangel* arrives – there were gunshots and explosions, cheers from the auditorium. 'This is our Liberation Day,' chuckled Alfie.

There were dissidents in our society. There were the intellectuals who opposed the regime, citing long-dead philosophers – they usually got one warning before they were shipped off to be re-educated, their homes requisitioned and their families moved into the worst houses, without running water. And there was an underground of those who took more direct action: digging escape tunnels under the wall, trying to organize trades unions or holding up half-hearted banners like the couple in Liberation Square. But it hadn't occurred to me that there were some who were open about their rebellion. They stood their ground with their clothes and their motorbikes, instead of political theories and clandestine meetings. If there was a vanguard of defiance, here they were.

I became aware of a ripple of movement outside. A rising of voices to match those within the building. A wave of noise – the Teddies shouting to one another, kicking their motorbikes into life. Alfie dropped his hand from my back and stared at the end of the street, where a commotion was flying towards us through the smog. Scores of policemen were rushing down, batons out, swiping left and right, knocking many of the boys to the floor. Their girlfriends screamed.

'The Bogeys. Blades up!' Alfie yelled over my shoulder

into the cinema. His shout was echoed and magnified within the walls until it became a roar. I felt a chill. On the few occasions I had seen real violence close to me – once a fight with broken bottles outside my local pub, once when the Nazis had caught a member of the Home Guard – I had felt every blow in my own flesh. The prospect of it happening scores of times in front of me made my chest clench around my ribs. As one, the boys snatched inside their jackets and back pockets for brass knuckles or knives, clicking out the blades and sprinting in defence of their friends.

They surged forward to jab at the police. I could hear the blows landing and the cries of pain before a crash above us made us look up, to see a window exploding, its glass falling just metres from where we stood. Through the empty casement we could hear the music as Lorelei welcomed the brave Soviet troops filing off the *Archangel*.

One of the Teddies drove his bike straight into the police ranks, leaping off when it struck home. Some of the boys, however, were riding in the other direction, away from the violence – whether scared or going for reinforcements, I couldn't tell – and stones were flying in the air in both directions. A few cracked into the wall beside us. Alfie pushed me towards one of his friends who was about to ride from the scene. 'You, go with him,' he shouted to me.

I stared back at the film poster, committing to memory what I had seen there. 'All right,' I said, jumping on the back of the bike. Something metallic sped through the empty air where my neck had been a second ago. The boy with the bike gunned the engine so that it deafened me and we wound through the throng. Over my shoulder I saw Alfie barge into a policeman, knocking him back, but the officer was a burly man and he grabbed the boy in a bear hug, dragging him down. In the last moment Alfie looked directly at me. Then he was lost in the tide of bodies and it seemed almost as if he had been swallowed by some sort of beast.

As soon as we were clear of the danger, the boy whose name I didn't even know dropped me off in a long, shabby street and roared away without a word. I was worried to see a police checkpoint where uniformed officers were going over people's cards – it could have been a result of the trouble nearby, or simply down to the increased security we always saw for Liberation Day.

Even though they couldn't possibly have suspected me of anything, I still felt worried walking away from them. It's strange, really, how successfully the government had ingrained this layer of anxiety – of paranoia, really – into all of us. I just trusted that it was a phase we would be able to leave behind when the state was more stable.

I asked a passing cabbie for directions to the Rising Sun pub and soon found it tucked away in a narrow backstreet, with a few young men standing outside with drinks in their hands. It looked to me like the interior was packed – not surprising, when people had a rare weekday off work.

'Excuse me!'

I froze as I was about to enter. One of the men standing outside was calling to me. 'Yes?' I did what Tibbot had told me to do: smiled and tried to look unconcerned.

He was a young man, with a hard body, standing with

two others like him. They had barely touched their drinks. 'Don't I know you from somewhere?' he said.

'Me?' I screwed up my face in a pantomime of trying to recall his. 'I don't think so. I don't think we've met.'

'No?'

'No. I don't think so.'

He paused while he and his mates scrutinized me. 'My mistake.'

My smile was fixed as I moved away. Did I know him? I didn't think so. But perhaps he knew me because my photograph had been handed around in Great Queen Street. Or was it a genuine error?

I fought my way into the rammed saloon bar to find the air wet with breath and a television bracketed to the wall showing the parade. Tibbot was at a table, nursing a drink.

'He hasn't come,' he said quietly as I reached him.

'Can you think why?'

'No.'

A sudden cheer rose from the bar and I turned to see what had caused it. The picture of the parade had disappeared from the television, to be replaced by a single fading white dot – the power cuts got even worse on Liberation Day as people held parties in their homes – but the cheer slid into a groan when it quickly flickered back to life.

I examined the lapel of my jacket and rubbed away at a stain. 'Is it a worry?'

'Could be,' he muttered. 'Let's go outside.'

'I think I know how the code works,' I said, as we shuffled towards the front.

'The key?' He sounded impressed.

'I think I've got it. Well, part of it,' I said. 'There was a fight near Liberation Square. The police went after the Teddies. I saw it there.'

'How?' I was about to tell him. 'No, wait. Outside.'

At the bar, the landlord was arguing with two men who were trying to persuade him to turn the television down and switch on the radio so they could hear the Liberation Cup final about to start at the Tottenham ground. 'No one wants the parade on, mate,' a thick-set older man was saying. 'Kick-off's any minute. Go on.'

'I can't turn the parade off, can I?' the landlord said, subtly nodding outside to where the three young men were sipping their drinks. 'So no.' The telephone behind him rang and he picked it up as we stepped out the door. 'What? No. It's the Rising Sun pub, mate. Frank who?'

'Wait!' shouted Tibbot, whirling around. 'Wait, that's for me.'

16

The landlord handed Tibbot the telephone. 'It's me,' he muttered into it. 'Yes.' The landlord gave us a suspicious look, but
obviously decided it was nothing to do with him and went off
to collect some glasses. I leaned against the back of a chair
and glanced at the men outside. They didn't appear to be
watching us, but how could I really tell? 'Why would that be?'
Tibbot mumbled into the mouthpiece, resting his elbow on
the bar. There was an undercurrent of concern in his voice,
but also curiosity. 'How recently? I see.' He tapped his fingers
on the bar. 'Yeah. But she ... Who could authorize that?
Right. Yeah, please.' He took a notepad and pencil from his
pocket and wrote something down. 'All right, ta. Take care.'

'Did he find it?' I asked, as soon as the receiver was
down. He kept looking at the telephone, tapping his thumb
on the bar thoughtfully.

'Yeah,' he said, almost to himself. 'But there's something strange.'

'What?' He looked over at the landlord, who was watching us through the corner of his eye. 'There are three men
outside,' I muttered.

'I've seen them.'

We chatted about the parade as we headed out, towards
the end of the street, and as soon as we were out of earshot, his features clouded. I looked at him keenly. 'It took

Kenneth longer than he thought to find the file; and someone came back from the parade early so he couldn't leave without it looking a bit off,' he explained.

'But he got it?'

'Yes.'

I waited. 'You said there was something strange.'

'Yeah, well, we have the name of the woman who bought this car. For now, we'll presume she's the one in the photo you found. She's Rachel Burton of 2 King Henry Road, Gravesend, Kent. She bought it in 1943. In 1950 it was requisitioned by the government as common property and transferred to the oversight of one Dr Richard Larren. No address for him, though.' I was impressed by his precise recall without recourse to his notebook, but no doubt he had spent forty years committing such details to memory.

'Who is he?'

'No idea. But it's strange to transfer ownership. Requisition cars, yes, but it's not normal to transfer to another private citizen. Even less so back then. So what's special about this Richard Larren?' I wanted to know that too. Someone profiting, somewhere along the line, meant someone who had knowledge and influence over what was going on. Profits certainly hadn't been banished to the old pages of history, they had simply been disguised as favours and rewards for loyalty. 'Of course, it doesn't mean he's in on anything. He might just have been given the car for being a good boy, or he knows the local Party chief, or he paid a backhander for it. But, whatever it was, it's something. So, we'll call on Miss Burton, if she hasn't moved, and hopefully she can also point us in the direction of Dr Larren. He might be able to fill in a few blanks.'

'All right.' Things were looking up.

'What was it that you found? The key.'

'I don't know for sure if it's right, but it could be. It's to do with the names and the dates on her posters. Think about *Victory Nineteen Forty-Five. VN* came up twice, remember? We need to go back to her house to check the other posters – they're in the bedroom, I'll show you.'

He mulled it over and sounded cautiously positive. 'All right.'

We turned on to the main road. A big car with darkened glass in the windows slowed beside us and I tensed. It had the hammer and compass in the centre of the registration plate and was immediately followed by another car, this one with the Soviet flag – their sickle in the place of our compass – indicating that it contained some of the Soviet officers who were here with their troops at the long-standing invitation of our government. A policeman waiting in front of a pair of solid gates stopped the traffic to let the two dark cars turn right across the road and in through the gates. Before they closed, I caught sight of a large, old house set back from the road.

'What is that place?' I asked.

Tibbot cleared his throat. 'I've only seen two types of people enter those gates,' he said. 'Party officials and young women. And I don't think it's a secretarial college. I suppose that's them celebrating Liberation Day.'

God knows my own background wasn't privileged, but I had never had to consider some of the ways people survived now. I wondered more about those girls than about the men – their backgrounds, their families, the homes they had left or never had. And I remembered that, while

Tibbot was helping me save my family, he too had had one once. I had been fearful at the thought of a life alone, but he was already living it.

I placed my hand on his arm. 'What happened to your daughter?' I asked.

He took off his square glasses to clean them with a handkerchief from his pocket, and I saw his eyes properly for the first time, the wrinkled bags under them hanging from age and drink. He was struggling with the memory and I wanted to console him, but I could sense an old-fashioned pride in him that wouldn't have it.

'Wasn't far from here, actually,' he said eventually, still looking at the spectacles in his hand. 'No, not far. There were rumours that NatSec wanted wider powers of arrest, but the police persuaded Blunt to refuse because we didn't want the Secs stepping on our toes. Julie was on her way to work in her pub and got caught up in a demonstration against the government. Students. About the elections and the Party winning like they did. No better than the Nazis, they were saying. They didn't know better back then.' We knew better now. He slipped the glasses back on and his eyes became bigger and less distinct for me.

'What then?' I gently prompted him.

'Some NatSec stooges, agents provocateurs, went into the crowd and started throwing stones at the police so the police charged at them. They knocked a few of the students about – not too badly, but enough to make the others start running, and Julie fell over.' His voice was a whisper for the final words. 'She'd had asthma since she was a kid.'

'She had an attack?' He nodded. I felt a deep mix of

sorrow for him and outrage for all of us. 'You're sure they were NatSec people who started the trouble?'

'Yeah. I did some asking around after, had a few words with some of the coppers who were there. The ones who started it were older than the students, dressed differently. All men. No girls. It was called a riot on the news and the Secs got their way because they convinced Blunt that these students were going to bring down the new state and the police were thugs. We knew what really happened, but we couldn't say nothing. Just had to cut our losses.'

I didn't know how to ask. 'Were you there too?'

'No,' he sighed. 'No, if I had been, I might have been able to do something.'

I gazed along the road. 'Do you have other children?'

'Just Julie. When I got a bit down with the job, I would think about her growing up.'

'Your wife?'

'Oh, Elsa's gone too now. So the answer to your question,' he said, 'the one you haven't asked me, is that I'm doing this because I'll be put out to pasture soon and this is all I can do against them. Not much. But it's something, isn't it?'

A strike back against the people who had taken his daughter from him. Yes, it wasn't much but it was something. What he wasn't speaking of, but I could sense, was the guilt he felt over his daughter's death, the guilt that he hadn't been there to protect her.

And that meant that I was taking advantage of a decent man's burden. Like everyone else, I suppose, I thought of myself as a good person but the new era had brought about changes. 'You're not frightened of them?' I asked.

He rubbed the bridge of his nose. 'Oh, what can they do to an old man like me?'

I thought for a second. There was the ageing man I had seen holding up a banner in Liberation Square, thrown into the back of an army truck.

The truth, really, was that they could do a lot.

It felt different being in Lorelei's house with someone else – this time the weeds outside were just weeds, rather than creatures to grab hold of me; the seeping smog was just the weather and not some smothering blanket. 'Nice place,' Tibbot said under his breath as we moved through. 'Hardly noticed it yesterday.'

'Nick lived here, with her,' I said.

'Very nice.'

As I passed the bathroom door, I couldn't help but look in. A thin shard of smoky light was slipping through the gap between the curtains and glittering in the long gilt mirror. Dust seemed to swim hypnotically in it, and, as I stared at the dark glass, straining to make myself out, pressure built in my head. And then, without warning, another figure slipped in from the edge of the glass, just as it had the first time I had seen it, when the room had been hot and damp and Lorelei's eyes shone under the water. I yelled and spun around straight into his outstretched hands.

'What's wrong?' Tibbot said urgently, searching my face for the cause of my fear.

I pushed away from him. 'Nothing,' I said, shaking my head, annoyed at myself. 'Nothing. Let's just get on with this.' He stood back and watched as I hurried to Lorelei's bedroom. 'There,' I said, as he entered the room, doing my best to sound grounded. I pointed to the posters on the wall. 'That's where the key comes from.' I showed him the list of codes I had copied from the book.

DD2261033445298	wfn
VN1081209994632	str cor
TW3284408109028	pro wfn
AM7126026369346	cor
VN4653310089328	cor str
DO55743010382201	wfn pro
TL2159414038033	nor

'Look at the first letters: *DD*; *VN* twice; *TW*; *AM*; *DO*; *TL*.' For each one, I indicated the corresponding poster on the wall: '*Daisy, Daisy*; *Victory 1945*; *The Whole Deal*; *A Month in the Country*; *Double or Quits*; *The Lucky Lady*.'

'Yes, I see,' he said. 'But what's the actual key? We have some posters and a string of numbers. How do the numbers relate to them?'

I pointed to *Victory 1945*. It was her attachment to that film that had given it away – using its title twice had been the detail that let me in. 'There are numbers on each of these posters. The date that the film or play is showing. Those must be the keys.' I wrote them down.

The Whole Deal	08/10/48
The Lucky Lady	15/04/38
A Month in the Country	16/06/39
Double or Quits	05/01/47
Daisy, Daisy	26/03/42
Victory 1945	10/09/46

'I hope you enjoy long division,' he muttered. 'You know . . .' He drifted off thoughtfully.

'What?' I said.

'These dates.'

'Yes?'

'Well, no. It's nothing. Forget it. Let's go downstairs and see what we can make of them.'

In the kitchen, we stared at the page again. I tried every mathematical formula I could think of to relate the date figures to the strings of digits in the book – taking one from the other, multiplying, dividing. None of the products made any intelligible number, though – nothing that was the right length for an identity card, telephone number or anything else. I had presumed that, having realized the posters were the key, it would all be over from then. That had been hubris and now I was being punished for it.

'Was she a maths genius?' asked Tibbot after a while.

'Not as far as I know.'

He furrowed his brow. 'Maybe we're looking at it the wrong way. Maybe they don't go together like that. You know I said about patterns being a way into understanding the cipher? Well, look at how many double digits there are. And a triple. That can't be completely random.'

He wrote the first string on his pad. DD2261033445298. Then he wrote the opening date of the play *Daisy, Daisy*, 26/03/42. 'Lots of the same numbers,' he said to himself, comparing the two. He started crossing out numbers from the first string. 'Do this,' he said. 'For every digit that you find in the date, cross off the first time it appears in the column.' He turned his page around to me. It now read

2̶2̶6̶1̶0̶3̶3̶4̶4̶5̶2̶9̶8. 'That's a telephone number for sure,' he said, his face betraying his satisfaction.

I jumped up, exhilarated. 'Yes. God, yes!' We quickly turned all the other strings into telephone numbers. The second column, of three-letter strings, was still a mystery, but we had taken a huge leap forward. Lorelei hadn't been some mathematical genius; she had simply dropped random digits, taken from the show dates, into the original telephone numbers. That disguised the telephone number. The rule was that each random digit had to be placed somewhere before it occurred in the original telephone number. 'How did you guess?' I asked as we went to find a call box, trying to keep my excitement in check.

'Those doubles. It's because she was lazy. Say she has to drop a false three in; it has to come somewhere before the first genuine three so she knows that the new first three is the false three. Sometimes she couldn't be bothered finding a random place for it, so just stuck it right in front of the genuine one. She wasn't always that lazy, but she was enough times for it to stand out.' I was impressed.

The street was busy again as people returned home from the Liberation Day parade. Across town, the Politburo would be taking its fleet of black limousines to the faceless prefabricated block next to the National Observatory in Greenwich Park that some unknown wag had dubbed the 'Concrete Kremlin'. From the top of that hill, they could look down on all eighteen million citizens of our new republic – or across to DUK London if they wanted to see what they were missing.

We entered the call box, ready to find out what Lorelei had been hiding. I dropped a penny in the slot and dialled o for the operator.

17

'What number, please?' she asked.

'Exchange 213; number 4598.'

'Please hold, caller.' I waited. So much was riding on this. There was silence, a few clicks, and then the operator was back. 'That number does not exist,' she said. I thumped the side of the box in fury.

'No line?' Tibbot asked, disappointed.

I didn't answer, as if acknowledging the failure would make it solid. I spoke again into the receiver. 'Try exchange 812, number 9932.'

'Please hold, caller.' Again, I waited. Then the same dead-pan voice. 'That number does not exist.' When the next number produced the same result, the operator's tone changed. 'Please stay on the line,' she said. I heard muffled voices, as if she were speaking to someone behind her. Then she returned.

'Caller, who are you trying to reach?' There was something frightening about that question, as if it were something she had been instructed to ask me. I hung up immediately.

'What's wrong?' Tibbot asked.

'She was speaking to someone. About us.'

'No, no, they get these calls all the time.'

'She was!'

He huffed and blew out his cheeks, not wanting to argue

more. 'Maybe they aren't telephone numbers after all,' he said, changing the subject. It couldn't be true – we had both been so certain. 'Still, let's try the rest.' I must have looked worried. 'It's fine,' he insisted.

I dialled o once more, hoping that it would be a different operator. It was, thank heaven – a warm Scottish accent asking me for my desired line. Still tense, I tried another number, hoping.

'That number does not exist.'

At that, Tibbot gestured to me to hang up. 'Hazel told you that the book has been up there since before her parents divorced, yes?' he asked, when the receiver was down.

'That's right.'

'So it's at least a few years old. And the phone network was improved a couple of months back: all residential lines got new numbers, didn't they? If these are phone numbers at all, it looks like they're out of date. Maybe Lorelei stopped whatever she was doing; or there's a newer list somewhere.' I didn't know what to say; it was crushing. 'Look, keep trying, but let's not get our hopes up.' I nodded and tried again. But there was only the message 'That number does not exist' that told me the call would not be answered. Then it was the sixth of seven entries. I read out the number without much hope and heard the familiar silence. Then a clicking. Then the operator's voice.

'Connecting you now.'

And then – incredibly – a distant ringing that said we had made a connection. Tibbot punched the air before pressing his ear next to mine so he could hear. We were on tenterhooks, barely daring to breathe in case it somehow caused the line to cut out. It rang and rang.

'Are they there?' Tibbot asked, frustrated. 'Answer the bloody thing.'

After a full minute without an answer, I gently placed the handset back in the cradle and pressed the button to return my money.

'But it's better than nothing. I suppose they haven't had their number changed,' I said, doing my best to remain positive. I pondered for a second. 'Is it just residential numbers that changed?'

'Yes.'

'So this one might be a business or government number?'

'Yes,' he said, nodding. 'Yes, you might be right. Try it again.' I hardly needed to be told. Once again, there was silence, clicking and the faint ringing, as if the other telephone were a few metres along the street and we could just reach out and touch whoever was standing beside it. But it rang and rang without a voice coming on. I hung up for the second time. Still excited, I tried the final number, but the result was back to 'That number does not exist'.

'We'll get there,' Tibbot said. 'We've got one that works. But let's go and find this Rachel Burton. She's tied up in this.'

I looked at my watch as we walked quickly towards Blackfriars Station. It was half past three. 'Where do your colleagues think you are?' I asked.

'Looking into some phantom theft of a box of coats from a shop.'

'Too dull for them to ask you about it?'

'That's about right. I'm old and decrepit, you see.'

His slight smile faded back to his normal grimmer expression. 'But you know I still have to be a bit snide about it. Especially now – they're talking of putting a political officer in every station so we're a bit on edge. Anyway, there's a chance we'll get stopped somewhere along the line – coppers or the Secs. If it happens, just let me do the talking. I'll say you're a friend and we're looking for a relative of mine who I lost track of during the War. Keep it vague.'

'What if they don't believe us? If they check up on it.'

'Well, if it gets serious, I can throw myself on the mercy of my inspector, say it's a personal thing I want to keep to meself. We go back, me and Jim. And I know a thing or two about him too.'

'Will that really work?'

'To tell the truth, I don't know.'

'All right.' I was more than happy for him to do the talking. If I had had to come up with some excuse for our enquiries on the spot, I would probably have gone to pieces anyway.

'So Miss Burton lives in King Henry Road,' he mused. 'Won't be that for very long.'

'What do you mean?'

'A bit too Royalist, isn't it? They're renaming all the relic streets.'

'Oh, yes,' I said, looking around me as if I could see the changing names. 'I suppose so.'

'Where are you from?' he asked.

It seemed strange to be getting to know each other on a personal level now, after we had been through so much together already. 'Herne Bay.'

'Nice. I used to go there with Elsa and Julie. Did you ever come up to the smoke when you were young?'

I told him how my parents brought me up for a day when I was ten or twelve. We had walked through Mayfair, what my dad had said was the poshest of London's neighbourhoods. 'I thought the big houses looked like palaces from a fairy tale.'

'The Jerries did for a lot of them. Real pity.'

'Oh.'

I wondered what it looked like now. The DUK might have rebuilt them – not, I hoped, as concrete blocks, like on our side. And it was strange to think that, as I had walked up the eastern pavement of Regent Street just the previous day, past the empty windows of the big old stores, the buildings on the other side of the Wall had once looked out on to the same road, with gleaming displays of plush furniture, jackets and boots, cots. Those frontages had since been sealed in by the concrete border that had been built right up against them, and the buildings had been turned around to face the other way as if the division between us was just too grotesque to look at.

'All this change,' Tibbot said. 'Do you even remember when the money had the King on it?' Until he brought it up, I actually had forgotten that there had been a time when Marx and Engels had been absent from those little tokens. 'Or all the other newspapers we had. *Sunday Pictorial. The Times.* Yeah, I bet you don't even know how much you've forgotten.'

It was only a few minutes' walk to Blackfriars, where we caught a fast train to Gravesend. Within an hour we stood

154

in front of 2 King Henry Road – or what was left of it. Most of the street, it turned out, had been demolished to make way for a new block of flats. There were cranes lifting big concrete slabs into place, guided by men in helmets.

'Lots of air raids around here just before D-Day,' Tibbot said, looking at the rubble. 'Going for the docks; and RAF Gravesend was a fighter airfield, part of Biggin Hill. These houses would've been hit a few times.' On the train down, we had seen Yak fighters taking off on routine patrol – a strange twist of history, really.

'You weren't in the War, though, were you?'

'Me? No, not this one. Far too old.' The first War, I guessed. A pals' battalion. Wipers or Gallipoli. Young men happily tramping off to what they had thought would be an adventure but finding only mud and drowning trenches. 'Mate of mine at the station was RAF down here, though. He says it was chaos – the Stukas spent months busting up all our fighters on the ground. That's why there was no air support on D-Day and the Luftwaffe had a free hand to bomb our boys on the way over. I'm glad I didn't have a son.'

The road faced on to the Thames Estuary but was cut off from the water by the familiar steel fence and watch towers.

A group of children, aged between six and nine, were playing in the rubble. They wore threadbare clothes, and their looks, as we approached, ranged from fear in the younger ones to defiance from the older, as if we had come to throw them off the only playground they knew.

Tibbot had a quick glance around to make sure there were no police nearby before addressing the boy who seemed to be the eldest. 'You look like a sharp gang,' he said. 'We're trying to find a friend of mine called Rachel Burton. Do you know her?' They shook their heads, glaring at us. 'There's a few bob in it if you do.' By some unseen signal, they turned around and marched away in single file. Tibbot called after them but they just ran. He shrugged his shoulders and pointed to a call box. 'Let's give it another go.' I nodded in agreement. We had tried the number twice more on the way without luck but weren't about to give up. We had to get lucky sometime.

I pulled out the numbers that we had taken from Lorelei's list and tried the sixth one. There was the usual rattling, then the long ringing. Just as before, it rang and rang without answer. I began to place the receiver back on its hook.

'Hello?' a tinny voice said through the line.

I jumped, pressed the button to talk and held the receiver so hard to my ear that it hurt. I had prepared something to say but it had spilled from my mind. Tibbot gestured to me to calm down, and I did my best to bring my speech under control. 'Hello. I . . . I'm sorry to disturb you,' I stammered. 'But may I ask who you are?'

There was a pause. 'You called here.' It was a woman's voice, suspicious and careful. I moved the earpiece so that Tibbot could hear too.

'Yes, I know.' I searched around for a reason to call. My mind was blank. 'Please, I have to know who you are.'

'I'm not really supposed to be answering this line at all. I'm just standing in,' she said.

'Just –'

'I can't.'

'Please!' I said, letting the emotion out.

I heard her breathing. Then a click and a mechanical hum to say she had hung up. I gasped and tried to call again. The number connected and rang until it cut out. I tried again. No answer.

'I can try to find out where that line goes, but I'll do it on the quiet when I'm back at the station,' Tibbot said. 'Better to keep things quiet.'

'All right.'

'We'll get there, honest. But for now, we'll try the neighbours about Rachel.'

We knocked on doors and stopped people in the street. After a while we tried a door in desperate need of patching up and painting – a lower corner seemed to have been kicked away. It was opened by a woman shrunken by age. 'Good morning, madam,' said Tibbot. 'We're from the council.' He didn't want any repercussions from these enquiries. 'We're asking about a woman named Rachel Burton. She used to live around here. Did you ever know her?'

The woman's lips twitched as she said the name to herself. 'Rachel. Yes. Yes.' I shot a look at Tibbot, keeping my excitement under control. 'Would you like to come in?'

'Yes, we would. Thank you very much.' She shuffled to a draughty front parlour and asked us to sit on a pair of upright wooden chairs that barely took our weight. 'How did you know her?' Tibbot asked.

'Oh. Oh, yes,' she said, staring at us, before going slowly to the kitchen. 'I would like some tea,' she mumbled.

'How did you meet her?' Tibbot called through the open doorway, gently pressing her. We waited, listening to the kettle whistle. She didn't reply until she returned with three cups of weak tea. 'How did you know Rachel?'

'This is my husband.' She touched a framed fading photograph of a man in clothes from the beginning of the century, on the crumb-laden table beside her.

'Your husband?'

She lifted his photograph. 'This is him. Lionel.' Her mouth quivered. 'The War, you see.' She meant the first War, the Great War. The carousel of battles had just kept spinning.

'I'm very sorry to hear that.' Tibbot waited until she replaced the photograph. 'And he introduced you to Rachel?' She looked away and dabbed the corner of her eyes with a handkerchief. 'Was it him who introduced you to Rachel?'

'Rachel?'

'Yes.'

She looked at me and squinted. 'Are you Rachel?'

'No,' I said.

She waited for us to say something more. 'Do you remember Rachel? Rachel Burton?' Tibbot asked again.

'Who?'

'Rachel Burton?'

She stared blankly at us. Tibbot smiled at her and we stood up. 'Well, thank you for your time,' he said.

'Thank you,' I repeated unhappily.

'Are you going?'

'Yes. I'm afraid we have to go now.'

'Oh. Well, please come again.'

'We'll be sure to,' I replied.

On our way out, Tibbot slipped a pound note under the cushion on the chair. She would find it later. 'She shouldn't live like this,' he said, as we felt the cold air outside.

'I know. Awful, isn't it?'

He rubbed his hands together against the cold. 'Streets like this, they used to leave their doors open. Everyone's gran.'

'I grew up on a street like this.'

We picked our way over rubble. 'I had a case last month,' he said. 'Postman found an old boy locked in a flat. The poor bloke was shivering – no heat in the place, hardly any clothes, covered in bruises. He wouldn't say a word, but it turned out it was his daughters knocking him about. Never let him out. Kept him for his war pension. Extra few quid. Never used to be like that. Never.'

I looked back at the woman's battered door. Age was something we couldn't help, but our families – they were supposed to stay with us. It was so unnatural to be cut off.

We tried more doors, but people had moved around so much – first when the Germans landed at Portsmouth after D-Day, and later when the Soviets had followed and started reassigning homes. Those old communities where people knew everyone in their street had been splintered and no one could help us. 'Well, that puts the kibosh on that,' Tibbot sighed.

'What about the doctor who was given Rachel's car?'

'Richard Larren. No address for him, and Kenneth couldn't find any more details in the records – he even tried the Medical Board, but they're closed today. I can call them tomorrow.'

'Tomorrow could be too late.'

'I know, but I can't see how else to go about it.'

'Perhaps Nick knew him,' I said, grasping at straws. 'Let's find out.'

At the end of the road there was a pub. It had a wooden telephone booth covered with messages scratched in ink – swear words, names and dates, a childish joke. I called a familiar number and the line was answered immediately.

'The consulting rooms of Nicholas Cawson. Charles O'Shea speaking.'

'Charles, it's Jane Cawson. I have a question. Does my husband ever have any dealings with a Dr Richard Larren?'

'Richard Larren? Not that I know of.'

'Can you check?'

'I'm looking through the addresses file now. There is no Richard Larren listed.'

'Oh.' I was disappointed.

'Who is he?'

I kept it vague so as not to arouse any curiosity. 'I thought he might be someone who could help get Nick released.'

'How?'

The truth was that I didn't even know the answer myself. But if I said nothing, it would only make him more suspicious. 'I think he can say that Lorelei's death was an accident.'

Charles paused. 'He will be in the medical certification directory.'

'What?'

'It's an annual requirement.'

I dared to see a glimmer of hope. 'Do you have it?' There was another pause, and I wondered if he was having second thoughts about becoming involved – with his family's history of supporting the Royal Family, he could easily end up without a job or home if he made it into NatSec's files. 'Oh, Charles, I promise you I'll make sure that nothing bad will come of it. In fact, if Nick gets out and the case is closed, it really makes us all safer. They won't be breathing down our necks.' There was a hiss on the line.

'Wait.' It went quiet for a minute, broken by the sound of movement in the background, as if things were being shifted around. Time ticked away. And finally there was a clunking sound as he lifted the receiver from his desk. 'Richard Larren's address is Willoughby Hospital, Willoughby, Kent. There are no more details.'

'Oh, thank you, Charles, that's wonderful,' I said. 'Thank you. I have to go now, but I'll see you soon.'

'Goodbye.'

I hung up. 'Shall we call him?' I asked Tibbot.

'Better to turn up in person. If he knows something, he's more likely to tell us face to face. Otherwise, he can just put the phone down.'

'Yes, you're right.' I was lucky he was there, or I would have blundered my way into dead ends.

'Let's try that other number, though.' We tried the number from the book again, but it wasn't answered. Still, Richard Larren's address held out a prospect of success. Tibbot checked a train timetable he had picked up when we arrived. 'Willoughby's just two stops back up towards London,' he said. 'We've got twenty minutes before the next one. Willoughby Hospital. Wonder what exactly he does there.'

We set off along the road, which had become gloomy in the twilight. As we walked, I pondered what we would find – something that exonerated Nick? Or something that proved him guilty of a plan I didn't yet understand?

I was distracted from those thoughts, however, by a

commotion – children running, adults hurrying, all in the same direction. I looked to Tibbot. 'Nothing to do with us,' he said.

'But what if it is?' There was such urgency that I thought somehow it might be connected to our search for Rachel. 'It's possible. We should see.'

He glanced in the direction of the station, then back at the clutch of running people. 'All right,' he relented.

We followed them to the fence along the waterfront, to find all eyes fixed on a small launch, barely bigger than a rowing boat, battering at speed through the waves. Steered by a young man, it shot eastwards towards the open sea. These attempts never happened in London because the Thames was too well defended there, but outside the capital people tried from time to time to escape by water. I had heard of night-time bids to slip from Herne Bay around the coast, although I had no idea if they were ever successful.

Everyone was watching the boat, willing it on. Above us, harsh searchlights picked out the launch, making the waves glitter. Then three cracks split the air and I looked up to see a guard in the watch tower lower his rifle.

I stared out to see if the young man had been hit. We all did. But the boat was still moving – the guard had missed. I felt my heart lift as if I were in the little vessel with that young man putting his life at risk to get to a northern shore. From the west, one of our patrol boats appeared, racing in his wake, hugging the shoreline.

'Will he make it?' I asked Tibbot, putting aside, for a moment, our own purpose that afternoon. But it struck me that our task wasn't unconnected to this sight. Whatever had, ultimately, pushed this young man to speed between air-cutting bullets in the Thames Estuary was surely the same cause that had left Lorelei shimmering under cold, drifting water in London. 'If he can get to the middle, he might. That's where the mines are – our boat won't follow.'

He was only a few hundred metres from the centre line. It couldn't take him long.

'Won't he set off the mines himself?'

'Maybe little boats don't set them off. I don't know.'

The people around us were egging the pilot on. The men in particular were shaking the wire fence. The children kept trying to climb the links but were dragged down and slapped by their parents, who pointed to the watch towers that were spitting more and more bullets.

'Will he get through?' I asked aloud.

'Yes!' a young man shouted back, abandoning discretion. Another patrol boat roared in from the east, but they were both holding back.

'What are they doing?' I said.

Tibbot jerked his thumb to the towers. 'Too many rounds. They don't want to get hit themselves.' The young man kept changing his course, apparently trying to make it harder for the soldiers to aim.

'He's going to do it!' shouted one of the men. But, just as he did so, there was another volley of gunfire and the pilot disappeared from view.

'Did he fall in?' cried one of the women.

'No,' Tibbot said quietly. 'He's in the boat.' The little craft began to steer a wild course, wheeling in a circle, before the engine cut out. It bobbed gently in the water, drifting along with the tide. There was silence now from the people watching. 'Let's go,' Tibbot said.

18

We walked quickly up the hill to find the railway line emerging around a corner. We bought two tickets at the station counter and sat in the small, empty waiting room. 'My wife was from Kent,' Tibbot said after a while. It was the first time he had spoken about her.

'From near here?'

'Quite near. Maidstone. She was devoted to Julie, of course,' he added, as if he hadn't stopped thinking of either of them for a second. 'Poor flowers.' I looked at him. I got the impression that he wanted to talk about it, but wasn't used to it. He stared at the floor.

'What do you mean?'

He shifted in his seat. 'Julie, she . . . It was Elsa's shift at the pub that she was going to when she was caught up in that demo. Elsa was poorly and I told Julie to cover it for her mum. She didn't want to because she was going to meet some of her pals, but I said her mum would get into trouble with the landlord.

'After it happened, Elsa and I never said anything, but I was always thinking, "If you hadn't got ill" and she was always thinking, "If you hadn't told her to take my place." Well, you can't stop those thoughts.' He cleaned his glasses and pressed them back into place.

I thought about my own mum and dad. How they had always done their best for me and how their own lives had ended, like so many others, with the indignity of TB. Really, though, I should be thankful that at least I had had a chance to say goodbye to them. Millions over the past decade had never had that.

A youngish man with neat hair and shining shoes sat on a bench on the other side. Tibbot glanced at him and quietly suggested we wait out on the platform.

'You're a teacher, you said?' he asked, as we emerged.

'Yes. Only I haven't worked for some time. No one will give me a job.'

'Why's that?'

'Because I trained in the old era. I can't be trusted. Do you know, there's been a standing directive for a few years: any children who were at school in the DUK before the Wall went up can't be in the same class together because they could form factions and pollute the others? It just seems normal now. God, that's awful.'

The train arrived and we boarded it. Tibbot was silent for a minute. Then he cleared his throat. 'Look, Jane, I'm sure I don't need to tell you, but we're crossing a line here. I can't tell them I'm a copper so we won't have that protection. If NatSec or whoever found out, we would be –'

'I know what we would be.' He didn't need to warn me. Maybe as a policeman he didn't experience the visceral fear that the rest of us had to live with. But it was as much as I could do not to catch the first train back to London and wait quietly at home for whatever was going to happen to me and Nick. 'I was wondering,' I said, changing the subject. 'Back in Lorelei's house, when we were looking at the posters, you started to tell me something but you stopped yourself. It was something you had seen in them.'

'Did I? Oh, yes, something did occur to me. Those dates on the posters – they meant something but not just the code in the book. Something else.' I waited again for him to explain. 'It's that they were all years ago. The last one was in '48. No more in the last four years.'

'So?'

'Oh, twenty years ago it must be. I was sent to a house up in Golders Green. I was living north of the river then. Actress by the name of – I won't forget it – Lillian Hall-Davis. She was a big star for a while. Silent era – before your time. Then the talkies came and the parts dried up. Well, poor girl did for herself. Do you think –'

'Lorelei would never do something like that.'

'How can you be sure?'

'Because she liked herself too much.'

It was fully dark when we alighted at a tiny station formed of nothing but a platform and a brick hut for the guard. The village it served was a vision of the rural England that used to be, and in my mind's eye I could see old maids cycling to church, waving to mothers with prams, while the menfolk played cricket on the village green. There were pockets of that left, with the new way of life taking its time to creep out from the towns and cities, but there was talk now of collectivizing the last remaining private farms to make them fairer and more efficient – no longer would the farmer have a fat belly while the factory worker starved, they said.

Following directions that the station guard gave us, we picked our way along a country lane. The hedgerows eventually gave way to a high brick wall that we followed for a kilometre before it opened to show a large country house, the sort a wealthy industrialist might have retired to in the last century. Thousands of these grand homes had rotted away after the Great War had left their owners' sons lying in shallow, muddy graves in Flanders and beside the Somme. Behind its closed wrought-iron gates we saw a little wooden gatehouse with a man inside dressed in a white uniform. He was reading the football reports on the back page of the *Morning Star* and looked up when I tried the gates. They were locked, I found. He slid open a window. 'We're looking for a Dr Larren. Is he here?' I asked.

'I haven't seen him go out.'

'But he does work here?'

'He's medical director.' He was becoming curious about us.

'Can you let us in, please?' Tibbot said.

'Visiting's over. Unless you've got an appointment, you can't.'

Tibbot pursed his lips. 'It's important.' I knew he didn't want to identify himself as a policeman.

The man was becoming irritated. 'Then make an appointment.'

'We don't have time.'

He went back to his match reports. 'That's your trouble,' he replied.

'We need to see him now.'

He refolded the paper. 'Piss off or I'll call security.'

We had already been frustrated today and this seemed our last chance. 'Police,' I said.

Tibbot stared at me.

'What?' the man in uniform blurted out, looking up from the page.

167

'He's police.'

I could see Tibbot mentally calculating the danger of admitting who he was. If we tried to slope off now, the man might well call the local station straight away and that would set a dangerous train in motion.

'Are you? Show me your warrant card.' He was suspicious.

Stony-faced, Tibbot drew out his warrant card. 'Here,' he said. He indicated a telephone on the wall inside the gatehouse. He had to brazen it out now. 'So we would like to see Dr Larren. That must be connected to the office, yes?'

The man still looked wary, but he took the telephone from the wall. 'What name?' he asked.

'Detective Sergeant Tibbot.'

The man stabbed the single button on the telephone. Tibbot kept that stony look on his face. I tried to catch his eye, to let him know that I was sorry, but he stared straight ahead. 'Police here to see Dr Larren. All right,' the man mumbled into the receiver. 'Asking him,' he said to us.

I looked across to the house. 'What kind of hospital is it?' I said. Perhaps Rachel had been a patient here, and for some reason Larren had taken her car to keep in trust. That seemed strange, though.

The man in white stared at me. 'Psychiatric.'

I gazed up at the wide building. I had never seen one before. It seemed so ordinary.

We waited a minute before the telephone squawked again. 'He wants to know what it's about,' the man said, the receiver still by his chin.

Tibbot was annoyed, and I was sure much of the anger was for me. 'Tell him it's about a car he received in 1950. Police business.'

The man narrowed his eyes. 'About a car he received in 1950. Yeah. I don't know.' We waited again.

'You know what kind of people are in these places?' Tibbot asked under his breath. 'You know it's not just for the sick now? There are . . . others.' He looked at me to see if I understood.

I did. It was what was detailed on that samizdat leaflet that I had found beside Liberation Square. The commitment to provide healthcare for everyone, including those with mental illnesses, had suited the government in a way that was never made public but was whispered about. It was something else we had borrowed from the Soviet Union: dissident intellectuals – and sometimes trades unionists or general troublemakers – were dumped in places like this and doped up until their words died on their tongues. The hospitals had become an extension of the political process. The Communists had told us from the beginning that everything would soon be political, but we hadn't fully understood them. We had thought it meant that the structures of society would be moulded to serve the public. We were – I was – beginning to understand that it meant that they would be bent to serve the requirements of politicians.

Eventually the telephone rang and the man in white put it to his ear. 'All right.' He placed the handset back in its cradle and looked us up and down, rubbing his palms over his hips. 'What's all this about a car?' he asked.

'I think you have to do as you've been instructed,' Tibbot replied, pointing to the telephone.

The man shrugged his shoulders. 'I'll take you up.'

He unlocked the gate and led us up a long and winding

gravel path to the twin-winged house. A very large ground-floor window on the left glared out light into the country evening. It held a number of faces staring out, hardly moving, while the corresponding window on the right showed only a smattering of faded furniture. Both were barred. With a clanking of locks from inside, the front door opened for us.

'They're to see Dr Larren,' the gatekeeper told a heavy-set man wearing an identical uniform, before returning to his post.

The new man told us to follow him, closing and securing the door with a key from a large bunch hanging on his belt. He smelled like he hadn't washed in a long time. 'This way,' he said.

We passed a heavy-looking door with a panel of wire-strengthened glass. It gave access to a corridor into the left-hand wing of the house. Next to it a security guard sat filling in some forms. The security was obviously tight, but still a thought arose: if Rachel had once been detained here, if her mind was unstable, could Lorelei have died under her hand?

We climbed a wide oak staircase scored with deep welts and approached a door of intricately carved wood, upon which the orderly thumped with his fist. From somewhere behind it, a voice told us to enter and we did so to find a short man in his shirtsleeves peering at us from behind a glass desk. 'Good evening,' he said. 'I'm Dr Larren. I'm sorry I said I was busy, but there's a lot to do right now. If I can help you, I will. You said something about a car?'

Tibbot showed him his warrant card. There was no use hiding it now. 'You were given a car two years ago. Well, you took one, anyhow.'

'I'm sorry, but no. No, I didn't.'

'Police records say you received a Sunbeam. Registration YXA 998.'

'I don't know what to tell you, Detective Sergeant, that's not my car.' He poured a glass of water and drank.

'We're trying to find the woman who owned it before you. Her name is Rachel Burton. Is she a patient?'

'No. We don't have any patient by that name.'

'You're certain?' Tibbot asked.

'Yes. We have fewer than forty patients. I know them all personally. I make a point of it. Only eight or nine have arrived in the past few years and she isn't one of them.'

'Could she have been here for a short time?'

'Even then I would have known her.'

'This is a most important enquiry.'

'I'm sure it is, but I can't help you.'

'Could you ask your staff?'

He looked amused. 'I'm afraid they would tell you the same thing.'

'You can't be certain of that.'

'But I can, officer.'

'Dr Larren . . .'

It was ridiculous and I could see no point going on with it. The man wasn't going to tell us anything. 'Look,' I said to Tibbot. 'Let's leave this and just go. Please.'

Tibbot seemed frustrated. He checked his notebook, although it must only have been to give him a chance to gather his thoughts. 'All right,' he said. 'The registration records must be a mistake. Thank you for your time.'

'I'm sorry I couldn't be of help.' Larren picked up a pen and returned to some papers on his desk.

Tibbot followed me out of the room and we were met by the orderly, who was waiting to escort us out of the building. As we went, I noticed how thin the staircase carpet was – little more than threads.

I turned to the orderly. 'Oh, I forgot to ask Dr Larren to do something.' He looked at me with little interest. 'Could you give a message to my cousin?'

His shoes were canvass, despite the cold and the fact that he seemingly had to tramp along country lanes to the hospital. 'Who's your cousin?' he replied.

'Rachel Burton.'

He glanced at the corridor to the other wing. 'All right.'

I felt a jolt of adrenalin but managed to stay composed. 'Just say Jane was sorry she couldn't stay. I'm feeling ill.'

'All right.'

We reached the lobby. 'Oh, she'll be so disappointed, though,' I said. 'I don't suppose there's any way of just saying a quick hello to her on my way out?'

He stopped and something seemed to occur to him. 'Past visiting time now. Shouldn't, really.'

'Yes, of course. It's a trouble for you. Perhaps I could pay you for your time.' I reached into my handbag and took a pound note from my purse. The orderly stared at it, then at the security guard, who was watching us. I added another note, and clipped my purse closed to show him that there would be no more forthcoming. The guard went back to filling in his forms.

'Just for a minute, no more,' Tibbot said, cajoling him.

The orderly swiftly stuffed the money in his pocket. He would buy the guard a drink later, no doubt. He unlocked the door to the corridor and took us to what I suspected was the room we had seen from outside the house, with the faces staring out on to the lawn. 'Be quick,' he said, as we stood on the threshold. 'A minute tops.'

'Thank you so much.' I was trying to appear calm and not too excited.

It was a linoleum-floored lounge with many small tables and hard seats. An unpleasant odour, like distant rotting fields, hung over the scene, emanating from a mass of dirty tin plates and wooden cutlery on the tables. The meagre remains of a meal were festering while twenty or thirty people, men and women, murmured or read battered magazines and paperbacks. Some of them had copies of Blunt's *The Compass* – doing so probably curried favour with the hospital authorities. A few posters of his image, emblazoned with quotations from his book, formed the room's only decoration, and below one such bill a heavyset nurse sat listening to gentle music drifting from a speaker.

She looked up as Tibbot and I entered, confused by our presence, but the orderly lifted his palm to say it was all right and I rapidly glanced through the room for any sign of the handsome young woman from the photograph in Nick's study. I must have stood stock still for a while, because the orderly spoke again. 'Go on, then, hurry up,' he said tetchily.

Unable to see her, but desperate to find her, I had to throw caution to the wind. 'Rachel Burton?' I called out, hoping she was there somewhere. The orderly looked startled, confused by what I was doing. 'Is Rachel Burton here?' The murmuring fell away and everyone turned to look. The orderly realized something was wrong and tried to take hold of my arm, but I rushed into the centre of the

173

room, hoping someone would reply. 'Rachel!' There was silence as all those faces looked blankly at me. The nurse shook herself into action and jumped up. 'Rachel Burton!'

Then, in a blur, the orderly was making for me, but Tibbot got in his way and they smacked against one of the seats, struggling. The nurse ran towards them too, sending a tray of food crashing to the floor, until Tibbot drew out his warrant card. 'Police,' he shouted. 'Let go.' The man did as Tibbot commanded, and there was an eerie sort of calm as we all stood facing each other.

The silence was punctuated by a quiet voice, timid as a shrew's, almost too timid to be heard. 'Over there,' it said. It was an old woman with straggling, near-transparent hair, thinning on the top. 'She's over there. Rachel.'

19

We followed the woman's thin finger to a figure in the corner of the room with her hands clasped together and her back hunched over so we couldn't see her face.

'Rachel?' I said.

She lifted her head and I caught sight of the features I had seen in the photograph from a few years earlier, but they were changed almost beyond recognition. Where the printed image had been of an attractive young woman, her dark hair tied back, here I saw her as if she had aged by a decade, her hair now matted and greying. And yet her eyes were keen as they locked on to mine.

'Rachel Burton?' I asked, as we edged towards her.

She made no reply but stared at the doorway. We spun around to find Larren looking furious. Another orderly appeared behind him.

'What the hell are you doing?' he demanded. 'Get out!'

'You said there was no Rachel Burton here,' I replied. His jaw worked as if he were trying to speak, yet no words came from his mouth.

'That car's stolen,' Tibbot added. 'Should we take a look in your garage? Now, we need to talk to her.'

Larren wiped his brow on his sleeve. 'Bring her to the visiting room,' he muttered to the orderlies. 'They're police.' I felt a thrum of nerves. So long as he kept thinking we were there on official business, we would be safe.

But if he began to doubt us, there was no guessing what the outcome could be.

The two orderlies led Rachel along the corridor with Larren and me walking behind her. 'Could she have got out of here a couple of days ago?' I asked. 'Got to London?'

'Of course not,' he replied angrily. I pondered how true that was. Certainly security was tight, but it wasn't a prison. And people sometimes broke out of those too.

The visiting room was a plain, windowless hole with a single iron-caged electric light, a smell of carbolic soap, and a table and four chairs bolted to the floor. I pitied anyone forced to meet a loved one in such a place. As we entered, Tibbot told Larren to wait outside and we would speak to him later. We sat at the table as Rachel took the chair opposite, with her face down. Tibbot placed a notebook and pencil in front of himself. Habit, I suppose.

'Hello, Rachel,' I said. She made no reply. 'How are you feeling?'

She looked up. 'Who are you?' her voice rasped, as if it hadn't been used for a long time.

'My name is Jane. Jane Cawson.'

'Cawson!' she spat, jumping up and clenching her hands into fists. 'That bitch!'

'She doesn't mean you,' Tibbot muttered to me, placing his hand on my arm to reassure me that we were safe. 'She means Lorelei.'

'Bitch.' She unclenched her hands, but remained standing over us, bristling with an anger that was all the stronger for having been repressed for years.

'Why do you say that?' I asked her, trying to adopt a soothing tone.

'Why?'

'Yes.'

She glared at me and pulled back her hair to reveal pale skin, wrinkling and lifeless; and from her left eyebrow up to her hairline, where it disappeared, a thin line of white scar tissue. 'This. I'll serve her back.'

'She's dead,' I said.

There was silence, then she sat back down. 'Dead.' She sighed heavily. 'I'm glad.'

'You're happy about that?'

'Yes.'

It was an ugly reaction, but I only needed her to tell me what had happened; her personal feelings weren't important right then. I checked the door was shut and lowered my voice. 'Rachel, I'm married to Nick Cawson.' She narrowed her eyes – it obviously made me untrustworthy, like Lorelei before me. 'We know you were involved in what she did. We have to know what it was.' If they really had been involved with a dissident group and crimes of subversion, then he was never coming home; but if it was something else, we might find a way. Rachel just watched us, still wary. 'We need to know.'

Tibbot spoke in a calm, relaxed voice. He must have been used to these situations. 'Rachel? Do you understand?' She nodded carefully. 'You and Lorelei Addington. Who was directing you?'

'Directing us.'

'That's right. Who did you deal with?' She winced, as if the memories were painful; as if she hadn't brought them to mind for a long time and now had to fight through a fog for them.

'Did you know? Did Lorelei say?'

'"My uncle has been in touch."'

'What?' Tibbot replied.

'She used to say it. "My uncle has been in touch."'

'When did she say that?'

'When the orders came.'

'Where did they come from? What uncle?'

She sighed again. 'Uncle Sam. Her joke.'

My breath caught in my throat. I had thought that Lorelei – possibly Nick – had been involved with some underground or dissident group, maybe one of the ones distantly encouraged by the Americans. But taking direct orders from them was so much more severe. We all knew that they recruited spies and saboteurs on our side, but I hadn't imagined for a second that was her life, her level of life-endangering belief.

'Rachel . . .' Tibbot began.

But I interrupted him. The only chance now was that Nick had played no part in what she had been doing, or that Lorelei had been the driving force and he had just gone along with it. If so, the courts might possibly be lenient – years in a camp, rather than the rope. 'Was Nick involved?' I asked, trying to suppress the panic in my voice. 'Was Nick . . .' And then she was gone. Without warning, we were in pitch darkness. I heard a rushing sound and a brush of wind. 'Rachel?' I called out, my nerves like ice.

There was whispering in the dark. Words I couldn't make out, followed by a thump on the table. I put my hands out, searching with them as if I could grasp the sounds.

'She's there!' Tibbot said urgently.

The whispering became faster.

'Rachel?' I called out. 'Rachel?' I probed again with my fingers but found only empty air. Then something appeared: a spark in the black to my side. Another spark. A fire-glow piercing it to create a face that flickered in the light. Tibbot was holding a steel cigarette lighter that cast a pallid glow over Rachel, pressed against the wall with a terrified look on her face. She was repeating something to herself over and over, as if reciting a prayer. I eased myself from my bolted-down chair to approach her, but she flinched away. 'It's just a power cut,' I said, with my hands open. 'Just the electricity gone out, that's all. Just the power for the lights.' She seemed as though she were trying to crawl into the wall. I wondered what happened there in the dark to make her so afraid of it.

'Just the lights gone off. That's all,' Tibbot reiterated, calmly. He stayed where he was, as she looked between us with her chest rising and falling. 'Happens all the time, doesn't it? Tomorrow the radio will say it was the Americans tampering with the lines or something.' Her breathing slowly returned to normal, and she timidly pushed herself away from the wall. The lighter threw a strange, elongated silhouette of her on to the wall.

She edged back to the table, with tears streaming down her cheeks. 'That's right,' I said. I took my handkerchief from my sleeve and handed it to her to wipe away the salt water. 'That's right. We're fine now.' I sat her down, and we all took our places again in the amber glow from the lighter. 'Rachel.' I put my hand on her wrist. 'I have to know. Was Nick Cawson part of what you were doing?'

She rubbed the sides of her head, as if she were in pain. Under her fingers I saw little patches on each side of her skull that had recently been shaved and now had a thin coating of stubble. 'Shocks,' Tibbot said under his breath. I tried to say something but couldn't find the words. It seemed barely human.

'Rachel,' I said again. 'Can you remember if Nick Cawson was part of it?' She looked down at herself with such sadness. 'Rachel . . .'

Perhaps my frustration was coming through in my voice, because Tibbot told me quietly to leave her for a minute. His breath made the lighter flame flicker. 'Who brought you here, Rachel?' he asked.

'A blue,' she mumbled.

'A policeman brought you here?' The bulb above us came back on, making us all wince, and Tibbot snapped off his lighter. 'Was he a local officer?' She nodded. 'How did he find out about you?'

'The nurse told him. The nurse. Another hospital.'

'Before this one?'

'Yes. For this.' The tip of her middle finger brushed along the line of pale dead flesh.

'What happened?' I asked.

'We fought. I said it was too dangerous, the Soviets . . .' She became confused again. 'She pushed me and I fell.'

'Did you fall against something?'

She nodded. 'Then I was in the hospital.'

What had she been before the War? A shop owner? A soldier's daughter? A theatre seamstress? I looked at her left hand, but could see no evidence of a ring. The only mark of a life before was the thin white one running through her skin. That was all that she had been allowed to keep.

'Why did she do it?' I asked more gently. 'This . . . work. What was Lorelei doing it for?'

'Money,' she said quietly. 'Excitement.'

They say that during the War half our agents in France were there for the thrill. Perhaps it wasn't so strange that Lorelei would do the same.

Tibbot met my eye and I steeled myself, hoping it was time to return to the question that I most needed answered. 'Rachel, was Nick involved in what you were doing?'

'Nick,' she whispered.

'Yes.' I spoke slowly, deliberately. I had to know. 'Was Nick Cawson involved? Please tell me.'

'Nick.' She opened her eyes and looked sadly at me. 'He ran it all.'

My heart fell to pieces. And for a second I wondered if I were really the one who was mad for refusing to acknowledge what should have been obvious from the beginning.

She was still speaking. 'I told that policeman about them,' she said thoughtfully. 'Taught the bitch a lesson.'

Coming to my senses, I began to argue with her, as if she would change her story. 'But Nick's not in government. What could he do for the Americans?' I said.

'He knows people, doesn't he?' Tibbot said quietly. 'Doctor to people.' And I realized something: that Tibbot had suspected this for a while, keeping it from me so that I would hold on to some hope.

Of course it was true. Nick had been angling to make contact with Ian Fellowman, Burgess's Assistant Secretary at the Ministry of Information, with a view to becoming his doctor. If he had succeeded, how the CIA would have loved knowing those men's state of health, what medication they were on, whether they were feeling stressed, whether they were going abroad the next month and where.

My fingers slowly scrabbled on the table surface. 'Was anyone else involved with you?' I asked.

Tibbot put a hand up to stop her answering. 'We don't want to know,' he said. 'Safer for them and us. It doesn't matter now.' And he was right: it didn't matter now.

Then, without warning, Rachel's hand flew across the table and snatched something. Before I knew it, she was leaping to the side, out of Tibbot's reach as he grabbed for her and I saw what she had: his lighter and a page torn from his notebook screwed up. In a second the paper was alight and she was throwing it at the window in the door. As it left her fingers, Tibbot managed to grab her arm, but it flitted and flickered through the air. It meant nothing as a weapon, but as a little act of defiance it meant every-thing. The door flew open and Larren entered with three orderlies. One pushed Tibbot aside, while another rushed behind Rachel and dragged her arms back. She meekly let him. 'I don't care if you are the police,' Larren barked. 'She's going back to the lock ward.' Another orderly pro-duced a gag, which he attempted to tie across Rachel's mouth. 'And if you want to speak to her again, you had better bring a warrant with you next time.'

Rachel suddenly wrenched the gag away and spat it to the floor. 'She said there would be new orders!' she cried. 'Big orders.'

'What orders?' I shouted back, but Larren and the other orderly were forcing us out. 'Rachel!' I tried to get to her, but Tibbot stopped me, taking hold of my arm. 'Let me go!'

'Leave her,' he said in a quiet voice. 'You can do nothing for her.'

'Yes, listen to him,' Larren said smugly.

One of the orderlies had her wrists, and another her ankles, as they wrenched her across the floor. She fought as well as she could, tearing one hand away to scratch at the burly man, drawing a line of red blood from his arm. He slapped her and she wailed into the gag. I tried again to reach her, but Tibbot put his body across mine. I knew what he was thinking – we were a hair's breadth from being exposed. 'Leave her alone!' I shouted helplessly.

Larren snorted in derision. 'Do what you have to do,' he told the three men. They dragged her away, ignoring her cries as she twisted over and over, struggling like a beast in pain.

20

We found an empty carriage on the train back to London. You could tell by the leather seats that it had once been First Class, although those distinctions had been among the first casualties of the new order, and now we could all sit where we chose. Cheap and reliable transport for everyone was so important to the Soviets.

And yet the London transport system had proved more treacherous than they had expected. A few days after the first fence went up along what was to become the route of the Wall, hundreds of people sped beneath it from our side to the other in tiny, underground carriages. It wasn't through the Tube – the Soviets had stopped those trains – but rather the little Post Office Railway, the network for delivering mail that the Reds knew nothing about until one of their friends in the Royal Mail ran to the Soviet HQ and told all. Their troops caught scores of people that day – men, women and children. They were lucky to get just a few weeks each in Brixton Prison – those who tried after, through the sewers or by climbing, usually got six months in solitary.

The Soviets learned from their mistake too. Instead of just closing the tunnels, they filled complete sections with rubble from the buildings that the Germans had destroyed during the relentless five-day bombardment that began their invasion. Most of those broken bricks had come from the East End – 'a hotbed of Jews and Trades Unionists', Mosley had informed the Nazi high command in advance. Well, those people had had their revenge in time, and Mosley's body soon lay broken on the street, next to that of his vile wife.

Coming from Kent, I had never really known the devastation that London had suffered until one night when Nick and I had climbed up on to the roof of a theatre on Shaftesbury Avenue, home to all the grandest playhouses. He had pressed a coin into the hand of an usherette during the interval of a musical, and she had surreptitiously pulled aside the chain that closed off the topmost flight of stairs.

'You see how some of these theatres have the roof missing?' Nick had asked me as the cool night air drifted about us.

'Yes,' I replied. 'The Blitz?'

'Not quite. This street's where the Home Guard made their last stand against the Nazis.' He shook his head. 'Old men up here with rifles and paraffin bombs against Panzers. Well, until the Luftwaffe blasted it all to bits. Poor blokes.' I tried to take it in, but it wasn't so easy. The official line that we were fed by the new state was that Churchill, in an act of supreme cowardice, had immediately signed the order of capitulation and saved his own skin by running off to Northern Ireland with the Royal Family. Others argued – discreetly – that he had been right to leave because someone needed to be in charge to direct the resistance, which was true. Well, you took your pick of viewpoints.

A night fighter on patrol passed overhead. Nick went right to the edge and peered down. 'Have you taken out life insurance?' I asked casually.

'Sorry, old girl, not a penny. So there's really no point doing it.'

'Pity.'

We looked to the other side of the Wall. Cars buzzed about with bright headlamps; there were omnibuses full of people; and bustling shops, despite the late hour. Sometimes, if you were close to the Wall and the wind was right, you could hear music coming over – that very fast, jumpy American jazz with guitars and singers that they played occasionally on Radio Free Europe. Young people – the Teddy Boys especially – would head to the basement milk bars of Soho to try to guess how the dances went, recreating the steps while they drummed on the tables with cutlery and fists. I had pictured Nick and myself over there dancing to the hot tempo music before laughing out into the street as the sun came up.

The train wheels crunched over tracks as Tibbot and I trundled back to London now. I looked out the window at houses passing in the night.

'He's lost,' Tibbot said. And he waited for it to sink in. 'I'm sorry, really, but if you keep on, it will only bring this down on you too. If they thought you knew anything about it, you would already be in one of their cells.' He was right. By delving into Nick's secret, I had made myself a target. And I had made Tibbot one too.

It was all so hard to take in. I understood that the state had its enemies – it never tired of telling us that – but I just hadn't seen Nick as one of them. I hadn't known him.

Whatever he had been doing for the Americans, though, I guessed he had stopped by the time we married. But then Lorelei had died and her death had somehow brought her

186

and Nick's activities to NatSec's attention. Whether her death was itself connected to their work, or was the product of something else entirely, didn't really matter – NatSec had learned about them.

'What do you think the "big orders" were?' I said.

'What?'

'Rachel said that's what they had fought about. She and Lorelei.' It was something so big they had come to blows. Yet, whatever it was, it didn't appear to have happened yet.

'I suppose it was all put on hold when she was taken in.'

'I expect so.' Perhaps that had been the final cause of Lorelei's death: someone had wanted to stop the plan or to take it over . . . or anything, really. All those possibilities of which we had no idea.

We pulled into a station and waited. The lights flicked off and back on. A door slammed. From further down the corridor, we heard a man's voice. 'Your identity cards!' It echoed through the train. Tibbot and I looked at each other, worried, and I pictured Larren on the telephone to whoever had transferred Rachel's car to him in return for keeping her quiet in his asylum.

'Two of them,' Tibbot said, putting his head outside the compartment. 'One's on the platform.'

I knew that I should have stayed put and calmly handed over my card, crossed my fingers and bluffed it out. I knew that. But panic took hold of me.

I jumped up, slid back the door and bolted into the corridor, away from the voice. Tibbot ran after me and grabbed me by the arm just as I was about to enter the furthest compartment. 'Calm down!' he ordered me. 'Breathe.' He checked over his shoulder. Luckily the man on the platform had his back to us and the other wasn't in sight.

'Identity card,' we heard again from one of the compartments.

'I'm sorry, I have it here somewhere.' It was a young man's voice, a local accent.

'What do we do if they recognize us?' I asked furtively.

'Come in and sit down.' He pulled me into the next compartment. An old woman in a shawl was sitting alone. Trembling, she held her card out to us.

'It's all right, that's not us,' said Tibbot.

'What do they want?' she asked in a feeble voice.

'Hard to say,' Tibbot replied.

I shot him a glance. I wanted to tell the woman it was us they were coming for, that she was safe, even if we were not.

She started talking nervously. 'Yes. A boy from my village, you see . . . I do my best, but you never know if the rules have changed and if someone is going to say something.' She took a handkerchief and dabbed her brow. She waved Tibbot away when he tried to put his hand on her arm. I heard the man's voice again, muffled by the door between us, but closer. 'And what then? What then?'

The door opened, but it was a girl, aged about eighteen, with her hair in the short style the Party encouraged. She sat down and no one said anything else. We just waited. The waiting went on for five, then ten minutes. Another door slammed and ours opened.

'Identity cards.' He was aged about forty – a little older than they usually were. NatSec preferred young men and women because they were more eager to shape the new world. It was the Secs' *belief* that made them so frightening.

I don't think I could ever have believed anything as strongly as they did.

I saw Tibbot look past the Sec, to the train door leading on to the platform. He was sizing the man up, then glancing at me. I could tell he was coming to the conclusion that it wasn't worth any rough stuff – he could probably handle himself, but not with me to look after too. The old woman and the girl who had sat down offered up their cards. They were taken, held up to the light, bent back and forth to test them and handed back without comment. Tibbot drew out his warrant card.

'All right?' he asked as he showed it. The Sec tried to take it from his grip. 'No need for anything, is there?'

'There is if I say there is.' His expression was challenging. He took the card from Tibbot and looked at it, then at him. 'This way,' he muttered. 'And you too.' I looked to Tibbot; he nodded. We did as we were told.

Stepping down on to a sullen-looking platform, we found it empty apart from the other Sec, a younger man, my age and athletic-looking. 'Now come on, mate,' Tibbot chuckled. 'What's this all about, eh?' A solitary light shone over a station sign that had been so broken and weather-beaten it was illegible. I guessed that we must have been close to Blackheath, the Closed Village where the Politburo lived with their NatSec minders.

'In there,' the senior man replied, pointing to the waiting room. The doorway was empty, with rusted hinges sticking uselessly out of the brickwork. Behind us, the train began to move off, the wheels whining as they strained to spin, and we watched the blank face of the old woman in the carriage disappear. 'I said in there.'

'All right, come on, a bit of professional comradeship,' Tibbot said, still trying to be pally.

'You're not my comrade.' Inside it was dark, with the smell of vagrants and what they had used it for. I started as I felt the younger man's hand on my back. 'Sit down.'

'I can stand,' I said.

'Sit down.'

'Just do it,' Tibbot muttered.

'Where have you been today?'

'Kent,' Tibbot replied, leaving behind the attempt at a friendly tone.

'Sergeant, you want to fuck about, you'll regret it.' I knew as well as Tibbot that he was probably right.

Tibbot lowered himself on to a backless bench in the middle of the room. He made the Sec wait before he answered. 'I was investigating a crime.'

'What crime?'

'Car theft,' Tibbot told him.

'Car theft.'

'That's right.'

The Sec pointed to me, then to another bench in the corner, behind Tibbot. His younger colleague took me by the arm and led me over. The older one resumed his questions. 'And just who reported this theft?'

'Sorry, that's between me and them.'

'Oh, yes?'

'Police business. Not yours.'

'Like I said, Sergeant, you fuck me about, you regret it.'

The younger Sec sat beside me. He had a small, pebble-like goitre bulging from the left side of his neck. He leaned in close to me. 'Your house,' he said quietly. 'Must be nice living somewhere big like that.' I stared dead ahead.

'Listen,' Tibbot said to the other man. 'You're pushing it and we both know that. Now, I know what you and your mates get up to in the basement of your HQ, but, unless you've brought a couple of rubber truncheons with you tonight, I'm going to cross my arms and sit here nice and polite while you piss off.' The Sec glanced at me. 'And you had better drop that idea and all, son.'

'Are you fucking threatening me?'

'Sounds like it, don't it?'

'You're a long way from home, Sergeant,' the older Sec told Tibbot, thrusting his face so close they almost touched.

'So are you,' Tibbot replied darkly. I was worried how this would end.

'You want to try, old man?'

'Been through as much as you.'

'You haven't a fucking clue.' I saw the saliva fly from his mouth.

Tibbot sat back, appraising him. 'What regiment?' he asked.

'One-four-two Commando.'

'Chindits?' The Sec nodded. Tibbot paused. 'And look at you now. Wingate wouldn't spit on a cunt like you.'

The Sec made eye contact with his colleague, who leaped up, grabbed the collar of Tibbot's jacket and pulled it down as far as his elbows, trapping his arms. The older man kicked Tibbot in the chest, toppling him backwards. He fell against my legs – if he hadn't, he would have cracked his head on the concrete floor. I bent down to help but the younger man dragged me back and I sat up again, my legs shaking.

'Fucking stay down!' the older man shouted at Tibbot.

Someone appeared at the door: a couple of kids aged thirteen or fourteen apparently attracted by the noise. They stopped at what they saw. 'Piss off,' the older Sec barked at them. They took his order and hurried away.

Tibbot was pushing himself on to his side.

'Are you all right?' I asked, afraid to help him up.

'Yeah.' But he wasn't breathing well and I hoped he was only winded.

The senior Sec took a notebook from his hip pocket, turned his back on us and marched over to a bashed-about call box in the corner of the room. He flipped through his book until he found what he was looking for, called a number and mumbled into the telephone. Tibbot pulled his jacket off and threw it angrily to the side. We all waited, freezing in the dank room as the Sec made his call.

A train, an express hooting its speed, came through in the opposite direction to ours. Distant road traffic provided a distorted chaos of noise. We waited, still. After a minute, the older man came back. 'The car is not stolen. There hasn't been any crime. It doesn't concern you any more, so you can go back to nicking pickpockets or whatever you normally do. Your inspector has been informed. I doubt he's over the moon.' Another train was pulling in on its way to London. 'You're getting on that one.'

'Are we?' Tibbot spat. I could hear the ice in his words.

'Yes. You are.'

Tibbot raised his head. He waited a moment before speaking. 'I've been in this game longer than you have, son,' he said. 'You learn some things.' He stood up stiffly, plucked his dirt-streaked jacket from the ground and walked towards the train.

As the train pulled into Blackfriars, I was reminded of the moment I had met Nick on the platform at Waterloo Station. Even after what had happened, the memory could still make me smile. But I had to come to terms with the fact that he wasn't coming back to me – what Rachel had said left little room for doubt – and if I ever saw him alive again it would be in a military court, where I would be giving evidence against him. I wouldn't have any choice about that. I would look at him across the room and it would split my heart, but if they ordered me to declare that I had witnessed him passing messages to American spies or that he had tried to recruit me to the cause, I would. He wouldn't blame me; he would understand.

'Well, thank you,' I told Tibbot as we stood on the platform. I knew that the moment he turned his back, the tears would flood out and I wanted to be alone with that grief.

'I didn't help much in the end.'

'No, but, well, I would have been much worse on my own.'

'What will you do now?'

'I'll have a talk with Hazel about her father. I think I need to prepare her for the idea that he may not be coming home . . . soon.' I didn't want to be the one to tell her, but I didn't want anyone else to do it either. 'What about you?'

'I'll go home, take a bath, make myself something to eat, fall asleep next to the radio, get up in the morning, go back to work.' He smeared his hand across his face.

'I first met Nick in a railway station,' I said. 'Oh, he could be charming.'

'That's probably why he was able to get away with it. For a while.'

'Probably.' The cold was beginning to get to me. 'Well, thank you. I suppose it's goodbye.'

'I hope it goes all right with Hazel.'

'Thanks.'

He slipped away towards the entrance to the Underground, into the sea of people hurrying in all directions and none. No one took any notice of this ageing man with an air of sadness about him.

'Hazel,' I said, knocking on her door, 'would you like to come down and have supper?' She opened the door. I could see she had been crying again. 'May I come in?'

We sat together on the bed. 'What about Dad?' she asked.

'Your dad's still where he was.'

'What did he do?'

I hesitated. 'Your dad is a good, brave man who always tried to help other people. If anyone says anything else, don't listen to them. He's a doctor. He helps other people, even when it costs him.'

'Are they going to let him go?'

'It might take longer than we thought.'

'Why?'

'I think you should eat something. Will you do that for me?'

'All right,' she said unhappily.

I took her down to the kitchen. There was much of

her mother in her, and yet there was a shyer grace in her movements – Lorelei seemed to attract attention even when she was standing still. I made an omelette with a little cheese, although I could hardly swallow mine. Then I saw her to bed and we talked for a while about Nick and what might happen now. I left her to let the thoughts sink in. Tomorrow we would talk more.

Sitting on my own bed, I couldn't stop thinking about how I had lost my own parents. I had been older than Hazel and had had time to come to terms with it – but even then it had been hard enough.

And I made a decision. I resolved to find a way to prevent that happening to her.

But what on earth could I do now? My mind went back to Nick's contacts. What if the Americans could help get him out? Some sort of deal. They did those from time to time: a man sent each way across the border, overseen by someone from the League of World Nations. But I could hardly walk into the American Embassy and ask. There had to be another way.

The more I tried to work it out, however, the more I realized how exhausted I was; and, in the end, I fell asleep without even undressing.

21

Sources within the RGB say the constant jostling for influence among the senior members of the Communist Party is crippling the country. Economic output is grinding to a halt, as internal bickering means state industries are run by bureaucrats with no experience of managing them. The result has been those companies teetering on the verge of collapse. As winter bites, shortages of food and fuel are already being felt. Scenes of great hardship are now expected in what was once the most fertile part of our island.

News broadcast, Radio Free Europe,
Wednesday, 19 November 1952

I woke just after eight o'clock the next morning, stiff in my clothes. I stretched and rubbed my limbs, but it did little good.

Nick had said that the concussion would take a couple of days to ease, and I lay there trying to recall more of that day when I had found Lorelei. I closed my eyes and pictured her there in the damp room as the light played on her skin. Her hands seemed to lift up to me and I looked deep into her glittering, searching eyes. But all that came back to me was a sense that there had been words on her lips: a cry of warning or distress. And what the words had been, I couldn't tell. I went to the bathroom and examined my face in the mirror above the sink. I asked myself how fanciful it was, that sense that I had that the division of our nation had in some way seeped into my own body, to divide me from my memories? Or was I just a silly woman wanting to blame her own failings on a political situation that had absolutely nothing to do with them? Well, maybe. But what did Socialism mean if not a connection between the individual and the state, one reflecting the other? At least on some level, even the most basic animal level of all, the injury I had sustained, the one that had beaten my memory from my mind, had been a result of the changes in how we lived – of the suspicions that we were forced to foster. The doubts about my own husband that had drawn me to Lorelei's house that day. On that level, it was no absurdity. It was a hard, physical fact.

As I washed, I turned to the more practical idea that I had had last night that perhaps there was someone who could help – one of Nick's contacts in the American CIA, if I could just find them. All I had, though, was that telephone number from her book.

The operator put me through. I knew how long the silence lasted – four seconds – and how many clicks there were – five – before it connected. Then the metallic ringing, like an idiot playing a distant instrument. 'Hello?' someone said. It was the female voice I had heard the previous day.

'Hello. I'm here.' I mentally begged her not to end the call as she had before.

'All right.'

'I called yesterday.'

'I can't . . . I'm hanging up.'

'No. Please. Just please.' I clutched desperately for a way to persuade her. She was the only chance, the only number in Lorelei's book that worked. I tried a wild lie. 'Are you married?'

There was a long pause. 'Yes.'

'I, I found this number in my husband's diary. I think he's having an affair, please, please, put my mind at rest.'

'That's nothing to do with –'

'Children?'

'Yes, please don't –' she began.

'I've got three. I just need to know that he's not going to abandon us. I don't know what I would do.' I put such tension in my voice I hoped she would break whatever rule she had been instructed to follow.

Her voice lowered, became more intimate. 'I don't know about your husband. This is a government number. I'm just the receptionist.'

'Oh,' I said. 'It's for' – I plucked a name from the air – 'Comrade Williams?'

'No,' she said, puzzled. 'Honeysette.'

Tim Honeysette. He was Nick's patient who had tried to introduce Nick to Ian Fellowman that night. The night when I had lost our child. Whatever this was, he was involved.

So maybe he could help.

'May' – my voice shook – 'may I speak to him? It's very important.'

'He won't be in until later.'

'When?'

She paused again. 'You said it was about your husband.'

'It is. It's urgent that I speak to him. It's government business.'

'So it's not about your husband.' I heard the suspicion rising.

'It's about him, but –'

'What's your name?' she demanded.

I hung up. I hoped she would be too worried about the consequences of having said too much to report it.

Up in Nick's study, I found a big red volume filled with his expansive looping hand. His handwriting was often hard to read, but with a bit of effort I managed to make out Honey-sette's address in Brixton, the commuter edge of London. Victorian clerks living there had taken trains to their jobs in the City, but it was better known now for its prison, where low-level political criminals sat out their sentences.

I stepped out on to the landing, already planning my journey, when a sound reached my ears – Hazel was in the hall talking to someone. '. . . W-S-O-N. Yes, that's right,' she was saying. I quickly descended the stairs and she looked at me, startled, lowering her hand with the telephone receiver.

'Who are you talking to?' I said.

'It's . . .'

I looked at her, waiting for an answer. Then I took the handset and lifted it to my ear. 'Hello? Who is this?'

A woman on the other end replied, 'National Security Police.' She sounded annoyed. 'Who are you?'

I slammed the telephone down. 'What are you doing?' I demanded.

Hazel looked scared and retreated a step. 'I wanted to help. I thought I could find some way to help get Dad out.'

For a second, I was speechless, chilled by the danger of what she could have said if I hadn't stopped her. I took her by the shoulders, trying to keep calm. 'You can't speak to anyone about this! Do you hear? It's very dangerous. It will make things worse for your father.' I paused, doing my best to soften. 'Hazel, I know you want to get your dad out, but you have to leave it to the adults.'

'You're not doing it, though,' she said. It wasn't bitter, nor was it an accusation, just a simple statement with the logic of a fourteen-year-old.

I wanted to explain but I didn't have time. 'Look, I know why you're saying that. I do. But I'm doing all I can and I can't tell you about it. Now, it would help me to help your dad if I can go out and leave you just to sit in your room and not do anything else.'

'I'll come with you.'

'No, you can't.'

She looked frustrated. 'All right. But will you tell me what you're doing?'

'Later. Please, please, just stay in the house and don't speak to anyone.'

After watching her retreat to her room, I went out on to the street, shaken by what she had almost done. I just hoped to God she wouldn't try anything like that again.

Honeysette's house was a solid-looking place, a few doors down from a row of bombed-out buildings where two vagrants were huddled at the back of the rubble, wrapping themselves in sheets and attempting to get a fire going from some broken wood they had scavenged. There was a lot of grey smoke but little flame. Compared to the thrilling colourful trips I had made to this city as a child, modern London often seemed like a flickering black-and-white newsreel.

I pressed the bell and steeled myself. It was risky, but if he refused to help Nick, or even to speak to me, I would threaten to expose him. The door opened to reveal

Honeysette wearing an overcoat, about to go out. He blinked, clearly surprised to see me, and glanced nervously over my shoulder before taking me inside without a word.

His large, warm parlour was decorated with pictures of Marx, Engels and Blunt, and with stacks of books all around. They were everywhere – old and new volumes – as was the sweet smell of cherry tobacco. I couldn't help but think of my father, who had infused our little house with the same scent. Comrade Honeysette stood upright in the centre of the room with his arms by his sides, waiting for me to say something.

'We met at –' I began.

'Yes, I remember.'

'I'm here on my husband's behalf.'

'He sent you?'

'Yes.'

'Why?' He was suspicious.

I thought it best to face him down; it was less risky than an excuse that could fall apart under scrutiny. 'He has business to attend to. It can't wait. And neither can I.'

He stared at me, evidently weighing up the situation. 'You know what this concerns?'

'Yes,' I said.

He paused. 'Then tell me.'

I kept myself in check as much as I could. There was only one thing I could think of. 'Orders from America.'

He pursed his lips, considering. He seemed to take in the expression on my face, the way I was standing.

'All right,' he said after a while, although he didn't seem entirely relaxed.

With his back to me, he went to a polished wooden box

on the mantelpiece, opened it and took out a brown envelope. He placed something in it that I couldn't see and handed it to me, hesitating just for a brief moment. I lifted the flap and looked inside. It held two five-pound notes. It was all so strange and I had no idea what I was supposed to do with them. There was little point leaving with them, though – they told me nothing. I tried to fill the pause, hoping he would say more so I could better understand the situation. 'Do you have a message for Nick?'

'No, that covers it,' he said, indicating the envelope and apparently waiting for me to do something, tell him something, take something – leave?

I tried to think of anything else to say or do. The wait became impossible and I began to lose control. I opened my mouth to speak but could only stutter the beginnings of words. I was utterly at a loss.

His eyes widened as realization dawned on him. Wildly, he snatched the money back. 'Get out!' he ordered me.

I didn't know what to do. He began to push me hard towards the door; he wasn't a strong man but he was stronger than me.

'Nick's been arrested,' I said urgently. He stopped dead and stared at me. Then he pushed me again, harder. 'You have to help him.'

'Just get out!'

'Please help him.' He pulled the door open and shoved me to the threshold. 'Just put me in touch with people who can help. I'll give NatSec your name if you don't!' I did my best to sound as if I would go through with it.

He threw me out and I stumbled over the step as he slammed the door. I tried knocking although I knew he wouldn't answer. The house might as well have been empty and boarded up. Not wanting to draw the attention of the neighbours, I walked away, but only to the end of the street, where I waited, thinking. For once the smog was a blessing, as it hid me.

Ten minutes later, with the cold seeping through my limbs, I saw him emerge. I planned to follow him but he opened up his garage, jumped in a car and drove off, so that I saw only his rear lights glowing as they sped away.

On the way home, I stopped to sit on a wooden bench to think. Above it, a hoarding depicted the Needle road as the tip of an actual syringe, literally sucking the blood out of the RGB.

Schoolchildren filed past me towards a large secondary school, and I deliberated whether, if I never saw Nick again, looking after Hazel would be a role that I could take on indefinitely. That would be if they let me, of course – the state often took away the children of dissidents, raising them in communal schools to drain them of their parents' divergent views.

It was a daunting prospect. After all, I had no experience of actually bringing up a child, and fourteen was probably the hardest age of all to take on – she would be old enough to rebel against my edicts but not yet able to take responsibility for her own. How would I deal with that? With great difficulty, I imagined.

The sound of the radio buzzed down from Hazel's room when I got home around eleven o'clock. Churchill was speaking. 'I walked through Regent's Park this morning to breathe the fresh air of freedom. It is a simple thing to walk along the road without fear, without let or hindrance,' he rumbled. 'To know that the man or woman that you pass is a friend and not the bully-boy agent of a state that treats its own citizens as the enemy. And so, to my friends on the other side of that ugly scar on the face of our nation, I say only this: courage. Courage, for . . .' And then the Internationale broke in with a loud and tinny whining, as our jamming stations locked on to the frequency.

The song was quickly replaced by a voice we all recognized. Usually our stations would simply pretend Churchill didn't exist but there was a man named Alec Mathers who had begun appearing immediately after Churchill's broadcasts to ridicule them. Like Fellowman, he was one of a handful who had defected from their side to ours. It wasn't satire that he broadcast – those shows poking fun at the ruling elite were long gone, leaving a hole in our cultural life – it was simply a foul sort of hatred.

The people trying to clamber over the Wall to the DUK were selfish ingrates who had been educated, clothed, fed and inoculated by the state, and now wanted to defect so they could make dirty money with the 'small-time Fascist gangster' Churchill, he claimed.

Even if there had been a nugget of truth in his words – albeit one twisted entirely out of shape by his hyperbole – it was completely buried under the bile. And I couldn't fathom how you could hate a stranger simply for wanting to live somewhere else, even if you disagreed with their choice. I was going to tell Hazel to turn it off when a sudden hammering on our front door stopped me.

I found Charles on our doorstep looking furious. His voice was like low thunder. 'I had the NatSec goons crawling all over the practice this morning. They went through the patient records,' he growled.

'Oh, God,' I said, panicked. 'Did –'

'I told you this would happen if you started poking around. Have you any idea what they could have done?'

'I'm sorry,' I said meekly.

He sucked on his cigarette and angrily blew the smoke out. It made my throat sting. 'Do you want to end up in the NatSec files? Because I'm bloody well in them now. I've never so much as listened to that radio station and now I'm in their records as some sort of traitor.' I understood just how serious this was for him. Because of his parents' support for the Royal Family he had already found it hard enough to find a job. Now things could turn far worse.

'What did you tell them?'

'What did I tell them? Nothing. Because I don't know anything. I have done nothing wrong. I don't know about your husband, but, as far as I know, he has done nothing wrong either. Whatever you are doing, it is making it worse for both of us – but you knew that already, because I warned you repeatedly.' And, amid the anger, there was more noise as the telephone rang, the bell demanding to be answered. I ignored it. 'All I have done is try to help you. And this is how I've been repaid.'

'I, I . . .' I stammered, unable to think of something to say.

He threw his fag on the ground, screwed it into the slabs with his foot and stepped into the hall. 'Well, if you don't think of me, think of her.' He pointed over my shoulder. Hazel was standing at the top of the stairs. 'You're putting her at risk too.' He was probably right but involving her raised my hackles. 'Listen –'

'No. You listen. Stop acting like a fool!' I said, losing my temper. The sound of the telephone bell was now filling my ears.

'I'm a fool?' He glared at me. The telephone continued to ring. Without warning, he swept it from the table and it tumbled to the floor.

'Mrs Cawson?' a hoarse voice whispered from the receiver. I made to pick it up, but Charles kicked it from me.

'I'm a fool?' he repeated. 'I have friends in the Party who can make sure your stupidity doesn't cost your husband any more than his time. So, from now on, you wait here. You look after her. Nothing else.'

'Mrs Cawson? Are you there?' the voice pleaded.

'Who is it?' I called out.

'Rachel Burton,' she said quietly.

'Rachel?' I gasped, amazed.

'Can you hear –'

But Charles was drowning out the words. 'So be bloody careful,' he growled.

I tried to push him aside, but he wouldn't move and I caught only a few more distant words from the handset: 'The orders are . . . where the bomb hit.'

I attempted again to grab it, but Charles got there first and slammed it into its cradle. 'It's for your own good!' And with that he stormed out. I reached for the receiver. There was only the dialling tone now.

'What's happening?' Hazel was visibly upset by the

scene she had witnessed. I stared at the telephone to see if it would ring again. Those words.

'Nothing. Just some trouble at the surgery,' I said distractedly, but I was thinking of those strange words of Rachel's.

An image formed in my mind: Rachel dragged from the room, spitting and screaming. She had cried out that she and Lorelei had fought about 'big orders'. I didn't want to think what she had had to promise an orderly in order to make a telephone call; she must have been desperate for me to know something. 'The orders are . . . where the bomb hit,' she had said. But her words made little sense.

And then they did.

22

Rachel's words made sense when I thought of what I had found in Lorelei's house. I lifted my head and spoke to Hazel. 'Can you go to your room for a bit? I'll come up and speak to you soon.' She reluctantly agreed, and as she returned to her bedroom I went into the back garden.

An aeroplane – civilian – rushed overhead in the direction of the coast. Flying in the other direction, a grey-and-black jackdaw soared and dipped, then came to a sudden swooping stop on one of the broken timbers that poked from the house's upper storey into the void a few metres above the ground – the remnants of what had been knocked down by a doodlebug in '44.

Above those exposed bones of the house was the uneven and ugly replacement back wall, thrown together in the months that had followed the peace. The lines of the bricks weren't straight, and the weather or subsidence had combined with the poor workmanship to prise apart two jagged expanses of them at the rear of Nick's study. He once told me that the gap led to the wall cavity, where the birds roosted at night.

The bird I was watching hopped along the projecting timber to the wall, sat for a while without moving, as if waiting for something to happen, then fluttered through the breach. I stared up at the brickwork, wondering. In the corner of the garden there was an old Anderson shelter that served to store some of Nick's larger junk, and inside I found a rickety and paint-splattered folding ladder. As I propped it up against the wall, the jackdaw emerged, looked down at me as if I had disturbed it and flew away.

The ladder shifted a bit as I climbed, but I kept on up until my face was level with the broken floorboards jutting out. The wood, I saw, had been baked and lashed with rain so many times since the night of the German air raid that it resembled something from a shipwreck, and when I took it in my hand, a piece tore away. I reached up to the gap.

'What are you doing?' I jerked my hand back and grabbed the sides of the ladder. Our young neighbour, Patricia, was framed by her open window.

'I . . . there's a birds' nest.'

'So?'

'They were making a noise. Disturbing Hazel. Nick's daughter.'

She looked doubtful. 'Where is Dr Cawson?' she asked. She had watched me and Tibbot leave the house yesterday. Someone might have told her to note down our comings and goings.

'He's at work.'

She crossed her arms. 'I heard one of Churchill's lying broadcasts coming from his daughter's room. Through the wall. Do you let her listen to that rubbish?'

'Oh, God, no. I'll make sure that's the last time.'

'It was this morning. My husband said we should speak to you.'

'Thank you. Yes. She's just a girl, doesn't know what she's doing. I expect we were the same at her age.'

'Were you?'

'Oh, I was a horror. But thank you for letting me know. I'll have a word with her.' *Go away*, I wanted to shout at her. *Just leave us alone.*

'She has read *The Compass*?'

'Yes, she has. At school, of course,' I said. That red paperback had never seemed so absurd to me as now.

'Good.' She paused and her face softened a little as she moved on to a new subject. 'Will Lorelei Addington be coming again?'

'I'm sorry?' I asked hoarsely.

'I saw her here when she came, oh, a few weeks ago.' Her face broke into a smile. 'She was my heroine when I was at school. Will she be coming again?'

I hoped Hazel wasn't within earshot. 'No. She won't, I'm sorry, I have to –'

'Did Dr Cawson give her the magazine?'

'What magazine?'

'She was in an old magazine I found, and I thought she would want it. I gave it to Dr Cawson to pass on to her. Did she get it?'

So it was this obsessed girl who was the source of the glossy publication I had found in Nick's surgery before Lorelei's death, the one that had made me imagine all sorts of false things.

'I'll see to it,' I mumbled.

'That would –'

'I really must get on with this.'

A pregnant pause passed between us, but it meant that she finally got the message and left me to it. I thought about abandoning what I was doing and going back into the house, afraid of what she might know or say in one of her Party meetings, but I pressed on. Stretching as far as I could, I managed to touch the sharp corner of one of the bricks at the edge of the gap, yet couldn't reach in any more than the sunlight could.

Back on the ground, I folded away the ladder and returned to the house. I couldn't access that narrow space from the outside, but it struck me that it might be possible from within the house. Passing Hazel's room, I made sure her door was closed, and then I entered Nick's study. I had made a mistake, I realized, when I had searched through it previously for anything that the Secs would have wanted. I hadn't thought of Lorelei's house. She had had a hiding place in the ceiling of Hazel's room. Wouldn't Nick have one too? Rachel had been trying to tell me where it was.

The back wall of the study was hung with a couple of framed watercolours that Nick had said he valued because they were so astonishingly ugly that they demonstrated immense talent. I had laughed then. Now I lifted them away and smoothed my hand over the plastered wall. There was nothing. Neither was there anything of interest behind his writing desk or any indication of a ceiling cavity. I drew back the curtains and checked behind them – and my eye fell on something I hadn't seen before. About half a metre up the wall, hidden behind the material, there was a large square wooden panel, with sides about forty centimetres long. I couldn't recall seeing anything like it in any other room. I knelt down and felt around it.

The sound of movement from Hazel's room made me stop. The subsequent silence told me that she wasn't coming, however, so, after first taking the precaution of locking the study door to make sure, I went back to running my fingers around the wood. There was a hair's breadth of a gap between it and the wall but the edge was too thin to get a grip on. I looked through Nick's desk for something I could use to prise it away. An old pen with a steel nib looked like it might work, and I stabbed it into the thin gap, but the only effect, as I tried to lever the panel away, was to bend and snap the nib. I needed something more solid.

I hunted through drawers, tossing aside envelopes, an ashtray and a few notebooks. Then, at the back of one, I found what I needed: a brass ruler, tarnished at the edges and its numbers rubbed away, but fundamentally strong.

I returned to the floor and shoved the ruler in hard behind the wood. It went in only a few millimetres, though, and, try as I might, that produced no leverage. I grabbed a hardback book from Nick's shelf – a medical textbook detailing the effects of hormones – and placed it against the end of the ruler. I shoved with all my weight and felt the brass slip in further, far enough to act as a lever. The wood didn't want to move; it was jammed in tight; but, little by little, working the metal back and forth, and then doing the same on the opposite side, I managed to draw the panel slightly towards me and into the room. Eventually, I could grip it properly and rip it away, to leave a gaping, rough hole in the plaster and a little cloud of dust seeping through the air.

Was this it? I bent down to find a cavity wall, with two layers of bricks. The external layer was the one with the crack in it. Then there was the cavity, then the internal layer. Some of the bricks had been removed from the internal layer, giving access to the cavity from inside the house.

The hole had then been covered by the wooden panel. It had been deliberate, I was certain of that.

I looked through into the cavity; yet, just as from the garden side, it was impenetrably dark, so I pulled over a reading lamp from the desk and shone it through, hoping there would be something there. I couldn't see much – dirty bricks, the same mist of plaster dust that I had sent floating up and the skeletal timber frame. Pressing my face right to the hole to peer around, I could smell the damp air, mixed with the odour of mould.

And then there was sharp pain and confusion – something was screeching at me and clawing at my cheek, drawing blood. I cried out as I felt its talons across my skin and its wings beating at my face, and I fell backwards, knocking over the lamp and scrabbling away, to press my back against a bookcase. The screeching went on and on, as if it were in my head, and at the same time I could hear Hazel calling out my name and then come running and trying the handle, banging on the door. 'It's all right, Hazel. I'm fine. I just . . . dropped something. Silly of me,' I managed to stutter.

'Can I come in?' she asked, hesitatingly.

'No, I'm . . . It's your father's things. His private . . .' And in the beam from the tumbled lamp, I caught sight of the glittering black eye of the bird that had scratched my cheek. I put my hand to the stinging wound. 'Please, just go back to your room.'

She sounded doubtful. 'All right.'

I stared at the bird. It was watching me through the gap in the plaster. And then it thrust its head through into the room and looked around, studying me with its head to one side, for a long while. I sat as still as I could, hoping it wouldn't fly into the room. Then it jumped back into the darkness, out of my sight, and all I heard was its wings flapping against the bricks as it flew away into the open air.

Recovering myself, I crawled to the hole and righted the lamp. Very carefully this time, I placed my face back to the breach. With the light I could see a bit more. There was a nest made from twigs and rubbish that sat on one of the floorboards, and beside it a pale and misshapen thing that I couldn't quite make out. It was about the same size as the nest, but not twisted together by a bird. Something man-made. I reached through, took hold of it and brought it back into the room.

On the floor in front of me, crumpled and empty, was a cardboard box similar to the one I had found in Lorelei's hiding place. It was a little larger but otherwise the same: divided into small compartments just like the ones that had held rifle rounds during my basic training. I unfolded it and shook it out. The compartments were empty – or so I thought, until I noticed, wedged in at the bottom of one, a circular piece of thin glass with jagged edges reaching upwards. It had clearly been broken off a larger item. Stuck to it was a tiny slip of paper with a single typed word, the letters stretching right to the rough edge. I held it in my fingertips and read it out loud to myself, rolling it on my tongue to try to make sense of it: 'Jacob'.

For a minute I remained still, hearing nothing. And then, with a rush of blood through my mind, I understood what I had missed.

I grabbed the stack of intimate letters from Lorelei that Nick had kept in his desk drawer. There was something in one that I needed to read again. I hunted through the lines about parties and acerbic comments about social climbers and fusty old men; declarations of love and laughing rejections of Nick's 'slushy' replies; and finally I found the letter in which she mentioned the American wartime colonel who had asked her about the Reds embedding themselves in British society. I pulled it out and scanned it. The name I was looking for was there in blue ink, as dark as when she had written it.

I looked hard at the box – I had seen others like it far more recently than during my Compulsory Basic. Maybe this letter could save Nick. If I were right, he was guilty of a crime, but it was nothing like what the Secs thought.

23

The League of World Nations has condemned an attempt by the so-called Democratic United Kingdom to hijack its proceedings yesterday. The truly democratic nations of the world, led by the Soviet Union, Jugoslavia and China, threw out a motion attempting to blame the Republic of Great Britain for the division of the British island. The democratic states refused to relinquish the microphone in the assembly chamber until the motion was withdrawn. They were roundly applauded by all the countries present.

News broadcast, RGB Station 1,
Wednesday, 19 November 1952

I took the Tube to the Aldwych. From there, I walked to the brass-studded front door of 60 Great Queen Street, a huge, faceless old building made of white stone blocks. I must have looked out of place and deathly nervous – the people freely entering this building were rarely civilians. After being searched, I was allowed inside to find a wide and tall lobby, plain to the point of austerity, where the reception desk was behind a thick glass window – thick enough to withstand a shot from a pistol, perhaps. I touched Lorelei's letter to Nick, held in my pocket, to confirm to myself that it was there. It was what I trusted to get me out of there safely.

As I approached the thick glass, a young woman in uniform glanced up at me without interest before returning to the paperwork she was involved with. There were four forms, each with two carbon copies, and she seemed to be filling them all out simultaneously with the same information. Twelve copies of that report to be sent through the offices of government, some to be looked at and ignored, some to be acted upon, some to be binned, some to be filed unread. I waited. 'Yes?' she mouthed after a while.

I pressed myself to the glass. 'My husband, Nicholas Cawson, is here. You . . . you suspect him of a crime.' A young man in a uniform that was too small for him was standing right behind me, making no attempt to hide the fact that he was listening.

'Yes?' the woman repeated.

'May I speak to someone?'

'About what?' asked the young man.

'I have some information.'

'Have you?' He sounded intrigued and a little pleased with himself. The woman, seeing someone else take the burden of dealing with me, opened a file and extracted another ream of forms that she began to fill out. 'You've done the right thing coming to us.'

It dawned on me that he thought I had come to provide information against Nick. I was about to tell him he was wrong, but it was more likely that I would have a hearing if I went along with his mistake. He took a key and let himself through a door in the wall, reappearing behind the glass partition. 'Your name?'

'Jane Cawson.' I spelled it out.

'And your husband's?'

'Nicholas Cawson.' He glanced at the scratch on my cheek that the bird had made. I put my hand to it. He didn't seem too interested, though, and wrote our two names on a piece of paper before going to the back of the reception desk to look through some cards. 'Wait over there,' he said, picking up a telephone and pointing to a line of chairs bolted to the floor.

On the wall was a poster of a man in a narrow alleyway, a shadow obscuring his face. 'Saboteur. Parasite. Black marketeer. You THINK he is your friend, but he is working against you. Report counter-social behaviour. No matter who it is.' There was a telephone number and I wondered how many people had called it – some proud to do their political duty, others ashamed and hoping no one would ever know.

I took the only available seat, next to an old man dressed in clothes that looked like they might once have been smart but were now torn and frayed. He had the air of someone who had felt his high hopes and ideals crushed out of him, and in between little sobs he opened a brief-case and pulled out what appeared to be pupils' exercise books – distracting himself by reading over them. A teacher who had welcomed the arrival of Socialism with open arms, perhaps, only to find his syllabus restricted and his students staring at him as a relic to be eased out and forgotten.

After a while, the loudspeaker in the corner of the ceiling began to whine, then bark. It was time for Comrade Blunt's address. '. . . banished superstition to the silvery pages of the history books. Our children will read of religion as they read of the Black Death – a terrible scourge that they will, thankfully, never encounter . . .' He didn't mention that his deceased father had been a vicar and he had been brought up a good Christian. Of course, Stalin had studied at a seminary, hadn't he? Perhaps it was the constant immersion in these ideas that had resulted in their violent loathing. Churchill and Blunt fighting over us with words and ideals – it never seemed to end. And the letter in my pocket set out the price that we had paid for their warfare.

It must have been ten times over the course of the next hour that I got up to leave, before losing the courage even to walk out the door. Finally, I decided for certain that I was making a terrible mistake and picked up my bag to go. At that moment, however, a man strode into the room – bald, but quite handsome despite it, and my heart sank. Instantly I was back in that cage, the smog seeping into the dark van as we wound through traffic, the smell of his breath and sweat. I had hoped never to see Grest again, but my name must have been linked with his in the files. He stopped and looked around the lobby, then came over to me. 'Mrs Cawson.'

I stared at him. 'I'm sorry, I've –'

'Come this way,' he said, as he led me towards two doors guarded by Secs with gun holsters.

'No, I was –'

'Come this way.'

His shoes clipped on the floor as he recorded my entry at the guard post. In the corridors on the other side, everyone had the same look of grim determination, as if we were still at war and the enemy were expected to land at any moment. I had to keep up with his pace, until he stood back with formal politeness to let me enter a plain room. The door was thick enough to prevent any sound passing through it.

I sat at the small table, trying not to think of the other featureless rooms in this building and what took place in them. Somewhere, Nick sat or lay. If he knew I was there, he might have felt some comfort or simply more fear. 'My husband,' I said, trying to speak with strength but finding that strength dissolving.

'Yes.'

'He's innocent.' Grest just snorted. I could see he was wondering what my plan was. Simple pleading? Vehement denials? Supply some rumour about Nick's friends in return for favour? He had probably heard it all a hundred times. 'Well, he's not entirely innocent. He's committed a crime but it's not what you think.' Now he looked mildly interested. 'You think he and Lorelei were working for the Americans. They weren't. Please. Read this.' I reached into my pocket and pulled out the letter I had taken from the stack in Nick's writing desk. I didn't want to think what would happen – to him, to me – if I were wrong.

Lorelei's letter told of the American colonel who, she suggested, was in a more underhand section of the army than the Education Corps to which he claimed allegiance. But before she wrote of him, she had described some of the other guests at the party – and one in particular:

. . . the town is also full of the worst sort of harpies ready to fall backwards with their legs in the air if it means an audition. Half

220

of them have a permanent grin like a hyena. It's stuck on with lipstick and regular injections from a doctor, Max Jacobson, who everyone here calls Dr Feelgood. I have no idea what's in those shots but I have to say that after I gave one a go I was dancing from Friday night until lunchtime on Tuesday. He was telling me how he could get hold of the latest medical drugs in big quantities when a Yank officer marched over, announced that his name was Colonel Hank Dee, that he was a huge admirer of mine and that he would be honoured to take me out for a drive. I politely told the good doctor I would talk to him later about his offer . . .

'I found this hidden in the house.' From my pocket I drew the broken piece of thin, circular glass with jagged edges that had been in the box. The typed label that stretched to the rough edge read: 'Jacob', the last few letters having been torn off. 'I'm sure it's the base of a medicine phial. I saw them all the time at the surgery.' The card boxes with their little compartments, those that had reminded me of the cartons full of rifle rounds, had held the delicate little tubes. And Tim Honeysette had handed me ten pounds at his house, expecting something contraband but vital in return.

So it had all fallen into place. Medical drugs. Everyone knew that the Americans had treatments years ahead of our own – antibiotics to fight infection, and medicines for your heart or blood – and this man, Jacobson, was offering them to Lorelei. Nick must have read and reread her letter, weighing the possibilities and the dangers. Even before the Soviets' arrival, it had taken years before American drugs had become legal here, and after our new friends arrived there hadn't been a hope in hell of getting them.

Grest examined the letter slowly and carefully. I could see him considering what I was saying. Would he be convinced by it? It wasn't conclusive proof, no, but it all seemed a damn sight more likely than Nick working for the CIA. 'Has he told you something like this?' I asked.

He gazed at me for a long time. 'I haven't spoken to him – it's someone else's case. But I haven't heard anything about this.'

'The other officer. Is he junior to you?'

'As it happens.'

'So you can take over the case?'

He brushed some dust from the desk. 'If I want to. Tell me more about this supposed activity of theirs.'

'They've been doing it for years. I think they were selling some to patients, and some was going to Party officials.'

Grest sneered a little as if the very idea were absurd. 'Which Party officials?'

I held my nerve. 'Tim Honeysette. Deputy Secretary at the Ministry of Food. He tried to buy some from me yesterday.' I felt guilty handing over his name – he had only bought whatever it was Nick was supplying him with – but I had no other way of getting Nick out of there.

There was a pause. 'Impossible,' Grest replied. But I knew he had believed me. 'And what was he trying to buy?'

'I'm not sure.'

The book had detailed the trade, each section noting a batch of orders smuggled from America. The first column, I knew, listed telephone numbers for the buyers. That was how they were identified. Then the second column, a string of three letters, probably recorded what they had ordered, but I couldn't decipher it. 'It cost ten pounds, though, and he might do you a favour or two if you let Nick out to keep up the supply.' He sat back and stared at me again. Most NatSec officers were true believers and Nick couldn't have approached them with such a confession and offer. But Tibbot had already told me that Grest had a history of looking the other way in return for a few quid. And here I was, also dangling before him the prospect of entry to the Closed Shops. 'It can all be confirmed by a woman called Rachel Burton. She's in a hospital in Kent. She was part of the group. There will be other buyers too. Maybe in the Ministry of Justice.'

'Who?' The prospect of rapid promotion was the most magnetic to him.

'I don't know. You'll have to find out.'

'How did they bring in the medicines?'

'I don't know.'

'I see.'

I gained a little courage. 'My husband isn't working for the CIA. I don't know why you ever thought he was – you half heard something somewhere and came to the wrong conclusion.'

He waved away my words. 'Can you get me the details – where they came from, who they were going to?'

'No, only my husband could do that.'

'If you're lying to me, Mrs Cawson, it will go hard with you, and with your husband,' he said. I nodded. He shifted in his seat. 'This Comrade Honeysette. Did he approach you?'

'No, I went to his house.'

A flicker of surprise. 'How did you know he was buying from your husband?' I hesitated. I didn't want to mention the ledger unless I had to – I wanted to keep a bargaining chip for later in case Grest went back on his word and kept Nick in custody. If I told him, he would demand I hand it over and then I would have nothing if he reneged on the deal.

'I heard him and Nick talking about it once,' I said.

He thought it over, drumming his fingers on the desk, before seemingly coming to the conclusion that it was at least worth considering. 'Wait here.' He left the room and locked it from the outside. There was a window with wire mesh over it, and I looked out to the street. People on the other side of the road stared up at the edifice, not seeing me. I knew everything that they were thinking, though.

Somehow I felt that I was betraying Tibbot by keeping all of this from him; but he really was better off not knowing. Good, sad Frank Tibbot could go back to his quiet life and retire, never having got revenge for his daughter's death, but all the safer for it. And I felt sorry for Rachel too. Like the dissidents, she had been dragged to an insane asylum to keep her quiet. No one listens to the mad.

I sat there for more than an hour, hearing that harsh building's distant sounds, until, finally, I heard a key rattle in the lock. Grest came back into the room, carrying a folder of documents. 'Your husband will be released,' he said.

I gasped. The joy I felt was as if I were the one being pardoned from a death sentence, not him. 'When?' I asked, jumping up.

'Tomorrow.'

'Why not today?'

He snorted. 'There was a set-to with one of our guards.

Stupid, really. Especially when Hopkins broke his wrist in return.'

I was secretly a little proud of Nick. 'But what's that got to do with releasing him?'

'You don't understand how this works, do you? If he had just kept a hold of himself, I could have been able to get him out today. But Hopkins might object if your husband walks out of here without a bit of a stay in the cells to teach him a lesson. You don't want to draw any undue attention right now.'

'Will he be all right? You need him too.'

'Hopkins and a couple of the others will stop by to make him understand. Nothing too serious. I'll make sure he can stand at the end of it.' I felt something harden in the pit of my stomach. 'Now go home. You'll see him tomorrow.' He opened the door for me. 'By the way' – he checked one of the documents he was carrying – 'it's not really "Lorelei". It's "Anne". "Anne Addington". It seems she changed it.'

'I didn't know.'

'No.' I wondered how many conversations like this had taken place there. Deals done. He examined me for a long time. I started to feel nervous again. 'Some of my colleagues,' he said. 'They hate people like you. Doctors, their wives.' We waited like that for a while before he gestured to the exit.

As soon as I got outside, a wave of relief broke over me, stronger than anything I had experienced in my life, and I cried out, laughing and clasping my hands together like a child. I didn't care about the strange looks I was gaining, I had never felt such elation. There was a busker playing old folk songs in the corner – badly. I gave him the entire contents of my purse. 'Good luck, lady,' he said, scooping up the cash. 'Good luck to you!'

'Thanks,' I replied. But before I could go home and wait excitedly for Nick's return, there was something else I needed to do.

Nick's safety had been everything for me. But now that I could almost feel him back with us, my mind turned to a different task, one that touched on my own safety rather than his. I was determined to recover the final memories of how Lorelei had died. Because someone had been there that day – I had seen them in the mirror – and whoever they were, they had let the suspicion of her death fall on us. What if they came back, preferring to see us all buried or imprisoned rather than able to expose them?

There was something I had once seen on a newsreel. A doctor had explained different methods of treating soldiers who had been badly affected during the War. One technique forced them to confront fears and situations that they had been shying away from in civvy street. It seemed to work for them, so I hoped it would work for me.

And so I stood again on the threshold of Lorelei's black-and-white-tiled bathroom, with my hand on the cold copper bath. The taps were stiff and it took much of my strength to turn them, until the freezing water burst out, rising rapidly while I turned my attention to the radio set in the corner. The face glowed for a moment when I flicked the switch, before light music played, and a woman's voice was heard, talking about her day. It wasn't Lorelei but, somehow, the more I listened, the more it seemed to become her voice, glistening like ice.

The level in the tub was lifting, and I felt my pulse speed as I forced myself to drift back. It began slowly, but, little by little, I felt the past seeping in, until I was behind the house again, opening the back gate into the dank garden, weeds pulling at my feet; stalking like a ghost through the kitchen that she never used; climbing the stairs, sure that Nick was with her; hearing a man's voice and her sharp laughter in reply. I felt every creak of the stairs, every step bringing me closer to her. Now my head was pounding, and the tide of the water was brushing the top of the bath. I gazed at it and heard a cold waterfall spill out and hit the floor, spreading across the tiles.

I fixed Lorelei's image in my mind then: the beauty, the arrogance. My eye fell on the gilt-edged mirror and I could just make out a form reflected in it, dark and indistinct. It was coming closer to me. But, as I stared at the blurred movement, something changed, something was very different. And in a moment I realized: I knew that this was no memory of the day she died. The cold air that I felt clutching my skin and the dark reflected image filling my sight were both there in the present moment.

I spun around to see a face I knew well, choking at the sight of it. Then something slammed into my cheek and I was in the air, tumbling across the room, feeling only fear and an arc of movement.

A noise rang out as the back of my head hit something hard and metallic – the bath – and everything was confused and there was water. The whole world seemed to be spinning. The tunnel of my sight told me that I was on the floor, looking down at a seeping flood.

Grest bent down to me. I could smell his sweat, just as I had when he had pressed his chest against mine in the thin blue light of the NatSec van, just as I had in that locked interview room at 60 Great Queen Street. His flesh was so close I could see the wrinkles in his skin. His lips parted. 'Give me the book or you end up like her,' he said quietly.

24

Grest was all that I could see. He stood up, flexed his fingers and shook his hand – the knuckles were red where he had punched me. 'It hurts me when I hurt you,' he said. 'I don't want to do it again. There's no need for it if you just give me the book.'

I lay there, unable to move. We imagine that at times of great fear our limbs will tear us away, but too often they lock us where we are. I could no more move than if I had been chained down.

He was looking straight down at me. His fingers balled into a fist once more. 'Mrs Cawson, you just need to give me the book and you'll be safe. Your husband and step-daughter will be safe.' He began to crouch down to me again. 'Mrs Cawson, do you want them to be safe?'

'Yes,' I croaked. 'Please.'

'Then you know what to do.'

Yes, I knew. 'The book.'

'That's right.'

'I haven't got it here,' I said.

'Then where is it?'

'I can get it. I can get it for you.' I was shattered into pieces. I would have said or done anything to make him leave me alone.

'Then we'll –'

And then the world shook again, and his arms stretched

out like wings, falling down, towards me, towards the tiles. I twisted to the side as his waist fell on to mine, thudding the air from me, and his cheek cracked against the floor just centimetres from my own, to make the tiles judder. His eyelids dropped.

'Jane?'

I turned my head and saw someone else standing where Grest had been. 'Are you all right?' Tibbot was breathing heavily and gripping his truncheon, one of the heavy wooden ones that the older policemen had kept from the days before the Soviets came. He dropped to his knees and pulled Grest's body from mine. 'Jane, are you all right?' he asked.

'I . . . think so.' The impact of Grest's body had left me winded, but no worse than that, I thought.

He pulled Grest's head up before throwing it back down with a thump. Blood dripped from the Sec's nose, swirling into the flowing water. Tibbot took a pair of handcuffs from his jacket, quickly locking Grest's wrists behind him, before helping me to my feet. Spots of light seemed to fly around the room, but my mind began to focus better.

'What happened?' he said, as he turned off the taps and put his hands underneath Grest's shoulders, dragging him out to the landing. But I couldn't immediately answer him. 'Jane, what's going on?' he asked again, frustrated by my lack of reply. He pushed Grest against the solid bannister, where he used the Sec's belt to bind his ankles tightly together.

I took a moment, trying to order my thoughts. 'It must have been him,' I said. 'No one else knew about the book. He killed her.'

Tibbot looked Grest up and down. I saw a hardness in

Tibbot's eyes that I hadn't caught before. It seemed to come from what he had lived through, what he had lost. I had seen a quiet sadness, but this cold determination was new to me. Perhaps it had always been there and I just hadn't perceived it. Something else we were all hiding.

'Go into the bedroom,' he said quietly.

'Why?' He shook his head. I could guess why he didn't want me here. 'No, I'll stay.'

'When it gets too much, go into the bedroom.' He stood rubbing his limbs. He hoisted Grest up and slapped his face a few times, until Grest started to whimper and turn away from the light blows. 'I'm glad you're awake,' said Tibbot. 'It makes it easier.' He stabbed Grest hard in the ribs with his truncheon. The Sec cried out in pain and struggled. 'Probably cracked one,' Tibbot said. 'I'll do them all soon. You've seen it from the other side. You know what it looks like.'

'I know who you are,' Grest mumbled.

Tibbot shoved him back on to the bare floorboards, took his truncheon and placed it across Grest's throat. He put his hands on each end and leaned on it, choking him. Grest tried to squirm away, but he was pinned too tightly and his eyelids fell. 'You think that worries me?' He lifted the truncheon. 'What did you do to Lorelei Addington?' Grest drew in air with a hollow, rattling sound. 'What was it? Did you hold her under the water? Was that what you did?'

The Sec didn't answer. The loathing that I felt for him – he seemed less than human to me now – worked against the aversion I felt for the violence.

Tibbot stood up. 'All right. You know, I haven't been

trained in this, like you have. Me, I arrest people who steal from their neighbours, or sell a few black-market tins of peas from their cars. So I don't really know what I'm doing with you.' He took his truncheon and brought it down on Grest's chest. 'Your heart's right where I hit you. Can that cause a heart seizure? I don't know. But you're young and fit, so you can probably take it.' He rubbed his brow. Grest's lips seemed to be searching for something to say. 'There's a science to it, isn't there? Things that the Nazis developed and the Russians borrowed. And they passed it on to you. I don't know about that. I'm as likely to kill you as get the truth out of you.' I couldn't tell if Tibbot's words were empty threats or if I had never really known him and what he was capable of. I hated the man on the floor, but the prospect of being there when he was killed made me stop and take a step back.

'Nothing to say? All right.' Tibbot went to the top of the stairs and looked down. 'We've got days. I could call in sick to work, spend a week here working on you. Leave you sitting in your piss all day, all night. You haven't told anyone you're here, we know that.' He walked back and sat down with his back against the wall. For a while there was just the sound of Grest's laboured breath. 'My daughter died because she couldn't breathe.' He looked down at his hands and the truncheon he was holding.

The adrenalin subsiding, I turned to stare at the wall, but I couldn't help glancing back to see Tibbot sit Grest up again so that the back of his head was against the bannister. He smacked Grest across the bridge of the nose with the butt of the truncheon – not a hard blow, but enough to make Grest's eyes stream with water. Then he pulled back his arm, ready to strike him fully across the face.

I wanted it to stop then and there. I rushed over, pulled Tibbot's hands away and dragged Grest's head up. 'Tell us!' I cried.

Tibbot thrust me aside roughly and grabbed Grest. 'I'm telling you now.' Tibbot shook his head. 'I'm telling you now that this time, when I start, I'm not going to stop. I'm too fucking tired of this.' Grest twisted his face up. 'So now, for the last time, I swear it's for the last time, what did you do to Lorelei Addington?'

Grest held his gaze on Tibbot. His chest rose and fell with rasping air. His lower lip was split and a line of blood was running from it. 'Held her under the water,' he mumbled.

Tibbot wiped his face with his sleeve. He stood silent for a long time, collecting himself. 'What did you want from her?'

Grest shut his eyes. 'The medicines.' He slowly licked his lips.

'What medicines?'

'Antibiotics. Other stuff.'

'American medicines,' I said. Tibbot stared at me. God, I had been a fool. I had sat there in a blank room with Grest, telling him things he already knew. It probably took all his effort not to laugh at me. What he had wanted all along was the book. And then I had blundered in and presented an easy way to find what he wanted. He had followed me right to where he thought I had it stowed. After that he could have done to me what he had done to her.

I told Tibbot everything. When I had finished, his head dropped and he sighed, as if knowing what lay behind it all made him weep. Somehow it seemed so tawdry. All this

233

because they wouldn't let us import the medicines we needed. I spoke to Grest. 'Then you got what you came for. You took the drugs. The book was there too – if you wanted it, why did you leave it?' He turned his head to one side and said nothing.

'I swear to God . . .' Tibbot began.

'I couldn't find it,' the Sec muttered. A little blood seeped from his nose, over his top lip and into his mouth. He spat it out and glared at me. 'You arrived and I stopped looking.'

So it had all turned on that. He had found the box of medicines but I had disturbed him before he got the book. If I had come just a few seconds later, things would have been so different. 'It had all the buyers and their orders,' I told Tibbot. 'He would have needed it to take over.'

Tibbot walked away a couple of paces. 'How did you get involved in all of this?' he asked Grest.

'I was a blue. Just like you.'

'Not like me. What happened?'

He swallowed painfully. 'Had a call a couple of years back, woman taken to hospital after a fight. Didn't sound like much.'

But the woman was Rachel, admitted to hospital after her struggle with Lorelei; and Grest told her that she would escape prosecution if she told him everything. Instead of reporting it, however, he had shoved her into Richard Larren's care, with her car as a down payment. He didn't want to arrest them; he wanted a cut.

Tibbot wiped his hand over his head. 'How much did you take to keep it quiet?'

'Thirty per cent.'

'Why did you kill Lorelei?'

And then Grest smiled, a horrible monkey grin. 'I didn't,' he said.

'What?' I whispered.

The life had returned to him. 'I didn't. She was alive when I got here, and still alive when I left her.' I didn't understand what he was saying. 'She told me where the stuff was, so I left her alone and went to the girl's room to get it.' He turned to look at me. 'Then I heard you come in.'

'Don't lie to me,' warned Tibbot.

'What then?' I demanded.

'You went in there and she says something.'

'What?'

'I don't know. "Who's there? I can't see." Something like that. Then there's all this splashing, like a fight.'

Sometimes we hear a phrase or name, and know for certain that we have heard it before. I was sure those had been her words. I heard them from her lips: *Who's there? I can't see.*

'And?' asked Tibbot. His voice was low and dangerous.

Grest spoke to me again. I could tell he was enjoying it now. My face must have betrayed my feelings, the sense of falling. 'I left you to it.' He laughed. 'When I came out the girl's room, you were bent over the bath with your back to me, so I just left.' He turned to Tibbot. 'Not what you thought, is it? Backed the wrong horse? You can smack me again and again, but you know it's like I say it was.' Tibbot threw him to the side and he crumpled to the floor. I placed my head in my hands.

'Did anyone else come in?' Tibbot demanded fiercely.

'No, mate.'

'He's lying,' said Tibbot.

But I saw the scene as he had described it. *Who's there? I can't see.* Lorelei was speaking those words, until they were drowned by surging water.

Grest shook with laughter. 'So someone killed her, mate, but it wasn't me.' He looked in my direction. 'They'll get what's coming to them, though.'

I ran to Lorelei's room, collapsing into the seat at her dresser. My hands dropped on to the table and under my palm I felt something hard and polished: her hairbrush. It still had some of her hairs entwined in it.

'Is he telling the truth?' Tibbot said quietly. I hadn't heard him come in.

'I think so.'

But what he was implying – it just couldn't be true. I wouldn't have done that. We know ourselves and our own lives, don't we? Or is that what happens when we begin to mirror the divided world around us? We become strangers to ourselves. No, it couldn't be true.

'We have to decide what to do,' Tibbot said. His tone was different. He was trying to work things out too.

I gazed at her hairbrush. 'Were you keeping a watch on me?' I asked. 'When I went to Great Queen Street?'

'And when you left. I had a feeling you weren't going to leave things alone. The thing about the Secs is that they just can't imagine someone doing to them what they do to everyone else all the time.' There was a pause. Tibbot looked around. 'She travelled overseas, didn't she? Met all those foreign actors and Presidents. I bet she brought stuff back with her. Perfect way of doing it. Besides, she's on our posters: *Victory 1945.* Pin-up girl for the Party. No one's going to stop her and go through her case. It would be like stopping Blunt.'

I hesitated. 'What about Nick now? Will they release him?'

'Yeah, I think Grest wanted your husband out of the way so he could get the contact information and take over – one hundred per cent is better than thirty. But Grest will be a good boy now. I've told him that if he doesn't, I'll have a word in a lot of ears. Spread it around.' He went over to the poster for *The Lucky Lady*, with Lorelei in a red silk gown, her face set behind a carnival mask made of red lace, and a spinning roulette wheel. There was a smaller image of her singing – it was a musical, it seemed.

'What will they do about her death? NatSec, I mean.'

He sighed. 'Blame it on an intruder, I expect. Burglary that went wrong. Close the file.'

'Are you certain they will close it?'

'You can't tell with these people. But I think so.' He wiped sweat from his brow. 'Jane?'

'Yes?'

'Will you do something for me?'

'Of course, what?'

'When your husband gets out, will you keep schtum about all this? Even from him. It's just that the fewer people who know, the safer it is for me, you understand?'

'Yes, of course.' I owed him that a hundred times over.

I grabbed on to the thought of Nick returning home to us, and looked to the speckled light slipping through the window.

25

I worried that, despite our leverage over him, Grest wouldn't keep his word about releasing Nick. All morning I wavered between staring out the front window and trying to find ways to distract myself. I didn't tell Hazel – even though I was bursting to do just that – in case it raised a false hope. Then, a little after eleven o'clock, as I was making some tea, there was a key in the lock and Nick stood on the threshold. I flew to him, and the two of us stood hugging each other as tightly as we could. 'God, I love you,' I whispered. And all the doubts and worries – how he had kept it from me that he and Lorelei had been involved in the black market and how it had come back to haunt us all – were buried under that truth. I would think about them later, but not now.

'I love you too,' he whispered back, kissing me. I knew that was true.

I wondered if he was aware of my involvement in his release, but I kept my word to Tibbot about not mentioning it – maybe one day I would be able to tell him. Luckily, the mark where Grest had hit me was small enough to be covered up by my rouge, and hopefully Hazel wouldn't say anything. Nick called up the stairs to her and she squealed at his voice, almost tumbling down to the hall.

I held them both until he fought away from me, telling me he did need to breathe every once in a while. 'Let's go to that café in Victoria Park,' he said. 'I have a craving for ice cream.'

I just burst into laughter and drew them both to me again. Hazel kissed my cheek.

'What was it like in there?' Hazel asked with an untouched dish of ice cream melting in front of her. She had been too excited to eat it.

'Oh, it was all right, really. Just boring. I spent most of my time thinking what I would buy you for your birthday,' he replied with a wink. At home I had helped him to splint and bind the wrist Grest said had been broken by one of the guards. Nick told us it was just a sprain.

'They didn't hurt you?'

'No. I think they knew they had made a mistake as soon as I got through the door; they were too embarrassed to admit it, though, so they kept me there for a while.' He kissed her forehead and she pushed him away. 'I won't be taking you there on holiday but it wasn't too bad. Now, do you want that ice cream or am I having it?'

'I'll have it, please. But I'm just going to the —'

'It's over there,' he said, pointing. I watched her go through the shabby door to the toilets. 'Has there been any more news about Lorelei? Anything from the police?' he asked me.

'No, I don't think so.'

'Hmm, well, I expect we'll find out eventually.'

I hoped so. 'What was it really like?' I asked.

'Not an unmitigated delight. Worse than I told her, but they didn't get the thumbscrews out. They threw a punch or two, but I'll live. Bread and cold clear soup three times a day – that was probably the worst of it. Really, I was telling the truth when I said I think they realized their mistake pretty early on, but they're NatSec, aren't they? So they can't admit to getting things wrong, or we little people will start to get ideas about them.' He ate a small slice of cake that the waitress brought him. We waited until she was gone before speaking again in lower tones.

'Was there questioning?'

'Twice, by the same man. He looked more like an accountant than a Sec.' That didn't sound like Grest – presumably they had people who specialized in interrogation. 'He was in this big high chair behind a desk and I had to sit on a low stool in the corner of the room like a child. Each time the questions were exactly the same: Why did I kill Lorelei? Who was I working for? Did she listen to Churchill's speeches? Did she have a normal sexual appetite or was she abnormal?' He forced down a grin. 'But that's when I knew I was safe – there was nothing that they actually suspected me of; they were just hoping I would volunteer something. And besides, they knew I was at Fred Taggan's house when she died. It was just them flexing their muscles a bit. You would think they had better things to do with their time. God knows why they thought I was involved in anything. Probably given some duff information by a Citizen Informant – one of my patients or a neighbour or something. Bloody CIs. They're vermin. Anyway, how did you bear up?'

'It wasn't easy. But I was OK.'

He took my hand in his. 'Was Charles any help?'

I thought back to how he had been. 'Hardly,' I said, trying not to sound too bitter.

He suppressed a smile. 'Well, he's not brilliant on the

sympathy front, is he? But he's harmless. Lorelei used to call him "Hopalong" when he wasn't around. His limp.'

'Did she?'

'Oh, yes. It was a bit rich from her, really.'

'How so?'

He started eating Hazel's ice cream. 'Oh, after the War she was taken round all the forces hospitals so the chaps could meet the lovely young actress and she could stroke their fevered brows. Lot of blokes with shell shock and the like. Charles was quite churned up and she kept the act up with him, asking him how he was feeling, telling him to let it all out, that sort of thing.'

'I see.'

'Yes, old Charles is all right. Actually, he can be quite warm sometimes.'

'He hides it well,' I said.

'He does rather.'

'Maybe he just needs a girlfriend.'

Nick almost howled. 'Now that's something I never considered in relation to Charles. I'm afraid I don't think he's much of a Casanova. From what I can tell, he wants nothing more than to marry some quiet girl who will love, honour and especially obey, before she pops out a couple of sons and they all spend Sundays in perfectly dull silence.' He looked a bit shifty. 'In fact, I'm not certain that he has ever "had" a girlfriend. If you catch my drift.' He winked. I smacked him on the shoulder. 'Perhaps that's why he's like he is.' I smacked him again, harder. 'Ouch! All right, I get the message. Now, tell me how you got on with Hazel.'

'Well. Yes, well.'

'Good. I'm really glad. God knows what the poor kid's

going through. I'll take some time off work and spend it with her.'

'Good idea.'

He rubbed my hands. 'I thought about you a lot,' he said.

'What were you thinking?'

'I was thinking that if I get sent to a re-education camp, all I'll have to look forward to are letters from you. And that's not much good because you may be an English teacher but whenever you leave me a note I can make neither head nor tail of it.'

'Do you want me to slap you?'

It was a joy just quietly cooking for us all that evening, making up a recipe involving the lard, flour and eggs we had in the house and the carrots and turkey ham we managed to buy on the way home. I created a sort of pie that was more successful than I had expected.

When Nick and I went to bed, there was absolute silence in the street for the first time that I could remember. No one was shouting at the neighbours; no police car was tearing along in pursuit of a petty criminal. The air was still and heavy, and I think being cooped up in his cell for three days meant Nick had a lot of pent-up energy that I was perfectly happy to help him expend. I lost myself then.

'I do love you,' he said.

'I hope so. My God, it was so hard with you in there.'

'I won't be going back.'

'Thank heaven.' I waited a minute, thinking. 'Nick, shall we have another baby?'

He kissed me again. 'Let's think about it later,' he said.

Well, having been through such a shock it was only natural that he wouldn't want to commit to something like that straight away. But lying there I saw a rich future with my belly swelling and knowing looks from other women on the Tube; followed by the two of us each taking a hand of our young child as we walked the corridors of the National Museum or through the grassy paths of Victoria Park.

My cheek rested on his chest and I could smell the musk on his skin.

The moon was poking through the misty sky when I spoke to him later.

'Nick,' I whispered.

'Yes,' he muttered in the dark, his voice muffled by the stillness.

'About Lorelei.'

He reached out and rubbed my back. 'It's over now. All of it.'

'It isn't, though.' I shivered in the night chill. I had been thinking about what Grest had said. His wild implication about me. 'We don't know what happened to her.'

'The most likely thing is that it was just an accident. You said she had been drinking.'

'Champagne. There was a bottle there.'

'Well, there you go. She got drunk on her own – not for the first time – and slipped down. Drowned. It happens sometimes. More often than you would think.'

'Still, it seems so strange.'

He sighed deeply, becoming more awake. I could see bruises on his stomach that were the result of his time with NatSec. 'People die a hundred different ways. The only thing you can be sure of about the human body is that it will keep surprising you.'

I rubbed my skull with my knuckles. 'What about the investigation now?'

'I don't know. I presume NatSec will continue with it, though I don't know why it's anything to do with them. They probably have "areas of enquiry" they're following up, or whatever they call them. It's nothing to do with us and I'm happy to be out of it now.' I understood. He had good reason to want to let it all go. But I couldn't. 'For Hazel's sake, I hope if she was killed by someone, then they catch him, but, otherwise, I just want nothing more to do with it.'

I stared through a gap in the curtains into the dark.

'Lorelei wasn't her original name, was it?'

'No. It was Anne,' he said.

'You never mentioned that.'

'Why on earth would I? Why do you care?'

'I used to see her in the films. It was as if I knew her.'

'She hasn't acted for years.' He was getting annoyed, but I couldn't stop.

'Did you get on with her? I mean, you saw her at parties, didn't you? And you had friends in common from when you were together.'

'We were polite to each other. We weren't friends.'

I pulled the blankets tighter. 'How did you meet?'

'Mutual friends.'

'And why did it end?'

'I was told she was having an affair.'

'Oh. Oh, darling. Who was it?'

He hesitated. 'Someone in the Party.'

'In the Party?' That hesitation suggested there was more to it. 'Someone senior?'

'John Cairncross,' he said through the dark.

'Cairncross?' The traitor Cairncross. At first I was amazed. But then why was that so unlikely? As the beautiful face of our idealistic young nation, she must have been introduced to them all. To those of us who lived in the Republic, the part she had played in the new regime was as great as Philby's or Burgess's.

'She denied it but she was lying, I could tell. She did that a lot, even to me, and I could always tell.' I had never before detected any real bitterness in him towards Lorelei. But then I had hardly asked him about her – deep down, I think I had been afraid of what I might hear. 'Lorelei and I were not friends. Yes, she was exciting to be with, but I can't say I liked her very much as a person – let alone as a mother to Hazel. Now, the past is past. Let's not rake it up.'

'I . . . yes, of course.' I came to myself. 'I'm so sorry. After all you've been through.' I wanted him to be open with me about her; but, if I were being truthful with myself, as I lay there in bed with him and there was silence outside in the street, I would have taken a future together over total honesty.

'Yes,' he muttered. His breaths slowed and deepened in his throat.

John Cairncross. I lay in the dark and worked it out. It had been four years since he had pleaded guilty to using his place in the Politburo to sabotage our food production in return for American money. Four years since Lorelei's last film and four years since the last story about her in the *Morning Star*. Surely that was no coincidence – his fall had resulted in hers, the taint running from one to the other. So she was no longer for public consumption. Even now, her death hadn't been reported – the censors had cut her out of our history.

I tried to settle down but a noise outside made me sit bolt upright. It was shouting – too far to hear distinctly, but not distant. Somewhere in our street. A banging sound, like a door being thrown open. There was more shouting and the sound of a car door slamming before the vehicle was driven away. Nick had woken up too. We heard a desperate knocking on someone's door. No answer. A voice calling out. The knock moved to a different door. Then another one. 'We can't get involved,' Nick said. 'Not now.'

There are many types of loss. Loss of a child. Loss of one's dignity. And loss of what you used to be. We used to be generous. We used to look out for those who lived beside us.

26

Nick went out with Hazel the next morning to spend the day with her, to talk about her mum and give her a chance to grieve properly. She hadn't even had that yet. 'I almost wish she had a bit more of her mother in her,' he had said to me. 'Frost inside. Instead, she's like you. A warm Victoria sponge.'

'Do I take that as a compliment?'

'Probably best to.' I tried to look stern but found myself unable to do so.

Just before ten o'clock, as I was sweeping the hallway, I answered a knock at the door to find a young policeman in uniform. There was a cardboard box at his feet. 'Is' – he checked a slip of paper in his hand – 'Dr Cawson here?' he asked.

'No, he's out. I'm Mrs Cawson.'

'Are you? Well, I'm handing something over. Some items, taken from . . . Mrs Cawson, you say?'

'Yes.'

'Second wife?'

I became instantly self-conscious. 'Yes.'

'Right. I see. These were taken from the house of . . . another Mrs Cawson.' He looked at me with . . . with what? Pity? Disdain? I couldn't tell. He must have thought that I was the next one on some conveyer belt of wives. Or maybe he was Catholic, a relic from the old era, and disapproved of remarriage at all. It was hard to tell. 'It's the stuff we took away for fingerprints 'n' that. Couldn't find any.'

'I'll see that he gets them.'

The possessions had mostly been taken from her bedroom and bathroom. I supposed it was anything that might have been touched by whoever had been there. Her identity card was on top and underneath it a few items of clothing, a glittering red lace mask of the type ladies once wore at society balls, tied on with ribbon of the same shade, a red gown made of silk – the one she had worn on the poster for *The Lucky Lady*, I thought – a pair of ash-trays, a long-player recording of one of Lorelei's plays in a paper sleeve, an ivory-inlaid cigarette lighter and a bottle of her perfume. A few cheap romance novels made my eyebrows lift – she led such a glamorous life, there was surely little reason to live another one vicariously through the pages of a shilling-book.

Flicking through, I found that they were not all classic romances either – a couple were American 'pulp' that mined the seamier side of life in the United States. The cover of one showed two girls with long hair tussling on the floor of a women's prison, their skirts riding up to expose their thighs. Another was set in the Roman Empire, although *The Lusts of Rome* looked little like the history books I had read at school. Tucked in the corner was a stack of letters, with all the envelopes torn open. I couldn't help but pull out their contents. A few bills; some fan mail forwarded by her acting agent; and a thick card with a gilded edge. It was an invitation, the rippled-edge, copperplate-script type that had once been for elegant weddings before they were denounced as bourgeois frippery.

You are cordially invited to join the party at Mansford Hall, Fetcham, Surrey. Masques from eight until midnight. Tuesday, the 25th of November 1952.

That was four days away. Those, and a telephone number at the bottom, were all the printed words, but there was more – a strange postscript scrawled at the bottom in near-illegible handwriting, as if the writer were in the grip of pain:

Nick knows you're selling him out

Nick. Seeing his name there felt like a blow. The card had arrived in an envelope postmarked the day before Lorelei's death, so whatever was between them hadn't completely ended until her death after all. 'Selling him out'? What did that mean? I searched through the rest of the box, pulling out lipsticks, silk scarves and pill-boxes; yet nothing else made mention of this gathering. Without thinking, I picked up the telephone. Nick's surgery was on our exchange so I dialled straight through.

'The consulting rooms of Nicholas Cawson, Charles O'Shea speaking.'

'Hello, Charles, it's Jane Cawson.'

'Mrs Cawson,' he said.

'Is . . .' But what would I say to Nick? Would I demand to know about the note and what it referred to? It was something to do with their black-market business.

The line hissed.

No, I should wait and calmly work out what to do. And one thing was certain: she was dead now, so it was truly over.

'Mrs Cawson?'

'Yes.'

'Your husband isn't here.'

'No?'

'No, he is out with his daughter.'

'Oh, yes, yes, of course. I'll speak to him later. Goodbye.'

I hung up and looked at the invitation again. There was something about it that was magnetic too. I had never been invited to one of these events; they existed for me only in the pages of Jane Austen or Baroness Orczy.

I opened the box again to find a few more unremarkable letters, and one envelope different from the rest. There was neither a stamp nor an address on it, only a single name: 'Crispin'. It held something solid and I ripped it open to find a slim paperback book: a copy of Sheridan's bawdy *School for Scandal.* Just her sort of thing, I imagined.

I opened the book. Tucked inside was a slip of thin paper with a smudged stamp that read: 'Citylight Prints, 2a Hannson Street, London W1'. It was dated five months earlier. There was also one of those 'this belongs to' gummed labels on the inside of the cover, sporting her spiderish handwriting, and when I traced over her name with my fingertips I noticed something: ridges under the label that told me there was something concealed underneath. I couldn't help being intrigued.

I tried to scratch back the label with my nails, but it was stuck on too firmly and tearing it away could have damaged whatever lay below. A sharp knife was also unable to lift it safely, so I had to resort to the kettle to dampen and melt the glue. The label slowly curled up, lifted by the blade, to reveal an item around which the glue had been carefully laid down so as not to stick it to the page.

It was a little square negative from a camera film. I gently brushed dust from it with my sleeve, put it to the light and squinted. The head and shoulders of a figure emerged – 'Crispin', I presumed. I could just about see that he had a slim face, glasses, neat mid-length hair parted on one side, but beyond that it was impossible to make out anything else. It was strange that Lorelei would have a negative of this man's image. It certainly didn't seem to fit with anything that I knew of their scheme.

The woman had so many secrets. Every time I thought I had discovered her, there was another layer below.

I took the box to our room, lifted out the backless red silk dress and held it in front of myself, looking at it in the full-length mirror. The silk was a type that wrinkled and crinkled to give it texture, not the smooth style that had been the norm before the War, and was the same deep red as her hair.

That afternoon, I passed Leicester Square's bronze statue of Kim Philby. His figure, poring over the lists of suspected Fascist sympathizers that he had personally handed to Beria, was dull in the lacklustre morning light. The pub opposite was named the Archangel and, as I walked under its sign showing the battleship floating on a serene Thames, I noticed a tin hoarding nearby covered with posters. One was an old bill for *Victory 1945*, but it was only half the poster, ripped off in the middle. Although the head and shoulders of Lorelei's on-screen boyfriend were still wrestling with a Gestapo officer, she was gone from it, no longer inciting a crowd to stand up to the Nazi occupiers. It seemed that when she had been dropped from the pages of the *Morning Star* four years ago, she had also been torn from the walls. Nick had once told me that the reason we had to hand in our newspapers at the end of the month was not only to reuse the paper; it was also to ensure that the only records of the past were in Somerset House. Can you rewrite history? Well, it seemed that we were trying.

Now I was in a district that I didn't know well and didn't want to. Shabby doorways were hung with strips of beads or gaped like broken mouths, and the tiles leading into them were broken and dirty. Some had small handwritten signs beside the doorbells. 'Jenny'. 'Roseanna'. I checked the street name against the address stamped on the slip of paper I was clutching and turned reluctantly down what looked like little more than a dead end. There I saw the shop. Citylight Prints was a dingy place in a dingy little street. The glass of the windows was covered with brown paper so that you couldn't see in, which didn't bode well, and the flaking shop sign had once been blue but now had hardly any colour at all.

'You all right, love?'

I turned to see a striking-looking woman with strawberry-blonde hair twisted up in the French style, standing in a shop doorway on the other side of the thin lane, tapping ash from a cigarette in a long holder, the sort they used before the War. 'You going in there?'

'I think so.'

She took a drag. 'You don't look the type. You do know what it is?' I gazed at the painted sign. 'You don't, do you?'

'A printer's?'

She hooted. 'That's what *they* call it. They do print stuff, there, love. Photos. Special type of photos.' I could tell what she was getting at. But why would Lorelei want to get that strange negative developed there? 'Sure you want to go in?'

'Yes,' I said.

'If you say so.' She pointed towards the shop with her cigarette. 'But if he gives you any gyp, you come out to see me.'

'I'll do that. Thanks.' I strode over and pushed through the strings of beads in the doorway.

It was a dimly lighted den, and the sole customer was a man in shabby clothes flicking through one of a set of boxes that lined the walls. As soon as he saw me he immediately left. I could hear a printing press thundering away in a back room. Behind the counter stood a young man, with little pictures tattooed on his neck in green-turning ink. He looked me slowly up and down, making me intensely uncomfortable, and wiped his mouth. 'You looking for work?' he said.

'No.'

'What, then?'

'I want a print from a negative.'

He shrugged. 'All right. Let's have it.' I handed it over. 'How big?'

'What's the standard size?'

'Whatever takes your fancy. Ten by eight's normal. Centimetres,' he said.

'That's fine. How much?'

'Eighty pence. Payable now.'

'Eighty pence?'

'Very discreet service here. You pay for that.'

I reluctantly agreed. 'A friend of mine recommended you.'

'Oh, yes?' he said with a chuckle.

'Lorelei Addington.'

For a split second he stared at me. Then he smiled. 'The actress? Don't think we've had her. I'd be on some beach in the South Seas smoking fat cigars if we had. Lot of trade on that.'

I couldn't tell if he was hiding something from me. 'When will it be ready?'

'Tomorrow at three.'

'All right.' I lifted it up. 'Can you tell me anything about it?'

He looked bemused. 'Like what?'

'Anything.'

'It's a neg. What the fuck else is there?'

'Sorry. No, that's fine.' I don't know what I had expected him to tell me. As I pushed through the doorway, I glanced back. His expression showed an animal wariness.

27

I went down the stairs barefoot the next day, Saturday, thinking that we could make pancakes for breakfast and pretend it was Shrove Tuesday – I had a little sugar and a lemon to squeeze over them. Pondering whether I had enough powdered eggs, I heard the postwoman arriving. 'You're up early,' she said, as I opened the door.

'So are you.'

'My job, though,' she chuckled. 'Sorry, looks like bills.' She handed over two brown manila envelopes before touching her cap and leaving. I put the malignant envelopes on the little table in the hallway for Nick. He could deal with them. It was then that I noticed something was missing.

A framed photograph that my friend Sally had taken of us as we had left our wedding ceremony wasn't in its place on the wall, even though the hook that had held it was still there. I searched around for the photograph and quickly spotted it on the floor by the coat rack. It couldn't have just fallen, certainly not to where it was now. It was a little strange, but I didn't think much of it.

As I bent down to pick it up and replace it in its spot on the wall, however, I noticed something underneath. It was a short white cigarette butt, the tobacco burned away. Nick's brand had a sky-blue band around the white, and there was none on this one. I had thoroughly cleaned the hallway just yesterday too, and was certain it hadn't been there then. Had someone smoked it and dropped it there, placing the photograph over it to ensure that it was found? It was said that the Secs did such things to disturb and intimidate. Or perhaps it was nothing and I had simply missed the cigarette when cleaning. I held it in my fingers, my pulse racing.

The waiting room of the South London Hospital seemed to cater to everyone without the right connections. Nick could probably have had me seen at Guy's alongside Party members if I had asked him, but I wanted to keep my visit to myself for now, because I was there to find out what had caused my miscarriage and I wanted to know whether it was good or bad news about having another child before I told him. He was doing his usual Saturday-morning surgery, so I hadn't had to come up with an excuse for where I was going.

There was a mass of people waiting at the chaotic reception desk. If there had ever been a single queue, it had long since broken down into an unruly shambles of young and old: aged women with walking frames crying at the back because they were too frightened of the pushing and shoving; young men forcing their way forward with hard looks; girls holding shrieking babies. Sometimes the nurses would wave at a young soldier who stood smoking by the doors, and he would amble over, bored, and push one or two of the young men outside, telling them they wouldn't be seen. After getting to the front and putting my name down, I was directed to a hard bench, where I waited to be called. I sat watching the sea of people constantly change yet remain somehow the same.

Three hours later – I wished I had taken a book with me – my name was shouted out and I was directed to a cubicle formed of curtains within a large room with a dirty floor. There were ten other examination booths; all were occupied and in some I saw women in various states of undress attempting to cover themselves as best they could with blue sheets. Yes, it was in a bad state, but it was free, I reminded myself. It was free for everyone in need.

A tall, slim man with untidy white hair hurried into my cubicle, checking a sheet on a clipboard. He had a harassed air about him. 'I am Dr Clement,' he said in a French accent. I guessed he was one of the refugees from '40 who hadn't returned to their ravaged land. 'May I have your name?'

'Jane Cawson.'

'Good, now what seems to be the problem?'

'I had a miscarriage.' It was the first time I had pronounced the words, and I hated every one.

'Oh.' He sat down and looked grave. 'I am sorry. When did it happen?'

'A month ago.'

'I understand,' he said, thoughtfully, noting down some details on an index card.

'I want to know what caused it.'

'What caused it?' he repeated.

'Yes. I want to have another child so I want to know.'

He looked a little troubled. 'Please tell me the details of the pregnancy.'

I told him, keeping my voice low so that it wasn't shared with the occupants of the adjoining cubicles. At the end, he took off his glasses. 'Mrs Cawson, it is probable that

257

nothing was the cause of the miscarriage. I am very sorry. It is something that happens sometimes. It is not your fault. It just occurs.'

'Has it . . . damaged me?' I asked.

'For becoming pregnant again?'

'Yes.'

'Well, there are tests.'

'I would like them, please.'

'Of course. I will first take a blood sample and a urine sample to see how healthy you are in total.'

He searched through a desk and found a jumble of instruments, including a hypodermic needle that he cleaned and sterilized in a jar of liquid. He fitted it to a syringe, rolled up my sleeve and drew out a line of my blood. 'Good,' he said, holding the tube up to the light. He labelled it and put it on his desk. 'Now, here is a pot for the urine.' He wrote on an envelope and placed a small glass phial inside it. 'Please hand it in at the desk outside and make an appointment to come back on Monday, I will examine you properly then.'

On my way back to that seedy print studio in a Soho backstreet, feeling my way through the thickening smog, I tried to guess what I would find there. There was no indication that it related to Nick and what he and Lorelei had been involved in. It was something personal to her. Something involving a man named Crispin, whose name had appeared on the envelope containing the negative. But still I wanted to know.

Inside the shop, the man with green tattoos on his neck greeted me. 'Got it here,' he said, reaching under the counter. He handed me a paper bag and I drew a print from it.

It was so confusing. The face on the picture was one I knew, and yet it had changed almost beyond recognition.

The thick-framed glasses were unknown to me. But the face. You could hide Lorelei's red curls under a side-parted gamine wig but you couldn't disguise her delicate face. 'That do you?' he asked.

'Yes,' I said, hardly able to speak. 'Thank you.' I began to leave but, as I was crossing the threshold, I turned to speak to him. 'By the way, do you know anyone called "Crispin"?'

'"Crispin"?' He paused. 'Don't think so.'

'All right. Thank you.'

Outside, the woman opposite was in front of her shop again, still smoking. She was even more striking-looking than the previous day, with immaculate make-up, a silver cameo choker on her neck and a large glittering mother-of-pearl comb in her hair. And, even though she was wearing a simple sort of white dress, there was something about the way she wore it. 'You're very glamorous,' I said, before I could stop myself.

She hooted with laughter. 'Nice of you to say that, love.' She reached out and took my hair in her fist, rubbing it between her fingers. 'You know, you could be a pin-up if you just paid a bit more attention to your make-up and did something with this. A wave. Bit of a tint. I'll do it for less than a quid.'

I looked behind her and realized that her shop was a hairdresser's. 'Like yours?'

'If you like.' Nick and I were going to the theatre that evening, and I thought it would be jolly to have my hair done for it. I was about to step in when something caught my eye: a line of men marching past the end of the street, clad in overalls. It was a work party of Germans on their way to dig up the road. Their guards were armed with guns and batons, and we watched them pass, some looking dejected, some angry and swearing in German. There were rumours that the Department of Labour was considering taking our own reported Parasites and putting them into these work details so they would learn the happiness of labour – I hoped that was just talk, though. 'Don't feel sorry for them. Not one bit,' said my new friend, watching them coldly. 'Me brother was at D-Day. He saw them shooting his mates on the ground after they had surrendered.'

People were often reticent about D-Day. Some claimed that it was Blunt himself who had supplied Stalin with our plans, and the Soviets had passed them on to Hitler so that our offensive would fail. The Red Army, they said, had stayed out of the War precisely so that we and Germany would knock each other to pieces, and they could then sweep through Europe when we were both so weak that we could hardly stand. Blunt didn't come across as that underhand, but how could you really tell?

The work party began to dig up some of the ruts in the road and shovel the dirt on to wheelbarrows. 'Your brother came back all right, then?' I asked.

'Yeah. He was a POW in Holland. Got home eventually.' It had taken six months for many of the POWs to make it back under their own steam, the Soviets not being too keen on the return of even the ragged remnants of our army. We had never been told what became of those who had surrendered to the Japs in Burma and Ceylon. She led me inside. 'Anyway, it's all over now, isn't it? So let's get you settled in. For a night out, is it?' she asked.

'I'm going to a show with my husband.'

'Lovely.'

I sat for an hour as she tinted and teased my hair into the same French twist that she wore. After that, she spent another five minutes redoing my rouge. 'Don't worry, no extra charge,' she said. 'Oh, and me name's Stephanie. Next time you come, ask for me.'

'All right.'

She continued to fuss over me. 'So what was it you wanted over there, anyway?' She tipped her head towards the print shop opposite.

'I found their details in an old address book of mine. I couldn't remember why I went there.'

She looked at me out of the corner of her eye. 'I see.' She clearly didn't believe me. But she just as clearly had a grudge against her neighbour. 'I could tell you some stories about that place.'

'Could you?'

'Oh, I could. They print all sorts there, they say. Dirty postcards; snide papers; magazines they say are French, though the girls in them are about as French as I am, and I'm from sodding Whitechapel, if you'll pardon the expression. Should wash me mouth out with soap 'n' water. Call me a gossip if you must but just telling what I've heard. Can't shoot me for that.' She stood back and flexed her back. 'Now it's seventy-five new pence, or have you got something to swap?'

'Not really.'

'Nothing? What's your job?'

'I'm a schoolteacher.'

'Oh. Pity,' she said sympathetically as she went back to my make-up. 'Seventy-five new pence, then.'

I handed over the coins and left, bidding her goodbye. The few cars on the road crawled through the smog at the same pace as the pedestrians, with their headlights shining to make them look like giant insects. A motorcycle, one that seemed to have been salvaged from the War, drove through the wet gutter, spraying dirty water over my legs. I absent-mindedly stopped to brush it off my stockings and noticed footsteps some way behind me.

I turned through a narrow alleyway that I thought must cut to the next road, though it bent a little in the middle so you couldn't see through to the end. The steps behind me turned down it too, echoing off the high walls of the buildings that hemmed us in. There were rumours that on days likes these thieves would walk beside their victims to slash through the side of handbags, grab their purses and then just walk off in the mist. We only had rumours, though, because the government hushed up news of most crimes.

I walked a little faster, but I tripped and my feet slithered when I came to a pile of rubbish and broken bricks that spanned the path. As I picked my way over them, the steps behind mine slowed. I glanced back. I could only make out a shambling figure close to the wall. Hurrying now, I squeezed past a dumped bedframe lying on its side, only to stumble on something that spun out from under my foot, making me drop my bag in the gloom. I wanted to leave it and bolt away, but it held my purse, so I had to nervously scrabble about for it. The figure stopped. I heard his silence.

28

Twenty-seven. Twenty-seven lives have been lost this year as our countrymen have tried to escape that prison colony that calls itself a republic. Twenty-seven families marking Christmas with an empty chair at the table. Twenty-seven diaries that will never be filled. The number lies heavy in my heart.

> Winston Churchill, Radio Free Europe address,
> Saturday, 22 November 1952

'Who's that?' I called out. There was no sound but the wind whipping down the alley like a spear. 'I can see you.' I raised my voice, hoping someone in the houses on either side would look out, but they remained lifeless. My searching hands found my bag and drew it to me. Clutching it, I stood up, spun on my heels and ran for safety. But as I rounded the corner I saw that the alley ended not in an open path to the next road, but in a high wooden gate topped with barbed wire.

The man hadn't come around the corner yet, but I could hear the shuffling of his feet, a snap and a metallic sound as he kicked a can. I pressed myself into the corner. The footsteps came closer. As he stepped out of the smog I recognized the rough green tattoos on his neck even before his face.

'What do you want?' I asked, holding my handbag to me as if it would offer protection.

The printer put his face right up to mine before grabbing hold of the bag. I tried to keep it from him, but he was too strong and threw me off. He searched inside and pulled out the paper package that contained the negative and print.

'Give that to me!' I shouted, snatching for it and hoping someone would hear. He pushed me away again and held me off as he fumbled inside his pockets, drawing out a lighter with no cap. He flicked the wheel and a spark flew up but no flame. He tried again, this time shooting up a bright jet. I didn't know what the purpose of those images had once been, but I knew they were important enough for him to tear them from me. He put the flame to the corner of the paper bag and I clutched for it again, but he dropped it into a metal tray that someone had discarded on the ground and I had to watch as the paper burned away, briefly leaving the print and the negative. I didn't understand why he had given me the print, and then followed me to rip it away. The plastic of the negative melted and shrivelled into a black mass before the print caught too. For a second by the light of the flame I saw Lorelei's face before it turned to ash.

He kicked the tray to shake apart the remains before picking up my handbag and pulling out my identity card. I felt too defeated to attempt to stop him. '"Jane Cawson,"' he read from it. 'Right. I know who you are now. So stay the fuck away from the shop. And if I was you I would forget that name you heard.'

So that was it. That was why he had given me the

print – it was only when I had subsequently mentioned Crispin that he had felt danger. There was something threatening about that name, or the man who bore it.

I felt angry afterwards that I had let that happen but still had to find my way to the theatre for Noël Coward's new play, *Three Days Without Wine*. Nick might know who Crispin was – one of Lorelei's friends, possibly. I would have to be subtle about asking him, though.

I passed a squad of young male soldiers dressed up for one of the dances that the state organized with the healthier girls – as chosen by their Pioneers COs or college political officers – in the hope that they would marry and soon have children to add to the strength of the state. Sexual desire and energy were to be harnessed for the march of the Soviet ideal by breeding a little army, we understood. I received a couple of wolf-whistles from the oily-haired young men, but the walk did me good, and I felt better by the time I saw Wyndham's Theatre's grand Victorian façade of patchwork bricks and intricate moulding.

Nick was in the lobby, buying tickets from the window with Charles beside him – I had forgotten Charles was coming. The ticket-seller held Nick's five-pound note up to the light and rubbed its paper between her fingers, eventually accepting it was real and not something he had knocked up in our shed. I thought it would be fun to surprise Nick with my dolled-up image so I put my coat in the cloakroom, positioned myself behind him and waited for him to turn around. But it was Charles who caught sight of me first. He seemed to halt midway through blowing a stream of smoke to the ceiling and stared. Then Nick himself turned. His eyes widened, then narrowed, and the tickets fluttered out of his grasp to the floor. I glanced about, to see what it was that had fixed his gaze, and that had made Charles stop too, but behind me there was only a fat old woman being helped to the door by an obsequious younger man. Something was very wrong.

Nick's voice was colder and harder than I had ever heard it. 'Why did you do that?' he demanded.

I looked desperately around again. I had no idea what he was talking about. 'What . . . what have I done?'

'You must know.' His jaw clamped down on the words.

I looked to Charles, hoping he would tell me what had made Nick so angry. But he simply looked back at me. 'I don't,' I said.

Nick lifted his hand. 'Are you saying this was an accident?'

'What is?' I was becoming frantic, checking again over my shoulder in case there was some clue.

He looked grim. 'Your hair. You dyed your hair red. Like Lorelei's. And you're wearing it like she used to.'

'It's just the same,' Charles said. 'You look just like her.'

The chatter around us seemed to die away. 'No,' I said, dragging a curled lock out of the French twist that Stephanie had created for me. 'But it's not. It's not like hers.' I turned to look at my reflection in a glass panel on the wall. I had thought it would be coloured like Stephanie's strawberry-blond hair. As I stared at it, I saw that it had, indeed, turned out darker. And it did look just like Lorelei's had at the party. I hadn't realized when I was sitting in the chair and Stephanie was teasing it into curls. 'I didn't know.'

'So much like her,' Charles said, reaching his hand up to touch it.

Nick's anger was growing. 'You're telling me this was just coincidence? You had your hair cut and dyed just like my former wife's purely by chance.' He seized me by the arm, led me to one side and shoved open a door to what must have been a fire exit. We were in a freezing, uncarpeted stairwell. 'What's this about?' he demanded. 'What on earth are you trying to do?'

I too felt a wave of anger, at the way he was treating me. Until then I had managed to suppress my frustration that he was hiding from me what had secretly been between him and Lorelei; but with his apparent accusation it all started to come out. 'Are you saying I can't even cut my hair how I want without your permission?' I replied.

'You're just like her.' He was speaking to himself, not me.

'No.'

'Yes, you are.'

I thought back to the party. How she had looked, how she had stood and moved. And just now, when he saw me, Nick had dropped the tickets out of shock. A thought crept into my mind: what if it wasn't shock or anger? What if, just for a moment, it had been hope?

'Nick? Did you –'

Behind him, the door opened. A short man with side-whiskers appeared wearing an evening suit. 'Excuse me, sir,' he said. 'This area is for staff only.'

'What of it?' replied Nick.

'May I be of assistance?'

'You can leave us alone.' His tone was unmistakable. There was to be no more talk.

The man silently withdrew. Nick just glared at me and shook his head before walking away, back into the lobby. I stood, feeling the cool air flowing in from the door at the end that led to the outside world. I knew I could leave through that door, and I probably would have done, once, nursing my wounds, but something kept me there. *Sticks and stones*, I thought to myself. And I thought again of that day when I had found her. Of the memories hidden from me.

I followed Nick out. He was talking quietly to Charles, who watched my return through the corner of his eye. Nick caught sight of me too and seemed to relent somewhat. 'Listen,' he began to say to me. But he was interrupted by the bell ringing to tell us to take our seats, and we reached a joint unspoken conclusion that the best thing would be to leave things to settle, so we traipsed in without another word. For the next hour we sat watching a frothy farce about a farm girl playing a buffoonish English aristocrat and an equally dim-witted and arrogant American banker off against each other.

Before the interval, Nick's hand crept on to mine and I shifted my weight so that my shoulder was against his. I felt him sigh. I knew he hadn't meant to be angry. It was just surprise more than anything else. I couldn't blame him, really, now that I knew why, and I regretted matching his anger with my own. Yes, it was annoying that he wasn't being wholly open with me about what had been between him and her, but that was just the world we lived in nowadays.

Still, as I sat there, I couldn't help but wonder again what had flashed through his mind when he had first seen me. Had some buried hope risen at the thought she was there in the room with him? Perhaps.

During the interval, we went to the bar to discover that

the miasma of smoke it enclosed was thicker than the smog filtering in from the street. Nick forced his way forward to get served, and Charles and I waited at the back of the room. 'Your husband is a very intelligent man,' Charles said, as we watched Nick's back disappear between the bodies.

'Oh, yes,' I replied. 'It was what first attracted me to him.'

He tapped ash out into a glass ashtray on the table beside us. 'I'm sure it was.'

I waited for him to say more, but he didn't, so I tried to fill the gap. 'How long have you worked –'

'And now you're wondering if you're the right girl for him?' I felt my face burn, and opened my mouth but couldn't make a sound. 'Mrs Cawson, I'm sure you are not a wicked person, I'm sure what you did this evening was an accident, but it seems to me that you and he might not be well suited,' he added, dropping the last of a cigarette into a discarded glass, where it hissed in the liquid at the bottom. 'Sometimes that happens.'

'I –'

'Where are you from?'

'Kent. Herne Bay,' I stammered.

'Family?'

'They died. TB,' I said hoarsely.

'I'm sorry, but we all have to live with such things. All of us. There's a danger that when we lose a family, we try to find a new one.'

'Charles, I've caused you problems, I know.'

He turned to face me. 'You make it sound like you wasted a day of my time. I received a letter today telling me that I had to move out of my flat within two weeks. It's being reassigned.'

How much had I set in motion? 'Is it NatSec?'

'I should say that's a given, wouldn't you?'

I had to. 'Where will you live?' I asked, my tongue tripping over the words.

'They sent me the details and I went to see it – it's a hostel, really. My own room, yes, but a shared bathroom and kitchen. All filthy. There was a man just sitting drunk in the hallway.'

I felt rotten. The knowledge that it had been a step on the path to freeing Nick didn't help much – ruin one man's life to save another's? It was a hard balance. 'I'm so sorry,' I said.

'And because of what you have done – I don't even want to know what it actually was – I might never get another job after this one.' He was right, no doubt. 'Don't worry. I haven't mentioned any of this to Dr Cawson. I can't because he's your husband and he's not likely to take my side, is he?'

'There are lots of flats that you . . .' I trailed off, realizing that I was talking like an idiot. He didn't want any useless advice; he just wanted me to understand my part in his harsher future. If only I could make up for what I had done to him, but I would probably only make matters worse. 'I'm sorry,' I said again.

'But that doesn't change anything, does it?'

I turned to watch the junior Party officials trying to use their position to push through the queue, and the young rakes out on the town.

Soon Nick returned with our drinks. 'Very kind,' Charles said, as Nick handed out the glasses.

'I'm sure Charles has been too modest to tell you,' Nick

began, with a glint in his eye. 'But it's largely down to him that I'm out of choky.'

'Is it?' I said, rather surprised.

'His connections. He made some calls; I'm sure that's what got me released.'

'I doubt it was that entirely, Dr Cawson.'

'But it must have helped.' Nick secretly winked at me. He didn't believe for a moment that Charles's attempts had helped.

'Well, perhaps,' Charles replied.

'Thank you for that.'

'Not at all. Although, Dr Cawson, I do believe now is the time for you to join the Party – this might all have been avoided with the right friends.'

Nick looked serious now. 'Yes, you might be right. I've put it off for a long time. But it's true.'

'I'm sure it is.'

'I'll need a sponsor,' Nick said. But as he said it he wasn't looking at Charles. Something was distracting him.

'Yes, one of your patients, I would say. Would you like me to go through the list?' He paused. 'Dr Cawson?'

'Hmmm?'

Nick was looking at a young man in the corner of the room who was confined to a wheelchair, his legs ending at his knees. There were others around him, but they were standing and talking over his head, and Nick's gaze took on that melancholy, faraway look I saw when he was back thinking about his War service. The man caught sight of Nick, and their eyes met. They seemed to understand each other. Nick raised his drink to the man and the gesture was echoed. They drank.

'Dr Cawson? Shall I make some enquiries among your patients who have influence? Discreetly, of course.'

Nick's attention returned to us. 'What do you think?' he asked me.

'I don't know,' I said. I never wanted to go through what had happened to us again, but, unlike Nick or Charles, I knew just how close NatSec had been. They might even have been in our house – the young man with the pebble-like goitre on his neck who had pulled Tibbot and me from the train, perhaps. They would never let Nick join the Party unless it was as their stooge, their blackmailed and beholden puppet keeping tabs on the other members. The Party was said to be rife with those.

'Yes. Well, go ahead, then,' Nick said decisively.

'I'll make the calls in the morning.' Charles looked satisfied.

It struck me that three days ago Nick had been in NatSec's cells; now he was planning to join the Party. All of our memories were becoming shorter.

29

The following evening saw me sitting at the kitchen table, leafing through a copy of the *Morning Star*'s thick Sunday edition. Despite its length, there was little in it: a long article about one Louise Archer, the mother of six children who was being lionized by the state as our own Stakhanov, explaining how easy and pleasant she found it cooking for a family of eight; and below it a warning to expect the heaviest smog of the year. There was still no mention of Lorelei, and I supposed that there never would be now.

Nick had just returned from spending the day in Waltham Forest with Hazel. She was still crying from time to time, but it had been almost a week, so I thought and hoped that she was over the worst. During six years of war as a country, we had got used to swallowing down our grief, so, sad to say, Hazel's experience was far from unusual. She had asked if I could come out with them, which was touching, and I wished I could, but I knew Nick wanted to be alone with her.

The telephone rang. When I went to answer it, however, a tinny voice was already speaking – Nick must have picked it up on the extension line in his study. The voice was too distant and hollowed out by the line for me to recognize it, and I was about to hang up when I caught a few words: '. . . and how is your wife?' They made me pause.

'She's bearing up. Things have been . . . difficult for

her,' Nick replied. I lifted the receiver back to my ear, placing my palm across the mouthpiece to deaden it.

'I'm sure they have.'

Who was this person, asking about me? I tried to work it out, but couldn't even tell for sure if it was male or female. Probably male.

'If she had started turning things upside down, it would have made it all ten times worse.' Nick was keeping his voice down, but sounded disturbed. 'She hasn't mentioned anything so I won't bring it up.'

'That's probably for the best. Do you think she knows?'

Nick sighed. 'No, I don't think so.'

'But she might.'

'Yes. She might. I'll do my best to prevent that.'

'This is all more dangerous now. I'm not sure we're going about it the right way.'

'Don't worry. You're always worrying,' said Nick, with more than a hint of irritation in his voice.

'Citizen Informants.'

'Oh, don't be bloody stupid.' There was a pause.

'Can you get more norethisterone?' the voice asked.

'Yes. I knew we would need more. That's good. But I don't want to talk about this on the telephone. Meet me there in an hour.'

'All right.'

'I could have put it to good use before, though,' Nick added, thoughtfully.

'How?'

'If I had had it before, Lorelei wouldn't have ended up like she did.'

'Yes, that's true.' The line crackled. 'Who do you think killed her?'

'Who can say?' He paused. 'But we can't let it distract us right now. The norethisterone. I found someone to test it.'

'A patient?' the voice asked.

'A private patient.'

'What was the outcome?'

'It works as predicted. Now it's time for them to start the course again.'

'All right. Well, I'll see you in an hour.'

'Goodbye.' Nick put the receiver down. I made to do the same. But, as I did so, I knocked the earpiece against the mirror on the wall. The glass rang and I gasped at the sound. My fingers wrapped so tightly around the telephone that all the blood drained from them and I held my breath, listening, praying that the person on the other end hadn't heard. There was nothing, only my heart beating. It was all right. I began to put the handset down.

'Is someone there?' It rattled out of the earpiece. I waited, staring at the receiver. 'Are you there?' the voice repeated, slowly and cautiously. Then a click as they hung up. I breathed out.

30

I couldn't stop thinking about that call even as I made Hazel breakfast the next morning. It had been – in part, at least – about me. Of course Nick would have occasion to talk about me sometimes, but this sounded very much like a conversation I was being deliberately kept from.

Hazel was wearing her navy-blue school uniform. I had worried that it was too soon for her to go back, but Nick thought it would be better for her to be with her friends than wandering about in our house with no one to talk to. Maybe he was right. 'Are you sure you feel up to it?' I asked.

'Yes.'

'Good.' With Nick around, things between her and me were warming by the day. 'What are you learning in English?'

She sighed. 'How Dickens depicts class conflict in *Oliver Twist*.'

Burgess and his friends had been clever. They had used our national love for literature as a way to open up our nascent political consciousness. So Tressell's *The Ragged-Trousered Philanthropists* and Orwell's *The Road to Wigan Pier* were required reading. And yet Lorelei had said Orwell had fallen foul of Burgess's assistant, Ian Fellowman, and ended up in a re-education camp.

'That sounds very interesting,' I said. 'I can help you with it if you want.'

'Yes, please.'

I was happy about that. 'It's a wonderful book,' I said.

'I'm really glad you're here,' she blurted out.

I hugged her. 'I'm glad I'm here too, Hazel. We're going to be fine,' I said.

After seeing her off, I took a tram heading south, watching the wrapped-up people and the bomb sites flit past. When I stepped down at the stop for the South London Hospital, a big black car slowed a little as it passed me. I briefly tried to stare into it before shaking my head and telling myself that I was seeing faces in clouds – that if they had wanted to remain hidden they would have done so, and if they had really wanted me to see they were there, they would have been a damn sight less subtle about it.

It was hard just getting to the hospital building. I had to push my way through a crowd milling outside the Irish Embassy, where at least a hundred people were clamouring for entry. I asked a young woman in a pinny what was going on and she said everyone in the scrum had an Irish parent so they were applying for Irish passports – apparently applications had just reopened after a couple of years, so there was a lot of pent-up demand. I wished her luck. I could understand their attempt, although anyone trying to get out of the country that way would have to endure months of harassment from the authorities. They would lose their job, and if they got another at all it would be the dirtiest in the city, kilometres from where they lived, just to teach them a lesson. After that, of course, the government might still refuse to grant an exit visa.

The scene at the hospital reception desk was almost identical to last time – a mass of people pushing and shoving, some demanding to be dealt with, some begging. Dr Clement was in his cubicle, writing on a card as he bid goodbye to a woman who was buttoning up her blouse. She left and he motioned me to a wooden chair opposite his that had been broken and shabbily bolted together again.

'Hello, Mrs Cawson,' he said. 'I have read the results from your blood and urine tests.' He rolled his lips over his teeth and bit down on them thoughtfully. 'They were to check your hormone levels. The reproductive hormones that you produce.'

'I see.'

'Yes. There is one that we must talk about.'

'All right.'

'It is called oestradiol. It is one of a group we call oestrogens that are vital for pregnancy to occur.'

'And?'

He cleared his throat. He seemed uncomfortable. 'Please tell me: what first said to you that you were pregnant?'

'How did I first realize, you mean?'

'Yes.'

'My periods stopped.'

He noted that down. 'Yes, yes. That is the way most women first believe they are pregnant too.'

'Well, obviously.' He avoided my gaze. There was something he didn't want to tell me. 'What is it?'

'Mrs Cawson.' He looked at a form on his desk. It was divided into sections, each with a few words of black type above red handwritten words and numbers. 'The tests we did. There was something we found.'

'What was it?' I said, now very worried – had losing the child meant I could never fall pregnant again?

'I am sorry to tell you that we find your levels of oestra-diol are low. Very low. Too low for you to have ever been able to conceive a baby, I must say. Too low for you to have been pregnant before.'

I was dumbstruck. It was impossible, what he was say-ing. 'But I was pregnant,' I stuttered. 'Before. That's why I'm here.'

He took his glasses out of their pouch and looked down at them. 'I am afraid not.'

I stopped. For a second my mind whirled. 'But I was. I had morning sickness. My husband, he's a GP. He did a test and told me I was definitely pregnant.'

'An hCG test?'

'Yes, yes, that's what he called it.'

'Perhaps he said that he thought you were, and you misunderstood.'

But, no – Nick had assured me I was expecting. I recalled how he had kept monitoring my temperature and blood pressure. 'I was pregnant!' I stood up and thrust the chair behind me. He watched me without moving. 'I had a mis–' I couldn't complete the word. The sheer pain of that night hit me like a wave. I sank back in the chair and put my hands over my face. I was going through it all over again: the feeling of having a part of me taken away. 'If I wasn't pregnant, what was that?' I insisted.

He put his hand on my shoulder. It felt gentle. 'I do not think you had a miscarriage. I think that was your period,' he said. 'For some reason we do not know, they stopped for a time; so it was more heavy than usual when they started again.'

My mind began to throb. My cycle had always been

very regular, so when it stopped, I had been certain it could only be one thing. I tried to speak, to make sense, to know what this meant for Nick and me. 'Are you saying I'll never be pregnant?'

He seemed to relax a little. 'Well, the good news is that there is much research going on into collecting or synthesizing hormones. We have extracted oestrogens from urine; already created a synthetic progesterone – norethisterone – and soon –'

Something leaped into my brain. 'Norethisterone?' I asked, interrupting him.

'Yes,' he said, looking at me curiously. 'You have heard if it?'

'Nick mentioned it once.' That unknown voice on the telephone had asked if Nick could get more of it. It was right after Nick had said he would do his best to prevent me from finding something out.

'Well, as I said, it is a synthetic form of progesterone, which is another of the hormones you make during your menstrual cycle.' He hesitated. 'Have you come into contact with it?'

'No. Why? What would it do?' He moved his glasses to another part of the desk and considered. 'Dr Clement?' I waited for an answer.

After a while he spoke, cautiously. 'I believe it . . .' He trailed off.

'Please.'

He looked at me curiously. 'Well, I believe it would stop your periods. But . . .'

My mind was hot. 'What else?' I interrupted him. 'What else would it do?'

280

'It could . . . produce nausea, cramps. Other effects too, probably.' He returned to that searching look I had seen.

'As if you're pregnant?' He nodded. 'And if a woman stopped taking it after a while, would her periods return?'

He nodded thoughtfully. 'I expect so.'

'And would the first be heavier than usual?'

'It is probable,' he said.

My God. What had happened to me?

I stood up and walked to the bed. I placed my fists on it and leaned on them, my head down, my back to him. 'And what is it used for? Its purpose?'

He fidgeted and glanced at the battered door. 'It is a little . . . something there is an argument about. The effect of halting the menses – your periods – means it can be used as a contraceptive. Something to prevent pregnancy.' He looked at me meaningfully. 'Of course, no doctor would prescribe such a drug. It would be disloyal. To the Party.'

On the wall outside was a poster of Louise Archer, mother of six Pioneers, bouncing a child on her knee. OUR STATE RELIES ON ITS CHILDREN, ran the slogan.

'Do people supply this drug? On the black market?' I asked. He hesitated. 'Please tell me.'

He cleared his throat. 'Doctors talk. I have heard of it happening. I do not know if what I heard is true.'

When the voice on the telephone had asked Nick if he could get more of it, Nick had said he had been testing it on a 'private patient'. 'It works as predicted. Now it's time for them to start the course again,' he had said.

'Would it be expensive?'

'I really could not –'

'It would, wouldn't it?'

'I imagine so.'

Expensive. Lucrative. So this was surely the basis of the new 'big orders' that Lorelei had told Rachel to expect. It was what they had fought about.

'What does it look like?'

'What does it . . . I do not know. I have never seen it,' he said.

'Guess.'

He sighed. 'A pill, a liquid, it is hard to say.'

'Would it taste of anything?'

'I really do not know. Maybe. Probably not. Mrs Cawson, is there something that you want to say to me?'

My throat was hoarse. 'No,' I managed to whisper.

Hardly able to think, I stumbled out of the room. My head spun with thoughts and images. I turned at random down corridors and through archways. In the end, I looked up and found myself in an unfamiliar corridor. There was a door beside me with the sound of voices behind it. I didn't know where I was and I needed someone to help me, so I pushed on the door and it swung open. The sight that greeted me made the ground shake underneath my feet.

I was looking into a huge ward of at least fifty beds. Occupying them were as many young women, sitting up under the blankets, leaning against the walls and breathing deeply or slowly walking up and down the room assisted by nurses. They were all, every one, just hours away from giving birth.

When I was a girl I had a collie dog named Sheba. When she died I screamed and ran out the gate, to the beach. I sat on the sand with my knees pulled up to my chin, trying to reconcile the images of my father who cuddled me on his lap at our warm dinner table, cheerily carving slices of meat while a pipe dripped from his lip, with the man who had tossed Sheba's body into a pit in the back garden without any emotion at all. Now that image came to my mind again, as the thoughts tumbled. Could it really be that Nick too had this side to him, something cold and hard?

I could hardly think as I wandered out of the hospital and along streets I didn't recognize, every step feeling like someone else was taking it, until I found myself at the Thames. My fingers twisted through the wire links on the fence that kept us from the water, and I hung there like one of the D-Day survivors who you saw on park benches staring ahead for hours on end.

Nick had hidden his continuing relationship with Lorelei from me, their involvement in black-market medicines. Had he also been using me as a test subject to see if the drug – a drug that mimicked the effects of pregnancy – worked? He had kept monitoring my heart rate and blood pressure. And the night that he was released I suggested that we try for another child and yet he had been reluctant – when he had previously been so happy that I seemed to be pregnant.

But then, sometimes women's cycles do stop for no special reason. So it could simply be that mine had halted for a while and the pregnancy test that he gave me was unreliable. And when Nick had talked on the telephone about testing the medicine on a private patient, he could have meant just that: one of his private patients. Equally, his reluctance to think about having another child at that moment was quite understandable, given the awful few days he had just experienced.

My mind swung one way and then the other.

I gripped the fence until the wire bit into my flesh. I didn't know where to go. I sat on the ground, feeling the wet sand and stones under me, and told myself I should return home, pack what little I owned and catch a train, stay with Sally while I tried to learn the truth of what had happened. And if it turned out that my fears were right, I could stay there, or in some town where I had never been and knew no one. There were so many rootless people these days I would simply be one more piece of driftwood.

And yet I knew that I couldn't leave, because no matter what had happened and what I had heard that day, I had never been as happy as I had been in the months spent with Nick. When I had gone through his desk, when I had followed ghosts in Kent and lied to NatSec, all of it was for him.

A sharp pain stabbed in my chest. Something was surging and I doubled over as my stomach convulsed, bile falling from my mouth in short, sharp jerks. It came in waves of nausea and pain, and when there was nothing left I sat on a mound of broken bricks. I stayed there for a long time, watching the birds glide and the sun move across the sky.

Back at our house – his house, really – I sloped upstairs and collapsed on the bed. All the way, I had been telling myself that I needed to know what had happened to me, just to have some level of certainty; and a thought had entered my head, a way of discovering the truth. It came from the look in Nick's eyes when he had seen me at the theatre – when, just for a second, he had seemed to think Lorelei stood in front of him.

I pulled the box of her possessions from the back of my wardrobe and delved through the books and compacts until I found her perfume bottle. I unstoppered it and let the sweet scent drift out. Then I found what I needed: the record of one of Lorelei's plays. It would be my teacher for a task that seemed reckless to me – but then the world had shifted and I had to change with it.

In Nick's study I placed it on his player. My fingers itched to open the drawer where I knew those letters from Lorelei lay, but I resisted and instead lowered the needle to the disc. The speaker on the side began to play the sort of music they danced to in nightclubs between the wars.

'Five pounds on red,' Lorelei called out. 'Yes, thank you.' With her scent on my wrists and her voice in the room, it was as if she had never gone.

I repeated her words out loud, listening to my own accent. It was a Kent coast sound, with shades of the London evacuee children I had taught. I felt ashamed of it.

'And now, all my winnings on black.'

'And now all my winnings on black.' It was better now. Had Lorelei been brought up in a country house and then sent to Cheltenham Ladies' College? Or had she looked into that society from the edges and moulded herself from clay? That is what an actress does, of course: she invents herself day by day and night by night. I had never fancied myself an actress but there was a seed of change in me now. For what I had in mind I would need her voice and talent for self-invention.

'Well, Mr Beckeridge, you're the last person I expected to bump into tonight. Would you care to try your luck?'

Her voice changed for the second sentence. It was still

285

of the English ruling class but it had added something, a coquettish undercurrent. I imagined what she would have felt carrying out what I had planned. She would have felt no fear at all, I told myself. Nothing but the thrill, like a rider galloping after the hounds.

'Why not?' answered a rough, gravelly male voice on the recording.

'And what stakes are you playing for tonight?'

'And what stakes are you playing for tonight?' I held the air lower down my throat, and the accent changed. The vowels became more rounded.

I kept listening to the recording, copying Lorelei's words and voice, until the sound of the front door opening alerted me to Nick's arrival home. I pulled the record from the player, locked the study door and dashed back to our bedroom. He came in just as I was pushing her box back into place in my wardrobe. 'Oh, hello, darling,' I said. 'Is the surgery all back to normal?'

'Awful patients complaining of imaginary illnesses,' he replied, taking his shoes off. 'So, yes, you could say that. I was looking forward to coming back to you.' I wondered if that were true. I hoped, still, that it was.

'Sally wrote. She's coming to London tomorrow to go to Moorfields Eye Hospital. She has to have an operation and needs someone to see her back to Herne Bay. I said I would do it. I'll stay at hers and come back in the morning.' I examined a pair of shoes. I wasn't used to lying, least of all to him.

'Fine,' he replied. 'Don't forget we have people for dinner on Wednesday.'

'Yes, of course. Nick, I've got such a terrible migraine, I

286

think I'll stay in the guest room tonight. I'll be restless all night and don't want to disturb you.'

'If you want.'

'Yes. That's what I want.'

He looked at me with a furrowed brow, as if there were something wrong, but he couldn't work out what it was. Then he dismissed the thought and took off his tie and jacket. I realized that I had been speaking in Lorelei's voice.

31

The next day moved past, the clouds rolling listlessly across the sky, and I pulled my coat tighter as I stepped from a train on to the platform at a village railway station in Surrey. The electric light above barely penetrated more than a metre of the night.

You are cordially invited to join the party at Mansford Hall, Fetcham, Surrey. Masques from eight until midnight. Tuesday, the 25th of November 1952.

The invitation had read. And then the words scrawled wildly at the bottom:

Nick knows you're selling him out

I could hardly believe I was there – that I had had the nerve to dress for it, buy the ticket, board the train. Each point had seemed like a border I was crossing. But whoever had sent Lorelei that card knew her secrets and Nick's, so they might know the nature of Nick's hidden work – and whether that drug really had found its way into my veins. In a strange way, that knowledge would map out the rest of my life. It's an uncomfortable feeling to realize that such knowledge exists and someone other than you possesses it. Nick had it, of course, but he was the one person

I couldn't ask. I had considered confronting him with the question, but to what end? Denials that I wouldn't be able to believe anyway? No matter what he said, it would bring nothing but sorrow.

So I was looking for the sender of that note, in the hope that the secrets they knew included what had happened to me.

I walked out of the desolate station to find two unlit lanes. I didn't know which to take, so I picked the left-hand path and walked, nervously gripping the small evening bag I was carrying as if it were a talisman and hearing nothing but my footsteps. I could only trust that the glint of light ahead was the village, and not an isolated farm building. The light grew as I walked and gradually I began to feel the path ahead was solid and open. It became the village high street, where the glint became a glow, the glow became a light, the light became a bright window.

Wide and low, the building before me was an inn of the oldest type: a rest-stop for travellers in need of a simple bed. The sign overhead said it was the Bell, and this was where I had telephoned to arrange a room for the night. Feeling relieved, I pushed through the heavy oak door to feel a wall of warmth wrap around me. Raucous laughter seemed to bounce off the brick walls and I struggled to see what the joke was until I caught sight, through a line of heavyset backs, of a little man attempting to drink a yard of stout as another timed him. Most of it was ending up on his collarless shirt rather than in his stomach but that didn't seem to put any of them off the game, least of all him.

Behind the bar a fat publican was laughing hard. 'Oh, Sam, Sam, you'll drown!' he shouted over. 'And none of us'll give you the kiss-a-life!' The party cheered as Sam finished his drink. The publican steadied himself on the bar as he shook with hysterics, and then brought himself up short when he saw me. 'Oh, beg your pardon, miss,' he said, looking me up and down. 'What can I do for you?'

'I'll have what he's having,' I said. 'But I'll just have a glass of it.'

The barman guffawed and handed me a smeared glass full of the treacly black liquid. 'There you go, miss. Eightpence.'

I took a swig of the stuff. It was thinner than I had expected, a cheap home brew. 'I telephoned about a room. My name is Lorelei Cawson,' I said, putting the money on the bar. Saying it to someone who could meet my eye felt unnatural, but not as unnatural as I had thought it would.

'Oh, that's you, is it?' he said.

'That's me.'

One of the men, with dirty black hair and strong gypsy features – a farmhand by the look of his frame – wiped his mouth on the back of his hand and ambled over to me. 'What brings you to Fetcham?' he asked in a low, guttural tone that suggested he didn't speak much day by day.

'I'm going somewhere.'

'Going somewhere, aye? Everyone's going somewhere.'

'I expect that's true. My name's Lorelei.' I held out my hand. He shook it warily.

'Pete. So where're you going?'

'Just a house.' I was beginning to enjoy the feeling of making other people hang on my words.

'Which one?'

'Mansford Hall,' I said.

His voice went cold. 'Mansford.'

I felt all attention on me. Perhaps I shouldn't even have

mentioned it – I hadn't realized that the name alone signified something. I had thought that out in the countryside there would be less suspicion and fewer conversations that you couldn't have, but were there CIs even here? There must have been. I could sense these men were as distrustful of me as I was of them now, and I wished I had been more secret, hadn't let my tongue rush before my head. I tried to bluff it out. 'That's right.'

'Mansford. The big house,' he muttered. He turned away from me.

'You know it well?' I asked his back. He slowly shook his head. 'Have you been there?'

'Once.'

'For work?'

'Not my work,' he said.

'Then whose?'

'My brother's.' The men around us looked uncomfortable and shifted on their feet but said nothing.

'What does he do?' He made no answer but rolled his shoulders backwards and stalked out the door.

'Mansford,' the publican said ruminatively behind me, as if he were turning the name over in his mind. 'What're you going there for?'

'A party.'

'A party,' he repeated. It sounded like the answer he had expected and didn't like.

I walked out after Pete. I could see a body moving in the gloom a hundred metres up the lane. I said nothing but he heard me and stopped. I walked slowly and deliberately. 'I don't know the way,' I told him.

'You'll find it.'

'I'm not from around here.'

'That road,' he said, pointing. I could hardly make it out. He came close to me. 'What do you want?' I said nothing in reply. 'People like you. Women like you.' He pursed his lips. 'All right, I'll show you the way.'

Eventually, we faced the gate of a huge square brick house – Tudor, it might have been. A clamour of voices and music was bursting out in a crash of sound, and there was something about it that reminded me of the madhouse that held Rachel. Here too there were guards on the gate and I looked at Pete. We both knew there was no point inviting him: he wouldn't want to come in and they wouldn't let him.

'Thank you for walking with me,' I said.

'Yeah.'

'Well, I know where to find you when I come back.'

'Aye.'

'Goodbye.' As his back melted into the darkness, I called after him. 'What's your brother's name?'

'Greg. Gregory.' And he disappeared.

'May I ask your name, ma'am?' said one of the gatemen.

'Lorelei Cawson.' Having been Lorelei to Pete and the other men, it felt more natural now.

'May I see your identity card?' I handed over the card, which had been in her box of possessions, thankful that it had been issued in her legal married name rather than that of the famous actress Lorelei Addington, or I would have been wholly unable to use it. In the darkness I looked enough like her photograph not to arouse suspicion. 'Just a moment, ma'am,' the guard said politely. He went into his hut, glanced at me and turned on an overhead electric bulb to examine the pass. I tensed as the light shone out over me and half turned so that he couldn't see me so clearly.

'So cold tonight,' I said to the other guard.

'Yes, ma'am.'

'I had no idea it was so far from the station.'

'Most of our guests have motors.' He said it in a way that suggested it was strange that I had come by foot.

'My husband crashed ours yesterday. Silly man. He's still up in town trying to get it fixed.' I was about to go on with the story, but could feel it spiralling away from me and forced myself to stop, surreptitiously watching the guard in his hut examine the card. He reached up and pulled the switch to turn off his light, and for a moment he didn't move. Then his silhouette began to shift and flow, back out the doorway of the guard post. 'Thank you, ma'am,' he said, handing me the document.

'Thank you.' Relieved, I took a few paces up the path before stopping to open my evening bag and take out the glittering red lace mask that had come with Lorelei's belongings. I tied it around my eyes and forehead. The house remained a block of stone, punctuated by beams of light glaring out on to the front lawn, and by its glow I noticed that the hem of my red dress was ripped, probably from bushes I had brushed against on the path. It was a stubby, jagged tear with threads drooping from it; I knelt to pull them away.

A black official car, with the hammer and compass on the registration plate, stopped in front of the house, and a thin man with a chicken-like neck and ridges of hair only over his ears eased himself out to stand imperiously still. On the other side, a sylph-like girl at least twenty years his junior was helped out of the vehicle. He slid a carnival mask over his face and ignored her as he strode unevenly into the house, taking a glass of fizzing wine from a waiter standing by the doorway. The girl followed.

The heels on my shoes shifted in the gravel as I reached the double doors, around which a classical wooden portico wound. I took a glass of wine as I passed into a small entrance hall, then into a large room with a haze of smoke so thick that I couldn't even see the ceiling.

Although more than half the room consisted of men in their fifties with girls in their twenties – not a pleasant sight, but one that I became used to – here and there I could see other young people milling around without attachment. Most wore masks, although there were a few army officers in dress uniform who wouldn't have dreamed of polluting their appearance that way. A couple of Soviet naval officers were drinking in the corner. The room was alive with conversation and flirtation, but these pursuits were taking a second seat to the room's main interest: gambling at tables set up to make a casino. It was real money being staked too, piles of it in wads of paper that were being handed to butlers in exchange for chips. Croupiers who had kept in practice since before the War dealt cards and spun roulette wheels. To my left, a plump and bow-legged man was speaking sharply to a woman who had dealt him a hand he didn't like. Behind him, his companions were doubled up in laughter.

'Will you be playing, ma'am?' asked a croupier.

'I'll watch for now,' I replied. I hadn't seen so much money in the world.

'Place your bets, ladies and gentlemen.' Even calling people 'ladies and gentlemen' would have been brave outside this house. I spent a while wandering around, watching the games, attempting to discreetly engage one or two of the young women in conversation as a ploy to comprehend who exactly was here, and who might be the one I was looking for – but they were as clueless about the other guests as I was, and I suspected that they had, in fact, been hired for the evening. I received some aggressive attention from the Soviet officers, but pretended not to notice.

As I was taking another glass of wine, someone whispered in my ear, 'Have you come out without your purse?' I looked around to see a man at my side wearing a white mask that covered all but his mouth, making him look a little like he had been in some sort of terrible accident.

'Yes, silly of me.'

'Oh, dear. Well, here.' He reached inside his jacket, pulled out a fist of paper and dropped it on a silver tray carried by a butler, who carefully flicked through, then measured out a stack of chips that my new friend indicated were to go into my hand.

'That's very generous of you,' I said.

'Jeremy. And you are?'

'Lorelei.'

'Well, off you go, Lorelei. Place your bet.'

I took some of the chips and placed them on the table. I recalled the line from the play that I had repeated over and over again to learn her voice. 'Five pounds on red,' I said.

'Bravo,' called my new friend. The wheel spun and the ball clattered through the numbers. A man in an evening suit and a woman in white, with a withering purple flower in her hair, were at the table. Two more men slipped in behind me to watch. 'Now keep your nerve.' I did my best. The ball fell into a red slot and I felt a thrill. 'Well done.' He patted me on the back.

'And now, all my winnings on black.'

One of the men behind me placed his chips in the black square too. We won. The third time I went for a column of numbers, and in the next moment I had sixty pounds in my grasp. The man and woman at the table had lost all they had.

'I'll take that,' said Jeremy, reaching for my pile of chips.

'You can have your stake back. The rest is my luck,' I said, passing him a few tokens.

He grinned and pulled his hands away. 'Quite right. Come this way, Lorelei, let's see how your luck holds at vingt-et-un.' But the table that he took me to was full. He mulled something over for a moment. 'On second thoughts, let's go outside,' he said.

'And what do we find out there?' I thought it useful to get the feel of the occasion before I pursued my true task.

'Oh, just a different crowd.' We passed out of a side door into the night, and he put his arm around my back to ward off the chill as we trudged towards some sort of low building made of Greek columns. There were lights shining, and, when the breeze blew towards us, I could catch a word or two from low voices. 'The pavilion,' Jeremy said.

'Which is?'

'A little outdoor home from home. Come and join the real party, Lorelei.'

'That sounds marvellous.'

'Oh, it is. They're Parasites all. Don't tell NatSec.' Inside the pavilion, what had once been classical and austere stone architecture had been transformed by satin oriental cushions and velvet drapes to keep out the cold. An old wind-up gramophone was playing jazz.

> It's one for you, it's one for me;
> It's two for you, yes, two for baby . . .

A group of people sat on cushions and wicker chairs surrounded by hot braziers. Niches in the walls showed the stumps of recessed busts that had recently been chiselled away. More history turned to dust.

'Here we are,' Jeremy said. He stooped at a table to pick up a fruit that I didn't even recognize – it was like an apple, but with soft flesh like a peach. He bit in and chewed a mouthful before throwing the rest aside; it skidded across the marble flagstones, leaving a trail of seeds and flesh. 'Grapes?' he asked, picking up a bunch.

'No, thank you.'

'Up to you.' He dropped them again, and I couldn't help but think that there was something awful about it all – absurd and impossible, that this could be happening, when outside the walls there were so many parents cutting slices of bread in half to share with their children. The scene was no different to a thousand that had taken place in country houses before the War, but still it struck me as wrong that it should continue to exist in a nation where such disparity was supposed to have been swept away. Privilege would always be with us, I supposed, yet it made my skin prickle that its beneficiaries should be so blasé about it.

'Jeremy,' a voice called over. I saw a man in his forties who looked to have been very handsome a few years ago, but those years had taken a toll in hollow cheeks and bags under bloodshot eyes. He was slumped on a wicker chaise-longue.

'Let's introduce you,' Jeremy said, taking me over. The man had his double-breasted jacket open as he leaned back against the armrest. 'This is Adam.'

Adam gazed at me. 'I had to beg for the wine,' he moaned. 'Shortages, apparently. Russians taking it all. Oh, how Socialist of them. Well, it doesn't matter now.' He was slurring his words and sounded utterly wretched.

'He's been like this all the time, recently,' Jeremy muttered. 'Very boring. You can look after him for a bit.' He walked away towards a table full of glasses and decanters.

'I'm Adam Cutter,' he said, more to himself than to me, holding out his hand.

'Lorelei Cawson.' I shook his hand and began to lift off my mask as the others had.

'Lorelei?' He seemed to wake from a dream. 'Oh, Lorelei, I didn't recognize you.' My fingers froze on my mask. 'Why didn't you reply?'

'Reply to what?' Tense, I tried to keep her voice in my mind, the way her vowels rounded and her consonants were like beats on a tight drum. I let the mask slip back into place.

'To my . . . note.' He lifted his head from the armrest, but the effort seemed too much and it fell back. 'Nick's heard that you're selling him out.'

I thought of the handwritten words on the invitation that had been sent to Lorelei. Presumably it referred to the medicines but how?

I sat beside Adam and put my hand on his leg sympathetically. 'You think I'm doing that?'

'Of course you are. Of course you are. To your friend up there.' He pointed towards the house.

So she had been betraying Nick to someone – and that person was here. 'Where is he?'

'Oh, where he always is now. The card room, making everyone think he owns the place, not me.' He closed his eyes and shook his head at the last words, then his eyes flicked open and his head burst up from the armrest. He stayed there searching what he could see of my face before slowly sinking back. I guessed that he was going to pass out any minute.

'What exactly does Nick know?'

'Hmmm?' He seemed to be slipping into unconsciousness.

'What does he know?' I repeated it more strongly.

He looked confused. His brow furrowed and his arm lifted up towards me. His fingers closed on my mask and began to pull it; I snatched them away, holding it in place. He sighed and seemed to drift away again. Then, without warning, he sprang at me, ripping away my mask. I grabbed for it, but it was too late. He fell back, agog. 'Who are you?' he drawled.

I thought perhaps I could shock him into sobriety. 'Jane Cawson. Nick's second wife.'

'Where's Lorelei?' he asked.

'She died. It was an accident.'

'Died?' He reached for a glass full of dark liquid – brandy, I guessed – which he poured into his mouth. 'My God, I didn't know.'

'She drowned in the bath. I'm here in her place,' I said. 'You can talk to me just like you talk to her.' He drained his glass and I put my hand on his shoulder. 'I need to know how Lorelei was selling Nick out.'

He waved towards the house. 'Ask him, not me. Card room.' I shook him again.

'Adam?'

'Please leave me.' He was so drunk that he couldn't even open his eyes and he folded into himself. A couple sat down on the chaise-longue next to him, laughing between themselves. I thought it best to go.

I walked over to Jeremy, whose mouth was a pit of fruit seeds and mush. 'Look after Adam,' I said.

'Utterly sloshed again? Yes, he does that,' he replied, lifting a peach from a tray and biting into it. 'Why don't you stay here for a while? I'm a little bit bored with the company, to tell you the truth. There's only so much time you can spend watching idiots lose a month's salary on the roulette wheel. I just come for the food nowadays.' I couldn't help but think how many coupons I would need just for what he had eaten in the last few minutes.

'Who's in the card room?' I asked.

'The card room? No idea. Take a look. It's upstairs.'

I put my mask on to walk back. The house was built on a slope that ran down to a dark lake. Beside the water a group of four or five young men had formed a circle around a waitress they had somehow enticed out there, and they were offering her money. She was trying to leave but they wouldn't let her. One grabbed her and she yelled, shoving her way out of the ring as they burst into laughter, continuing to call to her until she was out of sight. 'Three quid!' yelled one. 'More than it's worth.'

The card room was at the end of a short oak-panelled corridor on the upper floor. Two plain-clothes men stood in front of it, and, as I approached, one said to me, 'I'm sorry,

this is a private room. Would you please return to the party?'
I didn't know what to do. I didn't want to abandon the
course I was on, but there was no way they would let me
through. I was about to go back to the stairs when the door
opened and a podgy man with thinning brown hair
emerged, his stomach spilling out of his belt. Behind him, I
caught a glimpse of a room filled with blue cigar smoke. In
its centre was a circular card table with six or seven people
around it. The dim overhead light was dropping shadows
from their faces on to the green baize, making it hard to see
their features. But the dealer, clad in a drab grey suit, was
directly opposite me, and, as he lifted his face a little to push
the cards to his friends, I recognized him in an instant.

32

The door closed again. I knew it had been him, though. 'Please let me in,' I begged one of the guards. The fat man pushed past me. As he did so, his palms seemed to stroke across my waist.

'It's guests only,' one of the guards replied.

I couldn't think what to do. I turned and walked away. Then I started to hurry to where the podgy man was about to reach the top of the stairs. I stumbled against him.

'Sorry,' I giggled.

'Had a bit too much?' he said, a wide grin spreading across his face.

'Yes, a few too many glasses. It's all so nice, though.' I sighed and let my head droop on to his shoulder.

'Well, we could find somewhere for you to lie down.'

'Could you?'

'Oh, I'm sure I could. The bedrooms are through here.' He gently tugged me by the arm towards one of the closed doors.

'Oh, not yet,' I yawned. 'What's through there?' I pointed back to the card room.

'Nothing very interesting. Boring men playing cards.'

I stroked his chest drunkenly. 'Well, that's exciting. A real-life card game. Is it poker?'

'Three-card brag.' He glanced back at the guards. They were ignoring us. 'I think you need to lie down. You'll feel better.'

'I've never seen a real-life poker game. Could you show me?'

'I think –'

'After that, I'll have a lie-down. I'm so tired.' I yawned.

'Well –'

'Please?' I gazed up at him.

'All right. Normally I wouldn't but, well, just this once. I'm Piers, by the way.'

'I'm Catherine.'

'Nice to meet you.' His hand was clammy as it held mine. 'But when we're in there, we'll have to sit in the background. And we must be very quiet.'

'Like little mice.'

'Just like little mice.' Cautiously, he led me back to the card room. The guards opened it without reaction and we were inside. All the players at the table had the silver hammer-and-compass lapel badges worn by those who had been Party members when the Soviets arrived and a few glanced up, but paid us little attention. There were leather chairs at the side occupied by more young women, and Piers led me past them to a studded sofa. As I passed the table, I counted seven players and surreptitiously looked again at the dealer.

In his dull grey suit, vague in that cigar smoke, Comrade Assistant Secretary Ian Fellowman looked like nothing so much as a third-tier Party apparatchik. I hadn't seen him since the terrible night of the Comintern party at the hotel, when Nick had been so desperate to be introduced to him. The stark sight of him now brought back a sudden feeling of drowning in freezing water and I had to lean on Piers to stop myself from falling. Piers smirked, presuming the drink was doing its part.

Could Fellowman really be the one who had made a deal with Lorelei for contraband medicine? He had come over from the West in '47, an idealist among idealists. She would probably have known him, though, because of his control of our national broadcasting and her affair with Cairncross. And she had also warned Nick to stay away from him, saying that Fellowman was 'toxic' – which could have been her way of keeping Nick in the dark about her arrangement with him.

In the background, a record player was whining out an old speech of Blunt's. '. . . there is art too in the simple message of the Manifesto. This soaring first line . . .'

'I think we've heard enough from Anthony for a while,' Fellowman said, with a wry smile to the others. It was the first time I had heard him speak, and it was almost a surprise to know that he could. His voice was very deep, befitting his size, and he had an upper-class Scottish accent. They all chuckled, and a man I couldn't see in the darkness at the side of the room lifted the needle from the disc. 'Dealer has a flush,' Fellowman said.

Piers put me at the end of the sofa so I couldn't move away, and sat up against me, with his hand on my knee. We were in semi-darkness, the heavily shaded overhead light not reaching to the edges of the room. I resolved to watch from a distance for now and try to work out what to do. Although I was in the gloom, and Fellowman had seen me for only a few seconds the previous time we had met, I was thankful for my mask.

'These are some of the most important men in the country,' the fat man whispered in my ear. 'Senior Party men. That's Alan Turner. He's in charge of the railways now. And Ian Fellowman, he tells us all what to think.' He guffawed to himself. He believed that I would be impressed by these men. No doubt he was, despite his studied nonchalance around them. In the old days, people would drop the names of the local gentry, and those names would carry weight and inspire awe entirely because of tradition. Now it was commitment to the cause and the sheer power that these men had over the rest of us that impressed: the power to modernize, the power to destroy and rebuild. But the man by my side didn't know what I knew: the grubby depths to which at least one of them had sunk.

'Pair of sevens,' Fellowman said.

Piers returned to his normal voice. 'But it's going to be very dull for you, watching these men play cards. Why don't we find somewhere for you to have a rest? Have you had enough Champagne? I can have someone bring us some.'

'Do be quiet, Piers,' Fellowman muttered from the table.

'Sorry, Ian,' he replied.

'And a straight flush, well played.'

But Piers was fidgeting. His hand slid a little up my thigh, and I tried to brush it away without being too obvious about it. 'I haven't even seen you, properly,' he whispered again, his lips almost touching my ear. 'I think you should take this off.' He indicated the mask. There were chuckles from the table as someone conceded defeat in the game. 'Come on, off with it,' he said, reaching for the ribbons at the back.

'No, please,' I said, fending him off.

'Look – they've taken theirs off.' He pointed to the other girls in the room and reached up again. He disgusted me.

'I want to keep it on.'

He wasn't listening, but if I fought him off it would only draw more attention to me, so I let him tease out the ribbons and prise away the mask. 'There now. You are a lovely one.'

'Thank you.' I dipped my head down a little to hide.

'Another hand?' asked one of the men at the table.

'Oh, I feel like mingling for a while,' Fellowman replied, getting up and lighting a cigar. The game broke up and a few went to a drinks table, while another clutch huddled in a corner, laughing and slapping each other on the back.

I quickly placed the mask back over my face. Piers put his palm back on my thigh.

'I'm with someone,' I said.

'I don't see anyone here.' He sounded aggressive.

Then a voice close to us – somehow right beside us, although I hadn't seen him arrive – spoke. 'Are you not in the mood?' The sweating man jerked his head up at Fellowman's voice.

'No, not really,' I replied, tying the ribbons of the mask before lifting my face to him.

'Well, with fat old Piers here, who can blame you?' he laughed. 'Piers, you really must learn when a young lady isn't interested.' Piers laughed unnaturally heartily. 'Come on, why don't we find better company?' Fellowman took my wrist and lifted me to my feet. One of the players emerged from a corner and mumbled something in his ear. 'No. It's out of the question,' Fellowman told him. 'Guy has made up his mind and that's that. I'm not going to start second-guessing him.' The man ambled away. 'What's your name?' he asked me.

'Catherine.'

'Catherine. Are you enjoying the party?'

'Very much so.'

'I don't think we've met, have we?'

'I'm a friend of Adam's.'

'Ah, Adam.' We were beside a balcony. He stopped, thought, and forced the balcony doors apart. One was stiff and groaned as it opened. 'I need some air,' he said. Out on the stone platform, he sighed and leaned on the balustrade. I had no idea what he wanted or if he had somehow just taken a shine to me. 'Did you know Churchill once stayed in this house?'

'I didn't, no. That warmonger.'

He waved to someone inside the room. A young man appeared, and I knew in an instant that this was Greg, brother to Pete, who had walked me from the pub to the house. They had the same strong gypsy features, although Greg lacked the physique of a farm labourer. 'A cigarette,' Fellowman whispered. The younger man took one from a wooden case, lighted it between his lips and handed it to Fellowman, who placed it in his own mouth before gently touching him on the forearm in acknowledgement. He slipped away again, closing the doors behind him and pulling heavy curtains across them. 'A warmonger? Oh, I wouldn't call him that.'

'No?'

'It's empty sabre-rattling. For American consumption. Old Mr Churchill knows we could close the Needle any time we like and he's in our territory. Besides, our Soviet friends have twice as many warheads as the Americans, and who wants to fight a war that no one wins?'

'Well, yes,' I said. My nerves were still taut, but loosening.

He tapped ash down to the ground. Underneath was a

pile of what looked like chunks of collapsed masonry covered by a tarpaulin. I was surprised it hadn't been tidied up
and carted away for the party. Even here they had priori-
ties and some things were make-do-and-mend. 'Comrade
Burgess met him in '38, you know. That imbecile Cham-
berlain had signed the Munich agreement, and Guy was so
furious he went to Churchill's home in Kent to see him for
advice. In fact, Churchill had just received a letter from
the Czechoslovakian prime minister begging him to help
stop Germany taking over the country. "What can I do?
An old man without power, without party?" Churchill
said. It turned out that he was more in need of advice than
Guy was. Guy told him to go up and down the country
making speeches, to force people to listen to the danger.
He told old Winston that they would listen to him. They
didn't, though. Guy was wrong about that.'

He blew more smoke and tapped out his ash. 'Yes, Guy
was wrong,' he said under his breath. Then he looked me
squarely in the eye. 'Now, Mrs Cawson, will you tell me
why you are here?'

I shook with the blow. My mind raced to know if he had
recognized me when my mask had been pulled off, or if he
had known from the moment I bought a ticket to Fetcham,
his people keeping track of me all the way. I uncovered my
face. 'Lorelei had a deal with you.'

'What are you talking about?'

What did that mean? Had I misunderstood everything?

And yet he knew me, had taken an interest in me. So
surely there was truth in it somewhere. I suppressed my
panic and bluffed a confidence. 'Was it for the drugs?'

He stared at me as if I were mad. 'I fear . . .'

I stumbled on. One last push. 'What she was getting for you. From America – I can get them.'

'Mrs Cawson . . .' A bemused smile broke on his face.

'I can get them.'

I just stood waiting, hoping I had hit home. There was silence. And then he spoke.

'Why isn't your husband here? Why send you?' My heart was pounding so hard I felt it in my brow and my fingers. 'Ah. He doesn't know you're here, does he? So you're keeping this from him.' His mouth twitched. 'Maybe it's because you think he's keeping something from you.' I was right. 'Well, now, Mrs Cawson. You say you can get me the items the previous Mrs Cawson was supplying. I don't need any more for now. What she was offering – it was something more than just the items themselves.'

So I had been right after all. He must have dealt only with Lorelei, and that was why Nick had been so desperate to be introduced to him when relations between her and Nick soured.

'What was it? I can get it too.'

'You think so?'

'I'm certain of it.'

He drew in a mouthful of smoke and let it drift from his mouth. 'Well, I suppose we'll see if your self-confidence is misplaced. I was tired of going through middlemen. I wanted to buy straight from the source.'

'Why?'

His eyes bore into mine as he considered. 'Because I don't like having weak links in the chain.'

I could see his reasoning. Weak links can break; they can even get caught and talk to the police.

But there was more to it, I guessed. I glanced back at the room we had left. Yes. This way he could help out his friends in the Party's upper echelons, those with whom he had just been playing cards, perhaps. A favour granted, a favour returned.

'I can give you the contact,' I said, trying to control my nerves. 'What do I get in return?'

'What do you want?'

'What were you giving Lorelei?'

He cocked his head to one side in a look of curiosity. 'I don't see that it matters.' I waited. 'Well, it's nothing now. She wanted a marriage exit visa.'

A marriage exit visa. So Lorelei was engaged to a foreigner, someone who could take her to a new life outside the RGB. She wasn't just selling out Nick; she was also leaving the country.

'Who was she marrying?'

'I have no idea and no interest,' he replied. 'All that she told me was that she wanted the visa. I said I could arrange it in return for an introduction to her supplier in America.' He looked down towards the dark lake in the grounds. There was silence as we both lost ourselves in our private thoughts. 'No, no one listened to Churchill,' he said after a while. 'Instead we had the War and all that followed. Men chewed up by bullets and machines. Those camps. And people still ask us why we need Socialism. We need it to prevent men turning once more into savages. I don't want to see that again.' He threw the glowing cigarette butt into the night. 'Call our friend Adam when you're able to see this through.' He pushed back into the room.

I stared out. There were others like him in every street in

every city now, squabbling over the scraps of a nation that could barely muster eighteen million people. Lorelei's death wasn't the result of jealousy or anger. Not really. It was the result of small men scrabbling over tiny possessions. Such a grubby little country we had become. Socialism meant a minister and the wife of a GP haggling over the price of a box of medicines.

33

So he's been at it again, has he? That drunken buffoon. Did Churchill mention that it's the American arms companies lining his pockets? Who do you think pays for that huge mansion with so many servants licking his boots? Oh, my friends, I can't tell you how much freer we are in the Republic of Great Britain. So the next time the fat old fool comes on to make fun of you, turn it off.

Alec Mathers, broadcast on RGB Station 1,
Wednesday, 26 November 1952

It was the sight of my dress on the bare bedroom floor and a shard of morning light through the window that told me where I was. Downstairs in the pub, a girl was sweeping up. I paid her for the room, brushed some of the mud off my shoes and opened the door. Somewhere across the fields and streams stood Mansford Hall. I couldn't see it, but I knew it was there.

The railway station was bright in the morning sun, washed clean by the night's rain. Its telephone box shone spick and span. I dropped a penny into the slot.

'Mansford.'

'May I speak to Mr Cutter?'

'Whom may I say is calling?'

'A guest from last night.'

'Please wait, ma'am.'

There it was, that relic of the old way of things: ma'am. The woman's voice on the other end of the telephone was old too. I wondered if she had even served Churchill when he had visited.

'Hello.' The sound was cheerful. Adam might have been half-cut last night but he was fresh today.

'Hello, Adam.'

'And who might that be?' he called down the crackling and echoing line.

'It's Jane Cawson.'

A pause. 'Hello,' he repeated suspiciously.

'You do remember last night?'

'I do.'

'Good. Did Nick know that Lorelei was getting married?'

'What?' he blurted out.

His surprise was too sharp and quick to be feigned. 'She was getting a marriage exit visa.'

'But she . . .' He broke off.

'But what?' Silence. 'What were you going to say?'

'Just. . .' He broke off again, as if the words were restricted.

'Just what?' He was beginning to annoy me, acting like a child caught in a lie. I hardened my voice. 'Shall I show Comrade Fellowman the note you sent Lorelei about him? I don't think he'll like that you've been talking about him behind his back.'

'Please.'

'What do you think he'll do? Make your house his?' I changed my tone to sound more sympathetic. 'Adam, Lorelei's dead; there's no need to keep her secrets now.'

There was hissing on the line. I waited. Then he spoke three words in that quiet vocal parody of the old carefree upper class. They beat in my head one by one.

'She was pregnant.'

It was a shock, and a rush of thoughts crowded my mind at the news, but I tried not to let it tell in my voice. 'So it was this foreign man's.'

'No,' he said. He sounded reluctant to speak. 'It wasn't. It was . . . It was someone else's.'

The air felt thick. It seemed to weigh on me like in the hot moments before a storm, and I could feel something coming: a terrible knowledge. Words left my lips and I knew what they were, but I could hear them only from a distance. 'Who was –'

He didn't wait for the final sounds. 'Nick's. I think it was Nick's.'

A fit of anger bucked through me. 'No!' I shouted. I just didn't want it to be true. 'It wasn't!' He made no reply. There was just the crackling on the line. My head was ready to crack in two. 'Are you . . . Were they having an affair?'

'If you want to call it that.'

'But how do you know?' I demanded.

A pause, and he replied quite simply. 'She told me.'

'So? She could be lying! She was always lying.'

'I don't think she was about them having an affair.'

'Why?'

And then the final answer. 'I called him. He didn't even deny it.' And that was it. I sank down.

What did I feel then? What was it that racked my body in that little call box for so long that Adam asked if I was still there? It wasn't fury, or a sense of betrayal, that made me sob

314

and then retch. It was loss, I think. Anger and hurt were there too, but it was the loss that left me unable to see anything but a blur in front of me, and the flesh of my wrist going white as I twisted the telephone cord around it in coil after coil.

When I had overheard Nick on the telephone to an unknown hollow and metallic voice, he had said that the drug, norethisterone, would have prevented Lorelei ending up 'like she did'. I had presumed that referred to how she had died. But now I knew: he had meant it would have stopped her conceiving. I had no idea really if he had been using me to test that vile drug, but, somehow, even if he had, it was nothing next to this.

I breathed slowly and laboriously, like a hospital patient with infected lungs. 'Did Nick know she was pregnant?'

'I told him.'

There was a terrible pulsing in my head. It took me a while to speak again, as I tried to take in what he said and what it all meant – everything that had gone before, and everything that was still to come. 'What was between them?' I asked, keeping my voice as even as I could.

Adam sighed. 'Oh, who knows? They always seemed to want each other more when they hated one another.'

'What do you mean?' I needed to know if Nick's desire for Lorelei had crowded out any real feelings for me.

He sucked in a deep breath. 'Well, I remember a dinner party at the house.' He paused. 'Are you sure you want to hear this?'

'Yes,' I said firmly.

'Your choice. I remember dinner at their house – Lorelei's house now – all through the meal they were needling each other. "Nick thinks he's very amusing; it's lucky somebody

315

does." "Lorelei looks like she needs to be taught a lesson – better make it a simple one." In the end, she threw her wine at him and he jumped up, ran around the table and slapped her. After that we didn't see them for an hour, only heard them upstairs making the furniture bounce on the floorboards.' His voice drifted. 'You look so much like her, you know.'

So Lorelei was engaged to a foreigner, or to someone in the DUK who could get her out if she were granted a marriage exit visa. She had therefore made a deal with Fellowman: she would put him in contact with the American doctor who supplied the medicines in return for that visa. But Nick found out about their deal. And then Adam told him Lorelei was pregnant with his child.

'She met Ian Fellowman at your parties, didn't she?' I asked.

'Yes. But I –'

'What medicine was she supplying him with?' I wanted to know everything now.

Another pause. 'Well, you didn't hear it from me, but I was told Comrade Burgess picked up a dose of the clap – that's why he wasn't around on Liberation Day. Some nice little soldier, they say.' There had certainly been rumours about Guy Burgess for a long time. 'The Americans have these wonderful new antibiotics that clear it right up, so Ian was getting some for him. Besides, Guy could hardly go to one of the state doctors, could he? The Secs would be looking through his files before he had even left the room. No, the Party doesn't like nancies very much. All that sex without making babies. It interferes with your duty to the state. Very bad for morale.'

*

On the way home, the train passed a hoarding and I recognized the full-page advert of Britain cut in half, with ten occupied babies' cribs on the DUK side, nine on ours, and an empty cot bearing the words YOUR CHILD. STRENGTH IN NUMBERS!

Strength in numbers. In the new era, the state would take the place of the family, or, at least, that was what many had suggested. The regime itself was tight-lipped on the subject, probably because Blunt felt that we weren't yet ready to ditch our parents, our siblings and our children. It didn't affect me now. I had no family to speak of.

When I reached home, I dropped my mud-spattered evening dress on the bedroom floor, hid my winnings from the roulette table, bathed, washed my hair and put on more sensible clothes to go out into the afternoon.

'Hello, Charles,' I said, as I entered the surgery.

'Mrs Cawson.' He tore a sheet of paper from his typewriter. 'Damn thing keeps chewing up the pages.'

'You need a new one.'

'The licence is taking months to be approved.'

'That must be frustrating. Oh, by the way, I bumped into a friend of mine in the Ministry of Building yesterday. She said that they often send out notices of reassignment for homes but don't follow through on them. So you might find you're staying in your flat after all.' I had resolved that I would ask Fellowman to arrange for Charles to stay where he was, as part of my price for the information he wanted.

He looked cautiously hopeful. 'Did she? Well, that would be wonderful news.'

At that moment, Nick wandered out of his consulting

317

room and looked up from a set of patient notes. 'Hello, darling. What are you doing here?' he said.

'I just wanted to see my husband. It feels like so long since I saw you.'

'You're very sweet.'

The telephone on Charles's desk rang and he answered it. 'The consulting rooms of Nicholas Cawson, Charles O'Shea speaking. Yes, please wait.' He put his hand over the mouthpiece. 'The ministry.'

'I see. Better put it through, and by the way,' he said to Charles, 'a few people are coming to ours for dinner tonight. Why don't you join us?' He looked to me. 'That's all right, isn't it, darling?'

'Yes, of course,' I said. 'Seven o'clock.'

'Thank you,' said Charles.

'Oh,' Nick said to me, sighing. 'I was accosted by Patricia next door this morning, asking about Lorelei again. She said she heard Hazel playing a record of one of Lorelei's plays or something. I couldn't make out what she was on about.'

'It was probably the radio.'

'Probably. Patricia can be very tiresome. Well, let's hope she leaves us alone from now on.' He returned to his room and closed the door. I could hear him speaking on the line.

On the spur of the moment, I took Charles by the arm and led him towards the corridor. He was so bemused he banged his hip on the corner of the desk. 'Damn it!' he spat, screwing up his face and thumping the wood to distract from the pain.

'Oh, God, your wound,' I said.

'It's all right,' he muttered.

We moved out to the stairwell. 'Charles, what was Lorelei like? As a person.'

He pursed his lips. 'I don't know what to say about her, really.'

'Was she stepping out with anyone?'

He looked at his feet, embarrassed. 'I don't know. She wouldn't tell me things like that.'

'Maybe there was someone special? A boyfriend? Anyone foreign? Or in the DUK?'

'Foreign?' He had a blank look.

'Charles, I want to say something.'

'Yes?'

'You and I have had our differences in the past.'

'One or two but –'

'You've been very good to Nick, using what influence you have in the Party to help him. So I want to thank you for that. Thank you.'

'It was my pleasure, Mrs Cawson.'

'I'm glad. Charles.' I put my hand on his arm and left it there. 'Would you do something for me?'

'If I can.'

'Nick has been through so much recently. And now he's applying to join the Party. I worry that he's overdoing it.'

'Overdoing it? I wouldn't think so.'

'I expect you're right. You probably know him better than I do. But he has had a lot to deal with, hasn't he?'

'Well, yes, no doubt.'

'Today, for instance. He must have had lots of calls.'

'A normal number.'

'Do you recall them all?'

He looked proud. 'Yes,' he said.

'All work, I expect.' He furrowed his brow. 'Or some weren't?'

He hesitated and looked back to his desk. 'I should probably get back to work.'

'Yes, of course. But if you do find he's overworking himself, let me know and I'll do something about it.'

'Well, all right, yes.'

'Thank you.'

Sitting on my bed that afternoon, I supposed no one would ever know whether it was Nick who was the father of Lorelei's child or whether it was the other man, the one who was going to marry her and take her out of the country. She might not have known herself, of course.

When NatSec had suggested Nick was involved in Lorelei's death, I had thought the idea ludicrous. But, after what I had learned about norethisterone and what Adam had told me about Lorelei's plan to betray Nick, the thought had wormed its way into my mind. I had precious few facts, though, only suspicions and vague ideas.

There was still one thread I could follow, however. What Ian Fellowman had told me had also enabled me to work out the role of someone else: Crispin, the man who was to secretly receive Lorelei's disguised negative.

'Crispin could get me papers if I needed them, couldn't he?' I said to the man in the seedy Soho print store while the presses rumbled in the background.

'Get the fuck out of my shop,' he replied in a low growl.

I checked the street. Stephanie the hairdresser was

watching, ready in case something happened. The first time I had come here she had told me that producing 'snide papers' was one of the shady side lines the print shop operated; and, five months earlier, Lorelei had supplied Crispin with a photograph – the sort of drab, head-and-shoulders picture that you used for passports or visas – hidden in a book. When Fellowman revealed that Lorelei had later asked him for a marriage exit visa – presumably after Crispin had failed to come up with the goods – it was clear what she had wanted here.

'I'm going nowhere,' I said. He scoffed at me. 'No? All right.' I reached into my purse and pulled out a bundle of notes – some of my winnings from the previous night. His eyes widened at the amount of money I was holding in front of him and he wiped his mouth, as if thinking something over. 'How much for an exit visa? Will he do it for a hundred? I've got more if needs be.'

He was struggling with the decision. His hands seemed to itch for the notes, edging towards mine and flitting back. That told me all I needed to know.

'Jane!' It was Stephanie. I looked outside to see three men walking rapidly up the street towards us. 'Police!' she shouted.

I froze. I couldn't afford to have them asking questions and reporting on my movements.

'Christ, get in the back!' barked the man. He didn't want the police speaking to me any more than I did. He lifted the counter and I pressed through into a murky room. It had a paper-strewn desk along one wall, with big windows above; a white-painted stage in one corner was surrounded by photographic lights, and a camera on a tripod pointed at a stool in the centre. In the opposite corner, paint was peeling off what appeared to be an exit to the street.

I heard the shop door open, the bell above it clanking wildly. 'All right, Toby?' a gruff voice asked. I pressed myself to the wall beside the doorway. 'How's business?'

'Not been good this month.'

'I wasn't actually asking. I don't care. Come on.' The cash register opened. I bent my neck around to catch a glimpse. All I could see was the shopkeeper's back.

I tried moving across the doorway to see from a different angle, but didn't check where my feet were going and my left shoe connected with something hard. There was a metallic ring. I looked down to see I had kicked a pail a few centimetres. It wasn't a loud sound and I prayed no one had heard it, but everything had gone quiet out in the shop. 'I can get you more next month,' Toby said.

'Do you think I'm a fucking idiot?' the gruff voice demanded. 'What was that?'

'Just some tart. The usual.'

'Is it, now? I haven't actually seen that before. Could be nice. You stay here.' I ran to the other side of the room, behind the desk. A bear-like man with a heavy brown beard entered, followed by one of the other policemen. 'All right, love?' he said in a thick voice. I didn't reply. He appraised me and smirked to his mate. 'Don't know why you're here. You could do better. Magazines. Proper stuff.' The one behind him chuckled. 'Or for your old man, is it?' I didn't reply. 'Come on, speak up. I said speak up.'

My mouth was dry. 'My old man.'

'Bit of a game for him?' He walked slowly behind me. His breath had the tang of beer. 'He likes that sort of thing.'

I had to say something. 'Yes. A game.'

'Lucky him.' He moved out in front of me again. 'Well, don't let us stop you.' I stood there unmoving; the air seemed to smell of them. 'Come on. Been a crap day for us, so cheer us up.'

'How?'

'"How?" she says. Over there. In the light.' He pointed and waited. Terrified, I walked slowly over to the squalid stage and stood, blinking in the weak sun. 'Now show us something.'

'No, it's –'

'Don't annoy me, love. Show us something.'

There was silence as they stood stock still. I would have done anything to get out of there. I lifted the hem of my skirt. 'Come on, you're not a fucking nun.' His voice was sharper now. 'Show us something or maybe we'll make this more official.' I lifted the hem higher so that it reached my underwear. 'Not enough, love. We'll have to take you in, won't we?' The officer behind him nodded.

'What . . . do you want?' I stammered. He pointed to my blouse.

I was terrified of what they could do to me there, without anyone around to care, let alone stop them. I lifted my fingers to the top button but couldn't make them work – they felt stiff and numb.

'Go on!' His voice was rasping and brutal.

I tried to control my fingers. Slowly, I pressed the button through, letting the material of my blouse spread apart. Then the next fastening. The chill air made the skin on my chest prickle. 'More like it,' he said. I stood with it open. 'Not bad. Like I said, magazines.' I stood there, ashamed. 'Keep going.'

There was a crash from out in the shop and I could hear Toby saying, 'Told you not to do that.' The officer looked at his mate and jerked his head. They went out to investigate, and as soon as their backs were turned I rushed over to the rear door. It was locked, with no key in sight. I ran to the desk to look for it. I hunted through, shoving aside a toothbrush in a smeared mug, a box of tooth powder, envelopes full of negatives and a magnifying glass, but found no key. The panic was rising as I tried to think where this man might keep it – somewhere close in case he needed to leave quickly, just as I did. I dashed back to the door and felt along the top of the frame. It was there, cold in my hand, and I shoved it into the lock. The hinges were thankfully well-oiled and I slipped out, closing the door and locking it from the outside. I threw the key aside and hurried away, holding my blouse closed.

34

The house was quiet when I got home. Without taking off my heavy coat, I entered the parlour and was taken aback to see a woman a few years older than me sitting serenely in one of the pair of Queen Anne chairs that Nick had picked up somewhere. She was dressed in black with a pill-box hat that had a veil hanging across her forehead. But the veil didn't – couldn't – disguise the fact that she had a very pretty face. It was round, the type you saw in eighteenth-century paintings of nymphs and satyrs, expertly powdered. Beside her, Nick was in the other chair, his legs crossed. They were both silent, as if they had been waiting for me.

'Darling, this is Bella Singent,' said Nick.

'I'm so sorry,' I said. 'I didn't expect you until seven.' In fact, it had entirely slipped my mind that people were coming to dinner. Bella smiled sweetly and rose. She had long dark hair that shone in the sunlight. 'I'm so pleased to meet you.' I had been somewhat on edge about meeting these old friends of Nick and Lorelei. Bella and Lorelei had trained as actresses together decades earlier; but Bella had soon married someone steadfast and comfortably off and never set foot on a stage again.

'And you too,' she said, kissing my cheeks.

Nick went to the drinks cabinet. 'Would you like something?' he asked. I noticed that there were three glasses on the side table with a little white wine in each.

'Thank you,' I said. He poured out another half-glass from a bottle. They sat and watched as I drank.

'The soot really is terrible right now, isn't it?' said Bella.

I looked at my reflection in the wine glass. 'Oh, no,' I said, seeing a film of grime on my face. 'I had no idea.' I scrabbled about in my handbag for a handkerchief.

'Take mine,' she said, holding out a square of linen.

'Oh, I couldn't. I wouldn't want to make it filthy.' She shrugged and smiled again. I took it and dabbed at my face, making little difference.

'So you're going to be a new mother to dear little Hazel,' said Bella.

'Well, I don't know . . . I mean to say —'

'She's a real poppet. I do want to see her,' she told Nick.

'Yes, of course.'

'Nick tells me you're a teacher.'

'Yes, I am. Well, not at the moment.'

'Oh, I'm sure it's hard in London. A different sort of place from Herne Bay.'

'Yes. Yes, it is,' I replied, a little surprised that she knew quite so much about me.

The door opened and a big man with a jet-black heavy moustache and an unmistakable military bearing entered.

'This is Bella's husband, Major Kenneth Singent,' Nick said.

'How do you do?' I said, holding out my hand.

He shook it solidly. 'How do you do?' he repeated, taking up the unclaimed glass of wine and saying nothing more.

'So how are things guarding us all, Major?' asked Nick.

'We're doing our job,' he replied.

'I'm sure you are. The Major's regiment is currently

standing on top of the Wall, ensuring none of us are tempted to leap over.'

'We're making sure the Americans don't invade.'

'Yes, indeed,' Nick said. 'Cheers.'

'I went to Herne Bay years ago,' said Bella. 'So charming. However did you and Nick meet?'

'On the platform at Waterloo Station.'

'Oh, yes, that's right.' She looked at Nick. 'How romantic.'

'It has suited us,' I said. 'Hasn't it?'

'Yes,' Nick replied. 'Handsomely.'

'I'd better get started in the kitchen,' I said.

We were soon joined by Charles and by Nick's colleague Sanderson Morton, a neurologist at Guy's. Over vegetable soup, Morton told us how he had found a Parasite in his department and dismissed him. 'I'm glad to say that one of my more socially aware workers reported him. I should have informed the Department of Labour, but he had a family so I just gave him his cards and told him to go,' he said, spooning the soup to his mouth. I held myself back from taking him to task about this man and his family.

Nick followed with a funny story about a woman who had come into his surgery having mistaken it for a dressmaker's, and we all laughed. After that, we talked about the five-year building plan. Even Charles seemed to open up – perhaps it was the three glasses of wine that he had in him. Morton was expounding on the future frontiers of medicine. I chose my moment.

'What's norethisterone?' I said.

Morton jolted at the word. I thought back to that voice on the other end of the telephone when I had overheard Nick.

'Sorry, darling, what did you say?' Nick asked.

Unlike Morton, Nick's face betrayed nothing of what he was thinking. I wanted him to be off-balance, to tell me the truth, not what he had crafted as the truth. 'Norethisterone – is that right? Someone called for you today,' I told him.

'Who was it?'

'Just someone on the telephone. Didn't give their name, said they wanted norethisterone. Is it a medical thing?'

'I don't think I've heard of it,' he replied. He turned to Morton. 'Have you?'

'No,' Morton said.

'All sorts of things being discovered all the time; can't keep up with them,' Nick continued.

That might have fooled me once. Not any more, I thought.

'It must all be so exciting,' breathed Bella. Her soldier husband continued with his food, showing no interest in the conversation. He was used to straightforward men saying what they thought, direct and unvarnished. He didn't look for unspoken words. I was looking for them all the time now.

I broke a piece of bread and went back to eating. 'I thought it sounded chemical. Well, maybe I misheard him,' I said.

'It was a him, then?'

'Hmmm? Oh, yes, a him.'

Charles spoke, glancing between Nick and me. 'Dr Cawson, have you told Mrs Cawson your good news?'

'No, not yet.'

'Don't keep me in suspense,' I said.

'No. Well, I've made a bit of a strategic alliance. Do you remember Ian Fellowman, Burgess's Assistant Secretary?'

'Yes.' Where was this going? What had Fellowman done?

'His usual GP has finally decided to retire, so I've put myself forward for the job. The Comrade is considering it.'

'That would be quite an honour.' So it sounded like the Assistant Secretary was keeping all his options open. Only Nick didn't know that.

'Now you will have to join the Party,' Charles said.

'Probably,' Major Singent said with a subtle but unmistakable note of disgust.

'Indeed,' Morton added, decisively tapping his index finger on the table. 'Health is a public resource, not private. You have to join. The connections you will make will see you through to the top of the profession. You should take a research trip to Moscow. They are making such strides there in certain fields. I cannot tell you how much I learned during my own visit.' He was becoming animated, clearly getting on to a favourite topic of his. 'They have found entirely new ways to explain diseases of the mind. They understand now that it's all down to socialization or the lack of it. You know how I had some experience in psychiatry during the War – it's related to neurology, of course – but, next to them, British medicine is in the Dark Ages.'

'I'm sure Comrade Fellowman could arrange for a research visit,' Charles commented. 'I could accompany you.'

'I heard their asylums are full of dissenters,' I said.

Morton froze and slowly turned to me. He rested his elbows on the table, knitted his fingers together and looked at me over them. 'American propaganda. A few unstable agitators, no more. And where better for them? It keeps them safe, and it keeps society safe.'

The image of Rachel being dragged out of the room flashed before me. I wanted to tell him that I had seen inside one of these asylums. 'Couldn't they be left in society?' I said. 'We're social creatures, aren't we?'

He smiled politely and raised his eyebrows at Nick in humour. 'It's very interesting to have the opinions of women such as you, but I really think this is best left to the professionals,' he said.

'Then perhaps you can help me with something.'

'And what would that be?'

'Tell me this. What's it all for? I mean this new psychology.'

'For?' His mouth twitched in something that might just have been the start of anger and he rolled the word on his tongue as if it were distasteful. 'For. Mrs Cawson, I was in Vienna in 1938 to see Sigmund Freud only just escape the country with his life. His sisters lost theirs. What do you think the Nazis had planned for Britain? Can you think for one second where it would have ended? Fascism is built on psychosis – on megalomania. It is the only communicable disease of the mind. And it is a doctor's duty to fight disease. That is what it is *for.*'

'Yes, I see,' I said. There was strength behind the point and I felt guilty.

Charles changed the conversation. 'When will you speak to Comrade Fellowman?' he asked Nick.

'Not yet.'

'At the dinner?'

Nick glanced at me out of the corner of his eye, as if he had been keeping something from me. 'Perhaps.'

'What dinner?' I asked.

'Fellowman invited us to a big bash in honour of some Russians next week.'

'That sounds good,' I said.

'Yes.'

'When?'

He hesitated. 'I didn't think you would want to come.'

'Why wouldn't I?' He looked uncomfortable. It was strange – he was definitely hiding something. 'Go on, tell me.'

He cleared his throat. 'It's going to be at the Brookfield Hotel.' I closed my eyes and felt the pounding that I had felt the last time – the only other time – I had been in the ballroom of that hotel with Nick and Charles and Ian Fellowman. 'I –'

'No, it's fine. More bread, anyone?' I forced it away.

There was a pause, which Charles broke, nervously. 'I'll have some, thank you,' he said, reaching for the plate. 'It's very good. Fresh.'

'Deliciously so,' added Bella.

She began talking about a new bakery near her and people joined in, the topic of food always one to raise interest. And after a while, the atmosphere lightened again. Even Charles made people laugh with a story about being caught scrumping a crateful of pears when he was at school and being made to eat them all as punishment. He was apparently ill for days.

When I began to clear the table, he offered to help. 'Thank you,' I said.

'It was very nice, Mrs Cawson,' he said, as we entered the kitchen. 'It can't be easy making something like that from whatever's available today.'

'Oh, you find ways to get the ingredients.' I passed him a stack of plates and his hands wobbled a little. 'Can you take these through?' He was a lot more pleasant when he was squiffy, I decided. I would have to try to keep him like that. Dilute his morning tea with scotch? Make his coffees Irish to match his name? Some way to keep him mildly inebriated.

'My pleasure.' He went back into the dining room and I followed him carrying a china mug of water. Through the bannister I caught sight of Hazel watching us with a look of curiosity on her face.

We talked about the prospects for change at the top of the Party, should Blunt ever decide to retire – there were few other Secretaries with his stature and bearing, which meant it was hard to predict what would happen. 'But who could replace Comrade Blunt?' Nick said. 'I can't see . . .'

I lifted my drink but as I did so something struck me like a shard of light. Lorelei's last words, *Who's there? I can't see.* They echoed in my mind.

And then the mug fell from my hand, splitting in two and spilling the water everywhere. Nick pushed back from the table as it spread towards him, and Charles jumped up to grab what was left of the mug, setting the base upright again and mopping it up with his napkin. For his part, Morton just watched me as if he were studying a lab rat in a cage. 'Oh, I'm so sorry,' I said. But I said it with only half my mind on my own words. The rest was a jumble of thoughts and guesses. I kept turning the words over and over.

'It's all right, darling, it's quite all right,' Nick said in a soothing tone.

'I know it is,' I said angrily. 'I dropped a cup, that's all.'

'I didn't mean –'

'I know what you meant.' He meant that I was acting irrationally: arguing with Morton; feeling upset when I discovered where the dinner with Fellowman was to be held. Apparently smashing the damn crockery for no reason. At least he didn't suspect the real reason that my mind was churning. I had to keep it to myself for a bit longer. I left the room.

'Is there something I can do?' I heard Charles ask.

'No, just leave it,' Nick answered him.

In the kitchen I noticed my palm was bleeding – I had cut it on the sharp china when it broke. Running it under the cold tap numbed away the pain.

With a clean handkerchief pressed on to the wound, I went back into the dining room to find them all sitting silently smoking. It was the kind of silence that said they had been speaking in hushed tones the moment before but had stopped when I entered.

'Anyway, shall we go to the Duck?' said Nick in an unworried tone of voice, addressing the men.

'Why not?' Morton replied, putting a lighted match into the bowl of his pipe. 'I think we've finished here, haven't we?'

'I'll take a cab home,' Bella said sweetly to her husband. 'There should be some on the street.'

'Unless you would like a hand with the dishes, darling?' Nick asked me.

'I can do them – you go,' I said, taking the upper half of the broken mug and placing it inside the base.

Nick stayed back while the others went to the door.

'I'm sorry,' he said. 'It's where they have all these functions. I don't know if it's security, or if they just like it or . . .

oh, look, I'm babbling. I will understand if you don't want to come.' We were both straining to sound unstrained.

I looked him straight in the eye. 'I'll come,' I said. 'I can't get away from it.'

'No,' he said. He shifted uncomfortably on his feet. 'But it's so soon. I don't want you to . . . I think we have to recognize that it could make you feel unwell again. You've been a bit . . .' He took my hand in his.

'I'll survive. Who else will be there?'

'Oh, lots of people with important titles and empty heads. Jane, I really do think you should speak to someone about what happened to you. What you've been through.'

'I'm fine.'

'If you say so. Well, I'll be back soon.'

'All right.'

He joined the others outside. I watched them walk towards the pub. When they could no longer be seen, I ran out to the telephone box across the road and called Tibbot's number, eager to tell him what I had realized from the words Lorelei had spoken when I had found her.

There was a second of metallic clicking, and then the ringing tone. It went on and on and I willed him to pick it up. At the same time, I was watching through the glass panels, should Nick and the other men happen to return – they might decide the walk wasn't worth the candle, or the Duck might be closed, or there might be some other reason that would bring them back to find me making a strange telephone call from outside the home. I tried to think of an excuse in case I needed it, but none seemed plausible. 'Come on,' I muttered into the receiver. Eventually, I hung up and hurried back to the house. I would call him as soon as I could get away again.

Hazel was standing in the hallway, looking at me quizzically. 'Who were you phoning?' she asked.

'It's nothing. Just a friend of mine I'm seeing this week.' She looked at the telephone in the hallway. 'It's not working very well,' I said. 'So, now that the men have all gone out, what shall we girls do? Would you like to listen to the radio? Or play a game?'

Her eyes seemed to blur behind water, which she rubbed away. 'The Odeon's showing *Victory 1945*. Can we go?'

I pursed my lips. It was nine o'clock but seeing her mother's film might do her good. 'Well, it's a bit late, but all right.'

She perked up at my answer. 'Thank you.'

Soon we were on a tram as it bullied a car out of its path – Socialist transport took precedence over private vehicles. Hazel looked up at me. 'Will you come to my mum's funeral?' she asked.

'If you want me to.'

'Yeah. Please.' She bit her lip to stop herself grinning at a private thought. 'I think Charles is sweet on you.'

'Oh, I'm sure you're wrong.' But it warmed me to see her almost smile.

A bored seventeen-year-old in the ticket booth took our money and hunted around for a pen. 'Machine's not working. Got to write out your tickets,' she mumbled. Inside the crowded auditorium we found it was so hot with all the bodies that the condensation was running down the walls. A couple of Soviet guest soldiers entered behind us with their British girlfriends. They went to the best seats in the house, and the four occupants of those seats got up and moved. I didn't blame those girls, really. The Russians could get them extra coupons and into the Lyons Corner Houses. Our empire was over; theirs was just beginning.

The seats were covered with what had clearly once been velvet but had since been rubbed almost bare – not unlike the movie, which was also showing the ravages of time, its images old and scratched. And yet Lorelei still shone in it like the sun. Oh, they could rip her from the posters, but they could hardly cut her from the film. She mourned her executed boyfriend like Shakespeare's Juliet, and then raised a pistol to a Nazi officer. He fell and she showed no emotion. Our heroine. Our past and our future.

When the crowds on the screen cheered the *Archangel* steaming up the Thames, it occurred to me that these people just didn't know what they were letting themselves in for: the suspicions and doubts, the simple hardships of everyday life. I could feel the same thought flitting around the room too, and, as if to make the point, there was a brief power cut soon after. It came just as Lorelei began her speech about the coming dawn, the day when we would all live and build together. We had to wait in the dark for the picture to return, so I took the opportunity to slip out to the wooden call box in the lobby, telling Hazel I was going to the ladies' room. This time, the line connected.

'Tibbot,' he mumbled.

I was overjoyed to hear he was there. I began to blurt out everything without even saying hello. 'I know what was wrong when she died. I've realized now,' I said.

'What?'

'According to Grest, when I went into the bathroom,

Lorelei said to me, "Who's there? I can't see." But why? The lamp was on; it wasn't dark.'

'So the steam –'

'There wasn't any steam. The room was clear. But what if she meant exactly what she said – that she couldn't see. Her sight had gone.'

There was silence on the other end. He was contemplating it. 'It could be,' he said, but his voice was guarded. 'I can't tell why, though.'

'Could Grest have done that to her?'

'Well, if you beat someone badly enough they can lose their sight. But that would have left huge bruises, fractures probably. There weren't any.'

'He said there was splashing about, like a fight. That could have been her panicking to get out.'

Tibbot cleared his throat. 'It's possible.' I could tell he wasn't sold on the idea.

I came to the point. 'Either way, we need to talk to him. Can you meet tomorrow afternoon?'

'All right,' he sighed. 'Call me at the station in the morning. Eleven o'clock. Give your name as Mrs Stevens – I'll leave a message for you if I'm out.'

'Thank you.'

Back in the auditorium, Hazel looked at me curiously as I took my seat. The film had been resurrected after the power cut and Lorelei's speech played again. Beautiful in the sunset, her face filled the screen. As you watched, you could see the whole future of our country reflected in her irises. They eventually faded to black.

When the film ended, the lights came up to reveal Hazel's face awash with tears and her skin red. I hadn't noticed in the dark, and kicked myself for not guessing that seeing her mother move and speak, then disappear, would sadden her so. Hazel had never had a chance to say good-bye, and this was the closest that she would ever get. 'Are you all right?' I asked. An idiotic question, but one that we always ask at those moments, as if we don't know the truth.

'Mum was really beautiful, wasn't she?' she managed to get out, although her voice was strangled in her throat.

'Yes. She was.' And she was, really she was. Like a picture. But such beauty couldn't go unpunished by the world. Like Cassandra, her gift was also her undoing.

Where had it taken her? When Nick and Lorelei had first watched this film, they couldn't have known what the pictures would mean. They would mean Nick slowly watching the woman he had married slip away from him to become a part of the political world. And then the jealousy and pain as he learned of her affair with John Cairncross – an affair ended by a public trial and a confession of counter-revolution that would also cast Lorelei out of the spotlight. And the final image would be her lying under ripples of water.

35

Tibbot and I sat on a bench in Victoria Park as he threw bread to the birds on the pond. 'Bloody ducks eat better than I do,' he muttered.

'Better than most people. Well, this side of the Wall.'

'They had better be careful or they might just end up as a Sunday roast.'

'Is that your plan?' I said.

'Not this week. I don't have the mushroom sauce to do them justice.' He stopped and nodded towards the path.

A bruised figure was walking quickly towards us. He looked all around to see who else might observe him here, before sitting. 'What do you want?' he said in an angry tone. 'I'm busy.' I gazed at Grest's face, curious to know how he had explained to his colleagues the marks that Tibbot's fists had left on him.

'Doing such important work,' I replied.

'Tell me what you want or I leave.'

I didn't think he would, but there seemed little point in pushing him. 'You said before that on the day she died, you heard me go into the bathroom, and then she shouted, "Who's there? I can't see."'

'So?'

'Why would that be? That she couldn't see?'

He took a long look at me. 'You're a proper one, aren't you?'

'Mrs Cawson has a new friend,' said Tibbot. 'Comrade Fellowman. He's best mates with Guy Burgess, you know.'

'A true guardian angel.'

'So you really should answer the question. Was there something wrong with her sight?'

Grest waited again before answering. He was beginning to enjoy himself. 'Tart was blind as a fucking bat. At least she was then.'

So that confirmed what I thought. 'Did you do that to her?' Tibbot demanded. 'Smack her too hard?'

'No.'

'Stop lying to us!'

'I'm not, mate. She was like that when I got there.'

Tibbot looked at him suspiciously. 'Slipped your mind to tell us last time, did it?'

Grest leaned back casually, watching the truth dawn on us. 'Don't work for you, do I? I wasn't exactly in the mood to natter.'

'But you are now?'

He smirked. 'Well, I've been thinking about it. You see, Cawson called me the day before it happened. Said she was doing the dirty on us and I had to go round there to get the last of the stuff and the ledger. Now when I got there, I found her pegging out and myself in the middle of it all. So I had no choice – I had to keep the blues away from it and make sure no one investigated too far. You want to tell me the timing was coincidence?'

I understood what he was implying. 'But how could Nick plan it like that?' I said, confused.

'He's the doctor, not me. Something in her food, her

340

drink. That Champagne, I should think. It wouldn't need to be to the minute.'

No, it wouldn't have to be to the minute. Just so long as Grest was there around the same time, he would make sure any investigation was superficial. But then I had stumbled in and set everything awry. Poor us. Poor Lorelei.

'What did he use?'

'Don't ask me. Ask him.'

'What exactly did he say?' Tibbot asked, tapping his fingers together thoughtfully at the information.

'Just that. She was stabbing us in the back so I should get the stuff and bring it to him. Then things would go on like before, but without her.'

'Did he tell you to hurt her?'

'Not in so many words, but she wasn't going to just hand it all over tied up in a fucking ribbon, was she?' Tibbot looked faintly disgusted. 'Right, well, unless you want any more little stories?'

'Go on, then, fuck off,' Tibbot muttered to him.

Grest walked away, and we watched his back recede along the path. He had a rolling sort of gait now, casual, unconcerned.

'Could you have tests done on her body?' I asked after we had both sat, mulling over what Grest had told us.

'Well, her blood and hair could be tested for chemical traces, but it's a NatSec case, so I can't touch it. And, even if I could, we don't know what they should be looking for – they can't test for every drug known to man.'

'She's being cremated tomorrow. After that, we'll never know.' I stared at the monument to the Soviet sailors who had died in the battle for London. Their names were carved into the mottled marble block shaped like a cruiser. Someone had laid fresh red flowers on it – Pioneers, perhaps, or one of the Soviet guest regiments.

'My guv'nor called me in for a word this morning,' Tibbot said after a while. 'NatSec's been on to him.'

I understood what he was getting at. 'You think you'll be out?'

'The station's getting a political officer from next week. I know who it is. He's not a pal. So it's for the best if I toddle off, probably – well, retirement wasn't far off anyway. And that's that.'

I had the impression it was more of a blow than he was letting on. The police, after all, had been his life. 'What will you do with your time?' I asked.

'Fishing. Lots of fishing.'

'That's your hobby, is it?'

'No idea.'

'What do you mean?'

'Haven't tried it yet.'

'Never?'

'How hard can it be? Sit by a river. Pole. Bit of string. Worm.' I smiled. After a moment he spoke again. 'Jane, it looks like your husband has some responsibility for Lorelei's death. He sent Grest to her and that led to her drowning. But there's no real evidence that he drugged her.' He pointed to Grest's retreating back. 'Whatever he thinks or says – it can't be trusted.'

'But you think he's telling the truth, don't you?'

He looked pained. 'Yes,' he said after a while.

36

The bedside clock said it was after nine when I woke the next morning, Friday, in the spare bedroom. I had told Nick I was having a bout of insomnia and wouldn't want to disturb him – in truth, I just hadn't wanted to spend the night in the same bed as him. I wouldn't usually sleep nearly so late either, but recent events had left me exhausted. I heard voices downstairs. 'Who was –' I began, as the bedroom door opened. But it wasn't Nick, as I had expected, standing there. It was Sanderson Morton, observing me. I was too taken aback to say anything.

'Your husband has asked me to talk to you,' he said. He was carrying a black leather bag.

'Has he?' was all I could reply.

'Yes.'

'Why?'

'He thinks that you may be having a difficult time right now.' He walked over and sat on a stool in front of the dresser. 'You recently suffered something very distressing.' I couldn't think what to say. 'He told me you suffered a miscarriage. That must have been a terrible event for you.'

'Yes,' I whispered, knocked for six by the invasiveness, the directness.

He looked as if he were broaching a topic he found difficult himself. 'Mrs Cawson – this can be quite a delicate subject – you know about shell shock, don't you?'

'Yes.'

'It comes from being in a very stressful situation. Essentially, your mind attunes to that level of stress. Then it can't cope when you're in a normal situation. You suffer panic, insomnia, general unhappiness. That sort of thing. This is something that Soviet doctors have recently discovered and passed the knowledge on to us. So, believe it or not, what you are going through now is something like shell shock.' He opened the clasp on his bag with a click that seemed to ring off the walls.

'What do you mean?'

He turned on a small electric lamp. 'Lie back,' he said. My nerves were stretched taut, but I did so and he peered in my eyes. 'Look up,' he said, pulling down my lower eyelid. 'And now look down.' He released me and timed my pulse. His fingers on my wrist were oily. I watched his face as the second hand whirred around the dial on his watch. 'Do you think about it a lot?'

'Yes,' I said, truthfully.

'I can give you something that will lift your mood, so you don't dwell too much on it. From there, you can recover at your own pace. It's healthier in the long run.'

'I just want to deal with it myself.'

'I understand. And that is to be commended. But sometimes we need help from our friends and family.'

'Please just leave me alone.'

'I have treated many men with shell shock. Believe me, you will recover far more quickly if you give yourself a rest from those thoughts.' He took a phial and syringe from his bag.

'I don't want it,' I said.

'It will help you.' He drew a line of liquid up into the glass of the syringe.

'I don't want it,' I said again, pushing him away.

'Now, Mrs Cawson –'

'No!' I cried.

'Mrs Cawson!' He grabbed my wrist from under the blanket and dragged it up, exposing my arm. 'Do you want me to get your husband up here?' I struggled to get out of bed, but he was a big man and used his weight against me. All I could see was Rachel, dragged away in her hospital, spitting and screaming out in raw pain.

'Morton!' He and I both spun around at the sound, to see Nick in the doorway. 'What the hell are you doing? I said nothing of this.'

I wrenched my arm free. 'I said I don't want it!'

Morton glared at him, then at me, put a cap on the syringe and shoved it back in his bag. 'A word,' he muttered to Nick as he left the room.

'Jane –' Nick began, coming over to me and taking my hand.

'Leave me alone,' I said, drawing it away. He glanced at me, and then followed Morton out.

I lay there shaking. They were downstairs, arguing, but I couldn't make out the words. Morton seemed to leave, and Nick came back up. He stood at the foot of the bed and swept his hands over his hair. 'I don't know why he did it like that – that was wrong of him – but he was trying to help you,' he said, keeping his voice under control.

'He was attacking me.'

'It just got out of hand.' He sat on the edge of the bed. 'Christ. Morton and his bloody Russian ideas. I wish he had left them over there where he found them. He can't even see how brutal they are.'

Could any of us? Stuck, now, in the middle. Nick's American orders, Morton's Russian ideas.

'Will you leave me alone?' I asked.

He nodded. 'Yes, of course. I'm sorry. I'm sorry. I have to go to work anyway.'

He left and went to his study. I could hear him opening and closing drawers, and then his steps as he went down the stairs and out into the back garden. I hauled myself to Hazel's room, which overlooked the garden. Below me, Nick emerged from the shed hefting a rusted old brazier into the middle of the lawn. He crossed back towards the house and bent over to pick up something just out of my view before going back to the brazier and dumping what he carried into the iron cage. Small, folded pages spilled in. I guessed what they were. Pages that he had found himself unable to destroy, no matter how much he had wanted to.

After that he took a box of matches from his pocket and lighted the corner of one of the pages. The flame spread up the edge and along the other until the whole thing was a blaze of light. He threw it in and the brazier glowed, sending smoke up into the mist. As he watched them burn, I slipped downstairs to make a telephone call.

Tibbot answered. 'Nick's burning the letters from Lorelei,' I told him.

'Be careful,' his voice crackled down the line.

'I will be.'

I heard the handle of the back door turning. I shoved the receiver into the cradle and flew up the stairs as quietly

346

as I could, all the while listening to Nick's footsteps through the hallway. I heard him stop by the telephone. Had I put the receiver on the wrong way around? Had I moved it from where it was normally kept? But he opened the front door and I watched him from our bedroom window as he stepped out. He halted and I saw his head bow down. Then he turned around and looked up. For what seemed an age he just gazed at me. Then he turned back on his path and walked away.

'What happened?' Tibbot's voice crackled down the line an hour later.

I tapped my fingernails on the hall mirror. 'He came in.'

'Right.'

'Frank,' I said. 'I'm going to confront him. About Lorelei.'

'Oh, Jane,' he said, frustrated. 'What do you think will come of it? He'll tell you the truth? I spend days in rooms questioning people who have killed, raped, stolen. They don't confess even then. He's just going to tell you that you're imagining things.'

'I'm not imagining things.'

'He'll say you are.'

'What else do you suggest?' He was silent. He had to admit that he too could see no other move. 'Frank, I can't go on like this, wondering if he . . .' I broke off, unable to continue, and leaned against the wall, with the handset by my side. 'Can you come here by eleven thirty?' I asked.

He relented. 'Look, it's not easy today,' he said. 'There's some trouble: the Teddies are kicking off a bit, having a go at the coppers. Revenge for Liberation Day, that's the word.'

'I'll do it all. You can just sit in Hazel's room and listen.'

He disliked the idea, but I had known that he would. This would be the last time he would humour me, I suspected. 'All right,' he muttered. 'I'll be there as soon as I can get away.'

'Thank you.'

He hung up and I dialled again.

'The consulting rooms of Nicholas Cawson, Charles O'Shea speaking.'

'Hello, Charles, it's Jane Cawson. Can you put me through to my husband, please?'

'I'm sorry, he's with a patient.'

'Charles, this is urgent,' I said. 'Absolutely urgent.'

'All right,' he replied. He lowered his voice. 'Are you feeling all right?'

'Yes. Thank you. Just put me through, please.' Perhaps he would eavesdrop, but there was little that I could do about that.

The line went quiet for a minute, then there was a click as it was picked up in Nick's room. His voice came on. 'What's the matter?' he asked.

'I've got something to tell you. Show you, really. I don't want you to be shocked.'

'What?' he sounded surprised.

'It's about Lorelei. Her death.'

'What are you talking about? What's it got to do with you?' He was trying to control a burst of anger. It just made me more resolved. 'I had to get rid of a patient for this.'

'It's about her death, Nick. I know something about it.'

He paused. I could picture him struggling with all the possibilities. 'What do you know?'

'I've found something.'

'Then spit it out.'

'She was drugged. By the time I got there, she was already dying.'

Silence again. Longer this time. His voice was slow and measured. 'What on earth are you talking about?'

'She was blind when I got to her and she was dying. She hadn't been beaten up, though, so she must have been drugged.'

'How?'

'The bottle of Champagne. It was on the floor beside her when she died. I think it was in there. They sent over a box of things of hers today and the bottle was in it – they checked it for fingerprints but they won't have tested it for drugs. So it might have some traces in it.' Then I asked a question – a lot was riding on it. 'Do you think I should call the police and tell them?'

I waited. The line hissed and I heard him breathing. If he said yes, I would know he had had nothing to do with her death. If he said no, well . . .

'Take it to the police?' he repeated.

'Yes.' My nerves strained under my skin. 'Do you think I should?'

He paused again. I heard him working it through – what it would mean, how he should answer. Outside, two people were screaming at each other. Just another of the daily disputes we seemed to have these days. Then Nick spoke. 'No. No, I don't think so.'

'You don't?'

349

'No, I think it would be best to wait.'

'All right,' I said, my body collapsing a little. And I saw her again, under the water, her eyes as bright as coral. 'I'll just give it to you.'

'Yes. That's probably best.'

'You will test it, won't you?' Even then I felt a flicker of hope that maybe I was wrong.

He hesitated. 'I can't do it myself, but I know a toxicologist,' he replied slowly.

'And there's her hairbrush,' I said. 'She used it while she was in the bath. Lots of women do that because hair straightens if it's brushed while it's wet. There are hairs still in it – hairs soak up chemicals, don't they?'

'Some. I don't know which. It's not my field.'

'So that's also proof that she was drugged.'

He was being cagey now, instead of angry. 'Yes. Perhaps.'

'Good. Then meet me here at twelve thirty.'

'All right. Have you told anyone else?'

'No. I wanted to keep it between us for now.'

'Good. Yes, that's best. I don't want NatSec grabbing either of us again,' he said. No, I was sure he didn't. 'What first gave you the idea?'

'It just seemed so strange that someone would break into her house, kill her and run away without taking anything.'

'Yes, that's true,' he said.

And what was he thinking now? I wondered. Was he regretting the weeks that had passed? Perhaps he too was picturing her with the locks of her hair drifting out like threads in a stream. We were on each end of a line, trying to fathom what was in the mind of the other. 'Did she have anything worth killing her for? I mean, did she have anything stored from before the War or anything like that? Jewellery?'

'I don't think so. But she kept so much hidden from me it was impossible ever to tell what Lorelei was doing. So it's not out of the question.'

'No. Well, I'll see you here?'

'I'll be there.'

'I love you,' I said. There was a pit in my chest where those words sounded but didn't resonate.

'I love you too.'

I put the telephone down and went to the kitchen. I knew that I should eat something but couldn't. I sat at the table, surrounded by all his possessions, none of them mine, and wondered if he had ever meant any of it. I had. I had meant it all. I felt ill with my thoughts now. The smog had come down heavily enough to seep into the house through cracks in the plaster; you could taste the sulphur at the back of your throat.

One of the old pre-War magazines from the bottom of my wardrobe lay on the table. I opened it at the most-thumbed page to see a review of a play Lorelei had been in. It was some light comedy in which she had fallen in love with someone unsuitable – a writer of comic songs – and she had had to convince her father to approve of their marriage. It came off in the end, of course. According to the critic, the play was mediocre but Lorelei blazed 'like a firework'. So he was in love with her too. The review was printed below a photo of her and her co-star dancing in eveningwear.

I had to keep the nerves down – actors went through the same thing before they went on stage, I knew. Stage fright. I gazed again at Lorelei's face, made up of tiny dots on a page that from a distance looked like her but that, when you got closer, turned into nothing. I tried to pick out a shadow of uncertainty there, a sign that one day it might all fall apart. It had – but not in a way that anyone could have predicted.

Wandering out into the back garden, I found the brazier still smouldering but containing only ashes now. A jackdaw burst from the crack in the bricks where Nick had kept the drugs, sweeping up into the smog and disappearing within seconds. And, as he passed the neighbouring house, I saw a pair of human eyes watching me. Patricia was there again.

Anger got the better of me and I rushed through our house, out the front and hammered on her door. I kept it up until she answered, looking amazed. 'You're going to stop watching us. Now!' I told her furiously.

'What?'

'If I ever catch you watching or listening to what goes on in our house, I'll be putting in a call to the police about how you're always listening to Churchill and talking about buying a fake exit visa to get out. How do you feel about that?'

'But I don't –'

'It doesn't matter, does it? Want a NatSec investigation on your record? How will that go down with your Party branch?'

She looked dumbfounded. I thrust her away from her own door and pulled it hard closed before spinning around and returning to our house.

I stood in the hall, collecting myself. Perhaps that hadn't been the cleverest thing to do, but it was done now. I went to the kitchen and drank some cold water in the hope that it might cool me, but I stayed hot. As I placed the glass back on the sideboard, I checked my watch. Before Tibbot arrived, there was another card that I had to play: to dress the scene like the play that Lorelei's life had been. If Nick were guilty, it might wrong-foot him and lead him to reveal himself. If innocent, then, well, he would perhaps think I was mad, but at least I would know and could tell him it was the stress of the previous weeks but that it was over now. If he forgave me, we could try to rebuild our marriage. It was either that or leave.

I climbed the stairs, slowly, listening to my own breath, just as I had climbed the stairs in her house.

Our bathroom was smaller than hers. The floor was bare boards, not black-and-white tiles, and the bath was barely large enough for me, unlike Lorelei's, which was big enough to float in. Nick had framed and hung a few small propaganda posters on the walls. One showed a line of beetles crawling along a factory floor, with a booted foot about to fall on them. LET'S CRUSH THE PARASITES, read the slogan. IF YOU KNOW SOMEONE SHIRKING WORK, LET HIS MANAGER KNOW. OUR NATION HAS ENEMIES OUTSIDE AND IN.

I pressed down the plug and turned the taps. Tepid water flowed through the steel and fell to the bottom with a thud that quickly became a storm-like gushing.

It will all be over soon, I told myself.

From our bedroom wardrobe, I took the box of her possessions. There was the bottle of Champagne, which I carried through and placed on the floor beside the bath. Then, tucked away at the bottom of the box, I found the record from which I had learned to copy her voice. I removed Nick's player from his study, placed it in the bathroom and set the needle to it. That play, *The Lucky Lady*, started from the speaker once again.

'Five pounds on red. And now all my winnings on black.' All chance.

A knock on the front door told me that Tibbot had arrived. I hurried down to answer it.

But it wasn't Tibbot standing there. It wasn't Nick.

37

Our new land was born in the ashes of war. From the depths of human depravity, we have risen and said: 'No more!' No more will we take from one another all that we can take. No more will we cower before maddened generals. No more will we live in fear of another's force. Henceforth we live and build and work together.

Anthony Blunt, speech to the Communist Party of Great Britain Annual Assembly, relayed on RGB Station 1, Friday, 28 November 1952

'Charles?' I said, confused.

'Dr Cawson sent me to collect a bottle. He said you would give it to me.'

'Did he?' I was lost for words – I just hadn't imagined this move on Nick's part. I hesitated, leaving Charles on the doorstep, as I tried to understand. A cab, the one he must have come in, drove away.

'May I come in?' he asked.

'Yes, all right,' I said, unable to think what else to do.

He stepped over the threshold. 'A bottle and a hair-brush,' he said. 'Dr Cawson was most insistent.' Still I was bewildered. 'Mrs Cawson? Where are they?'

Automatically, I told him the truth. 'Upstairs.'

'Can you get them, please?'

'All right,' I mumbled. And I noticed something strange. Charles was sweating – great drops were oozing from his hairline and beads were running down his neck. It was a cold day and he was sweating hard.

'Mrs Cawson?'

Too confused to refuse, I took a couple of steps up. Then I looked back. And I saw him frozen, his face turned to the stairs, his eyes closed as if he were asleep. But he wasn't asleep: he was listening, transfixed.

Soft and sweet it was drifting down from the record player in Nick's study. Lorelei's voice. 'And what stakes are you playing for tonight?'

Nick would never have sent him for the bottle, of course.

And that's how I realized: Charles O'Shea.

Every time he had answered the telephone, I had heard it. I had joked to myself about making his coffees Irish to match his name. Nick had even told me his father was from Dublin, and yet I hadn't thought of it when I had asked him if Lorelei had a foreign boyfriend, the one she was going to marry and leave with once she got her marriage exit visa. All you needed was one Irish parent to claim a passport.

His eyes opened again and he seemed to wake from her voice.

'Oh, Charles,' I whispered. 'What did you do?'

His eyes met mine and he started to tremble. 'Go up,' he said, pointing. 'Go up.' And I felt no fear of him, only pity, because, as I stood on the stairs, in that moment when everything dissolved and reformed, I could see how it had happened. How, like me, he had been mistaken about those he loved.

But still, as he took a step towards me, I stepped back. Under my feet I felt water. The bath was overflowing and the damp was stretching down the stairs just as it had at Lorelei's house.

He climbed another step and I took one back. Then my limbs were working without thought and I was running to our bedroom. He came after me. And all the way my mind was turning between two poles: how I had misjudged Nick; how I had misunderstood Charles.

I dashed to our bedroom. And before I knew it he was there too, searching the dresser, hunting through my cosmetics, throwing everything on to the floor.

'Where's her hairbrush?' he demanded. 'Where?'

'I haven't got it!' I cried.

'What?' He stared at me.

'I . . . I was making it up.'

He stopped stock still, his mouth opening but unable to find the words. In a moment he too understood. 'You thought Cawson did it.'

'Yes!'

His body seemed to collapse into itself, the air escaping as he sat heavily on the bed and put his hands to his temples. The springs groaned, a harsh metallic sound like a cry of pain. I didn't know what to do, to think. My breath ran fast and shallow. I thought of trying to get out, but I would have had to push past him and could only stare. For a long time he was silent, rubbing his palms on his forehead as if trying to rub away a stain. 'I just wanted . . .' he said, more to himself than to me. 'I . . .'

'I know,' I said, blinking in the misty light through the curtains. 'I can see now. I know.' And I could see now, see

357

all the links in the chain that had brought us here. They were awful and corrupt and selfish.

The clock by my bed ticked. Lorelei laughed again, a reckless whooping cry that rose and faded, seeping into the hard bricks and plaster of the house. I felt that somehow it would stay locked in them, in the fabric of our house. Charles's eyes were a dark, searing red as they looked to me, then down to his hands. He wiped them with his sleeve, leaving little dark patches on the material, and his mouth twisted into a silent sob. Then his arm went back over his face to shut out the world. I recognized that pain, the very sadness of love.

'Were you going to go to Ireland?' I asked. He nodded, his skin glistening below his sleeve. Charles, who, Nick had said, wanted a wife and children more than anything. I guessed what she had told him. 'Did she say the baby was yours?'

He nodded again, a shallow little double dip of his head, gaze downcast, which spoke of a man whose life had slipped from his grasp a long time ago. 'But it wasn't.' It was little more than a whisper.

So that was how it had turned. Her death wasn't the result of ambition or money. Like so many others in our shattered land, she had just wanted out. But they had put a wall up around us, to protect our new state, and he had been her only way through it. So subtle, she had been.

'It wasn't,' he said, tears rolling down his cheeks.

I had to know. 'What did you do?' He didn't reply. 'Charles? What did you do to her?'

And then he spoke. 'I . . . tried to get it out of her.'

My eyes closed and I felt sick. Those final minutes she

had lived through in immeasurable pain. I couldn't help but picture them.

There had been something in her Champagne, yes. Charles had put it there to take away a child he thought was another man's.

He lowered his arm and looked at me. Wet streaks on his skin reflected the light. 'Please,' he said, reaching out a hand. 'Please.' His hands were open, the palms up, begging for understanding.

I had to get away from him, to dispel the image of the pain that had racked her. I knocked his hands away and grasped the mantelpiece, pulling myself to my feet, but my limbs were hardly working and I twisted my ankle. And then I was on my front with his knee on my spine, pinning me to the floor. 'No!' he said. 'Stop!' And a grey mist came down, as if my mind wanted to blot out what was happening. I struggled but his weight was too much for me. Pressing me down.

I tried to think of something to tell him, to convince him to let me go. 'I'll help you,' I said desperately. 'It was an accident, wasn't it?' And he paused, listening. 'Did she drink too much of it?'

He stayed there, unmoving. I waited, hearing his lungs wheeze, until his voice wheedled like a child's. 'I didn't want that,' he said. 'I didn't.'

'I know! I'll tell them that.' If he would just accept it could be true. 'Charles, I'm on your side.' A hesitation, and then he pulled up, just a little.

'Will you?'

'I'll tell them what you told me. Just an accident.' And, with another tiny move, almost imperceptible, his weight shifted away from the knee on my back.

I could feel the situation changing, moving my way, safety in sight. 'I can go –'

But, as I said it, something broke in: a sudden insistent sound from downstairs. The brass knocker on the front door was clacking, ringing through the hollow dark hallway.

'Hello?' a man's loud voice called from outside. I had no idea who it was – the postman with a package or a neighbour calling around. I just prayed it was something they wouldn't let go.

I began to form a word, a cry to beg for help, but, as I lifted my chest to draw in breath, Charles seemed to harden his thoughts and crushed his weight back down on to me, so that I could hardly suck in enough air to breathe. I could only croak out a cry for help so weak that it wouldn't have been heard outside the room.

The door knocker clacked again. The man was still there. I struggled, trying to turn on to my side, but Charles pulled my head back hard by my hair.

'Let me go,' I gasped. 'Let me go.'

The letterbox creaked open. 'Is anybody at home?' Looking in, whoever it was would see only an empty hallway. The letterbox closed again with a dull flapping sound, and we waited, listening, but there was only silence. We stayed there for a long time, long enough for the caller to leave and be swallowed up by the smog. I felt the hope that I had built slipping out of me.

Charles pushed himself away. I no longer had the breath and blood to get up and run. He sat on the bed, shaking still with his own shock and nerves. 'Sit there,' he said, pointing to the dresser.

I dragged myself to the dresser in the room I had shared

with Nick, the room where we had first made love after our wedding, looking at my cosmetics, at the compact and the rouge. Lorelei's voice came through the wall, speaking over a soaring violin. Charles sat staring at the floor. He couldn't let me go. I knew it. He knew it. If he did, he would get the rope. He was as trapped as I was.

And, even as we sat there, both of us unable to leave that room, each looking for a way out that couldn't possibly exist, I couldn't help but think the same thought that I had had on the balcony with Ian Fellowman: that this was the squalid natural ending to those dreams he and Anthony Blunt and Kim Philby and Guy Burgess and Arthur Wynn and John Cairncross had woven for us. This was where they ended: in ordinary people desperate to run away, but too fearful of the consequences that waited outside like bare-toothed dogs. All the words these men had poured into our ears and down our throats night and day – all they really amounted to when the light hit them was this havoc. This utter wreckage.

Something fell away in me then, leaving a numbness of feeling. It was like half my being had gone, leaving only my body. I didn't care any more. Not for any of it. There was nothing left to care. 'Charles,' I said quietly. 'I'm going. Please don't stop me. Just let me go.'

I pushed myself up and attempted to walk calmly across the room. And, as I took a pace, then another, reaching the centre of the room, I honestly thought he was going to let me leave.

But halfway across his eyes flicked open and I knew then, looking into them, that if he touched me I wouldn't see the day through. And, although my mind and body were numb, there is within us a sense of self-preservation stronger than almost anything else in the world that we can know. And so, once more, I ran.

Ignoring the pain in my ankle, knowing that he was a pace or two behind me, without an idea of where to go, I threw myself out of the room. I wouldn't get to the hall-way before he caught me, so by instinct I made for the bathroom, the only room with a door that could be locked.

My feet skidded on its floor, awash with water, just as Lorelei's had been that day. I tried to slam the door, but he was barging in and the force knocked me back against the bath. And then he grabbed hold of me and my face hit the cold surface of the overflowing water and it felt like glass.

Somewhere, Lorelei was singing. She was offering some-one Champagne to the sound of light music. Music to dance to.

I struggled for a time, twisting this way and that, catching glimpses of the air above, but the sounds of the world out-side became muted, slow and heavy. I couldn't understand them any more, I was falling asleep and they seemed to be coming from a place where I had never been and didn't belong. The strands of my hair drifted out like threads. The water was pulling me deeper, tangling my limbs and cooling my thoughts, until my mind was all washed through and strange. Images flickered past – people I had known, emo-tions; the poster on the wall above us, its political words picked out in red type. But they were all somehow indistinct and without weight or time. I felt nothing for them as they slipped away.

I fell into a closing darkness, and, deep down, I

understood it was all that I would have from now on. Everything was cold and hushed and empty. I would never go back. I would drift through an endless dark ocean, forever with a sense of loss.

38

I don't know how long I was in that darkness. It felt like seconds, weeks, years. It didn't matter. It didn't matter at all.

And then, after a while, something changed. The world began to shiver. The colour shifted. In the black there were points of light like distant stars, growing larger, and I could feel myself somehow being drawn towards them. They grew until I could see into them, and I was dragged faster and faster. In my veins, the blood was moving. My muscles were shaking. My arms were rushing through a river.

I burst up out of the water, spraying droplets and gasping for breath, ready to retch. My lungs were on fire as I sucked in all the air that I could. All I knew then was air – I had no idea of my own life until the memories flooded back with the freezing wet that was pouring down me. I twisted around and saw Charles looking towards the stairs. In a second I understood what had distracted him.

Below us, the front door slammed closed. 'Jane!' someone called. 'What's going on?' It was Nick. Charles's head fell as if he were in pain. 'Jane, are you there?'

I wanted to twist the knife, to tell Charles that Lorelei had despised him, that she laughed at him behind his back, but I couldn't form any words – they had been drenched out of me.

'Jane!' Nick's voice was in the hall now. Then there were footsteps coming up the stairs.

'I'm here!' I cried.

At my shout, Charles seemed to regain his strength and made for the door. Barely able to stand, I stumbled after, grabbing at him as he reached the landing. Nick, part-way up the stairs, looked stupefied at the sight of us. In the darkness of the hall he was holding the lighted oil lamp that he used to see through the smog, and, from the way I was grasping at Charles and the state of my torn and soaking clothes, he must have gained some idea of what had happened. Charles stopped when he saw Nick, and they both stared, until Nick began to move again, rushing towards us. Charles, seeing no other way out, leaped down the stairs, barging with his shoulder and hardly touching the steps. Nick was stronger and fitter, but Charles had the momentum. As he moved through the air, I yelled Nick's name, as if I could somehow protect him.

They met with a shout that rang in my ears long after they had crashed together and broken apart again. But it was mixed with something else: the bone sound of breaking wood. As I watched, a web of cracks spread through the bannister and a metre-long section exploded away, tumbling in shards and blades to the floor. Charles and Nick fell through it together, spinning through the air, lighted by a flickering flame from the lamp as it too dropped to the ground, splitting on the floorboards to spread paraffin on to the heavy hall rug. The lamp, the shattered wood and their bodies all lay, unmoving, on the floor. Wreckage again.

'Nick,' I gasped, as I ran down.

Time and sound seemed to have stopped as I looked from one to the other, both perfectly still and without signs of life. Nothing to say there was blood or warmth in them. I could hear the silence, long and bleak.

And then, with a groan, slowly and painfully, Nick stirred. My heart floated at the sight of his head lifting from the floor. With an effort, he got to his knees, a severe bruise welling on his cheek, and I made to throw my arms around him, but at that moment a flame leaped up from a pool of the lamp's oil at my feet, making me grab at the bannister for balance. The flare reflected on Nick's skin as he stood.

He looked deep into me and spoke in a low, severe voice. 'Go. The police.' He glanced at Charles, who appeared to be unconscious or worse. In a moment I felt just as I had done when he found me surrounded by police after Lorelei's death: gratitude entwined with guilt. Unable to say anything, I nodded and ran outside, stumbling over the bottles of paraffin for our heaters. The door closed behind me and the lock clicked into place.

That sound worried me – I couldn't say why, but here and now it seemed to be cutting me off from Nick for a second time and there was something threatening in that. I turned and shoved at the door. I hadn't thought to take my key and it was locked firm, but through the leaded side window I could see a bright glow that illuminated Nick's figure, bending down to pull the remains of the lamp's oil holder away from the fire – and, behind his back, Charles beginning to lift himself up from the floor.

I smacked my hand on the glass. 'Nick!' I screamed, desperate to warn him. His face turned to me; and then it burst away as Charles threw himself on Nick from behind, the two of them tumbling out of sight, slamming against the bottom of the door. 'Nick!' I cried out again.

I reeled wildly around, looking for anyone who could help. But the smog was so thick I couldn't see more than a few metres. I ran towards the end of the street, feeling for anyone there. 'Please help!' I yelled, tripping into the gutter and banging into low walls and cars.

A radio somewhere was broadcasting Blunt's Liberation Day speech once again. '. . . where the people who create the wealth have equal shares in that wealth, instead of being forced . . .' The crowd were cheering under his words. I ran blind, flailing about in the thick mist, hardly knowing in which direction I was moving. I blundered into the road, narrowly avoiding being hit by a car that was creeping through the blanket of smoke mixed with wet fog, and cried out for anyone to help. Anyone.

Then, from ahead of me, a shout answered mine.

'Jane? Are you there?' I recognized the voice, hardened by years of rough, cheap spirits. I couldn't see him but Tibbot was there somewhere. I ran towards the sound, hoping to touch him, winding my arms through the dirty air. His face came out of the mist, a severe look on his face. 'What's wrong?' he demanded, grabbing me by the shoulders.

'God, come quick!' I cried, latching on to his coat.

From the other side of the road I heard more footsteps running. A man sprinted past, followed a moment later by three Teddy Boys, whooping and shouting. One got a hand to the man's jacket and brought him down. 'Informant cunt,' one of the boys shouted, while the others kicked him. He struggled up, tore clear of them and began to run again. 'Off to the Secs?' they screamed at his back.

Tibbot and I turned and dashed back to the house, stumbling and catching each other. 'What is it?' Tibbot asked urgently.

'It's Charles. And Nick,' I said.

I went to the side window but all I could see were flames, divided into six by the lead-framed panes of glass, surging along the hallway. The pile of newspapers that we had to send each month to be destroyed in the National Records Office, the stack of our collective madness of accusations and denunciations and fury, was alight. The bottles of paraffin had exploded in the heat, fuelling the fire.

Something unseen was smacking against the wood from the other side – feet or fists. Tibbot put his shoulder to the door and I pushed against it too, but, whether it was the strength of the lock or the weight of the bodies on the other side, it wouldn't give. We heard someone cry in pain from the other side of the wood.

'The back door?' Tibbot shouted to me.

'It's bolted.'

'I'll call the station.'

'There's no time!' The heat was coming through the wood.

Tibbot scanned the ground and picked up a large stone from the garden. He pulled it back behind his shoulder and pitched it at the side window. But the leaded frame was sturdy, and, although the glass fractured, the window didn't give. He took the stone and used it to smash again and again at the frame, knocking it out of the wood to fall on the floor of the hall. A blast of hot air and smoke rushed out, stinging my skin and making me stagger back. Tibbot jerked his head away, doubling up to cough out harsh smoke.

Holding my sleeve over my mouth and nose to block out the smoke, I reached inside, turning the lock. Tibbot shoved the door then and it gave way easily – whatever had been up against it was gone, but as it swung back there was another rush of scalding air. The bottles of paraffin had showered the room with droplets of oil that flared here and there; the fire was licking high on the coat stand, and black smoke from the charring fabric billowed through the hall, making it hard to see. Nick lay on the floor and above him stood Charles, his hand and temple both bloody. He shook as his eyes met mine. I had no thoughts then but hatred of him. A second later Tibbot pushed me aside and rushed in; but the surge of air from the open doorway made the flames on the rug billow up, and they forced him back, coughing again. We both turned away from the stinging heat, and, when we looked back, Charles was running out through the rear of the house. The flames blew up again as he burst out the back door.

I took my handkerchief from my sleeve, held it over my face so I could breathe in shallow, panting breaths and flew to Nick, winding past the flames on the rug. He was lying on his side, turned away from me. I dropped to my knees and froze at the sight of his blackened face as Tibbot rolled him on to his back and put his head to Nick's chest. 'He's not breathing,' he said. There were broken pieces of bannister around us, smeared with blood where Charles's hand had touched it.

'Nick,' I rasped, my voice barely loud enough to be heard. On the rug, needles of glass from the broken paraffin bottles glistened in the firelight. 'Nick, can you hear me?' I bent to listen for any sound. There was nothing. I felt like I was holding his hand while he stood on a precipice.

'Look at me!' Tibbot ordered him, smacking Nick's cheek lightly. There was no response. 'Look at me.' He slapped again, more forcefully this time. I watched for any sign of life. The colour was gone from his skin. Tibbot felt Nick's wrist for a pulse, searching for it, seemingly unable to find anything.

'Is he alive?' I whispered, my heart thudding against my chest so hard that I thought I would break apart. 'Tell me.' A spray of oil flared by my hand, burning it. Tibbot glanced at me, a grim look on his face, as he moved rapidly to Nick's neck to feel for a pulse. Then he started pumping his hands up and down on Nick's chest, alternated with blowing into his mouth. I sat and watched, wondering if it would ever end. After a while, Tibbot checked Nick's wrist for a heartbeat, and then his neck again. He went through the cycle of actions again and again, each time feeling for a pulse.

And at the end, for ten, twenty, I don't know how many seconds, he knelt with his fingers pressed to Nick's neck, all the while looking at me. And then he slowly sat back and lifted his hand away. 'No!' I shouted. My hands searched desperately over Nick's chest, trying to find the heartbeat that would save us both.

'I'm sorry,' Tibbot said quietly.

'No!'

'He's gone.'

'I won't . . . no!'

Without warning, Tibbot grabbed me and dragged me aside, falling against the broken bannister. I looked back to see a bundle of flames and burning fabric tumble to the floor where I had been kneeling, the fire flooding out from it as it hit the boards. The coat rack was now a mass of light and more fell, separating us from Nick. The smoke was getting thicker.

'We have to get out,' Tibbot coughed, his chest hacking. 'He's —'

'He's gone. We have to get out!'

All I could feel was my skin burning. It could have all burned away. And, as I looked up, I saw Hazel in the doorway, standing just as she had done when a policewoman brought her to our house after her mother's death.

I ran to her, my arms outstretched, turning her so that she couldn't see the broken form on the floor. She put her arms around me and I felt her tremble with tears that began to wet my own cheeks.

All I could do was stroke her hair and pull her tighter. 'It's going to be all right,' I said. 'I'll look after you. I'm here. I'll look after you.'

39

What do we see, when we see the land ahead? We see endless possibilities. For our nation, our new way of political life presents a land ready to be filled with people and human endeavour.

Anthony Blunt, broadcast on RGB Station 1,
Monday, 3 August 1953

I walked all the way to Checkpoint Charlie today. I don't know what I was expecting to see. I stared at the gap covered by that impenetrable curtain of rope, holding Hazel's letter tightly in my hand.

The paper that she had written on was fine and heavy, the sort we had many years ago for correspondence but no longer use because there's no call for delicate and mannered words now. She was starting at a new school, and she told me about her teachers and some of the girls in her class. They're going to be studying *The Great Gatsby* later in the year, she said, so she'll be putting the copy that I gave her to good use. She had enclosed a photograph of herself in her new uniform, and I looked at it again in the afternoon light. It was green with gold detailing – so much cheerier than the heavy navy blue on our side. I found that somehow comforting.

Fellowman arranged it all, of course, in return for the name of the doctor in Los Angeles who supplied the drugs to Lorelei. I had expected at least some sort of reaction when I explained that the exit visa was for Hazel, not me, but he remained quite impassive, quite inscrutable, and I had the impression that this was the real Ian Fellowman, not the one I had seen at Mansford Hall. After all, it fits better with what he does. I should probably have guessed earlier, but, what with everyone else playing games, it's not surprising that one passed me by.

It was from him that I discovered Charles had listened to the telephone conversation between Nick and Adam Cutter the day before Lorelei's death. Adam, drunk as usual, had told Nick that Lorelei claimed to be carrying his child; and he asked if it were true they had been having an affair. Nick had only cursed her and slammed the telephone down without answering. That was what Adam had considered a confession. Anyone else would have thought Lorelei's claim to be no more substantial than her other stories but Charles took it to heart.

Such a fool he was for her. How she could make us doubt ourselves.

So the next morning, before he went to work, Charles brought Lorelei some Champagne to toast their emigration to Ireland. While she wasn't looking, he dosed it with something to end her pregnancy. Common rue from a greengrocer's, it seems. He found it detailed in one of the practice textbooks. He hadn't wanted to kill her; the opposite, really – he just wanted the life together that she had promised him.

Fellowman told me all this after the Secs told him. They

had found Charles sitting in his flat. I imagine he just wanted someone to listen to him.

Rue. Regret. Two meanings. I went to Southwark Library last week to look it up. There was a battered old volume in which medical students had made notes. 'Abortifacient effect,' it said. But it's hard to get the dose right. Adverse reactions: 'Gastric pain . . . renal failure . . . vasodilation and coagulopathy . . . systemic failure . . .' I didn't understand it all, but I understood enough. The book also mentioned that it produces little blisters on the skin if you handle it wrongly, so that was probably the rash I saw on Charles's hand that day at the surgery.

The book included a picture of the herb. It has pretty little yellow flowers, and I thought of Ophelia pinning it to her brother's chest before she drowns herself. She calls it herb-of-grace then: a blessing herb. A drowning herb too, really.

I spent a long time in the library, just sitting, thinking, until it closed at five and I had to go back to the boarding house I'm in now. It's warm and dry enough. The landlady takes all our coupons and sells some of them, I think, but I don't blame her: I suppose she's just trying to make ends meet like the rest of us. Everyone is trying. Frank Tibbot stopped by once to see how I was. He's a kind man. He's still in the police but says he has to look over his shoulder all the time.

Fellowman's office is right beside the one Guy Burgess now occupies as Deputy First Secretary and I can't help wondering how long it will be before they move up again, and how many of Fellowman's whispers will end up as our laws. I asked him what they intended to do with Charles but he didn't say. It doesn't matter now.

Who was the father after all? Was Lorelei even pregnant? All the secrets she's taken with her now lie as dust on the ground. And, in a way, I think it means she won out in the end.

I walked to Checkpoint Charlie from our house – what remains of it, anyway. Before leaving, I stood in the back garden and looked up at the charred brickwork. No birds live there now and at first it seemed to me that the garden was bare, but then, here and there, I noticed little slivers of paper and fabric – pinches of our everyday life that had floated out on the hot air. They had been soaked by rain and bleached by the sun; but still, under rocks and in crevices in the wall, they lingered as some sort of witness. I'm glad there's a witness.

So what do you think, Nick? Because now, in the end, I can admit that all of this is addressed to you. I'm speaking to you day in and day out, and I'm trying to tell you why I did what I did, because I don't think that drug was ever in my blood, and I don't know if you were truly guilty of anything except trying to make it through in the way that we have to now. And I miss you and I'm sorry. Just so, so sorry. It's not all going to work out for the best.

I watched our house burn. I would never have thought it possible that bricks and wood could take so long to burn to the ground. But there it was, for hours alight in the smog.

Oh, Nick, you once laughed at how badly I wrote for an English teacher. And you were right: I could write a thousand pages, but it wouldn't say anything more. It couldn't. And it still wouldn't be a grain of sand in comparison to what I want to say. So all I can tell you is that every minute of every hour I stare out the window and dream of going back and starting again. And that's all there is. All of it.

Except for Hazel. Yes, Hazel. Officially, she's over there until the end of her education and then she has to return, but that's hardly likely, is it? It's part of a new era of rapprochement with the DUK. 'Mutual acceptance of our different ways of life and an end to the destructive mistrust that has so long blighted our futures,' Blunt said on the radio yesterday. His tone was different in that address – more open to question. We're all reading so much into the speech, endlessly discussing it in hushed voices. Hazel even thinks it won't be long before I can visit her for a while. Perhaps. Things will need to change a great deal for that to happen. But things do change. And we have a glimmer of it now so let's just hold on to that.

There was a man at the Wall selling photographs of it to be used as postcards, just like the time you and I went there together. He was shuffling through the school groups and young couples to offer strings of the grainy images for a few pence. I was almost tempted to buy one when it was my turn to be approached, but in the end I said no and gave it back. He nodded politely and went off to try elsewhere. He struck lucky with a platoon of Pioneers, though, who handed him their money and took the cards to save or post home to their parents. One boasted loudly that he would be sending it to his girlfriend, until the others' jeers made him blush and bite his tongue.

I realized, as I waited, that it would be Hazel's birthday soon. I tried to guess what she would receive from the family looking after her – clothes maybe, or records. I'll send her more books, some that I loved at her age. So long as I choose them carefully, they should get through.

Eventually my watch told me it was six o'clock, the time she had specified in her letter, and I gazed at the mesh-covered breach in the concrete, knowing that she was on the other side, looking back. She had said that she would wave even though I wouldn't be able to see her. It was hardly further than the other side of the road but that gap seemed so far away, set behind the guard post and steel barriers chained together and bolted to the ground.

'Are you all right, miss?' It was the man trying to sell postcards.

'Yes. Just thinking about someone,' I replied.

He looked back at the Wall. 'Someone dear to you.'

'Yes.'

He stroked his jaw. 'I'm sure they're thinking about you too.'

'I think so.'

The sun had sunk lower towards the horizon, and I looked to where Hazel was standing. She was waving to me, I knew, sure that I was here on the other side. After all that had happened, she trusted me to be here. I watched for a while, seeing her in my mind's eye, waving to me in the light, as the postcard seller walked away.

Chronology

1939

- 23 August. Germany and the Soviet Union agree the Molotov–Ribbentrop Pact, which keeps the Soviets out of the War.
- 3 September. Britain and France declare war on Germany.

1944

- 6 June. D-Day fails; most troops are killed or captured.
- 29 August. Germany executes Operation Kestrel, the invasion of Britain.
- 30 August. The Royal Family escape to safety in Northern Ireland.
- 16 October. Britain capitulates. Winston Churchill is persuaded to join the Royal Family, now fleeing to Canada, so that he can direct the resistance to the Nazi occupation.

1945

- 11 March. The Soviet Union sweeps through Poland and into Berlin. With twelve million men under arms, the Soviets cut through the badly overextended German forces.
- 18 November. Soviet forces land in Britain, moving slowly through the country to mop up German troops and sympathizers.
- 29 December. United States troops, along with the remnants of Britain's armed forces led by Churchill, land in Liverpool and quickly occupy the north of England, Wales and Scotland.

1946

- 18 January. The Royal Family leave Canada for Scotland.
- 8 June. An agreement is reached to divide the nation in two. There is a separate division of London. The Soviets declare the birth of the Republic of Great Britain, to be ruled by a committee chaired by Anthony Blunt.
- 1 August. A fence is built to surround the DUK sector of London, soon to become a wall.

Historical Notes

For a detailed but readable history of the division of Berlin, Frederick Taylor's *The Berlin Wall* takes you through the power-plays at a good pace. Or, for a description of the tragedies and absurdities of life on the wrong side of the Iron Curtain, *1989: The Berlin Wall – My Part in Its Downfall*, by British journalist Peter Millar, is an entertaining narrative of his time as the East Germany correspondent for the *Sunday Times*.

For insights into the workings of the secret police and, in the new world, how to address the past, *Stasiland* by Anna Funder is an affecting work. It details not only how the Stasi murdered peaceful citizens, but also how they regulated the smaller aspects of life, down to strictly controlling licences for typewriters and children's printing sets.

Anthony Blunt died in disgrace in 1983. In 2009 the British Library revealed that it had had his handwritten memoirs since the year after his death, when they were deposited by a friend of Blunt. They are a fascinating document in which he claims that, while he had been recruited to spy for the Soviets for ideological reasons, in later life the reality of Soviet State Socialism had led him to reject it. He says that his treachery was the biggest mistake of his life and he had considered suicide in its aftermath.

Like the man, his handwriting is often hard to decipher.

It is made up of sharp lines up and down. The curves are crushed. The vowels – the vehicles of emotion – are suppressed. All we really see is the underlying meaning.

When the emotion does come out, it is often bitterness at the way that he has been portrayed. The preface, written in hand in black ink, concludes: 'It is written for my friends, who have stood by me with unbelievable affection and loyalty, and for the members of the public who are I believe more numerous than might be supposed, who want to know the truth about my life and actions, as opposed to the versions which have been served up to them by the press – I do not say "the gutter press" because that would imply that some parts of the press were not of the gutter.'

The *Archangel* was a real ship. HMS *Royal Sovereign*, a *Revenge*-class battleship, was lent to the Soviet Navy to protect the Arctic transports. The Soviets renamed her the *Archangelsk*. After the War, she was handed back to Britain.

Arthur Wynn was the founder of the Oxford Spy Ring – a group less prominent than their Cambridge counterparts but operational. He was recruited by Edith Tudor-Hart, who had also recruited Kim Philby. He was not exposed until the 1990s. John Cairncross was a self-confessed Soviet spy who may – or may not – have been the 'fifth man' in the Cambridge ring.

Lillian Hall-Davis was a star of the silent era. She took her own life in 1933.

The 1938 meeting between Winston Churchill and Guy Burgess at Churchill's country home was described by Burgess in 1951, with a recording taken in which he imitates Churchill's distinctive drawl.

No. 60 Great Queen Street, London, is the Freemasons' Hall, home to the United Grand Lodge of England, a very austere-looking building.

Dr Max Jacobson – aka 'Dr Feelgood' – was responsible for some of the liveliest Hollywood performances from the 1940s until the 1960s. His 'vitamin injections' – which were largely amphetamine sulphate – kept actors and actresses working with smiles on their faces. His clients included Bogart and Bacall, Marilyn, Elvis and JFK. In 1969 one of his clients died of an overdose and his medical licence was eventually suspended.

The London Post Office Railway operated from 1927 until 2003.

London's Great Smog of 5–9 December 1952 is believed to have killed more than 10,000 people, mostly through respiratory problems. At its worst, visibility could be as low as a single metre. Pea Soupers – so-called because the smog had a green-yellow tinge – had been common since the Victorian era, but this was the worst ever recorded.

Acknowledgements

First to Claire McGowan, Hannah Boardman and Ed Latham, who read early drafts of this book and gave some vital pointers. Also Dr Peter Mann, who advised on the medical aspects. My agent, Simon Trewin, and editors, Emad Akhtar and Joel Richardson, whose excellent ideas I have willingly passed off as my own.

garethrubin.com
twitter.com/garethrubin